The Chosen of the Light: Book Two
Soul Seekers

By

Jon Carlin Shea

Jon Carlin Shea © 2015

Editor: S.R. Howen

ISBN: 978-0-9985714-2-3

If you are interested in purchasing more works of this
nature, please stop by www.joncarlinshea.com.

Works by Jon Carlin Shea

The Chosen of the Light

Book One : Spirit Summoner
Book Two : Soul Seekers
Book Three (FORTHCOMING)

To Michelle, my own little sister who often accompanied me on journeys into fantasy.

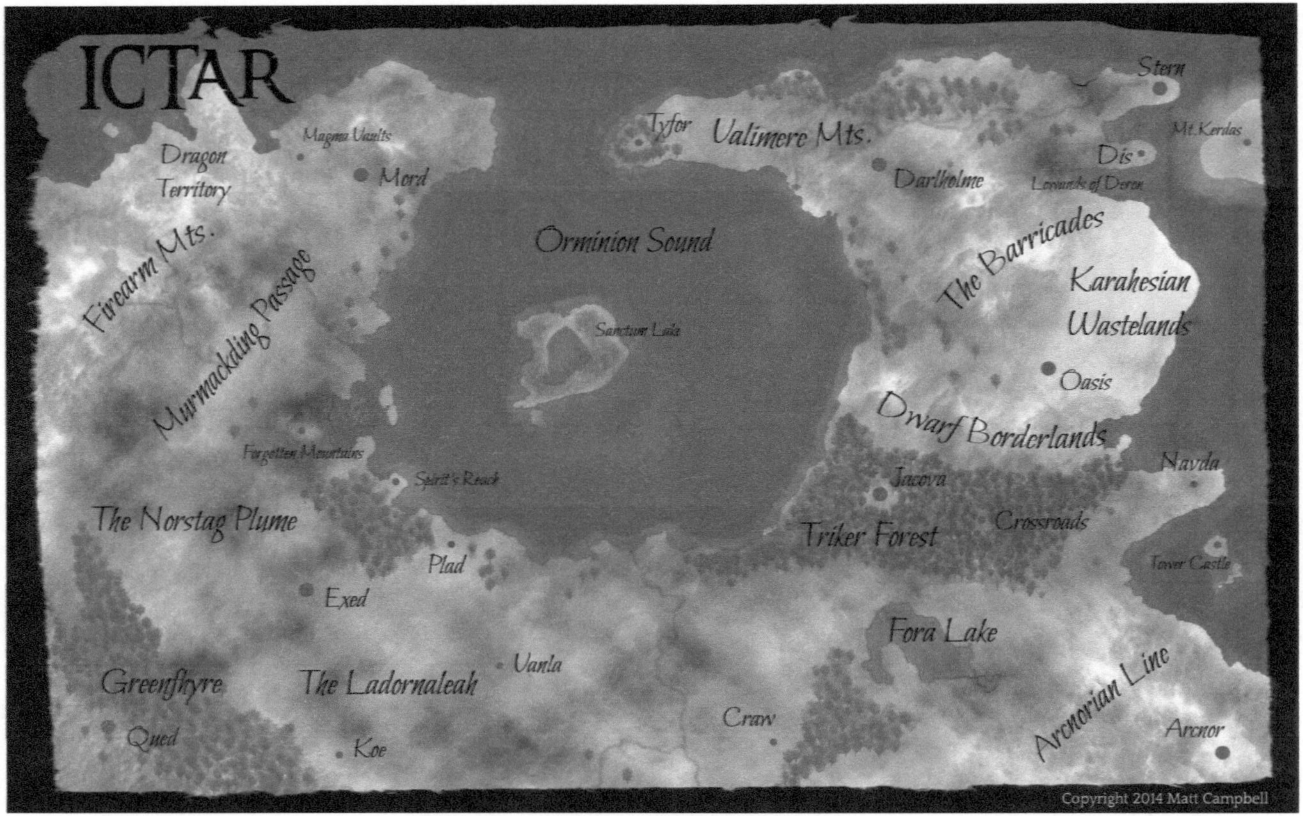
ICTAR
Magma Vaults
Dragon Territory
Mord
Firearm Mts.
Murmackding Passage
Forgotten Mountains
Spirit's Reach
The Norstag Plume
Plad
Exed
Greenfhyre
The Ladornaleah
Vanla
Qued
Koe
Ormininon Sound
Sanctum Lala
Tyfor
Valimere Mts.
Darlholme
Stern
Dis
Lowlands of Deren
Mt. Kerdas
The Barricades
Karahesian Wastelands
Oasis
Dwarf Borderlands
Navda
Jacova
Triker Forest
Crossroads
Tower Castle
Fora Lake
Craw
Arcnorian Line
Arcnor
Copyright 2014 Matt Campbell

Interlude

Kaeo shook out a ragged breath before gasping for another. His throat had gone numb and his lungs burned, but he lived, so he suffered through his discomfort. His breath erupted in angry clouds into the cold dawn air. His hands clenched at his knees where he knelt in the mud, the slick texture making it difficult to steady himself without digging his nails into the flesh beneath his pants. Beads of sweat ran down his face and the back of his neck. He shivered in response to the sudden chill beneath his tunic.

"We were searching the mires south of Jacova," Kaeo said. He took another breath before continuing. "South, where the forest begins to pull apart...they warned us..."

Kaeo stopped talking, overcome by sudden images. Despite his thirty-odd years and nearly a lifetime spent in the wilderness, he wept.

"Easy, now, hunter," the voice in the darkness soothed. "When you're ready, tell me the rest of what happened."

The calm in the other's voice gave Kaeo focus. The images tearing their way through his mind stopped, swatted away by the commanding presence before him. He couldn't be sure exactly who stood before him, shrouded in the lingering shadows of night, but he trusted this man. He must report what he'd seen. He couldn't let his fears eat him alive.

Kaeo spit into the mud and cleared his throat. "Before we left Jacova, we were given strict instructions to avoid dark areas, areas that could conceal the Soul Seekers. We were told to look for the mists in which they hide, but we were told explicitly to avoid any areas that looked suspicious. They told us to return to Jacova and report at once if we found such areas."

"Told so by whom?" the voice in the darkness asked.

"By Ariel Forn, the Cortazian King, and the Dwarf Elder Council. Didn't you know?"

"Of course. I knew, Hunter," the voice said. The words spilled out smoothly. "Continue with your report."

Kaeo shivered forcefully, a result of the sweat soaking through his clothes chilled by the early morning air. "My captain was a brave man, but he didn't believe in the Seekers. Even after hearing of the destruction in Navda, even after hearing of the savagery with which the Seekers fought, he didn't believe." Kaeo paused. Anger rose in his throat like bile and spilt from his lips. "How could he not believe? How could he disregard a direct order and believe his commander concocted fairy tales? How could he lead us so far astray without an ounce of regard for the orders he'd been given?"

"Calm yourself, Hunter," the voice in the darkness urged. "Keep your head clear. Keep your thoughts focused and tell me what happened next."

Kaeo trembled. He took another breath and swallowed hard against the lump in his throat. His emotions shifted inside, stirred and set aside by some invisible hand. His mud-caked fingers fell from his knees, and he folded them gently before him.

"Yesterday evening, before the sun set, I caught a glimpse of what I believed was smoke through the trees. My captain took us, all eight of us, down into the mires. It was so dark down there, and it was getting darker. I was the one who realized that it wasn't smoke, but mist. I told my captain at once that we should fall back, that something wasn't right. He laughed at me and told me I shouldn't give in to children's ghost stories."

Kaeo searched the darkness for the man before him, his vision clouded with sadness and rage. A vague outline settled in the shadows. He could almost put a name to him. Almost.

"Go on, Hunter."

A flash of red exploded in his mind, turning the forest around him crimson. In the crimson haze that had become his memory, he saw his captain exactly how he'd seen him last. Dark features twisted with hideous laughter. In the turn of a second, his captain's mouth widened into a cry of terror.

The mists around them turned inky black. A Soul Seeker rose up in front of Kaeo's captain in its tattered black robes. Silver claws lashed out in one swift motion that tore his chest and abdomen in different directions. As the remains of the captain's body fell away, his eyes, terrified, burned into Kaeo's memory.

"Dead..." Kaeo managed in a single forced breath. "All of them dead. First there was one Seeker, then two, then five. By that time, we were already outnumbered. Before we could even draw our weapons, three more of us were dead."

"And did you draw your weapon?"

Kaeo stared ahead. "I didn't have time. None of us could defend ourselves. Only one man managed to draw his sword, and he was struck down even quicker than my captain..."

"So what did you do?"

Kaeo shook his head, made frantic by the accusation in the voice of the figure before him. "Isn't it obvious?" he cried. "We ran. We threw down our weapons, and our supplies, and we ran. I ran. Every time I heard a man scream out behind me, I ran harder and faster. I ran until everything around me blurred into nothing. And when I heard nothing, I ran even harder."

Kaeo wept again, tears rolling down his face like a child lost and caught out in the impenetrable dark. No one would come to save him. The hunter sunk his chin into his chest. His great sobs slowed and then ceased altogether. The figure in the dark knelt down in front of Kaeo, but his tears hid the man's face from him.

Kaeo breathed deeply. "There's nothing more to tell. I ran as far and as fast as I could. I ran until my legs gave out, and that is where you have found me now."

The figure didn't move. Unease surged through Kaeo. He couldn't be sure why, but he suddenly and clearly realized he didn't know who he was talking to.

"Tell me, Hunter," the voice in the darkness whispered, the scrape of tooth against bone. "How many of the Soul Seekers have returned? How many did you feel at your back as you ran like a frightened hare?"

Kaeo's muddied hand slid to his thigh where he kept a knife strapped at all times. His fingertips found the handle effortlessly.

"Answer the question."

Kaeo kept his gaze locked on the shadow before him. "I can't be sure," he said. "It felt like a swarm of them."

In a swift, seamless motion, the figure rose up. A cold surge of satisfaction radiated from the man and into his own body. The hunter slid the knife free from its sheath. His muscles tensed. No friend stood before him.

Kaeo leapt to his feet, launching himself into the dark, knife drawn back and poised to fall in the middle of the shadowed figure's head.

"Useless." A hiss that echoed in Kaeo's ears.

Wicked green light flared in the dark. The earth beneath Kaeo rose up, enfolding him. The cold and the wetness of the dirt grasped him tight, pulling him down, its crushing pressure suffocating. The mud reached his chin, then his teeth. The cold seeped into his mouth. His breath escaped. His eyes widened, nearly popping from his head.

The face in the dark smiled.

"The Soul Seekers have come, Hunter."

Kaeo's lungs struggled for one last breath, but it was the darkness, the blinding blackness that finally, and so effortlessly, killed him.

Chapter One

"My story has grown tangled these last few weeks. Much has taken place within my troubled world, within the very walls of the city in which I live. My mind will not quiet the horrors I've seen, nor the joys. Only one question runs through my mind... Can the Chosen of the Light truly end the madness I see around me? Or will they disappear into the rising dust of this crumbling world?"

~From the personal writings of the Divine, Zander

The voice, so slow and quiet, startled Darr.

Confusion swept over him. Sawgrass encircled him completely, leaving a small radius of breathing room. He shook his lanky hair from his face. Startled, he whipped around. *How did I get here? Wait. Where am I?*

Above him, only the darkening skies were visible. The sawgrass rose up eight feet high, hiding any trace of the fields beyond. *Where's Jinn, and Feywen, and Conra? Where're the mountains?*

Faint glimmers of silver appeared in the grass around him. The blades of grass rattled gently. Darr's stomach turned into knots. He crouched, steadied his breathing. His fingers grasped for his long knife, but he hadn't thought to bring it with him. Darr swallowed hard, searching through the blades of sawgrass for something, anything that would clue him into where he was.

The voice echoed in his brain. Darr scratched at his head. *What is it saying? What are you trying to tell me?*

A pair of silver claws exploded out of the sawgrass. Darr cried out and fell onto his back, legs kicking wildly, but the claws were almost on him. The black tattered robes of a Soul Seeker materialized out of the grass. The Seekers' depthless hood stared back at him, empty of life. Darr squeezed his eyes shut, bracing himself for the killing blow.

"Darr!"

The Summoner's eyes burst open. The sawgrass parted

and Erec appeared. His brother leapt in front of the Seeker, followed by a whip of black hair. Strong arms came up, shielding Darr from the raking claws. Erec's blade struck out and cut the Seeker in two, releasing its magic. Dust scattered at Erec's feet.

"How many times do I have to tell you, little brother, not to start the chores without me?" Erec's words sounded harsh, but despite his anger, all he ever wanted was to protect his family.

"Thank you, Erec," Darr said, his voice still shaking. "I thought you were going to leave all this to me." *What am I saying?*

Erec snorted and smiled. "Could you imagine the look on father's face if I didn't help you?"

A scythe weighed heavily in Darr's hand. *When did I get this?* Erec helped him back to his feet. The sawgrass behind them fell away, presumably cut away by him and Erec. In the distance, his home, the village of Tyfor stood stark against the darkening skies.

Erec started working. His brother held a scythe now, too. Steadily, he cut the grass ahead of them away. Darr joined in, sweeping the blade along clumsily and much slower than Erec.

What am I doing? We need to get out of here!

The voice returned, but Darr shut it out. *I'm working. I have to get this done. Father will be furious if we don't finish.* Sweat dripped down his face, cold and damp. Darr shivered. When had it gotten so cold?

The scythe fell from his numb fingers. Black shapes rose from the fallen grass. Silver claws dangled at their sides. "We have to get out of here, Erec," Darr yelled. "The Soul Seekers are back."

Erec shook his head, laughing while he worked. "The Seekers aren't back, Darr." A smile played at the corners of his mouth. "The Soul Seekers never left."

Darr shook his head in confusion. Behind him, the Seekers rushed towards them. Tattered robes stretched out over searching claws. Darr scrambled to his brother's side and pointed at their approaching killers.

"What do you mean? They're right there."

Erec looked over his shoulder. The smile dropped from his lips. "We fought hard against them, didn't we, brother?"

Dizziness spun Darr around. He reached out and Erec caught his arm, holding him fast. The Summoner took steady breaths. Erec's scythe melted away and reshaped itself into a sword. His face contorted in rage. With his sword lifted high, Erec screamed and rushed into the wave of approaching Seekers.

Tears sprung to Darr's eyes. *No. Not again.*

The silver claws of the Soul Seekers ripped into Erec's body, and he exploded into ash. Darr fell to his knees, and his screams turned his ears numb. The black hoods and silver claws flew at him from all directions, their purpose fixed and hungry.

Instinct overrode rational thought. Darr, the Spirit Summoner, reached into the Currents and drank in the magic of the Fire Sephir. The power surged through the marrow of his bones, racing to his extremities along with the blood in his veins. It bled out through his pores. He stretched out his arms, fingers splayed, feet firmly planted. A geyser of flame erupted from his body, and the Soul Seekers disappeared in puffs of light and ash.

Darr's fire exploded into the sky, scorching the heavens and moving outwards to burn the surrounding clouds, turning them black and red. Fire rained down like thousands of flaming arrows. The flames burned away the sawgrass, his family home, and the Tyfran General Store.

Unfazed by the destruction, Darr let the magic of the Fire Sephir pour unchecked into the physical world.

Tyfor burned away in moments. The mountains and woods charred and fell apart. The oceans and lakes boiled, the water rising up into steam and dissipating into the air. Fields turned to charcoal, entire forests turned to smoke and ash. The ground itself splintered and cracked. Darr continued to scream, his rage taking the form of an inferno.

It ended when his scream died in his throat. The

Summoner dropped to his knees, naked. With blackened skin and blistered lips, he cried. Tears streamed from eyes he could barely open. The red glow of destruction burned his damaged vision.

A shadow, a band of darkness slipped down before him.

Thank you, Darr. You've become my savior. Your rage and arrogance have set me free.

Tears froze on Darr's cheeks. The voice, the voice. It belonged to the Devoid.

* * * *

Darr thrashed awake, throwing his blankets into a heap beside him. He sat up, taking huge gulps of the cold mountain air. A fire danced before his eyes, much less threatening than the fires of his dream.

"Is everything alright, Darr?"

Feywen's voice, not the Devoid's like in his dream. The Dwarf stood on the far side of their little campfire, concern lining his dark-skinned face. Another face came into view, rising up beside him, wrinkled and gray.

"Nightmares again?" Conra asked, his wizened features showing sympathy.

It was sympathy he didn't need or deserve.

"It's nothing," Darr said. He intended the edge in his voice to deter any further questions. At his side, Jinn slept soundly. Somehow, she'd been able to accept Erec's death. It'd been a couple of weeks, and she still wasn't herself, but at least nightmares no longer troubled her.

"Morning is only a couple hours away," Feywen said. He settled his body back down. "We'll begin climbing the pass tomorrow. You'll need your strength."

The pass through the Arcnorian Line would take them to the next Sephir. Once there, Darr would continue his quest to restore the Sephirs to their former glory, halting the Devoid's invasion into Ictar. His quest, and its madness, would continue.

The Spirit Summoner nodded to Feywen. He pulled the

blankets over himself. The firelight outlined Jinn's face. She was all he had left. Poor Erec had been lost to the Seekers, and he might never see his father again. Jinn, his little sister, would help to keep him strong, at least physically. Despite his deteriorating mental condition, he must ensure her safety, even if he no longer saw the point of it all.

He wanted to smile, a small gesture to prove his thoughts were musings, but Darr couldn't find the will to do so. Instead, he closed his eyes and rolled into his blankets, letting the nightmares consume him once more.

Chapter Two

"To answer my question, I looked first to the past. The Ancients, the men and women who called this world their home lived in ways I don't understand. They revered the world around them, and yet somehow, they let it slip away. Ignorance may be the cause, but I don't think that's the case. The Ancients, for all their power and understanding, suffered from the notion that they could take control over the life gifted to them."

~From the personal writings of the Divine, Zander

Night shadows retreated slowly across the city of Jacova, though the lingering darkness did nothing to stem the flood of activity both inside and outside its walls. In the east, where the night clung to the towering cliffs protecting the city's rear, Dwarves of all ages and creeds bustled about the streets. Some went about their daily business as merchants and tradesmen, while others tended to their homes, skeptical of the approaching battle.

At the city's southern section, its industrial center, blacksmiths pushed back the dark with the fiery orange glow of their forges. The busy clang of metal echoed along the walls, an orchestra of metallic sound. Outside Jacova's walls, the Tern bustled with like sound and motion. An interconnected series of ramps and earthworks, the Tern led from the forest below to the top of the cliff where Jacova sat, an eternal guardian. Beyond the Tern, the rock-strewn terrain writhed with activity. Cortazian men cut back the trees of the Triker, making way for the inevitable assault.

The Soul Seekers were coming.

Wrapped tightly within his familiar white robes, Nidic Waq watched the activity around him. From the tower on Jacova's main gate, he took in the sights and sounds, a hawk observing its surroundings, perceiving movement and life together. Both a Spirit Summoner and a prophet of the Archon of the Light, Nidic Waq had great insight into the

10

workings of the world around him. Though his abilities set him apart from the races of Ictar, the Soul Seekers would make no such distinction. They would destroy anyone they came across, regardless of their abilities, race, or beliefs.

The massacre at the Crossroads had proved that. Nidic Waq arrived in Jacova a day ahead of the Cortazian king, Ariel Forn, and his army. A trust set up between the Cortazians and the late Dwarf King, Gyrot Dery, ensured aid to the Dwarves in the fight against the Soul Seekers. No one, not even the Dwarf Elder Council, would deny Gyrot Dery's final wishes, but that didn't mean they'd make things easy. The Dwarf Elder Council, a petty bunch of old men, bickered for their own interests. Their leader, Brenan Jase, was the worst among them. The High Councilman stood not more than a few feet away, arguing bitterly with Ariel Forn and his general, Bru Kiln Tole. His words, previously a buzzing noise, grew more distinct.

"How can you expect me to draw over half of my troops away from the safety of the walls when I can't even be sure what we face?" Brenan Jase's hunched form coiled up, making him look like a frightened cat. A wisp of a beard trailed down his chest, and his eyes hid beneath his sagging brow. The Dwarf had the appearance of a lonely hermit, but nothing was further from the truth. Jase was a snake, always on the lookout to devour even the largest of enemies.

Ariel Forn remained motionless before the High Councilman, his body taut alongside the massive height and girth of his general, Bru Kiln Tole. "I'm not asking you to withdraw your defenses. I'm asking you to strengthen them. Since none of us knows what the attack will be like, we must assume the worst. The defense of Jacova will go much better if we can hold them at the bottom of the Tern instead of the top."

"That's exactly my point," Jase retorted. "They'll never make it to the top of the Tern."

Anger surged into Nidic Waq's throat, but he choked it back, calming himself. Brenan Jase based his knowledge of the Seekers on the few reports he'd read. He didn't understand the recklessness with which the Soul Seekers fought. They wouldn't stop at the bottom of the Tern, nor would the earthworks and traps in place deter them. They would scale the Tern in the same way the flow of a river works itself around a fallen log.

A sudden disruption at the gates below caused Nidic Waq's thoughts to scatter. Lacdur had arrived. Although he couldn't risk navigating the Currents, he could still feel their presence. Nidic Waq lowered his hood, knowing his startling green eyes and flaming red hair would draw them in. He turned to face Brenen Jase and the two Cortazians.

"Perhaps," Nidic Waq said. He kept his tone soft, but firm. "We should wait to hear what Lacdur has to say."

Irritation eradiated Jase's already pinched face. "The captain? He's in the field, not anywhere near..."

Jase clapped his jaw shut. Lacdur came into view at the top of the stairs. Dust covered the dark skin of his face. He'd endured much to get here all the way from Navda. Lacdur walked before Brenan Jase, his powerful body held rigid in the face of a superior, though defiance quietly burned in his eyes.

"Lacdur," Jase said with a croak. He leaned towards Ariel. "When Gyrot Dery was still alive, Lacdur led his personal escort, a position he's since relieved himself of."

Even without the aid of the Currents, the anger boiling within Lacdur was easily identifiable. Somehow, the Dwarf managed to keep himself calm. His resistance to Jase's taunts was a testament to his chivalry. Feywen and Gyrot Dery would've expected no less from him.

"What've you brought us, captain?" Ariel Forn asked, the blackness of his eyes washing away Brenan Jase's snide remarks.

Lacdur straightened himself. "I bring word from Feywen Dery regarding the Soul Seeker attack on Navda. I have valuable defensive and offensive information."

"Chaos," Jase said with a dismissive edge. "My scouts in that region would've alerted me of such an attack."

"With all due respect," Lacdur said, "your scouts in that

region are either dead or running for their lives."

Nidic Waq remained motionless, letting events move on without him. Bru Kiln Tole grunted in dismay and Ariel shook his head. Brenan Jase seemed unaffected, though the prophet could sense the beginnings of his fear.

"That is impossible. I had over two dozen scouts spread throughout the eastern end of the Triker..."

"And they're all dead, councilman, at least, the ones I found on my way here." Lacdur's features remained controlled.

Bru Kiln Tole took a step forward, his deeply scarred face otherworldly in the faint light. "Please, tell us what brought you here, Captain," he said in a voice so deep it shook Nidic Waq's chest.

Brenan Jase folded his arms across his body in a huff, but Lacdur ignored him.

"I've spent the last few months in the field with Feywen Dery, assessing the Soul Seeker threat. Two weeks ago, Feywen and I met up with Nidic Waq and a few others on an escort mission, something Feywen had committed to with the prophet." The Dwarf warrior nodded to Nidic Waq before continuing. "Our destination was the Dwarf city of Arcnor, but we were redirected at the Crossroads, a small village to the east of here."

"We've heard of the massacre that took place there," Ariel said. He gestured to Nidic Waq. "I'm sorry for what you had to go through."

Lacdur continued, keeping his thoughts to himself. "The Soul Seekers headed east to Navda. With our charges in tow, Feywen and I went to Navda to warn the people there of the impending attack. It took some convincing, but we were able to convince the Aratans to defend the city."

"Defend the city?" Bru Kiln Tole raised an eyebrow, twisting his features further. "My understanding is Navda has no defenses."

"That's about right," Lacdur said with a snort. "The city was unprepared to withstand any kind of attack, let alone the horde of Soul Seekers approaching. Feywen and I did our best to prepare a defense."

Brenan Jase shifted beside Lacdur, but he kept his arms crossed. "Why didn't you simply evacuate the city?" he asked with a hiss.

"An evacuation was impossible," Lacdur answered. "To flee to the west would've left us all exposed on open ground, and with barely a thousand men who could fight to protect us, we would've been caught and slaughtered. Evacuation by sea might've been possible, but the Aratans dismissed the Dwarf Navy weeks ago."

Brenan Jase started to object, but Ariel Forn shook his head and groaned. "What a terrible time to do such a thing." Jase took a step back, relegated to silence.

"How did you manage to survive?" Bru Kiln Tole asked.

Lacdur's composure faltered for the first time. His eyes shifted from Tole to Ariel, then to Nidic Waq. "We shouldn't have survived, none of us. The number of Soul Seekers that attacked Navda was in the thousands. In fact, the city was on the verge of being overrun when the Summoners...did something..."

Nidic Waq kept his stance rigid, his gaze riveted on Lacdur. He willed the Dwarf warrior to keep his words succinct.

"Over a hundred Spirit Summoners gathered to issue a prayer to the Fire Archon. When the Seekers broke through the city walls, the Summoners' prayer was answered." Lacdur paused, turning his head towards Brenan Jase. "I can't explain it fully. A fire erupted and swept through the city, taking every last Soul Seeker with it."

Jase paused, flinched, and gestured dismissively. "So, are we under attack, or has the Soul Seeker threat been destroyed?"

Lacdur ignored Jase's cynicism. "For the first few days, it seemed they'd been eradicated. I led several scouting parties along the peninsula, but we found no trace of the Soul Seekers. It wasn't until a week after the battle at Navda, when I finally departed for Jacova, that I discovered their presence again."

"And what kind of presence did you find?" Ariel asked, shifting his body closer.

"They're scattered, but I found traces of the Seekers beginning at the edge of the Triker," the Dwarf warrior said. He nodded faintly to Brenan Jase. "The scouts you mentioned earlier, I found most of them there, caught in the shadows of the forest."

Surprisingly, Jase kept his composure. "That doesn't necessarily mean the Seekers are coming back. The few that managed to escape could have killed my scouts as they fled from Navda."

Nidic Waq smiled without warmth. Brenan Jase couldn't admit to himself the danger he faced. He would make excuses in order to deny his fate, and when the truth finally arrived before him, he would cower. All ignorant men were the same, regardless of their race or status.

"You may be right, High Councilman," Lacdur admitted. Jase unfolded his arms and rested them at his sides. "But I fear that isn't the case. The Seeker mists, nonexistent since leaving Navda, built steadily the closer I got to Jacova. I tracked them to the south of here, which is why I took so long, but I didn't want to report to you without giving you some kind of estimation."

Brenan Jase shook his head. "And what estimation have you given us? Nothing you've said is clear enough to make any sense."

"I think he's been very clear, Councilman Jase." Ariel Forn spoke, his voice low and purposeful, his presence dark. If Ariel didn't have so much respect for Gyrot Dery and the Dwarves, he might've walked away from Brenan Jase a long time ago.

Lacdur leaned in close, his aura cold now. "The Seeker mists spread thick and wide to the south of here. I cannot estimate numbers because I've never seen the mists gathered so heavily before, but if what I saw at Navda is indicative of the force mounting against us, we could face thousands of Soul Seekers."

Ariel and Bru Kiln stood straight, their moods equally

sober. Brenan Jase didn't move. "This is all conjecture," he blurted out. His narrow body shook. "I don't see the point in investing more time and energy in a defense that may not be needed. Jacova's defenses are impenetrable, and from the good captain's report, it's impossible to know how many of these Seekers are out there. If all he's seen is mist, well that's not good enough for me, or the citizens I speak for. I need solid proof. Until then, the defenses which have proven sound for over two centuries must suffice."

Ariel Forn nodded curtly and Bru Kiln Tole took a step back. Lacdur remained motionless, his years of service to the king shining past his contempt for Brenan Jase. Nidic Waq came forward. He had a chance of neutralizing the situation.

The prophet lowered his hood. Jase's eyes narrowed when he peered up at him. "Everyone who's underestimated the Soul Seekers has been destroyed or close to it," Nidic Waq told him. "Those who haven't believed and been saved, have lived through the actions of those who didn't misjudge the Seekers."

Brenan Jase stood in defiance of the tall man. "Do not try to intimidate me, Prophet," he growled.

"I'm not trying to intimidate you, but instead reveal to you the truths from which you hide."

Nidic Waq let his consciousness slip carefully into the Currents. There was danger in what he attempted, but few options remained concerning Brenen Jase. Jase could no longer ignore the error of his ways.

The prophet reached out to Lacdur's Light, finding the memories of Navda's battle buried beneath the surface. Nidic Waq drew forth the images from Lacdur's light and thrust them into Brenan Jase, becoming a conduit for the memories in the process. Jase let out a gasp. The memories inundated his own Light. The Councilman's eyes rolled up into his head and his body began to tremble. Nidic Waq held him firmly.

Brenan Jase stood at the walls of Navda, watching and feeling the darkness when the Soul Seekers appeared from their mists, a silent wall of shapeless black and silver claws. Through the eyes of Lacdur, he rushed into battle against an enemy that fought recklessly, without caution for its own well-being. The Seekers ripped through anyone in their path, and Jase tasted the blood of those around him. He watched the glittering white souls evaporate from the bodies of the dead, taken forever by the dark creatures. Brenan Jase struggled for breath, fighting the memories and the battle with the Soul Seekers at the same time.

When Lacdur's memories had sufficiently played out, Nidic Waq removed them from Jase's mind. The High Councilman fell to his knees, coughing and hacking.

"What trickery is this?" he wheezed, unable to put any real force behind his words.

"No trickery was involved," Nidic Waq responded. He crouched down next to the crippled form. "I've given you a second chance, a chance to see through the eyes of a witness of the battle that took place in Navda. What happened there will undoubtedly happen here." Nidic Waq's voice lowered to a whisper, and he leaned close. "This isn't about the Dwarf nation. We're fighting to save all of Ictar. The Cortazians have come to your aid for this reason."

Jase began to protest, but he stopped himself, the words catching in his throat. He stared into the eyes of the prophet. Nidic Waq watched a flicker of uncertainty in the old Dwarf's face turn to fear and doubt.

The Councilman cast his eyes downward. "I fear I've made a misjudgment," he whispered. The others gathered around him bent close, except for Lacdur who remained at attention. "I've put this city and its defenders at risk. I must correct this."

With a shaking of his wispy beard, Brenan Jase rose up before the four men. He turned back to Lacdur and whispered a hasty apology. With a meek nod, he asked Lacdur to alert the senior members of the Dwarf and Cortazian armies. The defenses surrounding Jacova would be strengthened, effective immediately. With a final offering, Jase added he'd personally go to gather the members of the Dwarf Elder Council, dismissing himself with a bow.

Lacdur hurried after him. Bru Kiln Tole turned to Ariel

and said, "By your leave, Lord, I'll go with the Dwarf warrior and gather our officers."

Ariel consented and in moments, Nidic Waq stood alone with the Cortazian King. They remained silent for a time, looking down at the activity on the Tern below. The nature of that activity would soon change, though he wasn't convinced it would have anything to do with Brenan Jase.

"The Tern's defense will have to be completely rethought," Ariel said. His voice became an echo of his own dark features. "Do you think the council will actually work with us now?"

Nidic Waq bowed his head slightly. "Brenan Jase is not a fool. He'll work with us, and the rest will follow his lead. For now."

The first rays of sunlight were beginning to creep up over the cliffs backing Jacova, illuminating the trees of the west with an orange glow.

"In Navda, Lacdur said the Spirit Summoners prayed to the Fire Archon." Ariel turned to look up at Nidic Waq, but the prophet kept his gaze fixed on the trees. "That would be our Spirit Summoner, would it not?"

The prophet didn't immediately answer. "It was. Darr Reintol was there, and it was he who burned the Soul Seekers from Navda."

Ariel gave a barely perceptible nod. "Caeranol must've known what he was doing when he selected the boy. Such power. It's no wonder he's destined to find the Chosen of the Light."

Nidic Waq agreed. Caeranol, the Archon of the Light and guardian of Ictar, knew exactly what he was doing. Caeranol had chosen him as his prophet, after all. Ariel didn't know, or need to know, the fire Darr had summoned at Navda wasn't necessarily within his control. Worse, he'd tipped the scales balancing the Four Elements.

"We'll have to see if our combined tactics are enough," Ariel said. He returned his attention to the men working on the Tern below. "The Seekers won't do anything we expect them to do."

Cold crept over the prophet. "You're right about that, Lord Forn. All we can do is stall them long enough for Darr to discover the Chosen. Our only real hope rests with him."

Afterwards, Nidic Waq and Ariel kept silent. There wasn't anything more to say.

Chapter Three

"My understanding of the world that came before ours, the world of our guardian, Caeranol, is limited at best. The Ancients used a power I cannot fathom, a power born from their intelligence and not from the Sephirs. They understood how to combine the metals in the earth and the potions inherent in plants in ways that not only improved their lives, but sustained them as well."

~From the personal writings of the Divine, Zander

The staggering heights of the Arcnorian Line loomed before Darr. Even from the sheltered confines of their campsite, well below the Pass of Lore, the presence of the mountains caused his breath to catch in his lungs. How could something get so big? How could he be so small?

"It's something, isn't it?" Conra said at his side, his deeply lined face tilting up at the peaks.

The Summoner smiled even though he didn't want to. "Yes," Darr answered. "I can't believe we're going to climb up there."

Conra laughed and pointed to a wide cut in the Line that sunk down deep between two peaks. "That's the Pass of Lore, right there. It's a climb, but nothing like when we came through the Barricades. Arcnor might be out of the way, but the pass is regularly traveled. We shouldn't run into any problems."

"Except maybe for Ogres," Feywen said, causing Darr to jump. The Dwarf once-prince stood alongside him, his ability to move soundlessly still astounded Darr.

Conra snorted. "Ogres won't bother us. They keep to themselves."

From behind him, light footsteps crunched on the forest floor. Jinn came up behind him, her feel unmistakable in the Currents. *Why can't they just leave me alone?*

"Back in Tyfor, everyone believes the Ogres are savages," she said. "All we ever hear about them is that they're raiders, and brutally so."

Feywen shook his head, his blue eyes almost sad. "The Ogres are known to steal from time to time. Occasionally a group will get violent, but no more than any other race in Ictar. But because they keep to themselves, very few people ever see them as anything but thieves."

Conra kicked at a rock, sending it rolling away into the underbrush. "Doesn't matter anyway. We don't have anything of value, even to the Ogres. They won't bother us."

"I suppose you're right," Feywen said. He turned away, calling out behind him, "We should break camp and get moving."

Without another word, Conra stalked away, leaving Jinn and Darr alone. The peaks of the Arcnorian Line hypnotized Darr with their magnitude. Though his sister lingered beside him, he wished she would leave him alone. Let him have this moment of solitude. When she placed her hand on his side, it stung.

"Darr," she whispered, "I know you're not yourself. I know what Erec meant to you." Jinn took her hand away. "Just know that I'm here for you, when you're ready."

Darr nodded because that's what he needed to do and listened to Jinn's footsteps fade back into the sounds of the forest. Erec's death rested on his shoulders, and Jinn's attempts to dislodge his pain grew tiresome. He would use that pain to exact his revenge. He needed it, and he would not let it go.

The cold air from the mountains burned in his lungs. The Arcnorian Line no longer inspired awe. They were a massive hurdle, another in a long line of obstacles he'd have to overcome before he could see the Devoid destroyed.

Bitter, Darr stalked back to the camp to pack.

* * * *

The winter days hadn't quite started. Clear skies greeted Darr and his companions when they emerged from the southern boundaries of the Triker Forest. Sunshine warmed their faces, but the bite of cold in the air promised nothing of the mild fall air they'd experienced yesterday. The days ahead would be bitter, especially within the Pass of Lore.

Feywen led them south for a time before taking them onto a rock-strewn road leading up into the mountains. Deep ruts carved into the earth by wagon wheels indicated travelers frequented this route more often than Darr thought. Trees from the Triker swept up the mountainside, growing thicker where they approached the mouth of the pass, a great beard trailing from the Arcnorian Line.

They climbed through the morning and most of the afternoon. The road crisscrossed up the mountain, but Feywen followed it only when convenient. He favored the network of trails cutting across the road, a more direct path, but a steeper climb. No one said much of anything, even when they stopped to rest.

At dusk, they stopped and camped for the night on a ridgeline off the road leading into the pass. A caravan wound its way down out of the mountains, and together, the four sat by a small fire and watched the line roll to the forest below while they ate their supper.

Darr sat by the fire, but he didn't eat. Despite the arduous climb during the day, he didn't have much of an appetite.

"That's likely the last supply run Arcnor will get before the winter," Conra said while chewing on the tip of his pipe. The sweet odor of the smoke overpowered the campfire. "In a month, maybe sooner, the snow will hit and bury the city until well after spring."

Jinn swallowed her last bite of bread and said, "The Dwarves of Arcnor must know how to survive up there."

The bowl of Conra's pipe glowed red. He blew out a plume of smoke. "Arcnor has been around for a long, long time, since the advent of the Aeon Wars, as a matter of fact. The city has survived all this time, an impenetrable fortress in the middle of these mountains."

"Impenetrable maybe," Feywen said with a sigh, "but the Dwarves learned early on they couldn't stay within the mountains forever. Even during the Aeon Wars, they needed allies, and they couldn't find help by hiding. That's why they relocated to Jacova."

"But then why do they keep the Earth Sephir in Arcnor?" Jinn asked.

Feywen shrugged. "Before the end of the war, when the Dwarves finally claimed the Earth Sephir, they had it sent to Arcnor because there was an altar there, but also because it wasn't likely to be reclaimed."

"The Sephirs aren't commodities," Conra grumbled. "Everyone hoards them, but they should be accessible to all, not just one single race."

"Not necessarily, Conra," Jinn said. "Maybe the races hold onto them because they know to protect them and keep them safe."

The four lapsed into silence after that, for which Darr was grateful. The caravan disappeared into the shadows of night, though it likely had reached the shelter of the Triker Forest. The stars stretched out in the sky, a white blanket of pinpricks in stark contrast to the black earth rippling out to the horizon.

"I'll take the first watch," Darr announced. He turned away quickly so no one could dispute him.

He lost himself in the meeting between the sky and earth, catching a fading ragged line marking a mountain range he wasn't familiar with. The sounds of his companions disappeared, leaving him alone with his thoughts.

I've let everyone down.

Erec should be here.

The Chosen won't have to destroy the Devoid.

I'll do it myself.

I'll take everything the Sephirs have left to do it.

His thoughts repeated in an endless spiral, building in intensity with each rotation. Darr swallowed the lump building in his throat. Tears welled up in his eyes, burning with an odd sensation of anger and sadness. He wiped them away.

"Why do you keep punishing yourself?"

Jinn caught him by surprise. She'd seated herself beside him, but he hadn't noticed. "I don't know what you mean," Darr said.

His sister leaned in close, her huge green eyes shining in the star light. "You hardly eat, and you sleep only a couple hours each night, and when you do, you have nightmares. You rarely talk to us anymore." She touched his hand. "No one blames you for what happened to Erec."

Darr's face burned. "I blame myself," he snapped and pulled his hand away.

Jinn wouldn't let it drop. "Why? Why would you blame yourself for something you didn't do?"

"Because," Darr hissed, "if I'd just been quicker. If I'd paid closer attention, I could've stopped it all. 'Aos, I could've brought those firehounds out of the Currents before the start of the battle and saved hundreds of lives."

"Darr, what you did was terrifying, you know that, right?"

For the first time in weeks, calm confusion settled over the Summoner. He shook the hair out of his eyes. "What are you talking about?"

Jinn kept her distance. "You may've saved everyone in Navda, but think about what you did," she said without warmth. "You and the other Summoners released not just one or two, but hundreds of firehounds into the city. Elementals, Darr. Ictar hasn't seen that many elementals in one spot in well over a hundred years. We've all heard stories, but no one alive today has seen anything like that."

Darr shook his head. Was she reprimanding him for saving them? "Do you want me to apologize? I'm sorry I scared you all, but I was trying to save us."

Jinn reached out again, but she held back from touching him. "Don't misunderstand me. We're all grateful, but don't think summoning those firehounds earlier would've been any less horrifying. It might've been even worse."

"But Erec would still be here if I had," Darr said, his voice rising in pitch. "How can you say that? Who cares what the rest of Ictar thinks, at least our brother would still be alive."

"Darr," Jinn whispered, "at this point, I'd love to have just one of my brothers back."

The words stung, but his sister was right. Erec's death had brought about a change in him, something so drastic and filled with need that he wasn't the same. His need for revenge remained, but he knew something would have to change or he'd be lost forever.

"I'm sorry," the Summoner said. Jinn kept her face hidden, but her sadness radiated out into the Currents where Darr could share in it. "I've been consumed by this. I know I can't change what happened, but I want so much to end the Devoid and the Soul Seekers. I don't want them to hurt anyone else, ever."

His sister's hand touched his, and her round face turned to him. "You're doing that by continuing on. Every Sephir you restore will strengthen the Devoid's prison, and the further you travel, the more likely you are to locate the remaining Chosen. You will bring about the end of the Devoid, Darr, don't doubt that."

Jinn stood up, but knelt down at the last minute and hugged her brother close. "I meant what I told you," she said. "I just want my brother back."

Darr nodded and hugged her back. "I know. I'll do what I can to get him back."

He knew deep down that he wouldn't be able to.

* * * *

Dawn arrived frosty and cold along the ridgeline below the Pass of Lore. The grass that grew from the tundra had frozen into stiff spikes, and Darr's breath clouded in a heavy fog before him.

"I can feel the cold in my bones," he said over breakfast. It was the first bit of normal conversation he'd started in a while. "If this is the start of the winter, I don't want to be here in the middle of it."

Conra laughed, and Feywen smiled. "Don't worry about

that," the Dwarf said. "The journey to Arcnor will only take a few more days, then we'll be on our way."

"Snow shouldn't be here for a couple more weeks," Conra said. He took a sip from a mug. "We'll have to dress for the day though."

Before leaving Navda, they'd outfitted themselves with heavy coats, boots, and gloves specifically for this leg of their journey. They unpacked their gear, dressed, then kicked out the smoldering remains of their campfire.

They set out at once. Feywen took them up onto the top of the pass, keeping to the trails as they had the day before. The climb was much more difficult in their heavy gear, but the cold would've been worse. By midday, the peaks of the Arcnorian Line had engulfed them, and the Pass of Lore stood fully revealed.

"This isn't what I expected at all," Jinn said, nodding toward the cut of the pass.

Darr agreed. The top of the Pass of Lore wasn't really the top. The pass stretched onward for miles, a slow and steady rising of the terrain.

"The Pass of Lore was never intended to be a passage through the mountains," Feywen explained, his face obscured by his hood. "This is a passage to Arcnor, and only Arcnor."

Conra came up beside Jinn and nudged her playfully. "Don't you worry, Miss Reintol, there's still more climbing."

"At least it should be easier now," Darr said. He gave his best attempt at a smile. Conra laughed and followed Feywen, who was already moving.

Jinn looked up at him. "Thank you, Darr, for trying."

He laughed lightly before gesturing to follow Feywen and Conra. If only she knew what his insides were doing. He couldn't continue to carry on with his foul mood, but he couldn't ignore it either. His anger smoldered deep inside him, causing him physical pain.

Trees broke through the tundra in areas, but boulders and scrub brush comprised most of the landscape. Still, there was some beauty in it. Darr and Jinn had difficulty keeping up with the pace Feywen set for them during their continuous climb, though Conra appeared unaffected.

On their first night within the mountains, when Conra left before supper to forage for some ground roots, Feywen asked, "You know why Conra has no difficulties keeping up with people half his age?"

Darr shook his head.

The once-prince kept his voice low over the crackle of the fire. "Many Dwarves hold prejudice against the Elves," he explained. "You both saw it when Lacdur was with us. Those feelings come from the economic reasons I mentioned on our journey to Navda, but these are recent prejudices. The truth behind these feelings is because of what the Elves did to themselves during the Aeon Wars."

Darr shook his head in confusion.

Jinn asked, "What's that supposed to mean?"

Feywen leaned in. "Early on during the wars, the Elves used the Sephirs not to create elementals, but to augment themselves. They stole the Light from the Sephirs, using the elemental magic to sharpen their senses and increase their speed and endurance."

Jinn's eyes opened wide in shock. "That couldn't have been healthy."

With a shake of his head, Feywen continued. "It wasn't, not for the Elves or for the Sephirs. When the Dwarves found out what they were doing, they fought great battles to try to reclaim the Sephirs. Many Elves and Dwarves died, and in the end, the Elves abandoned their augmentations."

The sound of pebbles scattering across the rocks hushed Feywen into silence. Conra's gray head appeared over a rise in the rocks. A sly smile twisted his features.

"You know, you don't have to hide this kind of talk from me," the old Elf said with a cackle.

Feywen rose to his feet. "Conra, I would never...I meant no disrespect."

"Bah!" Conra set down the bag he carried, pulling free a twisted root, and crushing it into the pot simmering over their campfire. "All that stuff is ancient history, but I get why the Dwarves don't like us. All that magic got burned into our blood. It made us self-righteous and cocky to boot."

Feywen took his seat. "Still, I don't think it's respectful to talk about," he said. "Many Dwarves hold such ill will against the Elves over something that happened nearly a thousand years ago."

Conra pointed a gnarled finger at Feywen, and his face turned rigid. "But that's exactly the wrong take. I'm not saying the Dwarves shouldn't forgive the Elves for what they did, they should. But to forget it, well, that's something neither side should do. If you forget what happened, then you're doomed to repeat your mistakes. Better to keep it in the back of your mind, but move on."

The four lapsed into silence after that. They ate their supper and rolled into their blankets. Darr slept for a while, but his nightmares brought him awake far too early. For the remainder of the night, he watched the stars while thoughts of Erec and revenge played out in his mind.

An hour or two before dawn, Conra, who'd been keeping watch for the last leg of the night, knelt down beside him.

"You've been awake for a while now, Boy," the old Elf whispered. "You okay?"

Darr nodded. "Yes, just having trouble sleeping."

Though worry radiated out into the Currents, Conra's face showed none of it. "Well, would you mind if I went back to sleep? I can hardly keep my eyes open."

The Summoner sat up. "Go ahead. I'll take the watch."

Conra smiled and patted him on the shoulder, then retreated to his blankets alongside Feywen. Darr stepped over to the fire, warming his fingers over the gentle flame while Conra settled himself. In moments, the old Elf snored softly in the dark. He watched Conra, thinking of all the times he'd marveled at his keen senses and durability. How many of those skills came from the magic in his blood? Did other Elves share the same traits?

Darr sighed. His curiosity was fleeting at best. Once, learning new things about his world excited him, but now, it only bored him. Nothing mattered anymore, except finding the Chosen of the Light and the Devoid.

Darr snapped upright. His heart thumped wildly in his chest. Something lurked close by, seeping malicious intent into the Currents. He focused, letting his mind slip into the Currents, straining to sense what his eyes and ears could not. The spirits' voices were indistinct and garbled, the way they'd been prior to Racall's teachings. Deep breaths, he told himself. Relax.

Calm settled over him, but still, the spirits' voices came to him in indecipherable waves. He slipped further into the Currents, looking out into the wisteria lights of the spirit realm for signs of danger. Gentle shades of green, yellow, red, and blue wrapped through the ether around him, the Four Elements at work in the landscape. Small sparks of white light twinkled from nearby animals and insects, but nothing larger than a deer lurked in the dark. He withdrew his connection to the Currents, shutting out even the spirits' troubled voices.

What's out there? What am I sensing?

The Summoner rose, stepping past his sleeping friends to the trees at the edge of their campsite. The darkness of early morning masked everything around him, but nothing appeared out of place. Even in the shadows, nothing moved.

--Decept--ons--Summ--er-

--Get--He--

Darr's stomach churned, his heart pounded in his chest. He turned back to the campsite, the glare of orange from their fire an angry eye in the dark. A scattering of rocks at his feet warned him of danger, and Darr cried out. Something bit at his neck and his throat burned, preventing even a whisper to escape his lips. Burlap closed around his face, its smell suffocating.

The angry eye of the campfire winked at him before disappearing completely.

Chapter Four

"The Ancients succeeded in many things. They perfectly balanced the Sephirs and the Four Elements flowing from them. They lived harmoniously with the land and with each other, and while they lived here, this world prospered in ways unlike anything I've ever seen or known."

~From the personal writings of the Divine, Zander

Darr struggled awake. His tongue stuck to the back of his throat. He fought to open his eyes. When his eyelids finally rose, colors and shapes blurred together into madness. Rough, jagged rock bit into his back, and a white orb of brightness, maybe daylight, shone far in front of him. He shifted his body, finding himself able to move, restricted by leather straps around his wrists and legs.

What happened to me? How did I get here?

His mind, still too cloudy, tried to find reason in how he'd found himself in this state, but no answers could be found. The Summoner breathed deep, and familiar calm settled over him, allowing him access to the Currents.

Except the Currents, and the spirits, weren't there. The connection to the spirit realm snapped into place, but only numb silence filled his head.

Darr didn't panic. He'd gotten through most of his life without the Currents to aid him. Of course, he'd never been in a situation like this before, but his captors weren't likely out to hurt him, not yet anyway. He'd face this situation with the patience he'd known all his life. The thought reminded him of Erec, and the Summoner quickly shut it away. *Stay calm. Stay focused.*

The grogginess faded and his mind worked. The rough walls of a cave surrounded him, but nothing else. He likely hadn't left the Arcnorian Line, but then, he didn't know how long he'd been out. He remembered a little of how he'd gotten here, but the identity of his captors intrigued him more. The Soul Seekers wouldn't have bothered with a kidnapping, but who else were his enemies? Darr could think of no one.

The opening at the front of the cave darkened, and two blocky shapes moved into view, their bodies tall and gangly with unusually long arms, powerfully built even through the leather armor they wore. They were human in appearance, however no hair appeared anywhere on their bodies, and their ears pointed upward like the Elves, though they were much larger and wider. Ogres, Darr decided, though he'd never seen one to compare. Their skin color gave them away for what they were, a greenish-blue tone that had always accompanied descriptions of the Ogres.

The Ogres filed in and stood on either side of him. They carried weapons—wooden poles affixed with blades like a scythe, though narrower and shorter. Without the Currents to aid him, Darr couldn't tell from their appearance if they meant him harm. Roughly, they each grabbed one of his arms and lifted him to his feet, ruling out any merciful intentions.

A minute later, another Ogre entered the cave, this one larger and with a presence that suggested significance. His face, lined and craggy, supported the superiority he commanded.

The elder Ogre walked to him, his face suggesting defiance, though Darr couldn't imagine for what reason. The Ogre studied him a moment and said something in a thick, garbled dialect. Darr didn't know how to respond, so he remained silent. The Ogre spoke again, this time louder and with more force. The Summoner shook his head, but kept calm. With a surreptitious eye, the Ogre studied him another moment before taking a step back.

A sudden tugging from the Currents invaded Darr's mind, a strange sensation, but one he'd felt before. Someone pulled him into the Currents.

The Ogre was a Spirit Summoner.

Darr resisted, but his crippled mind couldn't focus...

...The wisteria glow of the Currents enfolded him and

the lights of the spirits danced wildly around. He spoke to the spirits, reaching out with his mind, but they couldn't hear him. He was as crippled in this world as he was in the physical world.

The mass pinpricks of light that identified the Ogre stood before him, imposing and commanding.

"You don't understand me in the physical world, but you'll understand me here," the Ogre said.

Language, it seemed, was universal in the Currents.

"Why have you brought me here?" Darr asked. "Why was I kidnapped?"

The Ogre drifted closer to him. "I have been monitoring you since you revealed yourself in the Dwarf city. Your power is greater than any Spirit Summoner. I want to know why."

How had the Ogre even managed to detect him? No one besides Nidic Waq knew how to access the Currents. Even the few Summoners in Navda he'd taken into the spirit realm knew little of how to find them again. Somehow, this Ogre had found the means.

His fear and frustration caused the spirits to swarm around him, but the Ogre Summoner swatted them away.

"You will tell me, Boy," the Ogre said, his words laced with anger. "How have you found this place? Why is your power so great?"

A flicker of doubt flitted through Darr's mind. Something seemed vaguely familiar about this Ogre, but he couldn't put his finger on it. Darr kept his thoughts from wandering. They would give him away.

"I don't know. I stumbled on it..."

The mass of light containing the form of the Ogre grew suddenly large, forcing Darr to shrink back. "You are a poor liar, Boy. You will tell me."

When he didn't answer, the Ogre's Light erupted, sending flashes of anguish lancing through Darr, physical pain somehow brought into an incorporeal world. He crumpled before the onslaught, his thoughts scattered. His defenses, fortunately, remained intact.

"You will tell me."

It took a moment for Darr to answer, to gather in the fraying ends of his emotions. "I already told you everything I know."

Again, the wave of negative emotion tore through him, forcing him to feel pain and misery. Satisfaction radiated out of the Ogre's Light.

"You have told me nothing, Boy," the Ogre said. "Ictar hasn't seen power such as yours since the Ancients left this land. What is it about you that makes you different?"

With much difficulty, Darr maintained control of his thoughts and emotions. How is this even possible? Why can't I fight back? The Currents were a reflection of his courage and resolve. Somehow, the Ogre had closed off these emotions, preventing him from fighting back.

"How do you like the effects of the dagroot?" the Ogre asked, responding to Darr's thoughts. "It's a special plant that grows in these mountains. When cooked properly, the juice of the dagroot acts as an inhibitor, depriving the mind of its capacity to feel. We use it to keep our prisoners subdued and calm, but the effects are doubly strong against a Spirit Summoner. Without the ability to process emotion, you have no power in the realm of the spirits."

The Light of the Ogre lingered in its expanded form before returning to its original size. Darr didn't move. His thoughts focused on nothing.

"You will tell me, Boy. I'll give you time to ponder your situation. Perhaps then you'll see the futility in withholding what you know..."

...The lights of the Currents vanished. Reality crashed in, dropping Darr to the ground like a rag doll. The two Ogre guards and their Summoner stood around him. Their pinched faces peered down at him with disdain. The Ogre Summoner said something to the guards in his garbled language. Without a second glance at Darr, the Ogre turned and left the cave.

The guards raised the Summoner back to his feet, and unbound the straps on his wrists. They each took one of his arms and lifted him off the ground, fitting each of his wrists into shackles fastened to the wall. He'd missed those on his initial examination of the cave. The Ogres hoisted him up, though Darr remained calm, a strange feeling. Panic should've set in by now. The dagroot really did keep him submissive.

Darr's feet barely touched the floor, and his arms, stretched out into the shackles, were already beginning to cramp. One of the guards turned to a hidden alcove in the rock wall. He fumbled with something for a moment and turned back holding a wooden cup. While the second guard tilted Darr's head back and held his mouth open, the first poured the contents of the cup down his throat, a warm, thick mixture. It tasted like bitter ale. The Summoner coughed up some of the liquid, but the guard poured more into his throat. Dagroot, he guessed, but he couldn't do anything about it. The dagroot would keep him subdued, leaving him no chance of getting out of his prison. Any help would have to come from outside.

Their duty complete, the two Ogres turned and walked away with little regard for their prisoner. Darr hung from the shackles on the wall, watching them go, his eyes growing heavy. His head dipped, his chin touched his chest, and he wished for someone to save him.

Chapter Five

"But the Ancients failed in some ways, too. They failed to recognize the seeds of destruction in their own ambition. When one among them decided it would be wise to examine the lengths to which one's life could be extended, the others encouraged him to do so. No one ever thought to ask if such a thing was a good idea."

~From the personal writings of the Divine, Zander

Atop Jacova's walls, Nidic Waq stood in the shadows between the torches. The Triker Forest shrank back from the Tern, torn up and cleared away. Pits flooded with oil replaced the trees and brush, scarring the once beautiful landscape. One thousand Dwarf troops stood alongside the Cortazian Army outside Jacova's gates and along the Tern, another decision that had been like pulling teeth with the council. In the end, the council had given in to the army leaders, allowing them to protect the city in a military fashion rather than a political one. Finally, Jacova was ready to withstand the Soul Seekers.

Nidic Waq pursed his lips into a scowl of concern.

The Seeker mists rolled in shortly after nightfall, the only siege machine Jacova would face. From their depths, the Soul Seekers would emerge, summoned into the physical world by the Devoid. While disconcerting, the mists were tangible. Their presence was manageable. Nidic Waq's unease came from the Currents. A sudden tension in the spirit realm prevented him from sensing anything beyond his own Light, like trying to search for something beyond the steely gray and white of a snowstorm. The disruption was an ominous sign.

The men gathered along the Tern appeared to feel the same way, their faces grim in the glow of the watch fires. Cortazian men stood alongside Dwarf foot soldiers on various levels of the Tern, each displaying the same look of fear of the unknown. Even if they knew the face of the enemy they faced, it wouldn't prepare them. The Soul Seekers, when they arrived, would trap them with their own fear. Such was their power.

Nidic Waq left the protection of the shadows, striding easily between the archers positioned along the wall. Those who turned cast wary glances. He'd gained some respect among the soldiers, but they feared him. The prophet of Caeranol remained a mystery to them, commanding forces that warranted fear.

The prophet stepped down the staircase to the army barracks positioned between Jacova's massive walls. The area abounded with the Cortazian Cavalry and the Dwarves' horse-driven warriors, the Daravens. He passed them all with the ease of fluid motion.

Near the inner wall, one of the barracks stood under guard. The leaders of the two armies needed a place to discuss their plans, so they'd converted this building into a conference room. A small nod to the soldiers standing guard earned him entrance, and he slipped through the door to the building.

Dim light and close bodies greeted him. Nidic Waq pressed against the wall and found the shadows between the light. A few faces he recognized among the leaders gathered around a table at the center of the room. Many others were present, likely captains and aides. Lacdur stood out among them, his grim face locked inside the wreath of light from a hanging oil lamp. At the center of the room, a debate began to stir up discontent.

"I don't see why we need to abandon our position at the Tern," Brenan Jase shouted. Stern puzzlement lined his face, and he pounded his open palm against the table before him. "We are safe. Reestablishing our lines at the front of the mists will only weaken the hold we have."

Ariel Forn stood rigid alongside the iron bulk of Bru Kiln Tole. The Cortazian King's black eyes bored into Brenan Jase. "We are not safe here. And we'll never be safe so long as the Soul Seekers are out there."

Blaque Eris, the commander of the Dwarf Army, leaned

into the light, his head a mass of shaggy black hair. Eris had served his army for nearly all his life, winning the respect of his soldiers and the Dwarf nation in the process. "I agree," he grumbled. "We should advance our lines and give them no quarter. Waiting will spread fear among our soldiers. By advancing, we give them purpose."

Jase cleared his throat. "I respect your opinion, Commander, but sometimes, you speak too loosely. As High Councilman, I decide what's best for our soldiers. They're Dwarf citizens and members of our democracy. As such, they fall under my protection. Advancing our lines against this unknown enemy will weaken their resolve. Keeping them here, inside the walls, is safer for everyone." The old Dwarf waved his hand dismissively. "What of our other plans? Why have the Daravens and the Cortazian horsemen been brought inside the walls?"

Behind Brenan Jase, a dark shape emerged. Tall and lanky, Vertain stepped into the light. He looked odd for a Dwarf, but he was likely the finest equestrian in Ictar. It was why he was captain of the Daravens.

"My liege," Vertain replied, "the Daravens stand ready to withstand an assault should the Tern's last wall give way."

Nidic Waq hadn't seen Vertain when he first entered the room. Not many people could hide themselves from him, even without the Currents to aide him.

Blaque Eris stood up from the table, his voice booming out. "There is sufficient room on the flats between Jacova's gates and the Tern's upper heights that will allow our cavalry to provide cover for a retreat inside the walls, if it becomes necessary."

Brenan Jase shook his head. "I'm concerned our soldiers will be less effective with the cavalry crowded among them. The soldiers of the cavalry would be better suited to fight beside our regular. In any case, the Tern has never fallen."

Ariel Forn rested his hands on the table, but youthful anger rose into his face, turning his features red and twisted. "You cannot be serious, Jase. You aren't a military advisor. You're putting your entire army at risk."

Jase remained calm, but his eyes smoldered with rage. "With all due respect, Lord Forn, you aren't my superior. I've no need of your criticism. I allow your army here only because of the conditions left behind by Gyrot Dery before his death. If you want my honest opinion, I don't think it necessary for the Cortazian Army to be here at all."

Silence fell across the room, thicker and harder than the building tension. Once again, the tenuous relationship between the Dwarves and the Cortazians unraveled from the words and actions of Brenan Jase. Someone would have to keep the councilman in check at all times.

"Now isn't the time to be bickering about our opinions," Nidic Waq called out, his voice carrying across the room. He stepped into the light surrounding the table, his composure calm. "Councilman Jase, you are aware of the danger posed by the Soul Seekers. While you feel safe within these walls, I assure you, your feelings are born of worry, rather than common sense." He raised his hand to Jase, whose mouth dropped open in protest. "Don't bother arguing with me. I've shown you what happened at Navda, and you know how unpredictable the Seekers will be."

Nidic Waq turned to Ariel, his voice purposely low. "And you, young King, mustn't let your emotions get the better of you. You are a diplomat."

Ariel gnawed at his lip, but he nodded in acceptance, adding nothing. The tension in the room eased, but the men around the prophet remained quiet and still. They seemed to be pondering what they were hearing, and weighing their options, though Nidic Waq couldn't be sure without the Currents.

"High Councilman, may I speak freely?" Lacdur asked. The Dwarf warrior had made his way to the center of the room. He held himself at attention while he waited. Brenan Jase hesitated a moment, then bowed his head.

Lacdur's gaze dropped to Ariel, but he addressed the crowd. "Some of you know me. My name is Lacdur, and I was once the captain of Gyrot Dery's personal guard." Something about the way Lacdur held himself kept the room riveted on his every word. "Your concerns speak volumes, Councilman, but I don't believe we should send away the Cortazian Army, nor dishonor their presence here. They've come here to help us, to aid us in fighting an enemy with which we're all unfamiliar. We cannot raise our expectations. We must be prepared for anything."

Brenan Jase stared across the table at Lacdur. He had no real fondness for Lacdur, and now, he probably regretted letting him speak. The entire room watched him.

At last, Brenan Jase looked back to Ariel. "I may have misjudged this situation, Lord Forn," he conceded. "I apologize for my offensive words." Ariel held his frame erect, but he gestured in acceptance. "If there's nothing more for me to do here, I think it would be best if I returned to the council. I will leave you to prepare without my politics."

The councilman lingered for a moment, keeping his eyes lowered. No one had anything to say. Even Blaque Eris and Vertain, two of Jase's most trusted men, let him go without another word. Jase made his way through the bodies around him to the door of the building, keeping his head down. When he opened the door and left, a weight lifted from the room.

With Brenan Jase gone, the army commanders went about their business unobstructed. Nidic Waq listened absentmindedly. He had faith in them. They would defend Jacova without jumping to conclusions, and they wouldn't give it up easily. Even though their tactics wouldn't succeed in the end, they'd do everything they could to keep that end from happening.

The bodies gathered around the prophet parted, and Lacdur stepped through.

"You did well, Captain," Nidic Waq said. "Putting Brenan Jase is his place before the rest of the leaders will likely have repercussions."

Lacdur shrugged, a wicked grin forming on his lips. "Jase wants to make this about a power struggle, so yes, we'll see repercussions. All that matters is that we hold Jacova for as long as we can." Lacdur shifted closer. "Have you sensed anything about the Soul Seekers, Prophet?"

Nidic Waq snapped to attention, though he'd never show it. He dropped his gaze to Lacdur. "I'm not able to detect anything right now. Something is being done to the Currents."

Ariel Forn, well outside of earshot, turned his head. "When did this happen?" he asked.

"It was when the mists first appeared," Nidic Waq said.

"Do you think the two events are related?" Lacdur asked.

The prophet smiled coldly. "I'd think it apparent they are connected."

The Daraven captain, Vertain, walked around the table. His lanky form slid easily among his brethren, coming up alongside Ariel. "So what you're telling us is the Seekers are disrupting the spirits you talk to. How does that help us in our defense?"

Nidic Waq stared at Vertain, refusing to back down from his cynicism. "It means we must be prepared for anything. It means the Soul Seekers could attack at any time and by any method."

"We should be with our men," Bru Kiln Tole announced, his words flat but not without meaning. Always straight and to the point, the Cortazian General was the rock upon which his army soundly stood.

With their meeting concluded, the leaders of the combined armies shuffled about, strapping on gear and weapons, preparing for battle. Nidic Waq turned for the door. He'd meet with the men shortly, but he wanted a moment alone to see if he could break through the distortion in the Currents and listen to the spirits.

The door to the building flew open, and a disheveled-looking Dwarf youth rushed in, his breathing rapid and face taut. His eyes opened wide when he saw Nidic Waq, but he shouted his message anyway.

"Commander Eris, the mists have vanished," he exclaimed. "The Soul Seekers are gone."

Nidic Waq turned back to the army leaders, words ready in his throat but stuck on his tongue. Without warning, the

Currents rushed into his mind, a tidal wave of voices and emotions, overwhelming him. Stunned by the force, Nidic Waq's trained mind wouldn't allow him to show his discomfort. He kept himself firmly planted in reality until he could make sense of what the spirits had indicated.

He blinked in disbelief. Jacova was on the verge of annihilation.

"What is it, Prophet?" Ariel asked, pushing to the forefront of the bodies around him.

Nidic Waq breathed deep. "We are in grave danger," he said. "Assemble the cavalry and have them meet me at the cliffs backing the city. Have all the men on the Tern prepare to tear down the walls for an evacuation."

"Evacuation?" Blaque Eris roared, his massive body clearing a path beside Ariel. "What's happening? You have to give us more than the order to evacuate the entire city."

Nidic Waq shook his head, spitting out the words. "We're being attacked from behind. In a few hours, you won't have a city left to defend."

Blaque Eris widened his eyes, but he made no effort to move. "How can you know this?" he asked.

Nidic Waq gave him a meaningful glance. With the Currents now clear, the prophet let him feel his certainty.

"Assemble the cavalries, Commander," Nidic Waq hissed. "You're all running out of time."

Nidic Waq turned, pushed past the frightened messenger, and hurried into the night.

* * * *

The heat of his emotions burned into Brenan Jase's face. He rushed from the barracks, his body barely containing the anger building in his muscles. The streets bustled with activity, but Jase heard none of it over the sound of his teeth grinding against one another. The world around him had become a blur of black and crimson rage, except for the Elder Council Hall directly ahead of him. Once there, he'd reclaim his city and evict the criminals attempting to oust him.

The Cortazians would take over the city if he didn't stop them. His commanders would allow them to do it. His control over the defense of his city spun away from him, but he'd tear it back. There were plenty of men loyal to him, men who would send Blaque Eris, and any other traitors, away with the Cortazians.

"Fools," he hissed, spittle flying from his lips.

The Cortazians had brought nothing but disorder to Jacova. No army, Seekers or otherwise, could ever get past the defenses of the Tern...

"Jase? What's going on?"

Furious, the Dwarf turned sharply at the sound of his name. He locked gazes with Councilman Bec, and his anger softened. As one of his most loyal supporters, Bec would be crucial in swaying the Council against the Cortazians.

"Bec," Jase breathed. "What're you doing out here at this hour?"

"I came to find you," he huffed. "You've been gone for a long time, and I assumed something had gone wrong with the Cortazians."

Excitement and relief buzzed through Brenan Jase. "You have no idea, Bec. Come. Walk with me."

Jase turned, resuming his urgent pace towards the council hall. Bec fell into line beside him.

"The Cortazians have gone too far," Brenan Jase said. He kept his voice low, laced with venom. "They want to use our army as their own, and worse, our own Blaque Eris is complicit with their demands. Before the end of the night, the Cortazian forces will command both our armies, and the Dwarf people will be at their mercy."

Bec didn't slow, but his eyes grew wide, panicked. "What...what are we going to do? This is an outrage."

Brenan Jase stopped, pulled Bec to the side of the road and away from any ears that might be listening. "Keep your voice down," he rasped. "First and foremost, we must retain the element of surprise. The Cortazians think I've fallen into line with them, but together, we'll muster the rest of the Council. Order will be restored."

"Yes, yes," Bec said, nodding his head like a toy doll. "We must hurry to the council hall then. I'll gather the others."

Jase smiled, his lips curling up. "I knew I could trust you, now let's get to work."

The two councilmen turned, but neither took steps forward. Jase's breath caught in his throat. Bec must've seen the same thing, but Brenan Jase dared not look over at the man. Such sights came once in a lifetime.

On the sheer cliffs backing the city's rear, several hundred feet in the air, a cascade of mist broke through the trees above and fell into the city below. The mist fell in a steady stream, a waterfall stuck in time, coalescing at the cliff base behind the council hall. The mist folded over itself, building up its mass. It heaved upwards into a white blanket that swallowed the council hall, moving steadily to the square where Jase and Bec stood.

White flashes of light flickered across the surface, and black shadows danced within the murk.

"What is it, Jase?" Bec asked, his words distant and confused.

Brenan Jase swallowed hard. Nidic had shown him these mists in memories pulled from Lacdur's mind from the Soul Seeker attack on Navda. The prophet was right. So were the Cortazians and his commanders. They were all right. He'd been the fool.

In the distance, at the city walls, a long cry from a horn warned of an evacuation. Too late, Jase thought. The black forms materialized out of the mist, dark and sinister, wrapped in tattered robes and armed with silver claws.

Brenan Jase whispered a silent prayer and closed his eyes. Cold washed over him and pressure built in his chest and arms. His breath stopped.

I should've done more.

Chapter Six

"Experiments led to further failure. Symdus, the Ancient tasked with unlocking the secret to everlasting life, was instructed to stop. I always wondered why Symdus tried to appeal to Caeranol and his fellow Elders to allow him to continue. He could have just gone into hiding, as we know he did, but no, he attempted to persuade the other Elders to his cause. I always believed the Devoid had possessed Symdus from the beginning, but I no longer believe this was the case. I believe Symdus could've been saved. All of this could've been prevented."

~From the personal writings of the Divine, Zander

Jacova erupted into pandemonium.

Against the eerie backdrop of mist spilling from the cliffs backing the city, screams rose up into the night. Innocent and torn from sleep, the Dwarves of Jacova cried out, unprepared for the death brought by the Soul Seekers. Nidic Waq's legs worked mechanically, propelling him towards the horrors he'd find waiting. In the Currents, there was only a roiling mass of fear and incredible sorrow.

You should've recognized this, he told himself. Somehow, the Devoid could manipulate the Currents. Caeranol didn't believe the Devoid was strong enough to extend its reach into the Currents, but he was wrong. All of Ictar was at risk, but especially Darr Reintol. The Spirit Summoner's presence in the Currents would draw the Devoid straight to him.

A band of Soul Seekers appeared out of the darkness of an alleyway and rushed him in a silent wave. The prophet drew out a thread of magic from the Fire Sephir, causing the robes of the Seekers to ignite. They exploded into ash, and Nidic Waq kept moving.

Lights flickered on in the surrounding buildings and clusters of Jacova's citizens flooded into the streets, alerted at last to the evacuation alarms. Somewhere behind him, the pounding hooves of the Daravens rumbled in his chest.

Another knot of Seekers appeared from a side street, their hunger drawing them towards the helpless. Nidic Waq turned the magic of the Fire Sephir on them, exploding them into ash before they recognized his presence. With his senses obstructed by the disturbances around him, the second group of Seekers emerging from the ashy cloud took him by surprise. Nidic Waq had enough time to throw out a spear of fire, scattering them before they overwhelmed him. The prophet backed himself along a butcher's storefront. The magic of the elements built on his fingertips. *Too slow.*

In an explosion of sound and motion, Vertain and his Daravens erupted onto the street beside him. The Seekers turned to this new threat, and Nidic Waq attacked. Golden light gathered on his fingertips. He threw out a whirlwind into the Seekers. The wind gathered them up and tossed them aside, allowing the Daravens to cut effortlessly through them. The gleaming spears of the horsemen tore through the black robes, leaving a scattering of ash in their wake.

Nidic Waq strode from the sidewalk to the closest rider, leapt up behind the Dwarf, and called out to Vertain. "The infantry will open up a path for escape, but we must hold the Seekers inside the city long enough for the evacuation," Nidic Waq called out.

Vertain gave a nod and called out to his men to follow. The Daravens hastened down the city streets, flowing easily between the clusters of evacuees running in the opposite direction, the horses responsive to even the slightest change in direction. Nidic Waq held tightly to the man in front of him, using the time to summon the Light from the spirits. He'd have need of the magic in the coming battle.

"Daravens, halt," Vertain yelled, bringing his men to a stop at a crossroads while Jacova's citizenry spilled around them.

From the city's west side, the heavy horse of Cortazian Cavalry rumbled to a stop before them. Their leader, Crusis Jiln, rode towards them.

"My apologies for our delay, Vertain," Crusis called out.

"We took the long route through the city's industrial center. We wouldn't have kept up with you with all the evacuees."

Vertain shook his head. "Doesn't matter, Jiln," he said with a shrug. He turned his black eyes to Nidic Waq. "Where are we going, Prophet? Where's the best place to fight back against these things?"

Nidic Waq pointed to the cascading mist falling from the cliffs above them. "The Elder Council Hall," he shouted. "The Soul Seekers are massing there. We must hold them for as long as we can."

Crusis Jiln shook his head. "With all these people about, my men will have to find another way around."

With a high-pitched whistle, Vertain signaled to his men. "Primes, stay behind and keep the street for the Cortazians open. Join us when they're clear." When he turned back to Crusis, he gave a nod. "No need to find another route now."

Vertain signaled again, riding off to the Elder Council Hall with his Daravens and Nidic Waq behind him. Pairs of Daravens broke off at regular intervals, controlling and herding the Dwarves fighting to escape the city. Soon, the Cortazian cavalry flooded into the streets behind them.

When the dark rise of the council building came into view, the challenge they faced took shape. Hundreds, perhaps thousands, of Soul Seekers poured into the square in front of the Elder Council Hall, a mass of writhing black shapes.

Nidic Waq released his rider and leapt to the ground, sending out the Light in a stream of white fire. The Light tore into the front ranks of Seekers. The Daravens and Cortazians collided with the mixture of bright fire and dark shadow, swords and spears lifting to tear apart their hated attackers.

The battle for Jacova had begun.

* * * *

Nidic Waq surveyed the battle raging below him, his vantage point critical to Jacova's defenders. From atop an abandoned warehouse, the Soul Seekers couldn't get to him, but for blocks in every direction, he could clearly identify their movements. The spirits aided him, both with their foresight and their magic.

The Cortazian Cavalry and the Daravens kept their numbers stable, but they lost ground no matter what tactics they used. Even with the leadership of Vertain and Crusis Jiln, and the support of his magic, the Seekers were too many. For every hundred Seekers destroyed, a hundred more poured from the mists. The Devoid gathered strength faster than even Caeranol knew, putting Ictar in greater danger than anyone suspected.

Despite the upset in the Currents, his magic was pulling through, a fortunate turn of events for everyone present in Jacova. Nidic Waq couldn't ignore the delicate balance in the spirit world, but he could work around it. He borrowed carefully.

A handful of Seekers tore through a group of Cortazian horsemen, threatening to break the line apart. Nidic Waq brought the Light to his fingertips and expelled it in a glowing white burst. The black forms disintegrated, and the battle raged on.

The resiliency of the cavalries was admirable. Both fought with equal determination, and while they came from different lands and endured distinct forms of training, they kept the Seekers at bay. From their high positions, the Daraven spears and Cortazian swords ripped easily into the onrush of Seekers, and their armored mounts resisted the tearing claws of their attackers. Ultimately, the Ictarians would lose this battle. The Seekers' numbers had nearly tripled since the battle began.

Another rush shattered the front lines, and Nidic Waq sent aid where he could. Neither infinite nor encompassing, the magic of the Light couldn't contain the numbers of Soul Seekers pouring through. The fragmented cavalry fell back. Nidic Waq rushed along the rooftop of the warehouse and leapt to an adjacent building. The cavalry passed on the street below. Nidic Waq summoned another thread of magic from the Fire Sephir. In a fiery explosion, the front of the warehouse behind him fell into the Seeker masses, slowing them.

The prophet ran along the rooftops, keeping pace with the cavalry. He loosened his connection to the Currents while he ran. He'd have to monitor what he used. If he continued using the Sephirs and the spirits, he'd have nothing to spare once he reached the walls.

A sharp set of cries caught his attention. Nidic Waq turned his hooded head towards the city walls. A net of bodies wormed their way along Jacova's streets towards the retreating cavalry. Bru Kiln Tole and Blaque Eris were mounting a counterattack. The foot soldiers would replace the cavalry, giving them a chance to regroup, and when the counterattack gave out, the cavalry would cover their retreat. Sound tactics from two of the most brilliant tacticians he'd ever seen.

Nidic Waq issued a small sigh of relief. The defenders would be able to hold for a couple of hours, but no more. The evacuation may or may not be complete when their time was up. The prophet listened to the Currents for a moment, sensing the loss of life coming from all around him. Many of the Lights consumed were Jacova's citizens, their flight too slow to escape the Seekers.

The evacuees needed more help at this point than the defenders. Nidic Waq gave the fighting armies a wilting frown before heading for the walls.

Chapter Seven

"After Symdus split from the Elder Council, he carried on his experiments in secret. When he began tampering with the Light, with life itself, he opened up the door to the Devoid. This is merely what I believe, of course. The Divine that came before me believed otherwise, that the Devoid found Symdus from the beginning and influenced him. Perhaps the Devoid was with Symdus all along, but perhaps not. Perhaps the terrible choices the man made brought the demon into him."

~From the personal writings of the Divine, Zander

Midnight came, and Darr Reintol despaired, hungry and alone.

The lethargy of the dagroot running through his system prevented any means of escape. His arms, cramped and numb, burned from the weight of his body. His guards kept careful watch over him, turning from the mouth of the cave every few minutes, regarding him like some kind of animal. They'd given him water once, several hours past now.

The Ogre Summoner hadn't returned. An ominous thought in Darr's brain told him it wouldn't be long before he reappeared.

The Ogre Summoner was something more than what he appeared. Robbed of his abilities, Darr couldn't figure it out, but his intuition told him to be wary. The Ogre Summoner had found the means to enter the Currents, but according to Nidic Waq, no Summoners in Ictar possessed that power. He couldn't have missed the presence of another Summoner in the Currents. No, something else worked against him here, something different.

Darr's maddened mind worked lazily in an attempt to find an answer. Conspiracy after conspiracy tumbled through his mind, but no sense came to him. He drifted, trying to find light where darkness cloaked his mind, laughing to himself when he failed and weeping when his laughter died away.

Deeply enslaved by the dagroot, his emotions came and went in uncontrollable bouts.

Shortly after midnight, the Ogre Summoner reappeared, this time leaving his guards behind. The man approached, his blue skin turned black in the faint light, his eyes yellow and bright. For several minutes, the Ogre stood before him, motionless. Pain lanced through Darr's head, a lingering agony, both cruel and debilitating. The Ogre pushed him into the Currents briefly before tearing him back to the physical world, repeating the motion for long minutes. Not only did the tactic weaken him, Darr saw no chance of escape. Before the Ogre Summoner, he'd become a prisoner in every sense of the word.

...The wisteria light poured in. The spirits swarmed wildly around Darr, feeding off his Light filled with despair. Their voices bored into him, drinking in his meager thoughts and emotions, dragging him into their mass. The intimidating brightness of the Ogre Summoner appeared before him, sending the spirits spinning off, rescuing Darr from their drowning grasp.

"I've saved you, Boy. Now you'll listen to what I have to say."

Darr didn't respond, could not with his mind so fractured.

"I cannot allow you to corrupt this realm. You've been brought here because your reach into this realm is vast and powerful. Even now, weakened as you are, your Light struggles to regain a foothold. You will not succeed. Your power is only as strong as I allow."

The Light of the Ogre expanded, enforcing its will on Darr. "No Summoner should be allowed to possess the power you wield," the Ogre said. "You swing your magic about like a toy sword, uncomprehending of its nature. How did you get a hold of this power? You will tell me."

Weariness swept through Darr, and he couldn't answer.

"Answer me, Boy. How have you found this power?"

Darr's thoughts drifted, his awareness lost in the wisteria lights. "I found it. It was shown to me..."

"Shown by whom?"

An image formed in Darr's mind, fragments of memory.
"A spirit...stone and trees...an Archon..."

"Why, Boy? Why did he choose you?"

"Because... to save..."

"Tell me why he sent you!"

Some inner well of strength bubbled to the surface. He
couldn't explain how, but Darr resisted the assault. A block
formed somewhere within him, denying him access the
answers the Ogre sought. He could sense whispered
warnings, the cries of the spirits giving him strength and
courage. The Currents shuddered in response.

"You think you can resist me. You are nothing..."

...Reality crashed back, followed by numbing cold. The
pain in Darr's arms and shoulders rushed in, stunning him,
but something had changed. Some part of his mind had
stayed in the Currents like an anchor. If he could submerge
himself, perhaps he could find a way to rescue himself.

The Ogre Summoner dashed to the small alcove in the
rock wall. He fumbled with a wooden cup, pouring thick,
dark liquid from a flask. The dagroot would work swiftly, and
once the Ogre had subdued him, he wouldn't let his
stranglehold slip again. Darr steadied his breathing, looking
for the line connecting him to the spirit realm, trying to find
what anchored him there.

His time ran out. The Ogre hurried over, the cup held
before his snarling face. Darr searched the fringes of the
Currents, fighting for a way back when a familiar sensation
washed over him. A rush of voices from the Currents swept
through him, there one second and gone the next.

The Ogre dropped the wooden cup, spilling its precious
contents to the floor. His eyes went wide and a guttural oath
spilled from his lips.

"You have no place here," a familiar voice boomed.

Darr craned his head and watched the wall of the cave
shimmer and melt, a cool green light emitting from the rock.
A shape emerged—broad, tall, and robed. Features and
appendages took shape, the solid face with eyes of emerald.

Darr could scarcely take a breath.

He'd summoned Racall, the Archon of the Earth, his teacher, his friend.

The Ogre guards appeared through the opening of the cave, their weapons lifted and poised to strike. Racall gestured dismissively towards them. Vines exploded from the rock, ensnaring the guards' arms and legs, holding them fast. The Ogre Summoner came at him, his face contorted in rage to the point where his features were of something else entirely. His eyes burned crimson, and he lunged at them. Racall stood his ground. The Ogre rushed forward. When he was inches away, Racall raised his hand, palm outward, and a spear of rock jutted up from the floor beneath the Ogre, sending him flying. He landed in a crumpled heap and didn't move.

Racall looked down. "I told you, young Reintol, I will always be your friend."

The Archon moved closer and picked up Darr gently by the waist. Greenish light sparked on Racall's fingers, and the metal of the shackles crumbled around Darr's wrists. He fell into the Archon's arms. At the cave opening, the Ogre guards struggled against their bonds, screaming out in frustration. Their attempts would be in vain. Racall set him on the ground, but held him upright.

"I summoned you, didn't I?" Darr asked, holding tight to Racall's arms for support.

The Archon's smile spread across his face. "How else, young Reintol? You were probably not aware, but in your dreams, you called to me for help. Though it was not a conscious request, you released me into the physical world. I waited patiently in the rocks below. I even found your friend, Feywen Dery, in a foolhardy attempt to rescue you." Racall gestured to the fallen Ogre Summoner. "When he brought you into the Currents, I held onto a small part of your Light. You must have sensed the connection, and in your desperation to be free, you brought me to your side."

Darr smiled lightly, admiration for the Archon welling up inside him. "Thank you, Racall."

"Your thanks are not necessary, young Reintol. It is enough that you are safe. But there is one more matter I am afraid I must attend to."

Racall set Darr back against the wall of the cave, leaning him carefully in place. He gave a reassuring smile, and took deliberate steps towards the fallen Ogre Summoner. The guards cried out at his approach, but with a quick motion from Racall, the cave opening sealed over with glittering stone, leaving them in silence and dim light. When Racall reached the Ogre, he knelt beside him and ran his hands over his body. He paused for several moments over the man's chest, his head lowered in concentration. When he was finished, Racall rose to his feet once more and walked back to Darr.

"Who is he?" Darr asked, watching the crumpled form warily from the corner of his eye.

Racall shook his head. "He is a man, a Summoner like any other, incapable of reaching the Currents without help. He will not trouble you any longer. Now give me your hands."

Confused, Darr placed his hands in Racall's. The Archon pulled him to his feet. Racall put his arm around him, holding him tight while blinding green luminescence surrounded them. Pressure held him tight. He began to sink, and a tremendous weight settled throughout his limbs, relaxing and warm.

When he opened his eyes, he found himself lying on grass, his body wrapped loosely in a blanket. The soft patter of rain played like music on the tree branches above him, followed by heavy drops on the ground. The sky, dark and ominous, didn't threaten him.

Jinn's face came into view, a smile of relief and warmth spreading across her face, and Darr knew he'd be okay.

Chapter Eight

"Demon or man, man or demon? It doesn't matter. What came out in the end was a demon, a creature of darkness in the body of Symdus. Seeking to absorb all life into itself, the Devoid began to consume the world of the Ancients. The great cities began to fall one by one, and thousands of lives were swept into the darkness."

~From the personal writings of the Divine, Zander

Nidic Waq found Ariel Forn on the city walls, ringed by his black-garbed kingsguard, his face turned out to the madness squirming on the streets below. The prophet followed his line of sight. A large group of evacuees fleeing the Soul Seekers ran into the Cortazians, effectively halting the counterattack while making themselves easy targets for the predators behind them.

"'Aos," Ariel swore, pounding his fist into his open palm. "Someone send word to General Tole about this lunacy. That break in the line must be fixed before the entire counterattack falls apart."

One of the kingsguard left without a word, rushing from the walls, presumably to deliver his king's message. Nidic Waq approached, keeping himself hidden in his hooded robes. The kingsguard tightened their ring around Ariel, but the young king issued the order to back off.

"Our time is growing short, Lord Forn," Nidic Waq said, ignoring the stares from the guards.

His face a mask of dark frustration, Ariel looked up. "That goes without saying, Prophet. We lost touch with the north end of the city, but the mists still pour from the cliffs above. Even if the Soul Seekers aren't expanding their numbers, I can't imagine we'll hold the city through the night."

"We won't," Nidic Waq replied, his tone blunt but sincere.

He turned and passed by Ariel, walking to the edge of the

wall looking out to the Tern. The soldiers put most of the ramps back into place. In some areas, logs had been lashed together to create bridges from one cliff to the next. The structure wouldn't support wagons and pack trains, but it would hold for the purpose of the evacuation. Crowds of Jacova's citizens gathered outside the city gates, held in place by soldiers and barriers until the Tern could safely accommodate them.

"We should begin the evacuation to the Triker now," Ariel said at his shoulder. He materialized from the shadows, his dark features unreadable. Nidic Waq felt his worry. "If we wait much longer, we run the risk of giving our soldiers inside the walls no room to retreat."

Nidic Waq shook his head. "I've never known much about military strategy, Lord Forn. Do what you think is necessary. I'll help where I can."

Ariel's black eyes met the prophet's gaze. He hesitated, but found his resolve. The young king called to one of his kingsguard, and a signal went out. Fiery brands fell into iron containers holding something other than wood, coal or some other mineral perhaps. The beacons exploded, an eerie yellow light, a signal to anyone looking to the wall that the evacuation had begun.

The evacuees filed out, slowly at first. Some pushed and shoved, running in fear, but the soldiers kept them firmly in check. There could be no more running about. Besides, with the Tern's ramps not fully in place, they didn't really have anywhere to run.

"Lord Forn," a voice boomed behind them.

Nidic Waq turned, finding Lacdur's familiar face, covered with grime.

"Three more ramps remain to be put in place. Our escape route is almost clear," Lacdur stated. None of his fatigue revealed itself. "The evacuees will be able to flee into the Triker as soon as they reach the base of Tern at the rate we're going. It isn't as ordered as I would've liked, but we should be able to get most out."

"Any word about the attack led by Blaque Eris and Bru

Kiln Tole?" Ariel asked. "You must've seen something on the way up here."

Lacdur shook his head. "We tried to get inside the walls, but too many people were coming out. There's still too much confusion down there."

There will be for quite some time, Nidic Waq thought. Inside the city walls, the glow of fire erupted into the night. The faint cries of fighting men echoed from the dark.

"I've given instructions to my men at the base of the Tern to begin leading the evacuees south towards Fora Lake," Ariel said, his attention focused on the evacuation. "Jacova is lost. Our defenses inside and out are shattered. There won't be any way to reclaim the city even once the Soul Seekers are gone."

"'Aos," Lacdur said, kicking at the wall. "Sad to see the city go like this, but Gyrot Dery would've been proud of the fighting we've done here today."

Sober nods came from all but Nidic Waq. Their best option now was to regroup and rethink their strategy away from the chaos of Jacova. But where? Nidic Waq wondered. Where could they possibly take another stand?

The wisteria light of the Currents flashed before his eyes, their appearance sudden and commanding. A summoning...

...*Nidic Waq submerged himself fully into the spirit realm, mindful of the fragmented balance in the elements. The lights of the spirits danced before him, but Nidic Waq focused on the brilliant shinning mass of light at the center of the Currents. His master, the guardian Archon of Ictar, Caeranol waited there for him.*

He flew to the shapeless form in a single thought.

"Why have you summoned me, Caeranol?" he asked.

--The Ictarians are fighting well, my prophet--

"I could be helping the Ictarians, Caeranol. You didn't have to summon me here to tell me that."

--Look then--

The lights shifted, and Nidic Waq fell to another level of the Currents. The elemental colors of blue, green, red and yellow wove together between the glittering white forms of men and women. *Fear and sadness overwhelmed him, but Nidic Waq followed Caeranol.*

The city of Jacova took shape, aided by Caeranol's ability to share his own visions with his prophet.

--The west end of the city--Do you see it--

Nidic Waq traced the walls around to the city's west side, but from very far above, like looking down at a map. The white shapes of the evacuees funneled into the streets, through the city gates and down the Tern. On the city's west end, an entire population of people nearly a thousand in number remained behind, trapped. The lights of the Currents shifted again, and the nature of the entrapment revealed itself.

"They're cut off," Nidic Waq said, his mind racing with the implications.

Concern radiated from Caeranol. --Forced into the wedge formed by the city walls, those people have been caught between the Soul Seekers and the Ictarian fighters--

"And once the retreat is ordered, the Seekers will go after their closest target. They'll be slaughtered."

--You must prevent this, Nidic Waq--So many lost lives will disrupt the spirits, and by extension, the Sephirs--This could be the keystone in the Devoid's escape plan--

Nidic Waq agreed. He must act quickly.

--Go--

...Nidic Waq reached out to Ariel Forn, grabbing his attention and pointing in the direction of the city's west end.

Ariel shook his head, confused. "What is it?"

"That portion of the city has been cut off because of the fighting," the prophet announced, loudly so Lacdur could overhear. "Nearly a thousand people are trapped there, and they'll all die if we don't find another way for them to escape."

"How do you know this?" Ariel asked.

Nidic Waq lowered his hood, his brow sunk into his eyes angrily. "You must act quickly, young Lord. We don't have time for this."

"Prophet, there's no other way out of the city," Lacdur

grumbled. "There's nothing we can do except fight the Seekers back."

"I don't think our fighters will be able to do that, but we must do something," Nidic Waq said. "If we abandon those people, we sentence them to death, but we also provide fuel for the Seekers. The spirit realm is already in distress, and this could break it apart entirely."

The four men stood motionless. Nidic Waq kept his gaze steady on Ariel, counting the seconds falling away, lost forever to indecision.

"Tunnels," Lacdur shouted out. His face turned rigid, his eyes hot. "There are tunnels beneath this city, left behind from the Aeon Wars. They haven't been used for decades, but they're there."

The Dwarf warrior turned away, facing the city's western flank. He wheeled back in excitement. "There's an old refinery, abandoned since the war. There are passages inside leading out of the city."

"But how do we get to them?" Ariel asked.

Lacdur took a step forward. "The army barracks stretch in regular intervals along the inner walls, with doors connecting them to the city for shift changes. We can use those to get past the hardest fighting. From there we can slip into the west end."

Ariel glanced briefly at Nidic Waq, nodding in consent. "Go quickly. Save everyone you can."

Lacdur gave a short salute. "I'll rally some men."

He started to turn, but Ariel shouted, "Take my kingsguards with you. You'll need all the help you can get."

One of the kingsguard came forward and whispered hastily in Ariel's ear, but he shook his head. "I appreciate your concern, but I will stay close by the prophet." The guard looked over him. He hid his fear, but Nidic Waq bowed his head, sending him a small sense of relief through the Currents.

The kingsguard hesitated, but he quickly found his place. He gave a sharp call to the men around him. As a unit, the kingsguard ran to catch up with Lacdur. Nidic Waq watched them disappear into the crowds of people and into the night. Ariel Forn, though young, knew how to act selflessly.

"How much longer do we have?" Ariel asked.

Nidic Waq's face tilted up to the night sky. "I can't be certain. But we must be ready when our time runs out."

* * * *

Time ran out an hour later.

A horn blew in the distance, long and mournful, followed by the heavy tramping of booted feet.

"The final retreat has been ordered," Ariel whispered.

Nidic Waq's wide brow knotted. "I won't advise you on strategy often, but I have something in mind that could ease our escape. Have your bowmen on the inner walls begin setting fire to the Seekers when they appear. Once the cavalry gets clear of the walls, get them away and out of the city. Do not let them linger."

Ariel nodded, turning away and issuing orders to messengers at the same time. Nidic Waq remained alone, taking his time concentrating. His mind slipped into the Currents, delicately feeling his way past the spirits and the elemental bindings around him. He kept himself firmly rooted in the physical world, his senses honed on what happened around him.

The Dwarf and Cortazian foot soldiers fled beneath him, their weary might flooding under the gates of the doomed city, following the evacuees to the Triker below. Fiery arrows launched into the night sky, silent and beautiful arcs. The cavalry horsemen rushed in to hold back the Soul Seekers while the fire archers cut them down. Somewhere on Jacova's west end, hundreds of survivors struggled to free themselves.

Through the filter of the Currents, narrated by the spirits, Nidic Waq saw and felt it all. Despite the order he sensed in it all, truly, chaos had broken loose. Panic set in. Men and women tumbled from the cliffs along the Tern. Morale had faded to nothing, resulting in soldiers and cavalry horsemen fleeing in much the same way. Such was the fear inspired by the Soul Seekers.

Time passed quickly in this state, but Nidic Waq held himself motionless.

"We have to get out of here, Prophet!" Ariel had returned to the wall, perhaps thinking he would save him.

Nidic Waq said nothing.

Frustrated, Ariel reached out and shook him, but Nidic Waq maintained his composure and concentrated.

"Fine. Die here," Ariel shouted. He turned away, rushing from the walls.

Archers and other soldiers fled now, including the Cortazian cavalry, likely because they were slower. Inside the walls, Nidic Waq could sense a handful of Daravens led by Vertain, struggling to survive.

The minutes ticked by. The perfect timing, promised by the spirits, was within reach.

Nidic Waq took a small step forward, then another. He found the first stair down from the wall, taking each consecutive step in turn, his focus unchanged. At the bottom of the outer wall, cavalry horsemen raced past, beating back the raking claws of the Seekers behind them. Nidic Waq slipped between them, oblivious but avoiding both hoofs and claw. Slowly, he walked through the city gates.

Ariel Forn, alongside Bru Kiln Tole, suddenly appeared at his side again. "Prophet, we're going to die if we stay here any longer. We must go!"

"Patience, Lord Forn," Nidic Waq said.

With an air-shattering set of cries followed by a volatile roar, Vertain and his Daravens came crashing through the outer gates. Dust flew in swirling clouds in their wake, along with the smells of sweat and blood. Nidic Waq's summoning tingled on his fingertip. He lifted his arms, palms up, and stretched out his fingers.

A bloody glow emanated from the space between the outer and inner walls, followed by a sheet of fire rising up across the open city gate. A handful of Soul Seekers managed to escape, but Vertain's Daravens cut them down quickly.

Nidic Waq raised his arms high. Twin orbs of crimson light encircled his hands, driving his summoning into the physical world. The red glow soared up into the night, growing brighter and more pronounced. Intense heat scorched the front lines, forcing the men behind Nidic Waq to back away. Smoke and ash rose in twisted coils, smudged black against the sky.

In an explosive roar, the dark sky turned golden. Flames, hundreds of feet high, soared into the night, their height stretching the entire width of Jacova's walls. The light hurt with its intensity, but Nidic Waq kept his attention focused on channeling the magic of the Fire Sephir from the Currents without interruption. Smoke filled his lungs. The searing heat sucked away his breath, but he drove his magic on. He sent the firestorm rolling across the inner wall and a dozen feet into the city, powerful and unpredictable.

The magic faded, and Nidic Waq stumbled forward a step. He took a moment to check the Currents. Distress radiated through the realm, but the bindings between the Four Elements were stable. Nidic Waq turned, facing the Dwarf and Cortazian troops cowering behind him. He commanded magic, a power forbidden to all in Ictar, a power not seen since the end of the Aeon Wars.

The prophet walked slowly to Ariel and Bru Kiln Tole. With a wondering stare, the king looked up into Nidic Waq's hood. "What have you done, Prophet?"

Nidic Waq didn't move. "I've given us an escape. The Seekers won't follow us this night. We'll be without them for a day or two. I won't be able to use that trick again for a while. No man should wield power like that."

Ariel watched him for a moment, but Nidic Waq turned away. Bright orange flames stretched skyward from the city walls, hot and intense. So beautiful, but still, so unpredictable.

"That man seems almost as dangerous as our enemy," Bru Kiln Tole muttered.

Nidic Waq smiled. Such was his place among the people of Ictar.

Ariel pushed past his general. "Let's get moving," he called out. "We have to find our men."

The prophet let a little distance grow between himself and the retreating army before he followed after.

Chapter Nine

"All hope fell away before the power of the Devoid. Symdus was a master of manipulation and deceit, and the Devoid now possessed his body and his powers. The Light it had stolen made it strong enough to repel any attack. Imagine trying to fight against a tornado. Where would you attack? Where would you run when your attack failed? The Ancients... they must've been so terrified."

~From the personal writings of the Divine, Zander

Darr's eyes opened, summoned awake by the stars above. He twisted his neck, loosening the muscles still tight from his captivity. He took in a deep breath, and tasted the coldness of the mountain air. The first signs of brightening in the east marked the dawn of a new day, still hours away, but it brought the promise of something new. Around him, his companions slept within the nestling folds of a small defile in the rock. Their presence didn't comfort him.

The screams from the Currents still echoed in his ears.

"You sense it as well, young Reintol?" Racall asked from somewhere beside him.

Darr smiled slightly, warmed by the sound of his protector's voice. He shook the hair from his eyes. "What's happening?"

Racall's darkened bulk shifted. "You hear the spirits crying out in despair. Many Lights have been stolen this night, and the Currents suffer."

Free of the dagroot now, Darr made the connection with the spirit realm easily. The spirits' voices rose up, hard and cluttered, and the unease they projected overwhelmed him. Darr focused, redirecting his confidence, giving himself space between the cries of the spirits and his thoughts.

"They are tormented," Racall said. His features hid in the shadows. "The cycle of their existence has been torn asunder, and with nothing else to do, they cry out their pain and swirl through their realm, attempting to make do with the

63

injustice served them." The Archon of Earth crouched forward and his broad features became visible in the starlight. "They are much like yourself, young Reintol."

The words sounded strange. Their truth weighed heavily, nearly crushing him with understanding. He resisted, and a dark shadow rose up, turning the light of understanding to ignorant blackness once more.

"The spirits are nothing like me," Darr whispered, keeping his face bent low so Racall couldn't see him. "They aren't even alive. They're little beads of light, fragmented memories and emotions floating in the ether. They aren't aware of what they're doing."

"You are wrong," Racall retorted with repugnance. "Your understanding of the spirits is small, and so you do not see the likeness I do."

The Archon rose and walked away, his massive form blocking out the light of the stars, swaying heavily across the slope of the pass. Darr let him go. He didn't feel like giving in to anyone's manipulations, but especially not from a creature pretending at being human. How could Racall know what he was thinking? How could he even relate? Suddenly furious, Darr leapt to his feet and stormed after the Archon. What right did a spirit creature have explaining how he should feel?

He approached Racall's black shape, massive in the surrounding shadow. An eerie calm fell over him, a manipulation of the Currents, but Darr allowed it to take hold of him. His anger drained away, replaced with what little tranquility remained inside him. For the first time in nearly two weeks, his mind cleared.

"You still do not understand the spirits," Racall stated. He did so with enough inflection he might've been asking a question.

Darr shook his head. "I understand them enough to know they're not alive like I am. What they feel, they feel as a whole."

Racall's position didn't change, but his presence shifted closer, more comforting. "The spirits are funny creatures, young Reintol. They are independent of the physical world, and yet they rely on it at the same time. After all, the world in which they live is nothing but a reflection of this reality. When a child cries in the darkness of reality, the spirits detect this and sadness shimmers through their realm. But there is almost always a balance, such as the smile on the face of a young lover."

Racall's massive form turned from comforting to commanding. "But now, in this time of fear and madness, there is little happiness to create a balance. Worse still, there are less and less spirits accumulating in the Currents to help sustain the impact of these emotions. They feel only the pain and suffering, and their cries echo that pain because they can sense nothing else from the outside world."

"But, there's more in this world than just pain," Darr said, lifting his head. Racall's presence withdrew. "Even though there's anger and suffering, there are small moments of happiness. I felt them tonight, when you and the others rescued me from the Ogres."

"So then, why do you continue to feel only pain?"

The question, though seemingly small, hit Darr like the pounding of iron against stone. It jarred him, ringing truth in his ears, forcing him to see something he'd been missing since Erec's death. Enlightened and horrified, Darr realized he'd done something terribly wrong.

Racall nodded slowly. "Yes, young Reintol. Now do you see?"

Understanding came slowly. "All this time, I've been blaming myself for Erec's death. I've been holding these feelings of regret and sadness and anger, feeding off them and not allowing myself to see beyond them. I held myself responsible for what happened to my brother, and I never stopped to look at what I'd done." Darr looked up at Racall's blocky form. "I did something bad, didn't I? What happened to me in Navda?"

The Archon shook his head. "I cannot answer that for you. You must find the answer for yourself."

The Summoner pushed past his immediate urge to

object. The answers lay within him. His memories of Navda returned, a tapestry of fragmented sounds and images, swiftly returning to startling clarity. The faces of the Summoners during his mass summoning gathered around him. The bleak and bloody landscape of the gardens forced him to recoil, but he dove deeper into his memories anyway. He remembered his time in the Currents, his struggle to rally the other Summoners to him in an attempt at a mass summoning. He relived his confrontation with the Archon of Fire, and the failure that ensued. The Archon wouldn't give him what he asked for.

"I wasn't in control of myself," Darr whispered. "I was too frantic and frustrated, and when I felt Erec's Light fade away, I gave in completely to my anger. I tore the magic of the Fire Sephir from its Archon."

"Yes," Racall answered, his voice clear, but not reprimanding. "In that moment, you became everything a Summoner should never be. You reacted to your emotions rather than to your thoughts and your needs. The Archon of Fire could not comply with such a demand, and so you took her magic."

Darr's jaw dropped open. "But the firehounds... I summoned them. I created them from the Fire Sephir's magic."

"Did I not once tell you that elementals are always born from unbalance?" Racall reprimanded. "You should have known right away what the presence of the firehounds implied."

Darr trembled. "But I didn't mean to do any of this. It just... happened."

"It does not matter, young Reintol. You are a Summoner, a powerful one at that, and you can never allow your emotions to control you in such a way. It was one of the first lessons I taught you."

Darr took a deep breath, his guilt profound. "How am I supposed to deal with this, Racall? How am I supposed to forget what happened to Erec and what I did to the Fire Archon?"

Racall placed his hand on his shoulder, the weight of his burden. "You are not supposed to forget, young Reintol. You are supposed to accept what happened. By accepting what has happened, you galvanize yourself against ever letting it happen again. Your brother has fallen, a chance of fate, a fault that lies nowhere except in the hands of the Soul Seekers. You must not let yourself be angry, for those emotions will stay deep inside you, even when you are in the Currents. If you accept what has happened, and you face your anger and your fear and sadness, you release it as well."

Racall lifted his massive hand and leaned back into the darkness. "As for the Archon of Fire, she holds no ill will against you. There is no way for you to return the magic you have taken, but if you succeed in your quest to restore the Sephirs, that power will be renewed."

Darr bowed his head like a child before the giant. Racall had been his mentor, but he'd also been his friend. For weeks now, he'd been stuck in a web of anger and regret, held fast by his own emotions. Racall had allowed him a release from those emotions, and he'd forever be grateful for the Archon.

"What would've happened if I hadn't realized this?" Darr asked in a whisper.

With eyes set, Racall answered firmly. "Had you tried a summoning, the Archons would have refused you. You would have been forced to take their magic once again, and the Sephirs, already taxed to their limits, would have collapsed. The chaos before the creation of the Currents would be unleashed, as would the Devoid."

Darr stood motionless in shock. "I could've...I could've destroyed everything I'm trying to save."

"You could have," Racall soothed, "but you did not."

The Summoner shook his head. "Is this what it means to be a Summoner? Am I supposed to close myself off from my emotions?"

"You know that is not the case," Racall replied. "Being a Summoner is about having self-control and gentle reflection rather than giving into the human condition. Your life will be different from here on out, but I encourage you to accept what you are rather than fight against it."

Tears welled up in Darr's eyes but he brushed them away quickly. "I have to accept Erec's death, and move on from it."

Racall smiled sadly. "Yes."

The path ahead held perils beyond comprehension, but the only way to protect those around him was to master his Summoning skills. This night, he'd discovered what an impact those skills could have. Now that he knew, he could move forward. The tiny stars above, solitary specks of brightness making up the whole of the sky, were much like the Currents. Like those stars, he had to find a way for his Light to burn independent of the others around him.

"You see, young Reintol, already you are charting your path."

Darr let a smile part his lips, swept up in the sudden gratitude for Racall's presence. "I don't think it'll be easy," the Summoner said.

In the blackness, the shadow of Racall's head shook from side to side. "This is true. The cries we have heard in the Currents herald the fall of Jacova. You have less and less time the further you travel, and worse, the Seekers will begin tracking you now. The Ogre Summoner who captured you was more than what he appeared. The Devoid knows of your presence, and it is trying to stop you. It can reach into the physical world now by manipulating the weak. It has done so with the Ogre Summoner, and it will try again."

A cold chill settled in Darr's stomach at the mention of the Devoid. How would he summon the strength to stand up to such an evil? Racall's strong hand fell on his shoulder, imbuing him with his own hidden confidence. "You are not weak, young Reintol. If you remain courageous and wise, you will be victorious. The Devoid cares only for the vices that bring about destruction. It knows nothing of virtue. From that, you will gain the upper hand in the battle ahead."

Darr understood, but the truth in Racall's words shocked him suddenly. "You said Jacova has fallen. How do you know for certain?"

The Archon withdrew his hand. "The Soul Seekers

caused anguish in the Currents when they took the Lights of many. Even though the spirit realm is clouded, it is easy enough to detect in which direction those cries originate. The spirits may not give information willingly, but their pain tells us what we need to know."

Darr closed his eyes and opened his mind to the spirits. He traced their pain, letting it pull him where it chose over the mountains and the forests, settling finally on a rocky rise at the western edge of the Triker Forest. The images were vague and the sensations muddled, but Darr knew without a doubt that he'd found Jacova.

"But we cannot know for certain that Jacova has fallen," Darr said, a silent hope.

This time, when Racall motioned in the dark, he nodded his head. "We know because the Dwarf city has an unforgiving defense. The only way such a massive loss of life could be perpetuated is if that defense was rendered useless."

Darr shook his head, thinking it over. He didn't know how to read the Currents the way Racall did, but he found it hard to accept the possibility the defenders of Jacova had failed. The loss, while tragic, couldn't garner any further attention. With his time limited, he couldn't ponder over how much time he had left. From now on, every minute would count until he succeeded in restoring the Sephirs and finding the Chosen of the Light. Darr didn't want to give the matter another moment of consideration.

"You should rest," Racall soothed from the darkness. "Tomorrow, we will reach Arcnor, and yet another trial for you to pass. Do not forget what you have learned here tonight."

Darr's eyes grew heavy, and the nodding of his head mechanical. "I won't," he said.

Darr let his feelings of pain and anger fade away into the dark. His emotions stuck with him, but they didn't interfere with his thoughts and dreams like they had over the days past, ruling over him like a tyrant king. They were a part of him now, bound inextricably to his Light despite the pain they caused. They no longer frightened. They became manageable and easier to accept.

Erec was dead.

The Currents were weaker because of him.

It didn't matter. He would make up for it and return the world to itself.

Chapter Ten

"I wonder how Caeranol felt during this time of destruction. Did he regret his confrontation with Symdus that had led to the birth of the Devoid? Did he despair at what could've been? I cannot believe he did. Caeranol pondered how best to save the life around him. That is why the spirits eventually chose him to become their emissary. That is why he is still our guardian today."

~From the personal writings of the Divine, Zander

Dawn light warmed Darr's face when he woke. He sat up and leaned against the log behind him, pushing the blanket from his body. How he'd ended up back at the campsite wasn't much of a mystery. Racall had carried him around before. Darr scanned the campsite. There was no sign of the Archon, but the spirits' tiny voices told him Racall hadn't yet returned to the Currents.

"You're awake," Conra said from behind the small cooking fire. His wizened features turned from mild interest to excitement.

Jinn poked her head up from somewhere behind the Elf, her task forgotten. A quick gasp escaped her lips and she dashed around the fire to Darr's side. She brushed the hair from his face and began checking him over like an injured child until Darr gently pushed her away.

"We were worried about you," she soothed. "Racall told us you'd been forced to eat some kind of poison. Conra gave you some herbs so you would sleep, but we didn't know when you would recover."

Darr smiled and he hugged her. The sound of his sister's voice comforted him deeply, reminding him how much he loved her. For the moment, his worries faded away, but he would have to make amends for the wrongs he'd committed.

"I'm fine," he said. He forced a smile but failed badly. "Where's Feywen?"

"He left at dawn," Conra answered, reaching out to Darr

with a steaming bowl loaded with boiled oats. "We're far enough away from those Ogres that they shouldn't be able to find us, but he wanted to be sure." The old Elf gave him an intense look. "You had us worried, Boy."

Darr accepted Conra's offering of breakfast. "I was worried, too."

Hungrily, the Summoner began eating while an eerie silence grew around him. With his hunger sated, he set the bowl aside. Jinn and Conra both stared at him, their features frozen and stoic.

"Racall told us what happened to you," Jinn said in a near whisper, settling her hand on his own.

Darr looked up suddenly in shock. "He did?"

"Said some Ogre Summoner was trying to torture you." Conra grunted.

Darr let out a small sigh of relief. He wanted to confess his wrongs, and fortunately, Racall hadn't done it for him.

"It must have been horrible." Jinn brought up her hand again and brushed the hair from his face.

The torture Darr had inflicted on himself had taken a greater toll.

"I want to apologize to you both," Darr began slowly, his voice strong but guarded. "Please, hear me out. I've been acting strangely ever since Navda. There's no excuse for how I've been pushing you all away."

He expected them to protest, but Conra and Jinn remained silent. The Summoner explained how he'd let his anger at Erec's death blind him, causing him to tear the magic of the Sephirs from the spirit realm. He'd blamed himself for Erec's death. He'd vowed to destroy the Seekers, and this quickly became his only comfort, but in the process, he pushed everyone around him away.

Conra and Jinn listened patiently while he talked, absorbing the words with silent reflection. Feywen, who'd returned from his foray, took a seat and kept quiet while Darr talked. When the Summoner finished he breathed a sigh of relief.

"There isn't anything we hold against you, Darr," Feywen

offered. "Your feelings are your own, true, but trudging through the suffering after the loss of a loved one is something we've all dealt with."

Conra shifted beside him and cleared his throat in the process. "I ran from my home and family to escape my troubles, and I saw you starting down the same path. You've done well despite your behavior the last couple of weeks. It took me nearly a lifetime to realize the mistakes I've made. You've done it in the span of a few days."

"It isn't just the loss of Erec," Darr replied, reaching out of habit to hold Jinn's hand. "It's what I did to the Currents. I could've destroyed the one thing we're trying to save."

"But you didn't," Jinn said with a slow smile. "Some part of you realized what was happening. You fought with your emotions for some reason, and in the end, you won. I think Erec would've been proud of you for that."

Darr wasn't sure if he agreed, but he wouldn't discredit his sister's kind words. He pulled her close and hugged her, grateful for her presence and perseverance.

Feywen exhaled sharply, rising to his feet. "It appears we've settled things. You should all be pleased to know there is no sign of the Ogres in the direction of Arcnor or back from where we came. We should have a relatively easy journey ahead."

"No."

Racall appeared behind them, his massive form sliding out of the rock of the defile. "This journey is just beginning," he said. "What you have all been through so far were merely stepping stones. Each of you will be tested in the coming days."

The Archon stood towering over them in the silence. "Have you told them, young Reintol?"

Darr shook his head, knowing what Racall expected him to tell them. He looked back to his friends, and his gaze settled on Feywen. "Last night, Jacova fell to the Soul Seekers."

"What?" the once-prince hissed, his feet rooted in place.

"We can't be certain, but there was a massive outcry

from the Currents last night. It came from the direction of Jacova."

"We can be certain now," Racall affirmed. "I have done some searching on my own. There is a mass exodus of Dwarves and Cortazians flooding south from the Triker. Their destination is Fora Lake, but at least we know there are survivors."

Feywen's expression turned from anger to confusion. "How could this happen?" he asked, wheeling away. "The city should've been able to withstand an assault for at least several days."

Racall shook his head. "I do not know how it happened. The specifics will have to wait until later. Right now, we must focus on the task of reaching Arcnor."

With sober nods and nothing more to say about the matter, the group rose and began packing up the campsite for their departure. Darr went about his work swiftly and with few words. Within a few minutes, they'd broken down their camp and packed. Feywen started into the pass without hesitation. The blackness of the Dwarf's mood rang through the Currents, filling the spirit realm with regret and grief.

With Feywen in the lead, the small company started back out into the pass. Conra followed behind Darr and Jinn, and Racall trailed far behind, seemingly not even a part of them. They moved quickly with clear skies overhead and the cool air. Urgency pushed them along. The fall of Jacova had marred them, reminding them nothing lasted long in this age of war.

Darr walked in silence beside Jinn, but nonetheless, her presence comforted him. The high mountain peaks of the Arcnorian Line nestled the rolling hills of the pass. For the first time since they entered, Darr felt their presence clearly. They weren't the mountains back home. They were huge, snow-capped monoliths that both reassured and awed him. The pass stretched on ahead, a winding river of green and gray that wound upward seemingly forever. Morning passed away, and the cool air turned colder. They stopped briefly for lunch, consuming a quick meal before starting again.

Shortly after noon, a massive wall rose up before them at a gathering of peaks. The pass suddenly swooped down into a little valley, split at its center by a crooked chasm. On the opposite side of the chasm, nestled in the gathering peaks, buildings and homes accumulated around a tall fortress. Strange, dark cloth stretched out from the huddled buildings into the plains within the valley, covering much of the greenery.

"What is that stuff?" Jinn asked, pointing to the dark cloth.

"Netting to trap the heat from the sun," Feywen replied calmly. "It keeps the fields from freezing. Without them, Arcnor wouldn't be able to support itself."

Racall took the lead from Feywen, and without another word, he started down the broad hillside into the valley. The day quickly waned with the sun already disappeared behind the mountain peaks. At the valley floor, a structure took shape, something Darr had missed on his first inspection. A bridge, enormous in width and height, spanned the gap and opened the path to Arcnor. The stone and wood of the structure had been painted or colored to camouflage it from anywhere except directly before it.

"This bridge is called the Galalin," Feywen explained. "Without it, Arcnor might've fallen multiple times during the Aeon Wars. It is the city's only defense." He pointed to a series of stone pillars on the opposite side of the chasm, chains extended to the bridge from them. "Those pillars contain the machinery that operates the Galalin. If the city is threatened, half the bridge can be pulled away while the other swings harmlessly down into the chasm. That, my friends, is Dwarf engineering at its finest." While Feywen's heart undoubtedly ached, the pride he felt in his people shined through.

On the opposite side of the chasm, a cobblestone road stretched up from the valley floor. Beneath their low-hanging nets, the farmland supporting the city stretched to either side of the road. The weave of the nets wasn't so tight sunlight couldn't get through. Humid heat rose from the fields, trapped beneath its blanket.

They climbed, leaving the warm protection of the fields. Low buildings of stone firmly planted in the earth popped up around them, some were built into the rock of the mountains. Despite the cold, gray of the buildings, Arcnor had a homey feel, a city at ease with its surroundings. They passed a few residents while they made their way up the hill, people who acted friendly, but nervous, a likely welcome for travelers not of Dwarf lineage.

Their destination rested at the top of the hill where it joined the mountains. The fortress, all planes and angles, was a dark-looking place stretching several stories up into the air. It had the look of some dreaded keep harboring torturers and tortured alike. If this place held the Earth Sephir, it did nothing to honor its residence.

Darr ran into Racall, who'd slowed to keep pace with him. The Summoner shrugged away his awkwardness and matched the Archon's step. "The Fortress of Gireck frightens you, young Reintol," Racall said, his gravelly voice soft. "I will admit, it looks forbidding, but its insides will hold more of what you were expecting. You have to remember, the fortress was built to defend the Earth Sephir, and it has done so for many years."

Darr tried to picture the era in which such a structure would've been born, an age much like his own. Depressing. "Can you tell me anything about the Ovid?" he asked, keeping his gaze on the path before him.

"The Earth Ovid has not been active for long. It is for this reason I have been able to accompany you." The Archon bowed his head and lowered his voice further. "The only advice I can offer is to expect anything. This Ovid is wicked, more so than the others, I think. It has not tried to hide its presence as the others do. The Earth Ovid has used the people of this fortress as its toys since it settled here."

Darr tried to envision a creature more wicked than the Shade of Water and couldn't. He had trouble making sense of most of the things he'd encountered over the past few weeks. Magic, spirits, and Archons, ghost tales told over a fire or in the comforts of the home. Now, he lived those tales, taking them in like a fine painting.

Except here, the paintings were frighteningly real.

Chapter Eleven

"Looking back at what had been was never an option for Caeranol. He had lives to protect and a battle to fight. When his first attempt at destroying the Devoid ended in failure, he knew his second attempt must succeed. Moving forward, he would make the ultimate sacrifice. He sealed the fate of two worlds, Contin that was and Ictar that would be."

~From the personal writings of the Divine, Zander

The dark oppression of the Fortress of Gireck sunk down on Darr. Racall said the insides would be more inviting, but such a thing didn't seem possible. The walls and parapets, inky black in the near dark, their length studded with murder holes like hundreds of empty eye sockets. The fortress gate stretched upwards, the gaping mouth of death.

"This place is right out of a nightmare," Conra muttered over his shoulder. Jinn shivered beside him. "I've heard of Arcnor's fortress, but I never thought it would be this ugly."

Racall shrugged and said, "The Fortress of Gireck is built into the very rock of the Arcnorian Line. At its base lies the well of the Earth Sephir where it burrows down hundreds of feet. Since the Ovid's subversion of the Sephir, the fortress falls steadily into decay, giving it its dark appearance." Racall smiled sadly and tilted his head back. "It is being poisoned, corrupted by the Ovid's evil design."

Before anyone could respond, a small door to the side of the main gate swung inward, a slow grating of stone and iron. From the darkness, a small figure appeared in the fading light. A Dwarf from the looks of him, his build small and slight, and his skin dark amidst his gray robes. Straight brown hair sat on his head like a bowl, and while his eyes were kind and wise, Darr didn't think he could be much older than Feywen.

"Racall," the Dwarf said. He greeted the Archon with a knowing grin. He passed the giant by and came straight for

Darr without a second glance. "You must be the Summoner."

Darr nodded.

A smile crossed the man's lips, so broad it consumed his face. "I'm pleased to meet you. You may call me Zander. I'm one of the few Divine here at Arcnor, and you will find our fates to be very much entwined."

Stunned by the small man's revelation, Darr kept his expression in check. A Divine at so young an age amazed him, but his remark about their shared fates gave him pause. He looked to Jinn and Conra for help. Feywen stood several paces away, shaking his head. Racall did nothing, a rock.

Darr fought to find something to say. "These are..."

"Your friends! I'm sorry for my rude behavior!" Zander said, looking past him towards Darr's companions and giving them each a nod. "There will be plenty of time for introductions. However, we've more pressing concerns, I'm afraid."

With a hurried bow, Zander turned and scurried off towards the door in the wall of the fortress. The Divine waved his arm in a sweeping motion without turning back.

"An odd one," Feywen muttered.

Darr agreed, but they didn't have a choice. Much like in Stern, they needed the Divine to get to the Earth Sephir. With his hesitation pushed aside, Darr and his companions followed. Zander allowed them a moment to shuffle in while he stood by the entrance. Once they were all safely inside, he shut the door, leaving them to stand in the darkness. Rather chaotically, Zander pushed his way to the front of the line, apologizing for his abrasiveness.

"It isn't far now, just straight ahead," he said followed by a sharp cough. "I'm sorry about the dark. I never think to bring anything. Just stay close."

With that, Zander's shuffling footsteps scurried off into the blackness. Darr followed, but not before Jinn's fingers fastened securely around the back of his tunic. The others would have to find some way to stay with them. Zander said the tunnel went straight ahead, Darr's fingers brushed across openings along the walls where other passages branched off.

After several minutes, Zander called a halt and began fumbling with something in the dark. Metal rubbed on metal, and after a series of small clicks, a door opened, splitting the blackness. A narrow streamer of red light shone into the passage. Outside, the bloody glow of sunset moved swiftly into place. Darr stepped from the passage with Jinn close at his side. She gasped in startled surprise.

What might've once been an inner courtyard of the fortress became a landscape blasted with horrific sights. The soil, hard and cracked at their feet, sprouted bushes and plants withered into thin, ebony stalks. Even the ruddy sky above seemed wasted and dark. Darr leaned in close to one of the nearby trees, examining the curiously grotesque shape, its surface stripped of foliage, leaving it with the appearance of charcoal. A strange looking knot along the twisted trunk drew him in. He reached out to touch it but drew his hand back. Fear coiled around him.

The knot, shaped like a human eye, was too real to be anything else.

Darr fell back into Jinn and together they crashed to the ground. Feywen and Conra drew their weapons and crouched into defensive positions. Zander calmly walked around them, shushing them while holding his hand out to Jinn, lifting her easily to her feet.

"What is it?" Darr hissed, picking himself up off the ground in the process.

Zander studied the trunk with its eye-shaped knot for a moment. Without turning back, he explained, "This garden lies directly above the well of the Earth Sephir. In times past, it's been a place of peace and beauty, but when the Sephir fell into the hands of the shade, this garden died instantly." When the Dwarf turned back, his face had gone slack. "Along with everything and everyone in it."

"'Aos!" Feywen swore, seeing the strange aperture in the tree's trunk for the first time.

"When the Earth Sephir was taken," Zander continued, "this fortress and the land about it fell into decay, and this garden was the point from which the sickness spread."

Darr glanced back at the eye. Other human characteristics began to reveal themselves along the trunk. A finger twisted into a shriveled limb and a foot embedded inside a protruding root, all turned into the same blackened wood of the tree. This Ovid truly embodied the word wicked. Darr turned back to find Racall, but he'd vanished sometime after they entered the walls.

"What happened to Racall?" he asked, but the others shrugged.

Zander shook his head before walking away. They followed the Divine, anxious to be gone from the horrors of the courtyard. He led them through a wide opening into the fortress interior. No one walked the silent halls beyond the door.

"I dismissed most of the guards after the Sephir was taken," Zander said. His words echoed quietly through the empty halls. "After what happened in the courtyard, it was apparent to me that no one but...well...you, Darr, could stop what was happening."

"And how did you know Darr was even coming?" Conra asked. His eyes narrowed in skepticism. Zander laughed and shook his head, providing no answer.

No less inviting than the outside, Darr could see how the fortress might've been grand once. Giant tapestries and paintings hung on the walls of the main hall, and the floors of granite were interspersed with fine rugs. Gloomy light infiltrated every corner of the place though, oppressing any life that might grow within. Zander led them down the hall, taking them past an imposing staircase that wound up into the fortress's upper levels, bringing them to a halt at a single ironbound door. Two soldiers stood watch at the doors, their faces emotionless, but weariness, sad and dark, shone within their Lights.

One of the soldiers acknowledged Zander with a nod and reached over to open the door. The oak slab hinged open without a sound, revealing a dark passage winding down into the bowels of the fortress. Zander took two torches from stanchions on the wall, passed one to Darr and kept the other for himself.

The bright look on his face disappeared, replaced by a mask of determination both frightening and commanding. "At the base of these stairs is the well of the Earth Sephir. That's where the Ovid has been since it appeared. It waits for us there. If any of you wish to stay behind, now would be the time to say so."

No one moved. Conra and Jinn stood resolute behind him, their faces hardened in preparation. Feywen came forward and took the torch from Darr. "I will bring up the rear," he said almost in defiance.

"It won't be what you expect," Zander whispered. No one showed any signs of staying behind. "Your fearlessness is greater than my own," the Divine said.

Then he turned and started down into the well.

Chapter Twelve

"To counteract the destructive darkness of the Devoid, Caeranol became a willing servant of the spirits. He took into himself their power, the full power of life and the Light. He became an Archon, one powerful enough to stand against the Devoid. But even then, Caeranol knew he could not truly defeat the Devoid. No one could. No one except..."

~From the personal writings of the Divine, Zander

Darr stepped through the door, casting a brief glance behind him. His companions shuffled into single file. The passage down wouldn't allow them any more space. The walls absorbed the torchlight into their cracked, blackened surface. If stone could rot, Darr thought, this is what it would look like.

The minutes ticked by. Soon the stone blocks of the fortress faded away, turning to jagged rock. The steps burrowed further down, showing no sign of ever ending. Anticipation rallied against Darr, but he ignored his wandering thoughts. He allowed his fear to rise to the surface where he could acknowledge it then smother it.

"Watch yourself," Zander called back.

A pile of rubble lay in the middle of the stairs. He managed a glance back at Jinn, making sure she saw the danger. He pushed himself against the wall, and the light from the torches revealed what he'd missed before. A hand and part of a head, carved from stone, lay amidst the rubble. Carvings too real for human hands.

Zander sniffed and coughed. "Poor souls. A group of soldiers attempted to protect the Sephir, but they all met with this fate. At least, that's what I believe happened. None of them ever came back, and I haven't been any further than this in several weeks."

Darr stomach knotted. He breathed, focusing, releasing his tension. They continued for a few more minutes, pushing their way through the dark until the stairs suddenly ended. A wide cavern opened up, its ceiling and sides lost in gloom. At its far end, something glowed fiercely, an emerald star in the dark.

The Earth Sephir.

But where was the Ovid?

Illuminated by the light of the Sephir, statues of soldiers in battle stood along the stark cavern floor. Some were shattered and lay in pieces around them, others stood in timeless poses with swords and axes lifted. Some appeared to be running away.

"So, you have come at last."

The voice belonged to Racall, instantly recognizable.

Darr stiffened at Zander's side, but curiosity drove him. Behind him, his friends filed out of the staircase. A sword slid free of its sheath, followed by the sharp click of a bolt sliding into a crossbow. Jinn's light breathing echoed in Darr's ears. He focused, easing himself into the Currents.

A dark shape materialized in the greenish light, forbidding and impossibly huge. Darr tried to relax but failed. Racall's features came into view, broad and smiling, but something wasn't right.

"Do you like my trophies, young Reintol?" the low voice asked, motioning his arms out to the parade of stone figures. "They tried to take the Sephir from me, but we both know they were doomed from the first. Only you have the power to do that."

A flicker of doubt insinuated itself into Darr's mind. Had the Ovid somehow subverted Racall, or was this actually the Archon? No. The features of the creature before him were rough and jagged with rock. Even the robes draped on its body seemed hewn from stone. The spirits whispered through the Currents, confirming what Darr now knew. This was the Ovid, as wicked as Racall had promised.

Movement flashed at the corner of Darr's eyes. Feywen edged towards the wall of the cavern, an apparent attempt to flank the Ovid.

--Your friends will die if they move--

--You must move forward alone--

Darr stretched out his arm, halting Feywen where he stood. "No one move. No one even think about going near it. It wants you close." He turned his head slightly, catching the desperation in Jinn's face. He couldn't falter now.

Darr waited for his friends to move back towards the stairs before turning away. The Summoner took short steps forward, making his way slowly towards the Ovid who wore Racall's face. The spirits came to him again, their voices clear and distinct. It seemed so long since they'd been of any help. They spoke to him in wisps of sound and emotion.

--The Ovid will try to trick you--

--You must be smarter--

--You will be smarter--

Darr breathed deeply, his mind working towards what he must do. The spirits' words were encouraging, their presence like a shield.

--Go to the Air Archon--

--Retain your focus and resolve--

--Your mistakes are behind you--

The spirits tugged at his Light, eager to push him into the Currents. Not yet, he willed them. He held himself firmly outside their realm.

"You think you can fight me now, young Reintol," the Ovid taunted. "The spirits will not help you. They are dead things, unknowing of anything besides what they knew in life. And the Archons, they will never trust you with their magic again." A wicked smile, chiseled in stone, formed on the creature's lips. "Why not bring your friends closer? Surely, they will aid you."

Darr kept his cautious approach. The Ovid attempted to goad him into failure, a gamble meant to tip the scale of his emotions so he'd make a mistake, a mistake Darr had made once before. He'd learned well from it. He kept his composure and his mind set.

"You are a child, Summoner," the Ovid hissed, its Racall-like features beginning to twist and warp into a mask of hate, something less human and more evil creature it was. "You are weak and unskilled and you will be ground into dust long before the Seekers and their creator wash all life from this world."

Darr stopped. The Ovid's voice turned from a slow hiss to the guttural sound of stone grating on stone. Its robes fell away and crumbled into dust at its feet. Its body glowed in a terrible green aura and doubled in size. Rocky spears jutted from its joints. Eyes and mouth sunk into bottomless pits of black. Darr took a step backwards.

"You will die here, young Reintol."

Darr blinked and swallowed the fear rising in the back of his throat. Jinn and Conra, Feywen and Zander would be the first to suffer if he failed. He tightened his fists, and his eyes lost their focus.

Then he plunged into the Currents with the swiftness of thought...

...*Wisteria light poured. The spirits danced wildly about him, a whirlwind of glowing white fuzz balls. A cloud of green fire closed on him, the Ovid, as it existed in the Currents. It could hurt him here. He'd seen it happen with Racall in the caverns beneath Stern, a fight in two places at once.*

--You will not escape me--

The wicked green fire of the Ovid reached out for him, hatred in its purest form, threatening to engulf him. The spirits darted away, leaving Darr to face the Ovid alone. Their wisdom lingered in the wisteria light, and Darr took it in like a breath of fresh air. The spirits might have nothing except the memories of their pasts, but those memories embodied knowledge, and in the realm of the spirits, knowledge turned into power.

Darr's mind snapped to attention, his thoughts on the Sephir of Air. One moment the green fire of the Ovid wrapped about him, ready to close. In the next instant, gold light replaced the emerald, burning it away with the brilliance of a miniature sun. Already, Darr could feel the brash, arrogance of the Archon within.

--Why have you come here, Summoner--

--To destroy the Ovid of Earth--

Glee vibrated from the golden light in gentle rays, followed by resistance.

--A futile act--The Ovids upset what the Archons balance--Their presence is necessary--It is the way inherent in all things from the time of our creation--

Too true, Darr thought. Let me ask a different way.

--The Ovid's presence in the physical world is unnatural--Grant me the power to return the Ovid of Earth to the Currents--

The Archon remained silent, but Darr pressed forward. He wouldn't allow himself to fail.

--Allow me the power to counterbalance the Ovid and return the Currents to their natural state--

--Why have you come here, Summoner--

A twinge of anger swelled within Darr's Light. Somewhere in the wisteria light, the Earth Ovid turned towards him, tracking his emotions the way a predator smells the blood of its prey.

--Tamas of Air, I have come to put balance back into the hands of the Archons--

--It is not your place to toy with balance--

Darr's thoughts, inflamed with bitterness, sent desperation flooding through his Light. He paused, catching himself. This same path had led him to the theft of the Fire Sephir's magic in Navda. Remain calm, focused, he told himself. His thoughts must be true, and his heart must drive them where they needed to go.

--Why have you come here, Summoner--

--To set right the wrongs I've brought upon my friends and my family--To make amends to the Four Archons and the spirits of the Currents--To return balance to a world I've helped upset--

A moment passed, an eternity in the Currents. The golden orb of light, the magic of the Air Sephir, flickered. Satisfaction, a small glimmer of it, spread out into the spirit realm.

--You might succeed in your endeavors, Summoner--

The Sephir flared, and gold light exploded into Darr, thrusting him from the Currents...

...Darr's physical senses returned, but he didn't fully stand in the physical world, nor did he remain in the Currents. His body pulsed with the magic of the Air Sephir, his flesh and blood an armor encasing his Light. The Ovid approached, but Darr stood his ground, detached but aware of everything. Somewhere in the back of his mind, the Archon of Air stirred, a shadowy presence sharing his thoughts and actions.

In front of him, the Earth Ovid screamed, a sound like stone scraping against metal. Unimpressed, Darr's gaze met the Ovid's empty eye sockets, his own height matching the giant's. Buffered by the Air Sephir's magic, Darr floated upwards, a condition of his summoning that awed him, but didn't surprise him. He glided forward on the currents of air, shoulders back and head held high. The Archon of Air didn't fear the Ovid, so why should he?

The Ovid, with its stone-hewn arms stretched wide, launched forward, its maw opened wide in howling rage. Its sudden movement caused Darr alarm, but the Archon of Air held him fast, turning his surprise into quiet rebellion. With a quickness defying its size and composition, the Ovid came so close Darr could almost reach out and touch its face.

The Ovid exploded.

The Ovid's body, a manifestation of razor-sharp stone, had burst into dust. The grit of it brushed against Darr's face, whipping past his cheeks and ears. The magic of the Air Sephir kept him safe from the brunt of the attack, but it appeared the Ovid had vanished.

--No--

If Tamas believed the Ovid still lived, then where had it gone?

"Darr!" Jinn screamed from the far end of the cavern, followed by similar cries from Zander and Conra.

The Summoner turned, but far too late. His awareness in the Currents brought understanding much quicker. The walls of the cavern moved like clay, shaped by invisible hands, sealing off the staircase where his friends waited. The Element of Earth bent around Darr, a reflection of the physical world shimmering through the Currents, reshaping to the wishes of the Ovid. Darr glided closer to the closing fissure, amazed that aged stone could move so easily.

Jinn peered out through the fissure, her eyes frightened. "Darr! You have to get out of there!"

Even if he wanted to, the opening had nearly closed.

He gave his sister a lazy smile. "It's okay," he told her. "I have my Archon for protection."

The fissure closed over, but the green of Jinn's eyes lingered for a moment after. Darr glided around and faced the center of the cavern once more, his actions in tune with Tamas. With the cavern now sealed on both ends, it had the feel of a stone cocoon. Of course, nothing could be further from the truth.

--I will crush you, Boy--

The nature of the Earth Element allowed the Ovid to be everywhere at once. It had become the stone of the cavern, insinuating itself in every rock, pebble, and grain of sand, and Darr floated through its belly.

On the far end of the stone cocoon, a face appeared in the rock, eyes sunk deep and a grin filled with malice.

--This will be your tomb--

A spire of rock jutted out of the ceiling above Darr, a giant thumb seeking to crush him by surprise. Darr whipped himself out of the way, a sudden breeze scattering across the cavern. The stone fell into the floor and folded back into itself. Another spear came at him from behind, followed by another from below, but Darr glided away from the attacks. With Tamas to keep him grounded in the Currents, the slightest change in the Four Elements redirected his body and thoughts.

Darr focused, bringing the Air Sephir's magic from his Light and out into his body. His fingertips buzzed with power, and he thrust out his hands, sending a spear of lightning into the Ovid's grinning face. Pieces of stone flew apart on impact, shattering small parts of the hideous visage.

--Fool--

From above and from his sides, more of the rock spires exploded across the room, racing from side to side and floor to ceiling. Darr dodged the attacks, but this time he had a difficult time making his body do what he wanted it to. Tamas struggled against him, created small lags in the movements Darr made.

He grit his teeth. A dozen more rock spires came at him, and this time, one of the blunt stone edges caught him on the shoulder. Pain ratcheted through his arm, instant and sharp, and he spun to the wall.

--Stop trying so hard, Summoner--

Tamas spoke to him, his voice taking his pain away, but Darr ignored him. He glided back to the wall of the cavern to confront the Ovid, but the creature's face had vanished.

--You are exposed now, Summoner--

Was it Tamas or the Ovid speaking to him? It didn't matter. Just because the Ovid's face had vanished meant nothing. The Ovid, hard and unyielding, embodied the entirety of the cavern. It could be everywhere at once if it chose.

The elements behind him shifted. Darr tumbled away, too slow. One of the Earth Ovid's arms erupted out of the wall, slamming into Darr. He flew across the cavern, hitting the opposite wall with jarring force. The magic of the Air Sephir swirled about him, protecting him from injury, but the impact of the blows reverberated through his body.

Lightning danced and buzzed in his palms. Darr thrust his arms out once more, sending jagged shards of white lancing at the Ovid. The first of the strikes landed, shaking the room. Darr sent more bolts after, chasing the ragged shape of the Earth Ovid dodging around the room, a small animal trapped beneath a bed sheet.

In the back of his mind, a voice reprimanded Darr for the futility of his action. He dropped his guard. More of the rock spires erupted behind him, a maze of crushing rock. Darr dodged them, but with his strength rapidly draining, he suffered more than a couple blows. He flung himself across the cavern, stopping briefly to catch his breath.

Even with the aid of the Air Archon, the Ovid still only toyed with him.

--That is because you have not used my help, Summoner-- Tamas reprimanded him through the Currents.

What does that mean? Darr wondered. *I've been using your help this entire time.*

--You have been using the magic of the Air Sephir, but you have not yet used my help--

The Earth Ovid's head rose up from the center of the cavern, its hollow eyes glowing wicked green and its mouth split wide. It came to finish him. Darr resisted his impulses to fight back or to flee. His first summoning in Stern had gone this way. The Water Ovid nearly won against Racall in the beginning, but it couldn't withstand the joining between Archon and Summoner.

But that doesn't apply here. I'm already joined with Tamas. Aren't I?

I'm not.

Darr flinched. The magic of the Air Sephir, the golden light gifted to him in the Currents, flooded his Light and coursed through his body. Even though Tamas had given him the magic, even though he shared his physical body with the Archon, they had yet to join.

With a slow smile, defiant in the face of the Earth Ovid, Darr reached into the Currents. All around him, the golden aura of Tamas's presence swirled, a reflection of the wind carrying him. Darr let his Light swell and mingle with the Archon's Light. They pulled together.

The magic burning within Darr intensified, a raw hot sensation. His thoughts merged with Tamas's own. He understood the nature of the Ovid, how it would move and think. Tamas grew more defined, a force not only of raw physical power, but also of freedom and intuition. The knowledge flooding Darr's mind, knowledge born of the elements and older than the land, rang clear in his mind, guaranteeing his victory.

His body exploded with the magic of the Air Sephir, a

sensation he knew to be true without actually feeling it. White lightning buzzed in his ears and coursed through his veins. His flesh glowed with the charged power of a hurricane. The Ovid closed the distance between them with its mouth agape, prepared to crush the life out of its enemy.

Darr's flesh of wind and his blood of thunder erupted out of his body. The magic collided with the Ovid, a concentrated burst of power so raw it slammed the creature hard enough to crack its stone body.

The Ovid's monstrous head separated from the cavern floor, but Darr and Tamas held it in place with the whirlwind they commanded. The wind of Darr's body became a raging tornado, pinning the Ovid at its center. Darr's fists rained down from every direction, jagged shards of lightning, tearing at the creature's face, stripping away its rock frame one miniscule grain at a time. The cocoon of stone around the cavern began to shatter, torn and cracked apart by the terrible force of Darr's summoning.

In slow increments, the Light possessed by the Ovid died away, its binding element torn away and no longer able to sustain it. Darr howled, and his voice became the howl of the wind. His body became a cylinder of dust and wind, spinning madly across the height of the cavern, letting not even a grain of sand escape.

Darr's eyes grew heavy. Sleep approached, but without a body, he wondered how such a thing could be possible. The magic lent to him by the Archon of Air faded away in miniscule droplets. With each falling bead, Darr's body closed about him, its weight settling, and the tiredness in his mind sunk into his bones. The wind and lightning and roaring thunder faded away, and with it, any sign of the Earth Ovid. The Light fueling its imbalance had vanished, returned and scattered into the Currents.

With a shudder, Tamas disconnected his Light from Darr, the summoning now complete. Darr's body became whole once more, his flesh and bone joined with his mind. The maelstrom of his body dissipated, and at its center, a brilliant green spark fell to the floor.

The Sephir of Earth, released at last from its Ovid.

* * * *

Darr fell through the wisteria light of the Currents, caught in the shimmering dance of the spirits while he dreamt. *Is this really a dream?* The realm of dreams lay in line with the realm of the spirits. Both consisted of truths and falsities wrapped in images, and both gave reflections of the physical world.

As he fell, faces passed before him in the white shimmer of the spirits, reflections belonging to Jinn and Feywen, Conra, and the Divine named Zander. They gathered around him, checking him for injury before lifting him off the ground. They carried him deeper into the center of the cavern. Jinn stroked his cheek, and while her love resonated with his Light, fear echoed within her. Fear echoed within all of them.

His thoughts drifted away. Conscious, but sleeping, Darr let them carry him to a small room beyond the main cavern. A strange metal obelisk, the altar of the Earth Sephir, sat on a narrow ledge dropping away into the bowels of the earth. Jinn held what looked like a shimmering emerald teardrop, its surface glassy and brilliant, and set it gently atop the altar.

Darr fell deeper into the Currents, losing all connection with the physical world.

The faces of his friends and their mixed feelings disappeared. The spirits entertained him for a while, but soon they vanished. The wisteria light lasted a few moments longer before the cool rush of darkness engulfed him.

The darkness, so deep Darr couldn't even detect his own presence, spread out to eternity. Alone and forgotten, only the small spark of consciousness which remained within Darr allowed him to exist. He drifted more than he fell now. It occurred to him he no longer existed in the Currents. This was the real world, a world consumed in dark nothingness. The small fragment of self-identity remaining in Darr prevented him from disappearing completely.

"Remember yourself, young Reintol."

Racall's voice.

"Your deeds are honest, and your will is strong. The power of the Spirit Summoner which resides within you is true."

Power, Darr thought. *This power turns me into something I'm not.*

"You are wrong, young Reintol," the voice soothed. "Your power turns astray only those who are false in their emotions, those unwilling to exercise control."

When I use it, my body isn't mine to control. The magic and the Archons take it and put it to their own uses.

"No, Darr. The magic does what you command it to. If you ask the Sephirs for help, the magic does only what you ask. When your Light is tainted by your emotions, therein resides the danger in summoning. That is when the magic becomes unstable. In such a state, fusing with an Archon makes the magic impossible to control. You become a leech, feeding off the magic of the Sephirs through their Archons."

I can't control this power!

Gentleness, in the form of a green aura, surrounded Darr, comforting him and calming him. The darkness faded, bringing Darr peace.

"You do not need to control the magic. You only need to bear it and wield it with a clear mind. You only need to allow yourself to be carried where you have asked the Archons to take you. That way, you can walk at their side, and they can walk at yours."

Darr didn't respond. The emerald light radiating through him expanded outward into the darkness, chasing away the shadows and bringing life back to the world. Sinewy plants twisted and shot skyward, blooming and spreading into leafy canopies growing from rich, black soil. Darr stood at the center of the world while it grew around him, his awareness and purpose returned.

"You have done well, young Reintol. And you will do well in the tasks ahead."

Wrapped in a cocoon of tranquility, Darr spun into the heart of his dream and found peace.

Chapter Thirteen

"The Chosen of the Light. Only they would be able to undo the damage the Devoid had done. Only they could send it back to where it came from. Caeranol laid the groundwork carefully, leaving the spirits to guide his magic where it needed to go. When he was ready, Caeranol, the Archon of the Light, used the magic of the Sephirs to seal away the Devoid for thousands of years."

~From the personal writings of the Divine, Zander

Clean linen encased Darr, a soft cocoon keeping him warm and safe. Daylight probed at his eyelids. The crisp smell of the sheets kept him rooted firmly in the moment. Time turned slow. In the space beyond his tiny shell, birds chirped outside a nearby window and fallen leaves rustled in the wind.

Darr's lips curled into a smile. Fall. At last, the season began to return to Ictar, a direct result of his efforts to restore the Sephirs.

He didn't want to interrupt the moment, but Jinn and Conra watched over him, their presence in the room easily identifiable through the Currents. For a while longer, they'd remain unnoticed. Once he opened his eyes, his journey would begin again, and he didn't know how long before he'd see a real bed again.

Ready at last, Darr opened his eyes and let in the soft gray light of the room. To the left of his bed, a picture window looked out into the courtyard surrounding the Fortress of Gireck. The yard, now clean and clear of the Earth Ovid's trophies, indicated someone had been working there. Perhaps the altered bodies returned to the earth once the Sephir returned to its altar.

"Darr?" Jinn's voice sounded like it came from some distance, but Darr knew better. His mind focused.

"Darr?" his sister asked again, her voice steady. "Do you know where you are? Do you remember what happened?"

"Give him a minute, Girl," Conra whispered.

Darr turned his head slowly towards them, his eyes adjusting to their familiar faces. "We're in Gireck. And I remember..."

The words stuck in his throat. He wasn't afraid of what happened to him during the summoning of the Air Archon, nor did he have trouble understanding what happened. His hesitation came not from the event itself, but by how easily he'd accepted it. A smile wormed its way into his face. Darr's eyes drooped, but he'd never felt so awake.

"I remember everything," Darr said.

* * * *

As best he could, Darr explained to Conra and Jinn how he'd defeated the Earth Ovid. He didn't shy away from the details even though the Currents hissed with his friends' unease. While he described his interaction with the Air Archon and the magic that resulted, Conra listened intently, but with fear in his heart. Jinn looked lost, her eyes both unsure and afraid. However, the longer he talked, it appeared they began to understand.

"Harnessing the magic alone isn't enough, is it?" Conra asked, his face awash in wonder now.

"No, it's not, and that's what confused me for so long." Darr turned back to Jinn. She hadn't said anything since he began. She no longer looked afraid, but she kept her face blank.

Darr leaned in close. "Are you okay?" he whispered.

A slow smile crossed her face, and she answered wistfully. "Yes, I'm fine. Go on."

Darr wasn't convinced, but he could talk to her later. He continued, explaining how he and the Archon, Tamas, had finally merged and defeated the Ovid.

Conra cleared his throat. "So let me get this straight. You destroyed that monster by merging with one of the Archons."

"Something like that. That's what summoning really is." Darr shook his head and looked down at his sheets. He hadn't gotten out of his bed yet.

"I think I understand, though," Jinn said. The distant look on her face remained. "If I hear you correctly, it's like you and the Archon trade places. You stay in the Currents, while it comes here."

Darr shook his head once more. "I was in my own body, but the Archon was with me, too. Its body, the physical expression of its element, they were all a part of me. We were like two completely different individuals, but we shared the same body, the same soul." The Summoner looked up at them with frustration. "I'm sorry. I guess I don't understand things as well as I thought I did."

A long peal of laughter cackled out of Conra's mouth until he had to hold his hips to calm himself.

"You understand things a whole lot better than you give yourself credit for," Conra said at last. "I'll confess, I don't follow half the things you told me, but there is one thing I know for sure. You've finally made sense of things for yourself. You've grown."

The words made Darr smile, not for himself and his own accomplishments, but from the fact that in Conra, he had a better friend than he ever would've imagined. Conra gave a sharp nod before rising and turning for the door.

Conra stopped short and said, "I spoke with Feywen this morning. He doesn't plan on leaving today. We'll stay in Arcnor for tonight before heading out early tomorrow."

The old Elf gave a quick nod, and then he stepped out into the hall, closing the door softly behind him. Darr sighed, and before he could look over at Jinn, his sister leapt from her chair and rushed to his side. Jinn threw her arms around him, tears streaming down her face.

"I don't want this, Darr. I don't want any of this."

Dumbfounded, Darr held her while she cried.

* * * *

Jinn had never been one to be afraid of change or the unknown. Even at the death of their mother, Jinn adapted to the tragedy with unnatural ease. A realist, Jinn wasn't willing to let the horrific change of events upset her life and the lives of others. Life went on, and while many people used the saying without meaning it, Jinn did.

As Jinn wept into Darr's shoulder, he couldn't help but wonder at how he could help her. Never before had he seen Jinn so completely distraught. Was this because of his summoning beneath Arcnor or something else entirely?

After a while, her sobbing became less intense, and she quieted, resting her head heavily against his arm.

"How are four ordinary people supposed to stop the Devoid?" she asked.

Darr shook his head. "There's a lot we don't know yet," he replied. "Is that why...you're..."

Jinn sat up next to him and wiped at her eyes. "Upset. Confused. Scared...no, terrified."

"Yes," Darr said. His concern washed through the Currents. "All of those things. But like I said, there's so much left to know about the Chosen. The magic you're supposed to command, the Moonstone, seems like it'd be powerful enough in itself to destroy the Devoid. Imagine what the other three Chosen will be able to do."

Jinn's eyes flashed with anger. "But that's just it. All I can do is imagine. No one has told me anything more about what I'm supposed to do." She lowered her head. "After seeing what the Ovids can do, it scares me that I'm going up against something blind."

Darr smiled. "Well then let's see if we can put an end to that. Let's talk to Zander. He said our fates were connected, and Nidic Waq told us the Divine would be able to help. Maybe he knows something about the Chosen."

Jinn hesitated, but finally nodded her head. She could always see the light of reason, even when standing in shadow. Jinn left the room, and Darr threw back his covers. He quickly washed and dressed. Someone had set out new clothes. Darr couldn't imagine what his old clothes must've looked like after his battle with the Ovid.

Dressed and ready to go, Darr met Jinn in the hallway.

"Are you hungry?" she asked, and after he nodded, she pointed down the hall. "The dining room's down there. We should eat something before we venture out."

Jinn led the way, her features calm now. Without trying, Darr detected her fear like a shadow trailing behind her. The hallway opened up into a broad foyer. At its center, a massive staircase wound up into darkness. They walked across the foyer and into a dining room where an array of food awaited them, spread out on a long oak table. Darr licked his lips. When he'd recovered the Sephir in Stern, the Divine, Herdas, had kept them hidden in a room.

A Dwarf appeared and seated them before going about serving them breakfast. Darr glanced at Jinn, finding a look of shy humility on her face, likely the same look he wore. Having someone perform the menial task of serving breakfast embarrassed him, but Darr kept his mouth shut and smiled.

The two siblings ate in silence, both eager to get on with the day. Halfway through the meal another Dwarf entered the dining room, dressed in what appeared to be a formal guard's uniform.

"Excuse me," the guard said softly, but without making eye contact. "Feywen Dery gave instructions to tell you he will be gone for most of the day. However, he will be back in time to meet you for dinner."

The guard started to turn away and caught himself. This time he slipped, and met Darr's gaze. "Your friend Conra departed moments ago. He says to find him in town once you finish your business with the Divine."

With a short bow, the guard turned and walked swiftly from the room.

A fragment of curiosity flickered in Jinn's eyes. "How could Conra know what we talked about?"

Darr shrugged, chewing a piece of fruit while he answered. "Conra's been around a long time. Maybe he only suspects." He swallowed. "But maybe it wasn't Conra who gave the message. Maybe it was Zander."

They finished their meal. Darr thanked the man who

served them, and with Jinn in the lead once again, they headed back to the foyer and the main entrance of the fortress. Another guard opened one of the massive double doors of the keep allowing them passage into the courtyard beyond.

"Take the pathway leading north from the fortress," the guard told them when they passed by. "The Divine waits for you in the vahl."

It seemed Zander expected them after all.

After leaving the fortress, they stepped into the courtyard they'd walked through the day before. Darr took another quick scan, expecting to see more of the horrors they'd seen coming in, but there was none. Shrubbery and flowerbeds stretched out before them, a beautiful courtyard scattered with trees.

They walked along the cobblestone path from the fortress in silence. The air outside brushed playfully against Darr's uncovered head. This late in the fall, and especially this high up in the mountains, he should've been freezing. Even with the Earth Sephirs return, the elements continued to tilt out of alignment. The flowerbeds glowed with color, but the blooms curled in on themselves, wilting in the morning light. The lines of trees and shrubbery along the walkways kept their leaves but with a gray cast to them. Darr sighed. His work wasn't finished.

When the path broke to the north, Jinn hastened her pace. She wasn't hurrying, but the urgency boiling within her spilt into the Currents in a hot wave. The path wound off a ways, working itself back towards the flank of Gireck Fortress where a thick copse of birch stood high. The masonry wall of a building nestled there, peeking out from behind the branches.

"Is that the vahl?" Darr asked, but Jinn kept moving. He didn't know why he asked. The Cortazians didn't have vahls. He didn't even know what he was looking for exactly.

The thicket of birch closed around them, and mixed with the gray daylight, they became temporarily lost among the white trunks. Then the light began to harden, and Darr could make out stone blocks set against the harsh face of the mountains.

The trees fell away and a clearing spread out at the end of the path. At the center of the clearing, a squat stone building, its walls painted white and trimmed with cedar planks turned silver with time, caught his attention. The building's roof arched upward so high it nearly doubled the height of the building alone. There were no windows set into the walls and only one small door. The windows were instead set at regular intervals along the surface of the roof.

"Glad to see you are doing well, Darr," a voice called from somewhere off to the side.

Zander appeared from a small flowerbed at the building's side, poking his brown face up from his work, smiling fiercely.

"Good morning to you, Zander," he called.

Jinn said nothing. With a clap of his hands, the Divine walked forward through the dust cloud emitted from his hands. "Just checking the roses," he announced, his face beaming. "I was afraid the sudden change in the elements might've killed them. Quite the opposite though. Sleeping soundly now if I were to comment."

But you did comment, Darr thought. Zander shook his head and chuckled softly.

"Good morning to you as well, Jinn." The Divine stuck out the palm of his hand, the fingers bent slightly inward, a greeting perhaps.

Jinn did nothing. Anger, deep seated and hot, spread out from her and into the Currents. So far, Zander had done nothing to warrant such behavior, but Jinn's anger stemmed from her fear. It wasn't an excuse, but Darr tried his best to send her a feeling of calm without being too invasive.

Jinn's face turned red, and her anger melted into embarrassment. She reached out to Zander's outstretched hand, unsure. The Divine smiled back and reached out with his other hand, placing it over Jinn's hand. He pulled her hand towards his own outstretched fingers, interlocking them.

Jinn smiled and laughed. "It's how we say greetings in this part of the world," Zander soothed before letting his hand fall away. His face took on a serious cast. "But then, friendly greetings aren't why you two are here, is it?"

Darr and Jinn said nothing.

Zander appeared to understand. "Come inside," he said. "I have tea waiting for us."

The Divine turned and shuffled towards the door, looking like a fast moving turtle in his heavy robes. Darr and Jinn followed him, though Darr bit down on his tongue to keep from laughing at Zander's appearance.

Chapter Fourteen

"The Ancients, no longer able to survive in this land, left it for another. Caeranol put the races of what is now Ictar into hiding before his battle, and after the ground settled following the Devoid's banishment, the races emerged."

~From the personal writings of the Divine, Zander

The inside of the vahl looked nothing at all like what Darr expected. The walls of the low stone house constricted when they passed through the door, but the insides were warm and cozy. A woodstove sat in the corner beside a small table, and next to it, a bed. Cabinets filled with books lined the walls. At a small break between the cabinets, a narrow door nestled into the wall. Darr's compulsion to go straight to the door and fling it open nearly overwhelmed him, but he resisted the urge. Jinn appeared to fight the same urge.

Zander went to the kitchen, oblivious of his guests impulses. He took cups from one of the cabinets and set them on the table. As he poured tea from a kettle, he encouraged them to sit. Jinn sat down in front of one of the steaming cups, but Darr stood in place. The door across from him contained something that resonated in the Currents, though the spirits kept silent on whatever it might be.

"Darr?" Jinn called softly.

The spell broke, and the Summoner shook away his thoughts. He sat beside Jinn and took a sip of the tea. The strong taste caused the back of his tongue to tighten.

"Is there anything else I can do for you before we begin?" Zander asked with intense and inquiring eyes.

"What's behind that door?" Darr asked abruptly. His mouth ran ahead of his brain.

The Divine laughed and shook his head. "I thought I saw you looking. That door leads into the vahl."

"But I thought this was the vahl," Jinn said with an upward glance.

"No, no." Zander looked embarrassed. "This is merely my humble office and home. The other Divine have quarters within the fortress, but I like it out here, close to the vahl." He trailed off distractedly before recovering himself. "You've never been to one before, have you?"

Darr shifted uncomfortably. "I don't think so."

"Well, the Divine north of the Borderlands don't use them," Zander continued. "The Cortazians are more concerned with keeping the magic safe and less concerned with doctrine and spirituality. They've no need of vahls. That might change one day, but I suppose it isn't important for our discussion."

Zander reached out and took a sip from his cup. When he looked up, his eyes, clear and blue, looked sad. "Now, even though you want all the answers up front, I should probably start from the beginning." He paused. Darr and Jinn waited patiently. "Well, the history of the Divine is long, but I will explain it as best I can in the time we have."

Zander cleared his throat. "After the disaster which resulted in the fall of the Ancients, there was an uprising in the land we now call Ictar. The five known races of Ictar were mostly in hiding during the Ancients' reign, keeping to themselves in scattered tribal states. When the Ancients vanished, the tribes began to occupy the lands that were once strongholds of these vanished people."

A slight sigh came forth from Zander's lips. "It was during this time of confusion that the great Archon of the Light, Caeranol, appeared before a historian and explorer named Wyntol Ictarus. This man, Wyntol, became the first of the Divine."

"I've heard of Wyntol before," Darr interrupted, remembering lessons from his childhood. "He found the Sephirs after the fall of the Ancients, and many of the charts he made are still in use today. His work was invaluable in bringing an end to the Aeon Wars. But I'd never heard that he started the Divine."

"You wouldn't have," Zander stated. "The true origins of the Divine have been kept secret since its inception. Wyntol felt the institution of the Divine would better serve as caretakers of the Sephirs. The truth is, Caeranol entrusted Wyntol with a vast amount of information. Wyntol recorded this information in a series of books he called the Covenants. These weren't promises or pacts as the name implies. Most of what Caeranol passed on was knowledge of life before the rise of Ictar."

Zander took a deep breath before leaning close. "But there was one true covenant, one true promise passed to Wyntol that Caeranol would uphold. The Devoid, the cause of the old world's destruction, would return one day to reclaim what it'd lost, and the Chosen of the Light would appear to destroy it."

"But how do we know for sure what Caeranol said is true?" Jinn asked, her voice hard. The question intrigued Darr. "No one else has ever seen Caeranol, and besides, what if Wyntol misinterpreted his words? This 'promise' of the Chosen of the Light saving Ictar could all be a fantasy."

Zander inclined his head, weighing his response before answering. "I cannot lie to you, Jinn. It's not impossible that Caeranol's words could be misinterpreted, and having never spoken with the Archon myself, I can't say for certain how Wyntol might've been affected by the experience." The Divine's depthless eyes fixed and stared at her. "How about you let me finish my story? Then we can talk about how much of it you believe."

Jinn sat motionless for a moment, her jaw clenched. Eventually, she relaxed and agreed.

A smile tweaked the corners of Zander's mouth. "As I said, Caeranol's teachings were passed down orally to Wyntol and he recorded them into the Covenants. With this task finished, he was to go out into Ictar and gather people from the races that would protect the Sephirs. Of course, this was a disguise for the true purpose behind his sect, which was to keep safe the lessons passed down by Caeranol. Some of these lessons would be shared with Ictar, teachings that would help better its people, but the rest of Caeranol's teaching would be kept protected until time called them forth."

Zander leaned on the table, folding his arms before him. "Wyntol went out into Ictar, and he gathered a few trusted individuals from the races, each of whom would guard one of the Covenant books and the teachings within. These Divine took apprentices, choosing one among them to pass on the Covenant for the next generation. For hundreds of years, the Divine functioned in this manner. The sect grew in size as caretakers of the Sephirs and spiritual teachers, leaving a few Covenant Bearers who knew the truth about their origins."

A heavy sigh escaped Zander's lips, and his eyes drooped. "Like everything else in Ictar, the Aeon Wars warped and changed even our little sect. No one knows exactly how it happened, but somewhere near the end of the Wars, the Divine experienced an uprising from within. Viewed as harbingers of dark secrets, the Covenant Bearers were thrown out of their vahls without warning. Some managed to remain hidden, however, only a few did so."

Darr watched Zander in silence. The sorrow radiating from the Divine struck him profoundly.

"The Divine split after that," Zander continued. "The Covenant Bearers, those who weren't cast out, blended in with their sect, passing along their secrets only when they were positive they wouldn't be found out. Those who were cast out went into hiding. To date, it's impossible to know how many Covenant Bearers there are, though I suspect they no longer live in hiding."

Zander shook his head. "The Divine changed drastically, even though many of the Covenant Bearers still lived among them. The sect remained as protectors of the Sephirs, but they were no longer driven by teachings and lessons, rather they began to conquer the hearts of men using fear and complicated rhetoric. I'm not sure what their intentions were in making such a drastic change, but I'm thankful the Divine faith has not spread to all of Ictar. They no longer teach and instruct, seeking a life more in tune with the Sephirs. Now they hold to rules that no one can possibly live by."

"You don't hold a group you claim to be a part of very

highly," Jinn said. The somewhat hostile statement startled Darr.

Zander sat motionless for a moment with the barest indication of a smile. He appeared to be thinking something over, but not once did his gaze divert from Jinn. "I speak as I do out of sadness, not anger. Most of the Divine today seek to control and manipulate. It tarnishes our true purpose."

"You're a Covenant Bearer," Darr said, an attempt to break the tension.

Again, the faint smile passed Zander's face. "Yes, Summoner. Like my fathers before me, I am a bearer of Caeranol's trust."

Darr's face brightened. "There was a Divine in Stern that helped us," he said. "Herdas. He helped us return the Sephir of Water to its altar, preventing us from scrutiny by the governor. Was he a Covenant Bearer, as well?"

Zander shook his head, but he looked amused. "I'd like to hope he was, but there's no way for me to know. Any contact between the Covenant Bearers after the purge was strictly between bearers of the same covenant. I will say that a Covenant Bearer would be much more understanding of your abilities than a typical Divine."

The Divine took another sip of tea and pushed back from the table. He rose to his feet and said, "I think we should step into the vahl now."

He shuffled towards the door at the rear of his office without waiting to see if his guests followed. Zander fixed his hand around the door's handle, pushing it inward with a creak. A flood of harsh, gray daylight spilled into Darr's eyes, filtered down through the vahl's high windows. He squinted, giving his eyes a moment to adjust, and soon he found himself standing in a long room that burrowed into the side of the mountain.

Chairs and tables of stained mahogany ran along the granite-tiled floor, stretching to the far end of the vahl where a bookcase nearly twenty feet high ran to the ceiling. And books! So many books filled the case. There had to be thousands.

Zander hurried off across the room while Darr looked up at the mountain of books. Jinn bumped into him from behind, her face bewildered. He imagined he looked much the same. Recovering himself, he followed the Divine. Zander walked to the high bookcase and pulled a wide tome from the shelf at waist height. He reached into the empty space and fiddled with something that clicked. Smoothly, and without sound, a small section of the bookcase fell inward and Zander slid it away.

Zander stood by the black entrance and waited for Jinn and Darr to approach. When they stood before him, he produced a small glowing stone from within his robes. "Even today," he whispered, "we Covenant Bearers must be wary of those around us. Persecution wouldn't be far off if we were discovered."

He stuck his arm into the opening, indicating he wanted the siblings to enter before him. Darr looked back at Jinn, expecting to find a hint of worry on her face. He found anxiousness in her eyes instead. He reached back, found her hand, and led her into the darkness.

The Divine slid the section of the shelf back until the same clicking sound snapped it into place. Jinn and Darr stood motionless, listening while Zander shuffled past them and deposited the glowing stone into what looked like a simple jar. When the stone touched the interior of the jar, brightness flooded the room and its sparse periphery. Shadows stretched out and gave lines and definition to a small writing desk, a couple chairs, and a chest that appeared bolted to the floor.

Zander walked past the table and pushed one of the chairs around so they stood side by side, giving a nod to Darr and Jinn to sit. The Divine produced a key from around his neck and fitted it into the brass hasp on the front of the chest. The tumblers of the lock released with a sharp clicking, and Zander raised the lid. He reached into the walnut box and pulled out a bundle of linen.

"As I said before," Zander said in a low voice, "this Covenant was passed down to me by my father, and his father before him. It's been in my family for generations, and it'll stay so for as long as the tradition is needed."

The Divine set the linen bundle on the table and carefully released the tome within. Bound in oiled leather and about the size of an egg-crate, the book looked like any other despite its unusual size.

Zander set his hands evenly on the book's cover and took a deep breath. "What I'm about to tell you has been privileged to my family alone for nearly two hundred years. While the Divine as an institution does not encourage marriage, my family has found that bloodlines are necessary to ensure the Covenant passes into dependable hands. I trust you both. Darr, because he is the Summoner trusted with restoring the Sephirs, and you, Jinn, because as one of the Chosen, the knowledge is of utmost importance."

Jinn tensed up, her surprise a quake through the Currents. "How did you know of my connection to the Chosen?" she asked.

A smile spread across the Divine's lips. "Racall, of course. I don't possess a connection to the Currents, but sometimes the Archons speak to me in dreams, a world that borders closely on the spirit realm. Racall came to me shortly after the ordeal with the Ovid last night, just as he came to me before you arrived."

"So what is it?" Darr urged. "What does she need to know?"

Zander's gaze fell on the Covenant beneath his hands. "The promise Caeranol made that the Devoid wouldn't survive a second coming was not without conditions," he replied. "The Chosen of the Light will only be as strong as they choose to be, and only when they each hold the talismans that are their birthright."

A whisper broke the silence. Zander opened the cover of the book and began leafing through the pages. "Once the man named Symdus had been completely overcome by the Devoid, the Ancients themselves became its victims. First, the Soul Seekers destroyed the populace, sending them running in fear as their cities burned behind them. Then came the plague, sent by the Devoid out of its hatred, intent on preventing any chance of interference. Out of sheer desperation, Caeranol, the High Elder—not the Archon—retaliated in force."

Another page flipped by. "Using all of his resources, magic and science both, he and a small group of men and women formulated a plan to overcome the Devoid. Their plans failed horribly, and any hope that they would regain their homes was lost."

Zander's eyes lifted, and another page turned. "What transpired during that battle isn't chronicled in the Covenants, but before becoming the Archon of the Light, Caeranol discovered the errors they'd made and promised the Devoid wouldn't return to Ictar a second time. Caeranol's promise comes in the form of the Chosen, flesh and blood mixed with his own Light, allowing each to control powerful magics. Each of the Chosen are to play a vital role in the Devoid's destruction, and each is to be in possession of a talisman."

"But what are the talismans for? What purpose do they serve?" Jinn asked, the urgency thick in her voice.

Zander cast his eyes down briefly before meeting her gaze. "I do not know, Jinn. Caeranol never gave a detailed description as to how the Chosen would overcome the Devoid, presumably to protect that information. He says each would hold a certain talisman, and when the time came, each would know what to do."

Darr's heart sank. Like Jinn, he'd been sent blindly into Ictar to embark on a journey with no expectations, but at the very least, he received some guidance. Jinn had nothing. She had no connection to the spirits or even the Currents. Even Nidic Waq seemed to know nothing more about her than what he'd already told them.

Darr leaned forward and asked, "What about one of the other Divine? Could someone else know the secrets about the Chosen?"

"It's possible," Zander replied. "Stories and legends once possessed by the Ancients have inexplicably passed into our world. I don't think that's the case with the promise of the Chosen though. Even if Wyntol Ictar had divided that information amongst the Covenants, there is no way of telling if the book is even in existence today after what happened during the purge."

The frustration radiating from Jinn caused Darr to shudder. He severed his connection to the Currents her feelings were so overwhelming.

"So that's it," Jinn whispered through tightened lips. "I have to go forward blind."

"Oh, no," Zander soothed, stretching out his hand to Jinn with a warding motion. "Blind perhaps, but never defenseless, and not without company. The other Chosen, once they're found, will be there to stand with you at the end. Each of you will hold a key to defeating the Devoid, and each will know what to do with that key. It's in your blood, and in the Light within you to know."

Jinn's shoulders sagged. The tenseness in her body drained away, but her hopelessness echoed clearly in the Currents. Darr reached over instinctively to comfort her.

"Oh," Zander breathed, turning the pages of the Covenant with a little less care. "Here." He flipped the book around to face the siblings.

Drawn among the archaic writing was a picture of something close to the size of an egg but perfectly round. Lines of definition gave the object a spherical impression, and white ink colored the drawing. Oddly, washed lines of green colored the outside edge. Perhaps the object wasn't white after all.

"What is it?" Darr asked.

"It's called the Moonstone," Zander said, his voice charged with awe. "It's for you, Jinn Reintol, for the Healer of the Light. This is the talisman that you will carry and use to defeat the Devoid."

Hypnotized by the drawing, Jinn reached out to the book and her fingers grazed the aged parchment. Quickly, she drew her fingers back, and her eyes glowed in anticipation.

"What is it?"

Smoothly, Zander turned the book back around. His eyes lowered. "I'm afraid I don't know for it's a relic forged before the time of the Ancients. The purpose of the Moonstone, like the purpose of all the Chosen of the Light, is not known to me. But it doesn't matter to me what the Moonstone can do. What matters is that I know where it can be found."

Darr and Jinn both stared in silence.

A smile crossed the Divine's face. "For generations the knowledge has been guarded within this book. I know the location of the talismans that are to be held by the Chosen of the Light. If the spirits will it, and if you listen very closely, I will tell you how to find them."

In the immediate stillness following, Darr's heart thumped furiously in his chest.

Chapter Fifteen

"For a time, we lived in peace as we rediscovered our new world. Caeranol guided the first of the Divine towards the Sephirs, perhaps in an effort to protect them. What happened was the opposite. The Sephirs, once in the hands of the races of Ictar, became objects of power to be possessed, not shared."

~From the personal writings of the Divine, Zander

The Covenant I bear speaks of four talismans that each of the Chosen of the Light must wield if the Devoid is to be defeated. These talismans are well hidden, and each can only be claimed by the one chosen by the spirits to take them up. To attempt to do otherwise will cause harm, so do not deviate from the directions I give you.

What I say to you is directly translated from the Covenant.

To the Warrior of the Light, a mantel of power, liberated of physical form, will be freely given by the spirits of the Currents. The shape this power takes will vary depending on the person to which it's bestowed at the time of their choosing. However, the mantel of power will have one condition laid upon it that will not be changed. The ability to summon the Light shall be the Warrior's one true weapon. Without this talisman, the Chosen will fail.

To the Guardian of the Light, the power to wield the Vedin Kael will be freely given by the spirits of the Currents. The strength of the Vedin Kael relies on the strength of its user, and the Guardian will possess such strength. The relic will not be easily found for it resides locked away in a forgotten stronghold. It's location will only be known to the spirits, and by extension, the Guardian. Like a moth to flame, the Guardian will be drawn to the Vedin Kael, utterly unable to resist its call. Without this talisman, the Chosen will fail.

To the Healer of the Light, the power to wield the Moonstone will be freely given by the spirits of the Currents.

A weapon forged before the rise of the Ancients, the Moonstone possesses power known to destroy its user. The Light imbued to the Healer ensures immunity from the Moonstone's destructive power. The Moonstone is well protected, hidden on the spirits' edge. Beware the termites. When light leaves you, reach beyond the edge towards the peak of dawn to claim the Moonstone. Without this talisman, the Chosen will fail.

Finally, to the Bearer of the Light, the power to wield the Azlude will be freely given by the spirits of the Currents. The Azlude, forged during the Ancients' darkest hour, is a power feared deeply by the Devoid. So deep was its fear, during the Azlude's first and only use, the Devoid seized it and hurled it across Ictar, altering its shape in the process. Drawn by the calling of the spirits, the Azlude will find its way into the Bearer's hands. Without this talisman, the Chosen will fail.

These talismans will be needed if the Chosen of the Light are to succeed, and I now leave it in your hands, Darr, to help the Chosen find them. You are bound to the Chosen by the will of the spirits, and in turn, you are bound to their talismans. You must remember what I have told you, and you must decide how to put this information to proper use. Remember, these passages were written purposely so to keep them safe. They may translate literally, then again, they may not. You will have to discover that for yourself.

And be wary, young Summoner. The Covenant Bearers west of Arcnor are few and far between. You head into territory that was among the first to purge them from the Divine. Unlike me, the ones that do exist will not expose themselves to you. They will stay hidden. If I were you, I would not trust in the Divine at all. Remember, your abilities are a threat to them, and they would lock you away if they knew what you can do.

Trust the spirits and trust your friends. But most importantly, trust yourself.

That is all the help I can offer.

Chapter Sixteen

"The Sephirs contained magic, and we could draw out that magic and use it for great and terrible things. A power struggle erupted, and the once peaceful races fought each other to control the Sephirs. They did so at the cost of their own lives, for the Sephirs also held control over the Devoid's prison. The danger we put ourselves in during that time was born of pure ignorance."

~From the personal writings of the Divine, Zander

Over supper, Darr and Jinn discussed with Feywen and Conra everything Zander had told them. With Jinn's help, Darr retold the history of the Divine, the Covenant, and of Zander's knowledge of the Chosen of the Light.

Surprisingly, Conra took the news about the Divine and their clandestine history the hardest.

"I always knew they kept secrets," the old Elf breathed, leaning against the table and shaking his head. "I never suspected they were so corrupt, though."

By the end of their meal, Conra stewed in his silence, a trait he didn't often display. Feywen took the news mildly, his face intrigued but not surprised. In all reality, the Divine and the men who sat at the heads of Ictar's governments probably shared many of the same secrets. As the once-prince of the Dwarf monarchy, Feywen surely knew a great deal more about the Divine than he'd ever let on.

"Does anyone know what 'spirit's edge' refers to?" Jinn asked, looking first to Conra, then hurriedly to Feywen.

"There's a lonely mountain west of Plad in the Elven territories called the Edge," Feywen answered, shrugging lightly. "I don't know if that's it though. From what I've heard, the Edge is a dangerous place."

Conra snorted and laughed at the same time. "You got that right. Yes, that's the place. I've known that place since I was a child, but we called it Spirits' Reach. Do you know why? Because you become a spirit if you go there. Lots of

116

people have gone there and vanished without a trace."

Jinn leaned forward, her fingertips white where they met with the surface of the table. "Well, we have to go there. It's the only lead we have," she said. "Can you take us?"

Conra sighed heavily and shook his head. "Can Zander be trusted?" he asked, his arms folded across his chest. "After all you've told us about the Divine, can we really believe what he told you is true? Deviating from our course and going to Spirits' Reach takes us a long way from Qued. Time is not something we can afford to lose if this Divine is off his rocker. Certainly, we can't be putting you two at risk."

Darr and Jinn looked at one another, but neither said anything.

Feywen's calm voice broke the silence. "The Divine keep secrets, yes, but so do we all."

Conra looked like he might object, but he lapsed into silence.

Feywen continued. "There may still be a wealth of secrets being hidden from us, but thus far, Zander has been forthcoming with what he knows. He went to Darr and Jinn with his knowledge, and he should earn a small amount of trust by that gesture alone."

"Except a lot of what he told us was vague and confusing," Jinn said. It appeared she questioned her own beliefs now.

Darr's gaze shifted from face to face, marking the tension he saw in each. "In the beginning, I had reservations believing what Zander told us," Darr began. "Suddenly, my quest had expanded beyond simply restoring the Sephirs. Not only do I have the Chosen to locate, I have to unravel the riddles of Zander's Covenant as well. All of this responsibility has been thrust on me without my permission."

He paused, looking down before returning his gaze to Jinn. "Yet at the same time, I possess the magic needed to restore the Sephirs, and something within me will find the Chosen. I accepted these as I might accept a hand dealt to me in a card game. I could throw down my cards—I wanted to throw them down—but I kept them, and I'm still playing them, because leaving them on the table isn't an option. Why not do the same with the tasks set before us by Zander?"

No one said anything, not even Jinn. The defeat on each of their face, born from their uncertainty, would need action rather than words to fix.

Darr took a deep breath and exhaled. "I've decided. Spirits' Reach is at least in the direction of Qued, and we cannot afford to sidestep it. We must go there and see what we can find."

The look of skepticism on Conra's face was palpable, and the feelings of continued uncertainty from Jinn stung. Feywen alone showed unswerving faith in Darr's decision.

"If you are sure, Summoner, I will do nothing to stand against this," the once-prince said.

Darr smiled in relief. At least one among his companions trusted him.

With a casual shrug, Feywen pushed himself away from the table and stood up. He hadn't cleaned up since returning from wherever he'd been for the day. Haggard and worn, with dust coating his clothes and small abrasions on the backs of his hands, whatever Feywen had been doing couldn't have been easy.

Feywen gave a slight nod to his companions and said, "We leave Arcnor at dawn tomorrow. But we won't be leaving by way of the Pass of Lore."

Feywen turned and walked from the dining room. Darr watched him curiously, trying to figure out what he meant.

Chapter Seventeen

"The Divine, though they could've helped Ictar understand the danger they put themselves in, did nothing. Some helped to educate, but they were met with scorn and sometimes death. Mostly, the Divine leveraged themselves into positions of power where one day they might have control over the Sephirs themselves."

~From the personal writings of the Divine, Zander

The smooth waters of Fora Lake lapped gently at the shoreline, not quite touching the bottom of Nidic Waq's robes. Across the waters, far to the north beyond the dark smudge of the Triker Forest, smoke continued to rise in thin ribbons from the ruins of Jacova. Three days past the city had fallen, and three days later, it continued to burn. Sadly, Jacova wouldn't be the last city to fall.

Nidic Waq lifted his head and his hood fell away, green eyes squinting. A group of survivors approached, too far yet to detect with his physical senses in the falling light of the day, but the Currents revealed them without effort.

Ariel Forn would want to know.

The prophet wheeled about, bringing the ash-coated hood of his robes about his head once more. His steps, strong and measured, carried him along the edge of the lake towards the encampment where the Dwarf and Cortazian forces regrouped, though the term encampment might be an understatement. While some supplies had arrived from neighboring towns and cities, basic needs like food and shelter remained scarce. Watch fires glowed in the dusk light though, so at least they had some measure of comfort.

Heads turned towards him at his approach, but Nidic Waq kept his gaze level with the ground before him. An odd mixture of respect and fear trembled through the Currents, an expected reaction to his presence. At the center of the camp, a tent stood upright, one of only a few. Nidic Waq walked hurriedly towards it.

The ring of soldiers around the tent parted, letting him pass without question. Mere steps away from the tent entrance, the flaps parted and Ariel Forn appeared, his dusky face serious and black hair disheveled. The young king hadn't slept more than a few hours since the fall of Jacova.

His dark eyes burned with excitement. "Survivors?" he breathed. Nidic Waq nodded. "My scouts just informed me. Are you going?"

He didn't answer, but Ariel took notice and led the way, striding from the tent with two guards falling in line behind him. Nidic Waq followed at his side. No words passed between them. While inside the camp, Ariel held his head high, his gaze direct. With the loss of the Dwarf Elder Council, Ariel Forn led both armies. Soldiers, Cortazian and Dwarf alike, stood and saluted him, but he waved them away dismissively.

On the outskirts of the camp, two more soldiers and one of Ariel's scouts joined them, the latter taking point and leading them along the lake's north shore. The dark of night had nearly fallen, bringing fresh danger with it.

"Can you see anything of the Soul Seekers?" Ariel asked. He kept his voice quiet, but his words were freer with the camp behind them.

Nidic Waq held his gaze forward. "Nothing tonight. The Currents are not disturbed. But make no mistake, the Seekers will recover."

"Do you have any idea how long we have?"

Nidic Waq frowned. "A few days. Perhaps."

Ariel hunched his shoulders forward, a warding motion. "Supplies should arrive from Craw and the outlying cities by tomorrow morning. Maybe then we can recover some strength and sanity."

The prophet didn't reply.

The scout led them onward for a few long minutes, the silence building until at least it ceased. A line of a couple hundred or so Dwarves, made their way out of the shadows toward them. Mostly they were women and children, ragged, dirty, and bloodied, but alive.

At the forefront of the line, the familiar shape of Lacdur led the way followed closely by one of Ariel's kingsguard, a younger man Nidic Waq didn't remember.

"Roelian," Ariel breathed, quickening his pace. "Roelian. Lacdur. You've returned to the land of the living."

Roelian stopped and knelt, his face lowered but it didn't hide his distress. Lacdur stopped behind him. He grunted and waved the people he led around them.

Ariel beckoned Roelian to stand before turning to his guards and the scout. "Show these people to the camp," he ordered. "Let them get a few hours rest before moving them on to Craw."

The guards followed their orders and ushered Jacova's survivors back towards the camp. Ariel and Nidic Waq led Lacdur and Roelian towards the shore. There they could talk in some privacy.

"Tell me what happened," the young king urged. "Where are the rest of the kingsguard?"

Roelian paused, searching for words, spilling his memories into the Currents unknowingly. Nidic Waq heard whispers of the death he'd seen from the spirits even before the kingsguard opened his mouth.

"We secured the west flank of the city, my lord," Roelian said. His words tumbled out. "We gathered all those we could find as we made our way north. We had nearly three hundred Dwarves with us when we reached the refinery hiding the tunnels. Our evacuation began with no resistance."

Roelian lowered his head. When his gaze finally returned to Ariel, it burned with weariness. "There was an explosion at the walls. We could see flames rising up into the night, and as soon as it happened, the Seekers came for us. There was no time to prepare ourselves. Nate didn't even have a chance to draw his sword before he fell. Captain Tilis was ripped apart before he could rally the rest of us. We all fought with our hearts, but it was not enough."

Roelian suddenly fell to his knees, his head lowered to his chest. Beside him, Lacdur hung his head. "It wasn't enough, my lord," Roelian rasped, his voice shaking. "I couldn't save any of them. All of them are dead, and I did nothing for them."

"All?" Ariel whispered in disbelief. "The kingsguard are the most skilled Cortazian soldiers, and Tilis had been a kingsguard for my father. How can they all be dead?"

Lacdur raised his head, and his terrifying hazel eyes burned with hatred. "The Seekers rob even the most skilled of us of our senses. Caught unprepared as we were, it's fortunate any of got away."

Ariel recovered himself. "Stand, Roelian," he commanded. The kingsguard snapped to attention with unwavering loyalty, his despair cast off. He stared boldly into the eyes of his king. "You have performed admirably. The deaths of your comrades are staggering to say the least, but the responsibility for their deaths lies only on my shoulders."

"No, my lord..."

"Stop," Ariel said. The word came out hard. "I alone command the kingsguard. I must deal with the consequences. You must concern yourself with relieving your guilt."

A hint of refusal lingered in Roelian's eyes, but within moments, it vanished. "I will do my best, my lord."

Lacdur stood beside Roelian, his face showing nothing except the practiced hardened stare.

"What of the Dwarves that were rescued from Jacova?" Nidic Waq asked in an attempt to drive the conversation towards what lay ahead rather than dwelling on the past.

"Roughly three hundred escaped," Lacdur replied. "A hundred or so, those more seriously injured, went north to a village near the mountains. No way would they have made it this far south, but we don't know if they made it to the mountains either. Those who were strong enough came with us, though you can see not many men made it out. Many stayed and fought to cover our retreat."

"And the Seekers?" Ariel asked.

Lacdur shook his head. "We've seen no sign since Jacova."

Ariel studied Lacdur for a moment. Lacdur remained silent.

"I want you at the meeting tonight," Ariel said, his composure recovered. "We are to meet in about an hour. There is a tent at the center of the camp--the only one we were able to piece together. Norris Dane will want to hear your report."

"Dane?" Lacdur questioned, his features confused. "He sits on the council, but..."

"He is the only councilman left," Ariel said. "As far as we can tell, Brenan Jase and the remainder of the Dwarf Elder Council perished in the initial attack. Dane was at the walls consulting with one of the captains when the attack came. It's the only reason he escaped."

Lacdur shook his head, his disbelief evident. "But Dane is an engineer. That's how he earned his position on the council. He's no leader."

Ariel nodded. "I know. That's why he's given all leadership responsibilities to me. For the time being, both armies are under my command. Still, Norris Dane and Blaque Eris are trusted advisors. I need them both to help manage relations between the two armies."

His words faded to strained silence afterwards. His emotions raged, a buzzing in Nidic Waq's mind where it connected with the Currents. The weight of responsibilities crushing down on Ariel Forn overwhelmed him, but the young king managed to keep a strong exterior. Nidic Waq sent him calm, but eventually, Ariel would have to face his demons.

"Roelian, report to Bru Kiln Tole once you've had something to eat," Ariel said at once. "I want you reassigned to my personal guard. You've both done Ictar a service, and I am thankful you've returned." Ariel saluted curtly to the kingsguard and gave a perfunctory nod to Lacdur.

The two men saluted in response before turning away and walking briskly to join the other survivors. Ariel spun about, walking out to the water. His emotions crashed down on him, and a terrible cry echoed through the Currents.

Apart from his guards, Ariel stood alone at the shore, suffering silently. The Dwarves and Cortazians needed Ariel desperately if they were to survive. Nidic Waq would have to do something to help him.

He crossed the distance to Ariel in the span of a few steps. "Your courage is faltering, young king," Nidic Waq whispered. "You must not let it."

Ariel started noticeably. His eyes flashed with anger before settling into quiet resignation. "I didn't see you there, Prophet. What do you need?"

Nidic Waq remained silent for a moment, his gaze settled evenly on the ground before him. Ariel had already turned his attention back out to the water. "In the history of the Continese," the prophet began, his voice soft and detached, "nothing broke their spirits more than the coming of the Devoid. They'd suffered before, but with the Devoid, their lives turned to that of animals running on instinct alone. They were a people without hope."

Ariel turned abruptly, his eyes burning again. "What're you saying, Prophet? The Ancients were an advanced race, far beyond our limits. What do we have that they did not?"

Nidic Waq's lips twitched into a cold smile. "We have a promise given to us by Caeranol himself."

Ariel craned his neck, his body settling heavily. "The Chosen's efforts will do us no good until the Devoid is destroyed."

"True," Nidic Waq replied. "But our hope lies with Darr Reintol."

Curiosity washed over Ariel's face. "The boy?"

Ariel had never heard his name before. Nidic Waq nodded. "Two of the Sephirs have been restored. The shackles binding the Devoid have grown much stronger."

"Then why are we doing any of this?" Ariel threw up his arms wildly, gesturing back towards the army. "Why aren't we out there protecting the Sephirs? If restoring them is all it'll take to end this, why must we fight this battle?"

Nidic Waq refused to acknowledge the young king's anger. "If this dilemma rested solely with the Sephirs, none of this would be happening," the prophet spoke. "The Sephirs bind the Devoid to a prison from which it cannot escape, but this doesn't change the nature of this particular beast. The Devoid is a conjurer of dark forces, and even in its prison, it can send magic out through the barred windows. For centuries, it has worked at the restraints holding it, first by sending Ovids to drain the Sephirs, and now with the Soul Seekers. Restoring the Sephirs strengthens the Devoid's prison, but the summoning bringing life to the Seekers will continue until all the Sephirs find balance. If we wait, the Devoid will grow stronger and its prison will fail that much quicker."

"But is it not better to ensure the creature remains locked away?" Ariel asked, calmer now. "We can mobilize forces to go to each corner of Ictar. If we restore the Sephirs now, then we'll have nothing to fear from the Soul Seekers or the Devoid."

Nidic Waq acknowledged him with a frown. "You've forgotten an important piece of the puzzle. The Sephirs must be free of the Ovids to regain balance, and the Ovids can only be defeated with magic. A thousand of your soldiers wouldn't stand a chance. Besides, if we don't give any attention to the Seekers, they'll destroy Exed, and we both know what that means."

"Then why are you not securing the Sephirs? Surely you are better equipped to deal with the shades than this boy."

"Darr Reintol is no mere boy," Nidic Waq said. His throat burned with anger. "He is a Summoner of untapped potential, capable of one day rivaling even me. He lacks experience, which is why he is securing the Sephirs. You will need me here."

Nidic Waq bent close. "The Devoid has had millennia to plan its escape, and it has positioned its troops precisely. If we pull attention from either the Sephirs or the Seekers, it will win. This war is not the meaningless one you make it out to be."

Ariel stared defiantly. Understanding flickered in Ariel's Light, enough that Nidic Waq knew he'd come to terms eventually. For now, he stiffened with quiet anger.

"So that's all of it," Ariel said. "We are to fight an enemy we cannot see and that can rebuild its ranks at will. We are to fight until this Summoner completes his task, or until we are all dead."

The prophet shook his head in a slow back and forth glide. "While it's possible your armies will fall before the last of the Sephirs is restored, I don't believe that will be the case. Every time one of the Ovids fall, the Devoid's control over the Soul Seekers slips. It's not much, but it should provide enough time for your army to regroup."

"How much time?" Ariel asked.

Nidic Waq breathed deeply. "For the time being, the Currents are unclouded of the Seekers' presence, and so far, there are no weakened points in which they might reform. But that time will come. Four days, maybe five."

"That would allow enough time for supplies to arrive from Craw," Ariel replied.

"Even if the Devoid regains control before that, the Devoid must obey the laws of the physical world. The Seeker mists will reform at the point of their last summoning."

"Jacova?" Ariel asked.

"Yes. That will take another few days if the wind stays calm."

A slow breath escaped Ariel's lips. Hope stirred in the Currents. They had some time. Not much, but enough to rebuild some of what they'd lost. Supplies would raise morale, and a new strategy would strengthen their resolve.

"Why tell me these things, Prophet?" Ariel asked unexpectedly. "You will be present at the meeting with the generals tonight. They will want to know this."

Perceptive. A laugh danced in Nidic Waq's chest, but he refused it. "I've told you this because I trust you to be honest and straight forward. The men who lead this army have little trust in me. They will believe easier if my words come from you."

Ariel smiled lightly, but it faded quickly. "You give me too much credence. You have the power to influence the leaders of the army better than myself."

"It is you who misplaces credence," Nidic Waq said. "The Dwarves may wish it otherwise, but you are the head of this army now. Your heart is the greatest, your courage the strongest. Do you know why?'

Ariel shot the prophet a questioning glance. Nidic Waq smiled cryptically. "You know the real danger taking place. You know what will happen if we fail."

An image, bleak and dark and filled with death flashed in Nidic Waq's mind, and he sent the image spinning into Ariel's Light. The image would be familiar to him. It was a mirror of the one he saw when he met Caeranol over the summer.

Ariel's senses returned slowly, so stunned was he by the images he experienced with his own Light. When he looked up at Nidic Waq, strength and determination returned to his face.

"I will speak for you," Ariel said, his voice strong and clear. "But you will be present."

Nidic Waq stood motionless. "I'd have it no other way."

Ariel gave him a perfunctory nod, and then walked past him to his guards. Nidic Waq smiled at the way the young king carried himself, his steps measured and his shoulders set squarely. Confident. Calculating. The leader the Ictarian Army needed.

Ictar would need many men like him.

Chapter Eighteen

"The Aeon Wars lasted for thousands of years. The Elves drew the magic of the Sephirs and changed their bodies. The Dwarves created monsters to fight for them. The Men to the North used the magic to lay waste to the land around them. The Ogres, when they possessed it, used it to wall themselves away. Only the Dragons stayed neutral. Why do we do such horrible things to each other? I'm not looking for the answer to that question though."

~From the personal writings of the Divine, Zander

Darr basked in the dying glow of the day, sitting atop a rise running high along the southern slopes of the Arcnorian Line. The ridge looked out over a morass of forested land, uncharted territory belonging to the Ogres. Far off into the horizon where twilight melted into darkened land, some unexplored mountain range stood low and solitary.

Darr watched the jagged line, tracing the shape from end to end, wondering if the mountains had a name. Surely, they did for the Ogres had occupied the southern lands of Ictar for as long as anyone could remember. Perhaps even the Ogres didn't go that far south. Perhaps the mountains, and whatever lay beyond, were a mystery even to them.

Darr's curiosity died away. Reason settled in. Plenty remained for him to wonder about on his journey across Ictar. Once he completed his journey, he'd be perfectly content to see the familiar lands around Tyfor again. A sigh parted his lips, and bittersweet memories flooded his mind. A pang of regret welled up in response, but he forced it away. He had a long way to go before he could think about returning home. Besides, returning to Tyfor would bring memories of Erec, and Darr wasn't quite ready to face those yet.

A sudden burst of laughter echoed across the ridge, rough and deep, issued from the mouth of Geraul, the Dwarf who'd guided them out of Arcnor. The orange glow of their

128

camp fire bounced off the distant cliff face. He returned his attention to the forests below the ridge. After the trek they'd endured over the last two days, the need for time alone with his thoughts was a necessity.

"Still trying to hide, I see." Loose stones scattered behind him, but Darr already knew Jinn had found him.

He smiled lightly and shook his head. "Not anymore, but I suppose some company is in order."

Jinn sat next to him, her face and eyes showing the worry she felt. Darr could tell without checking the Currents. Until the end of time Jinn would be giving him that look anytime he was frustrated, depressed, or generally not himself. Jinn's nurturing side always forced her to try to make things better.

"I was thinking about our night in the tunnel," he told her without taking his gaze off the horizon.

"We came out of that tunnel today, but it feels like a part of me is still down there," Jinn replied, her tone suddenly cold. "I still feel those walls closing in."

Darr coughed. "I understand why Feywen wanted to go that way. With both the Ogres and the Soul Seekers a potential threat, finding an alternate route made good sense. But, I've never felt that way before and I never want to feel that way again."

The tunnels running from the Fortress of Gireck to the ridgeline along the mountains' southern edge had provided little space to breathe, let alone move. Even with Geraul to guide them, the tunnels turned into an unnavigable mess.

"I still don't understand how you got us free," Jinn said, breaking the momentary silence.

Freedom. That's what they'd needed so desperately after Geraul lost his way. They wandered for hours until Geraul forced them to a halt in an attempt to sleep in the blinding black of the tunnels.

Darr blinked, remembering. "I listened to the spirits." He tilted his head towards his sister. "So much has been going on. The Ovids and the Soul Seekers and...Erec...I closed off my mind to everything, the spirits included. I thought the dagroot the Ogres gave me was still in my system, but it wasn't. It was me. And it wasn't until everything was quiet that I began to listen again."

Jinn scrunched up her nose. "And they just told you how to lead us out?"

Darr narrowed his eyes and shrugged. "They told me how to get free because I think I was asking them. I don't know for sure, but my mind was racing, searching for a way to get us free. Nidic Waq and Racall both told me the spirits have answers if I ask."

"So what did you ask them?" Jinn asked.

A soft laugh spilled from his lips. "I asked them for a way out. They told me to get up. They told me how to move. Anytime we reached a junction or a low spot, the spirits told how to proceed."

Darr turned away. The nightscape unfolded before them, the blackness of night overtaking the twilight. Jinn didn't understand. Her confusion, so clear in the Currents, felt like a small itching sensation in the back of his head. He hated how certain emotions forced their way into his head, whereas others lay buried.

Jinn shook her head and turned her attention back to the night. When she did so, the feeling of confusion went with it. Darr admired her ability to let a puzzle go. Too often, he thought on mysteries until they mired him with their intricacies, like the Chosen and his place among them.

"What's bothering you?" Jinn asked, easily reading his mood.

He answered without looking at her. "I can't get past this feeling I'm supposed to do more. I can't believe my path ends with the Sephirs, that someone else will continue the fight after I'm done. It just seems so pointless given all that I've sacrificed." He shrugged his shoulders and turned towards Jinn's round face, washed white in moonlight. "Am I wrong for thinking that?"

"No," she said without hesitation. "You've always been one to follow through, Darr. When we were younger and father would set us all to a task, Erec and I always found a way to leave something unfinished if it proved too tedious. You always followed through and finished no matter what the situation. It's the same thing here. You've been given a responsibility, one that would've frightened away a hundred others, and once your responsibility is completed, it'll leave a loose end. Everything you worked so hard to accomplish can still be lost if the Chosen don't follow through and destroy the Devoid. So of course, I don't think you're wrong for wanting to be involved. I hope you can be there with me right up to the end."

Darr set his hand over hers. He could sense a deep pit of fear opening up in her, and he lent her what courage he could. With a gentle nudge, he sent it into her Light.

"You know I'll stay with you even after the Sephirs are safe," he stated, puffing up his chest.

Jinn shook her head. "What if you can't? None of us knows what the battle against the Devoid will be like. We don't know where it'll take place, and what to do when we get there. What if you can't follow where I must go?"

"Then I'll go as far as I can."

Her fear had lessened, replaced by doubt. There had to be a way to help her, but nothing came to mind. Besides, maybe he couldn't help. So much of what lay ahead remained in shadow. He hoped Zander's advice would guide them on the path forward.

"How do you think the Moonstone works?" Darr asked, searching for something more to say.

Jinn's face darkened. "You're asking me?"

"No. I guess I'm just wondering. Nidic Waq told us what it does, but I wonder how it all fits. Are you supposed to use it against the Devoid?"

Jinn looked away. "I suppose it must be something like that," she said, hesitating a moment. With her hesitation, her doubt clouded the Currents. "What's it like using magic?"

That's why she's so afraid, Darr realized.

He didn't have a good answer for her. His magic was innate, a condition of his being a Spirit Summoner. He didn't know what it would be like to use a talisman containing magic.

"I don't know, Jinn," he said. "I'm sorry."

"But all magic comes from the Currents, doesn't it?"

He sighed, searching for a way to help her. "When I call up my magic from the Currents, it comes through the Archons. Once it's unleashed, it's like my body has been taken over, and I become a spectator." He looked thoughtfully at her. "Maybe it'll be like that for you."

When she looked over at him, her smile turned frigid. "You mean maybe the Moonstone will take my body and use it for whatever purpose it serves? No thank you. I'll refuse, if that's the case."

"You mean you would give it up?"

"No," she whispered. "I won't let it control me."

Darr approved of her suggestion, even if it was futile. A talisman composed of magic would surely exact some kind of a price, most likely to the user who wielded it. Jinn didn't need that weight on her shoulders though.

A scattering of rocks behind them broke the silence, and Conra's stooped form appeared out of the growing darkness. The old Elf crouched down next to them with an audible popping of his joints.

"Legs aren't what they used to be," he grumbled. "I have supper ready if you two want to join us."

"We'll be along in minute," Darr replied, shrugging.

Conra studied his face. "You two doing alright? You look as if the weight of the world rests on your shoulders."

Darr almost laughed. "We'd be doing better if we knew a little more about all this business."

"Bah!" Conra grumbled and waved his hand dismissively. "One day you'll both be at the end of your lives and you'll realize there's not a whole lot you know anyway. Life is full of uncertainties. That's what makes it exciting."

"But our uncertainties could mean death over life," Jinn said.

The Elf shook his head furiously. "So what? If you knew everything that's going on, you telling me you'd be off into the sunset, fists up and ready to fight?" Jinn began to answer but Conra cut her off. "It'd be nice to know what you're up against, I know, but life just doesn't work that way. You'll never understand fully what trials lay ahead of you."

With a soft clap of her jaw, Jinn's retort stuck in her throat. Conra continued to eye her fiercely, but he placed one of his gnarled hands on her shoulder.

"It's better, Jinn, if you stop and look at what's around you." The edge had gone out of his voice, softening his tone. "Most times, that's all the answer you need. You're safe, and you're among friends. You have a beautiful night sky over your head. As for your future, you've only a handful of vague possibilities. They're gonna give you a headache if you try to sort through them."

Darr thought for sure Jinn would lash back at the old man, but she looked away. Her ability to let things go continued to amaze him. Conra rose with a swiftness that ignored his earlier comment about his aging body.

"Now come on, the both of you," he ordered. "Get warm by the fire and eat some hot food. That Dwarf we picked up in Arcnor has a head full of stories, so we won't be lacking for some entertainment."

Conra waited while Jinn and Darr rose from their spots before starting back towards the orange glow of fire. Jinn leaned over and gave her brother a warm smile, and with a whip of her hair, she followed.

The doubt Darr had suppressed during his conversation with Jinn returned . Would he find the Chosen? Would they destroy the Devoid?

"Get moving, Boy," Conra called out from the dark.

Darr smiled and thrust his thoughts away for another time to ponder.

Chapter Nineteen

"As the Aeon Wars finally began to wear down, the Divine assumed responsibility for the Sephirs. Many of the Divine did so from a religious standpoint, one born from control. Only a few of the Covenant Bearers remained in the world, and we hid ourselves among the wolves, remembering our true purpose. I'm so grateful to count myself as one of the few."

~From the personal writings of the Divine, Zander

At daybreak, Darr Reintol watched Geraul gather his things, preparing for his return to Arcnor. The Dwarf said almost nothing as he packed, and Darr could tell he felt guilty for having led them so far astray in the tunnels beneath the Arcnorian Line. Before heading off, Geraul pointed at Darr and told them all to listen.

"If his sense of direction is as good out in the open as it is underground, you'd do best to keep him in sight at all times," the grizzled Dwarf said.

Heat surged into Darr's cheeks and he smiled nervously. Even though he grew more accustomed to his abilities every day, he didn't like calling attention to them. Geraul gave a wave and walked briskly along the ridgeline towards the mountain wall in the east. In moments, he disappeared into the gray and green landscape, gone back to his life before Darr and his companions had pulled him away.

Feywen informed them they could be out of the mountains by the end of tomorrow, but he did so anxiously. His eyes shifted constantly, and he paced their campsite impatiently while they collected their gear. Darr made a mental note to talk to him about it later rather than probe the Currents. Something bothered Feywen, something important.

They broke camp shortly thereafter and started working their way westward along the ridge. Darr walked alongside Jinn and Conra, letting Feywen take a considerable lead. The old Elf conversed in short bursts, his eyes ever watchful of their surroundings, a tracker always. Feywen kept entirely to himself, focused on their path.

Clouds had been moving in from the south all morning, bringing with them a chill that left Darr numb. When they stopped to rest around midday, they found shelter beneath a massive pine. Feywen sat by himself at the base of the tree, his body blocked off from the others, but Darr had no trouble finding him. Feywen's dark eyes scanned the western horizon, but they flashed irritably when Darr walked over to him.

"Do you mind if I sit with you?" the Summoner asked.

Feywen managed a smile. "My ears are open to you."

Darr took a seat, unsure of how to proceed. He didn't want to put Feywen on the defensive by questioning his sudden aloofness. He certainly didn't want to demonstrate a lack of faith in his ability to lead them.

"Where do we go from here?" he blurted out awkwardly. Feywen's face remained blank. Darr fidgeted. "I mean, once we're out of the mountains, where do we go?"

"These mountains," Feywen said, his voice trailing off with a slight edge to it. "They've been quite troublesome for us, haven't they?"

Darr noticed how easily Feywen had evaded his question and turned it around. More likely, Feywen knew why he was there.

"Is that why you've been so distracted?" Darr asked, avoiding a delicate approach.

"Am I that transparent?" Feywen asked with a quick arching of his brow. "I guess so. I've traveled in these mountains several times in my life, and never have I had such a trying experience. There are forces working against us, and that puts me in a difficult position as your guide. I try to keep you all safe, but I find myself guessing between which routes are merely dangerous and which routes will get us all killed."

Doubt. The word whispered in his mind, from the Currents or his own thoughts, he wasn't sure. Doubt fueled

Jinn's fears and his own. It seemed this whole quest attracted doubt, not only in the journey itself, but in each individual.

"If the Seekers wanted us all dead, wouldn't they have succeeded by now?" Darr asked. "Sure, they've tried, but we keep them back. We continue forward in the face of our tragedies."

Feywen lifted his head, curiosity crinkling the lines around his eyes. "It sounds strange hearing that from you, Summoner. You've lost your brother because of your commitment to this cause. I don't consider that a success for us."

Darr shook his head adamantly. "No. Erec died in Navda because he was courageous, but he was also unwilling to listen to reason. He knew what he was getting into." Tears welled up in his eyes, but he pushed past them. "I miss Erec, and I wish he could still be here with us, but he didn't die because of some unexpected attack. He walked right into the maw of the beast thinking he alone could make the difference."

Darr wiped away his tears and straightened himself. "But look what we've been through since. The Ogres, the Ovid of Earth, those tunnels beneath Arcnor--none of them kept us down. We got ourselves free from each of those situations. We survived when we never should've, when anyone else would've given up or worse."

A sardonic smile crept along Feywen's hard features. "You are right about one thing. We did survive. But we survived because of you and the power you command."

An objection burned in Darr's throat, but he held it back, shaken by Feywen's words. Racall rescued him from the Ogres, a summoning brought out by his sheer desperation. They conquered the Ovid and navigated the tunnels beneath Arcnor because of his connection to the Currents. His newfound strengths and abilities caused his companions to doubt themselves. Had he really become so powerful?

"Do you see now why I'm concerned," Feywen whispered. "I'm here to guide you, but I have no power over the dangers that threaten us."

The once-prince shook his head miserably. His despair knifed through the Currents, a sharp wash of pain.

"Maybe you don't need power over the dangers that face us," Darr replied. "Your leadership and courage are power enough. Maybe you don't know the dangers ahead, but you've always remained courageous in the face of them. What's more, you lend us all that courage when you do so. I think that's more important than simply having a means to an end. We don't expect you to know everything, only that you'll lead us through it."

Feywen took in Darr's words with a slow smile. When he looked over finally, skepticism sat plainly on his face. "Your ability to read me is uncanny. You knew what to say to ease my lack of faith, didn't you?"

Darr shook his head in defiance, but a disturbing thought managed to worm its way in. He'd become so attuned to the Currents, he no longer had to go there to read what others were thinking. The spirits whispered to him, telling him it was the truth.

"I'll admit, my connection to the Currents allows me to feel things in other people, but I've always been good at figuring people out by their body language. I guess it makes it easier for me to know what to say."

Feywen watched him silently for another moment. "Well, whatever it is, it worked," he said. "You wanted to know our next move, and I suppose Jinn and Conra do also. Let's go talk to them."

With a wink, Feywen pushed himself up from the tree trunk. As Feywen moved further from him, his mind grew quiet when not more than a moment earlier thoughts swarmed his head. No, not thoughts. He'd been listening to the spirits, and they'd told him everything he needed to know about Feywen.

I'm a puppet for the spirits. A willing participant is whatever agenda they have in store for me.

The thoughts startled him.

* * * *

Feywen told them all what they wanted to know, however, he waited until they were back on the trail before doing so.

"I've given a lot of thought about how we should proceed," Feywen began, his voice clear in the open air. "Jacova has fallen, and unless the entire Cortazian and Dwarf armies have been wiped out, its army will move south. Fora Lake will provide ample space for their numbers to regroup, not to mention fresh water will be a high priority right now."

Feywen glanced sideways at Darr. "Eventually, they'll head west toward the Elven territories. The Elves have the resources and strength of numbers needed to withstand a prolonged assault. Obviously, we want to avoid any contact with the Soul Seekers, and the easiest way to do that is to avoid the Dwarf and Cortazian forces. If we're to believe the Divine, our destination is Spirits' Reach, however the land between here and there is the only place the army would be able to regroup."

"That makes it difficult to avoid them, don't you think?" Conra's brow arched.

Feywen ignored him. "Once we leave the Arcnorian Line, we can secure horses in Craw and head west. We'll be able to find a crossing at the Wilamedde River south of Walvor Bridge. From there on, we'll be in Elven Territory, but we should be able to cross well before the Dwarves or Cortazians do. Then we head northwest, straight to Spirits' Reach."

"But we won't know until we get there, will we?" Jinn asked.

The Dwarf nodded his head, but he said nothing more.

They continued west along the ridge in silence. The day waned towards dusk, slipping away with a gradual darkening of the light filtered through the overcast skies. Once the sun finally lowered into the western horizon, darkness fell rapidly. The temperature fell with it. Even with the Sephir's delicate balance, winter had arrived in the Arcnorian Line, bringing a vengeful wrath of black clouds, threatening wind and rain.

Fat drops of rain began to fall when Jinn spotted an overhanging rock shelf along the mountain's northern slope. Feywen, preoccupied with pushing them forward, missed the shelter several hundred yards in the wrong direction. Jinn turned them around and they raced for the safety of the overhang.

Despite the onset of rain, they dropped their packs under their shelter and began searching for firewood. With the dropping temperature, wind, and rain, they'd be in trouble without a fire. They spread out from the cliff, working their way along the rock face grabbing branches and anything else that would burn. By the time they made it back to their camp, rain fell in a steady rhythm in the black of night.

Their wood, mostly wet, didn't survive Conra's patient hand with kindling and a flint. Soon they had a modest fire. They stripped off their wet clothes and wrapped in their blankets while eating pieces of dried meat and bread, watching the storm rage beyond their little shelter. The cliff hanging over them kept most of the wind at bay, but every so often, it would blow raindrops into the hungry fire, hissing and sending up trailers of steam.

They passed an ale skin back and forth, and the night deepened.

"I'm surprised at how fast this storm moved in," Conra said. His eyes fixed on the black world beyond their fire.

"Yes, it came out of nowhere," Feywen said, shifting his body so he could lean in closer to the fire. "Winter didn't even exist until this afternoon."

Darr listened, but kept silent.

They woke the next morning to bitter cold and half a foot of new snow. The storm had passed, but the skies remained clouded even in the dark hour before dawn. Fearing the weather would turn worse, Feywen wanted to get them out of the mountains by the end of the day. They ate a quick breakfast, dressed, packed, and started off across the snowy fields of the ridge.

With cloaks and hoods pulled tight, they trudged through the wet and cold. Darr's toes turned numb with cold after the first hour, and not two hours into their trek, they had to stop and build a fire to warm everyone up again. Feywen estimated they'd be in front of the snow by noon.

Feywen's estimation proved correct, though their overall progress dragged out much longer afterwards. While the snow had vanished to trace amounts, the soil turned muddy and loose. Their footing became unreliable, forcing them to inch their way along the ridge where it wound out of the Arcnorian Line. Dusk fell upon them by the time the terrain turned solid again, but darkness would fall before they reached the foothills. Craw, it seemed, would have to wait another day for their arrival.

Feywen set up their camp at sunset on a rocky outcropping overlooking the ridge channeling down the mountains to the foothills below. Far in the distance, Fora Lake glittered faintly with the last remnants of daylight breaking through the clouds.

Conra built a fire, and by the end of supper, warm and content, they all began talking again. The bitter cold didn't account for their moods, though it certainly didn't help. An oppressive cloud had been hanging over them since Navda, built from the doubts they all shared and the looming dark on the path ahead. On this night, at last, those feelings faded into the ether.

They started out again at daybreak. The sun's brightness managed to penetrate the overcast skies, and though rain threatened overhead, they remained dry. By midmorning, the Arcnorian Line turned into a rock wall behind them, and the broad plains of Borland unrolled before them.

After a brief rest, they started out once more. If all went well, Feywen thought they could be in Craw before nightfall. Evergreen trees ran in long lines down the foothills, interspersed with great boulders. There was no trail to follow, but Feywen knew the way, angling them in a southwest direction to the base of the hills.

Around noon, Conra called a halt. "Something is tracking

us," he said in a faint voice, drawing up close to his companions. "I thought maybe it was a forest creature, but in the past few minutes I've caught glimpses of something in the trees. It's nothing I can get a clear view of."

Feywen shook his head and said, "Not Soul Seekers then. They would've left no signs of their passing, and they don't hide."

"So what could it be?" Jinn asked, a hint of fear in her voice.

"There are any number of wild animals in these hills," Feywen answered. "A bear. Perhaps a cindercat."

"It's neither one of those," Conra acknowledged with a shake of his gray head. "The tracks I saw are subtle and fine, almost like a snake."

Recognition flickered in Feywen's eyes, but it disappeared quickly. "All we can do is keep our eyes and ears sharp," Feywen said. "Darr, is there anything you can do?"

He thought about it for a moment. "I could look into the Currents, but if it's Seekers, I might alert them to my presence."

Feywen eyed him, concentration tightening his features. "Do it," he said. "Even if you alert whatever it is, at least you'll draw it into the open. It's a risk, but I really don't think it's the Seekers."

Darr opened his mind to the Currents. His perceptions drifted into the spirit world, but his physical senses stayed firmly rooted. The Currents became a lens for his eyes. He scanned their surroundings in search of anything out of the ordinary. It didn't take long. In a stand of pine a few dozen yards south, a Light glimmered, something alive. Its emotion, dark and predatory, wormed its way into Darr's Light, a feeling unlike any he'd experienced before. There was hostility in this creature. There was bloodlust.

"There," Darr said and pointed. His friends turned to look.

The pines exploded in a shower of needles and broken branches, knocking everyone but Feywen backwards. A dark shape rose up against the skyline, a black cloud coiling into a single spiral. With a silent snap, it unfolded and expanded outward in a hiss of rage. Feywen reacted out of instinct, and across the Currents, his intentions screamed like a murder of agitated crows. *Protect! Flee!* Darr got up and reached for Jinn, and Feywen reached for Conra. They sprinted along the hillside, racing for an open space bathed in sunlight.

Feywen stopped them, and he turned to face their attacker, his sword flashing wickedly in the bright light. Nothing chased them now. Their attacker vanished, melted somehow back into the shadows.

"What was that thing?" Conra hissed at the Dwarf's shoulder.

Feywen looked around in confusion, his gaze shifting across the clearing. "It's called a laechin," he said. "It's a kind of snake, but like everything else that came into existence during the Aeon Wars, it's been altered by magic." Feywen turned, searching in all directions. "There hasn't been one in this part of the world in centuries though. I didn't even think they existed anymore."

"How do we fight it?" Conra asked, his arm coming up with his crossbow ready.

"I don't know," Feywen replied, his voice a hiss. "It cannot survive in sunlight, but that's all I have to go on. That's the legend anyway. But it doesn't matter, because as soon as those clouds cover the sun, we'll be a target again."

The clouds overhead drifted dangerously close to the blinding white of the sun. Their shield began to dim and falter. Darr attempted a deep breath but he failed. Against his shoulder, a light movement fluttered. Jinn stood next to him, her eyes wide with fright but she bit down against her lip. He noted her look for a moment, taking from her what small strength he could. He wouldn't let anything happen to her.

With new resolve, Darr dove into the Currents...

...the bright lights of the spirits swirled around him, glittering in the wisteria lights, whispering their words of warning. Death was close they told him, but help was closer.

--What do you mean--

The spirits didn't respond.

He'd have to figure out how to fight the laechin himself. It couldn't survive in sunlight, but how could that information help? The sun was about to be blocked by the clouds above.

--But what if there were no clouds-- The spirits whispered, a playful radiance.

Knowing satisfaction filled Darr's Light. The Archon of Air could move the clouds. A single thought sent Darr across the Currents. Golden light surrounded him, angry and filled with arrogance.

--You try my patience, Summoner--This magic is finite when it is sapped from me with every passing moment--

--What else can I do--

--Do you seek my advice--

Frustration washed through the youth, but he pushed it down, focusing his thoughts. --Tamas, take these clouds away--

Cruel glee erupted from the Archon. --Your efforts are wasted, Summoner--A creature summoned by the Devoid will not be caught so easily--

Darr refused to give in to Tamas's heckling. The Archon clearly wanted nothing to do with him. But why? Without a way to defeat the laechin, they'd be killed. Why wouldn't Tamas allow his magic to be summoned?

Unless Tamas knew the magic of the Air Sephir would be ineffective.

--Good, Summoner--Now you are beginning to see--

--What else can I do--

--Ask the spirits--They hold the key to what you need--

The spirits? The spirits were nothing but fuzz balls of light containing memories of the dead. They didn't even make their presence known in the physical world.

--Not true--

--Our reach extends into the physical world everyday--

Darr didn't agree with the spirits. --For a Spirit Summoner, maybe, but not to the rest of Ictar--They don't

143

even know you exist--

--They may not see us, but we are there--

--We give life to everything living--

Understanding flooded Darr. Yes. The spirits reached into the physical world all the time. They passed the Light into the physical world, allowing life to flourish. A memory flashed in Darr's mind, a flicker of white fire erupting from Nidic Waq's fingertips.

--Our gift to the living--

--A gift of protection to those who preserve life--

Satisfied and with a quieted mind, Darr expelled himself from the Currents.

But not completely...

...The ground beneath Darr's feet drew up and hardened, and air flowed into his nostrils. He opened his eyes to the physical world, tinged in the wisteria light of the Currents. Feywen and Conra crouched before him, a mix of color and white light, their weapons lifted and ready to strike at the first sign of their stalker.

Jinn held tightly to him, green eyes searching his face. "Did you find something that will help us?" she asked.

"I think so," Darr said. His voice sounded strange, hollow. "You must do something for me."

Jinn complied with a shallow nod.

"Whatever happens next, just let me be," he said. "Don't talk to me and don't touch me. If you have to run, then run. Leave me alone, no matter what."

Jinn's eyes flash from fear to anger and her jaw tightened. "We're not leaving you here."

Certainty, cool and direct, flowed from Darr's Light, spiraling down his arm and into Jinn. "You must. This thing will hurt you, but I have the spirits on my side. Please, do what I ask."

Jinn started to say something, but her voice caught in her throat. She swallowed, nodding hastily, and pulled away. "Okay. Be careful."

Darr straightened his body, staring ahead. His emotions drained away and focus took over. The spirits, tiny fireflies, drew near to him, summoned by his thoughts.

"Here it comes," Conra yelled from somewhere near, but with a hollow voice that suggested he was far away.

The laechin approached without sound, a mass of fluid black motion, ink spilled across the grassy landscape. Feywen and Conra stood their ground, weapons drawn. Jinn straightened and drew her hunting knife, her fear a glowing star within her Light, shielded by her refusal to run. Darr knotted his fists, feeling and seeing everything happening around him. The spirits danced in the space before his eyes, touching him, mingling with his Light and physical form equally. They, too, were a part of everything happening around him.

The laechin's inky body slid into the sunlight. It'd been toying with them. Tamas was right. Infused with the Devoid's power, the laechin resisted its normal weakness. It rose up, a tower of scales and muscle, but with an opaque cast to it as if birthed from discarded shadows.

The laechin hung suspended in the air, its baleful yellow stare burning and daring them to approach. It coiled in on itself, wrapping tightly around, and with a sudden jerk, it sent its tail whipping outward. Conra shielded his face moments before the laechin's body crashed into him, sending him rolling a dozen yards out into the field. Darr remained motionless. His fear and anger rose to the surface. The spirits swirled madly around him, and he forced his emotions back down.

Feywen charged with his sword drawn back, undeterred by Conra's sacrifice. The once-prince dove forward with a series of quick slashes. The laechin hissed and reeled backward, coiling in on itself again. Too quickly, it recovered and whipped back at Feywen, slamming into his chest. The sword flew from his fingers. Feywen spun away and landed in a heap.

Emotion rose to the surface, and Darr forced it away. The spirits reacted to his emotions, distracting them from giving him what he needed. Why didn't they respond?

--*Let us in, Summoner*--

--Allow us to see--

Jinn held her hunting knife before her. She backed into Darr, guarding him. The spirits turned into a storm of flashing lights. Panic began to boil within him.

"Darr," Jinn said without turning around. The laechin hung back, hissing and jerking its body back and forth, uncertain. "Now would be a good time to do whatever you're going to do."

The Summoner cleared his emotions, but he sifted through his memory, searching for an answer. Nidic Waq told him he could summon the Light by walking in both worlds, by using his strength of spirit.

--We must join with you, Summoner--
--We must be a part of your Light--
--We must be a part of your need--

He walked in both the physical world and the Currents, but help still didn't come. He kept his emotions in control, his knowledge intact, and still nothing. The spirits swirled about him, asking to join with him. He let them touch his Light.

No. They appeared to touch him, but he refused them. His defenses remained in place. In the Currents, he had to resist the lure to mingle with the spirits, but here, anchored in the physical world, would he be able to do such a thing?

The laechin hissed, an angry sound, and it coiled for the last time.

Darr surrendered to the spirits. They swarmed and coalesced, and before he could think better of it, they merged into his Light. His thoughts became theirs, and theirs his own, and for the briefest moment, the spirits of the Currents lived in the physical world once more.

The laechin struck out, and Darr pushed Jinn aside with one arm, bringing the other up to defend them with the spirits' white fire. The Light burst from his fingertips, a blinding comet exploding into the laechin below its gaping mouth. Wounded, the laechin thrashed and sunk down into the tall grass, melting away. The Light surged into Darr's fingertips once more, and he thrust both hands forward. A pillar of white fire surged across the field, finding its mark in the laechin's black mass, reducing it to ash in a soundless puff of smoke.

Darr froze. The Currents faded and the spirits retreated. His head ached and his fingers tingled. Everything around him felt heavy.

"Darr," Jinn said. She placed her cold hand on his face.

The Summoner started. His sister leaned over him, and his hands fell limp at his sides.

Dumfounded, he asked, "What happened..."

Chapter Twenty

"Here we are today, thousands of years later, the people of Ictar. Like the world of the Ancients, our world begins to burn away, swallowed in the flames of the Soul Seekers. The Devoid has yet to break free, but it is coming. I know because the Sephirs are weakening, but perhaps not for long."

~From the personal writings of the Divine, Zander

The Wilamedda River swept down from the southern territories, a sluggish flow cutting deep into the surrounding highlands. A gentle breeze followed, bringing cold and numbness. At the apex of the highlands, where the converging hills turned into a plateau split by the pounding river, Walvor Bridge rooted itself into the surrounding land. Twin spires of marbled granite rose up on either side of the plateau, housing between them the iron and stonework marvel. Since the end of the Aeon Wars, Walvor became a monument of peace, a physical and metaphorical bridge.

Lacdur spit on the ground. "A waste we're going to throw it away."

The Dwarf warrior stood on a promontory of rock stretching over the river south of the bridge, watching the Ictarian Army go about their work. The Cortazian King, Ariel Forn, and his last kingsguard, Roelian, stood alongside him, a silent specter. Lacdur wanted to be down with the other soldiers, but Lord Forn wanted him here surveying their defenses. No one else in the Ictarian Army camp knew what he knew about the Soul Seekers.

"We're not throwing it away," Ariel said, his tone thoughtful. "We're repurposing it for our survival. The fact that the Cortazians and Dwarves are here fighting side by side is a testament to that."

Lacdur groaned. "It'd be nice if the Elves would make an appearance. We're in their land. You'd think they'd have shown up by now."

The Cortazian King didn't reply. Lendor Terwin, the King of the Elves, wouldn't likely let them down. He'd gone with Ariel Forn and Gyrot Dery to find Caeranol and learn about the threat of the Soul Seekers. Still, not a single Elf presented themself after crossing the river, and that fact alone caused Lacdur considerable indigestion.

"When do you think the next attack will come, Captain?" Ariel asked.

Lacdur scanned the horizon, letting his gaze settle on the white mass of Seeker mist growing west of Fora Lake. "Tonight. Make no mistake. They're coming whether we want them to or not."

He shifted away from the troops crossing the bridge and setting up camp in the Elven lands to the west. "You know how lucky we were in getting here, don't you?"

Ariel's face, dusky and dark, showed nothing. "I know."

"Aos, we're lucky we escaped Jacova at all," Lacdur said with a grunt. "We managed to get resupplied and then moved all the way here without a single confrontation with the Seekers. Luck's on our side, but I don't think it'll last much longer."

In silence, the three continued to watch the troops setting up camp and building defenses around the bridge. Yesterday, Bru Kiln Tole, along with Blaque Eris and a few others, made the decision to collapse Walvor Bridge if the Seekers breached their lines. Ariel hadn't been one of those men, but his general, Bru Kiln Tole, had been. The disagreement caused tension between the two, likely prompting Ariel to bring Lacdur to stand alongside him today.

"You're making the right move, Lord Forn," Lacdur said, kicking a scattering of pebbles off the edge of the promontory. "Even if it isn't going to help in the long run."

Ariel shrugged, his head bowing in defeat. "There has to be another way than tearing down this structure, tearing down something that means something to everyone in Ictar."

"It might buy us some time," Lacdur advised, turning away. "It probably won't, but we have to know when to make a stand and when to fall back. Especially in a war against creatures like these."

Ariel's reply, when it came, sounded frail. "I fear we won't make a stand until we're pressed up against the gates of Exed."

Lacdur almost smiled, but he didn't want to disrespect the young King. Ariel knew how to lead, but he still didn't understand the rules of the battlefield, especially when cheaters like the Soul Seekers wandered onto it. *Anything can happen in a battle like this, where our enemy has nothing to lose.*

"My Lord," Roelian called out in warning. Ariel started, but Lacdur turned without much interest. The faint sound of the prophet's approach didn't bother him, not after tracking the Seekers.

"It's alright, Roelian," Ariel soothed. "I will see him."

Nidic Waq climbed up the low rise and stopped beside Ariel on the promontory, his cowl showing nothing of the craggy face beneath. Lacdur returned to watching and listened.

"How fares the Army?" Ariel asked. "The generals are doing what they see fit. I'll keep my distance for the time being."

"I'm not convinced collapsing the bridge will help us," Nidic Waq answered, his voice softer than usual. "Nonetheless, we should be in agreement before going to battle."

Nidic Waq turned his head faintly. His robed arm stretched and pointed to the bridge below. "The engineers have everything in place," he continued. "Most of the reinforcing supports have been removed from the bridge, and winches have been installed at set intervals along its length. If a retreat becomes necessary, one man will be able to pull in the winch to remove the pins in the support structure, and the east side of the bridge will fall down into the Wilamedde."

Whether it works or not, it's still a good plan, Lacdur thought. "It's lucky Norris Dane survived Jacova," the Dwarf warrior grumbled. "Without his engineering skills, I doubt any one would've figured out how to rig that bridge to fall."

Ariel Forn took a step forward, peering over the edge towards the bridge below. "Fortunately, the removal of the pins will take away only half the bridge," Ariel said. "The other half will be left structurally sound until it can be rebuilt."

If any one's alive to rebuild it, Lacdur thought darkly.

"Any news on the Soul Seekers?" Ariel asked, stepping back.

Nidic Waq lowered his arm. His hooded head turned to the east. "This morning, the mists were at Fora Lake, but they'll be here by nightfall. So far, I can see nothing behind us, or to the north or south, but that could change quickly."

Lacdur laughed but without humor. "Aos. All we can do now is wait and hope they fight us head on."

Nidic Waq nodded grimly, but Lacdur didn't need the prophet to confirm it for him.

* * * *

The darkness of winter descended over the Wilamedde, a rapid fading of the light. Watch fires burned on the eastern side of the river, a wall blazing three hundred yards out and a mile long.

Bru Kiln Tole, a mass of muscle and bulk, shifted uneasily at Lacdur's side. "Do you think my men are prepared, Captain?"

Lacdur didn't answer right away. "They've seen what the Seekers can do. They'll know to expect anything," he answered. "But no, they won't be prepared."

The Seeker mists rose up outside the glow of the watch fires, a seething mass of white, heaving against the skies. The soldiers of the Ictarian Army stood before them. Everyone waited, anxious for something, anything to happen.

"You sure don't beat around the bush," Tole grumbled, shaking his head. "At least it's an honest answer."

An image of Feywen Dery, the once-prince of the

Dwarves, his charge and friend, flashed in his mind. Lacdur laughed through his nose. "I do what I can, General Tole," he replied. "I'd much rather be out there with the rest of the soldiers though. That might be a better use of my skills."

The Cortazian general crossed his arms and set his feet apart. "Not going to happen, Captain. Lord Forn was clear to all of us. If the Seekers plan to trap us here, as they did in Jacova, you and the prophet are the most likely to catch it early. You're staying back here where you can keep an eye on things."

Lacdur set his jaw. A warrior since childhood, he wasn't accustomed to taking the sidelines during a fight. He wasn't accustomed to ignoring orders from his superiors, either.

Bru Kiln Tole dismissed himself, leaving Lacdur alone with the soldiers and archers defending the bridge. The Cortazian general parted the soldiers, making his way to the front lines, a massive beast demanding space and commanding respect. Near the watch fires, Bru Kiln Tole would join Blaque Eris, and together they'd lead the Ictarian Army against the Seekers' initial assault, whenever it came.

On the army's right flank, the Cortazian cavalry led by Crusis Jiln stood ready. On the left, Vertain and his Daravens waited. Archers prepared themselves along the heights of Walvor Bridge and along the chasm falling down to the Wilamedde. With arrows wrapped in thick burlap and soaked in oil, the archers could spread fire to the Seeker ranks should they close in on the bridge.

Lacdur stiffened. The air brushed against his neck, an alien feeling. With the approach of midnight, something had changed.

"Here we go," he grumbled. Then again, louder. "Here we go. Prepare and stand ready."

His words rose and then faded into a silence so deep it defied logic. Out in nature, sounds should carry and mingle, interacting with other life and at the very least, the elements. Lacdur's words, the sounds of them, disappeared into the vortex of the Seeker mists. The Dwarf warrior took a deep breath, studying the mists fiercely. They churned.

A low wail rose into the night and usurped the silence. Lacdur strained to make out the sound, but it sounded like many voices, all talking over one another. No, not talking. Screaming. Crying. Suffering.

The mist caved in on itself, splitting down the middle, and wind poured out onto the field before the Ictarians. The watch fires flashed wildly, and some disappeared. Lacdur, nearly a half mile away from the source of the wind, shielded his face. He choked on the smell of it—foul and pungent, the smell of death.

When he looked up, the Seeker mists had dissipated into the night. Beyond the flickering light of the fires, something approached in a slow and ponderous march. Vaguely sketched out in the fiery light, the figures moved nothing like the Soul Seekers.

"Get a message to Ariel Forn," Lacdur growled to one of the runners beside him. "Something new approaches. We may need the reserve troops sooner than expected. They should be ready to cross the bridge at a moment's notice."

The runner scurried off. Lacdur steadied himself. The first of the dark shapes passed between the watch fires, illuminated by the bloody light. It towered nearly eight feet in height, helmeted and armored in dull white plate. Its tattered robes flew like ribbons around it, but in order to cut through the robes beneath, they'd have to penetrate the armor. Glittering silver danced now in the firelight, a sword or mace held tightly in the creature's claws.

"Those aren't Soul Seekers," Lacdur whispered, his disbelief profound. "These creatures are here to devour our souls."

More devourers passed through the watch fires, their armor immune to the flames. Three. Ten. Two dozen now. Like rolling smoke, the devourers charged for the front lines of the Ictarian Army. With a mace lifted high, the leading devourer flung its arm wide, scattering the foremost soldiers. The men blew away, leaves on the back of a strong breeze.

A buzzing tore into Lacdur's brain, and his face burned. He reached back for his battle-axe, its handle a perfect fit in his hand, and he charged off the bridge, following the red haze on the horizon. Shouts rang out around him, urging him to stop and come back, but he ignored them. Ariel Forn wished him to remain on the bridge to better sense a Seeker trap, but there was no longer a point in doing so. The trap was already set and sprung.

Lacdur ran, his blood racing through his veins, his lungs burning, but the fire of battle carried him on. The rear troops of the Ictarian Army let him pass, their confidence and formations shaken. The forward troops disappeared in droves.

These weren't the Seekers Lacdur was used to fighting, but he'd find a way to destroy them anyway. He and Feywen had done it before.

The closer he got to the front lines, the more disorganized the troops became. Some men fled, others stood in open shock. A few fought for their lives, charging the approaching devourers. Lacdur went with them, battle-axe swinging at his side.

The troops around him thinned, and the red light of the watch fires contrasted the black and white specters of the devourers. The screams of men fighting and dying became a dull white noise in Lacdur's ears, his own cry included. The closest devourer towered before him, its faceless head covered in a helmet of bone. Its sword thrust upwards and fell in a wide arc, threatening the lives of three Cortazian soldiers caught in its path.

"Aos, with you, demon," Lacdur roared, his axe held before him like a shield.

The Dwarf warrior leapt in midair, knocking the devourer's sword aside. He successfully deflected the blow, but barely. The devourer possessed tremendous strength and uncanny speed for something so big. Before Lacdur regained his feet, the devourer lashed out. Lacdur rolled away, and the giant sword smashed into the ground, splitting the soil.

Too strong and too fast for a front assault.

He'd attracted the devourer's attention, leaving its back exposed.

"Don't stand there. Attack it," he yelled to the soldiers whose lives he'd save moments ago.

The Cortazians scattered and flanked the devourer. Lacdur dodged sword strikes that would otherwise cut him in half, rolling and crouching, back and forth. The soldiers hacked and chipped away at the bone plate protecting the devourer, but it would take much more force to cut through it. Like the Seekers, the devourer's armor would have to be torn away in order to release the magic binding it.

Lacdur's distraction no longer proved interesting. The devourer whipped around, and with a monstrous swipe, cut away the soldiers attacking it from behind.

We're not going to last long like this, Lacdur thought. He rolled to the side, gained his feet, and bolted away from the fighting in search of a different tactic.

Thunder rumbled in the distance, the pounding of hooves against the earth. The Cortazian heavy cavalry had arrived, raking the devourers with swords and axes capable of shattering their armor. Their speed protected them from counterattacks, but not completely. The devourers, unlike their Seeker brethren, acted like trained fighters, capable of thinking for themselves. They turned on the cavalry within minutes, cutting them down in swaths when they passed by too slow.

Lacdur raced behind a regiment of Dwarf soldiers who'd managed to overtake one of the devourers, pinning it down. As a collective, they hacked and chopped at its armor while the devourer struggled to rise.

They're going to take one down!

A Dwarf mace crashed on the center of the devourer's breastplate. The shell cracked open like an egg. A high-pitched whistle pierced the night, and dark smoke streamed out of the devourer's chest. Lacdur's stomach knotted up, his sixth sense screaming. He scrambled back in retreat.

A volcanic boom pealed across the battlefield, masking the sounds of fighting. The fallen devourer exploded into ash, but not without consequence. The Dwarves crowded around it fell flat, pushed back by the blast and torn apart by fragments of the devourer's armor.

Lacdur cried out to them, far too late to make any difference. *It isn't enough that they can die. They have to kill us even after we kill them.*

Despair fell away. An idea formed in Lacdur's mind. The Dwarf warrior strapped his axe on his back and made his way back through the flood of soldiers. He wouldn't find what he searched for here.

'Aos! Hurry!

Minutes ticked by. Lacdur kept his gaze steady on Walvor Bridge. He shoved aside the soldiers who stood dumbfounded, and weaved between those edging forward. Once he was finally free of the rear troops, Lacdur raced for the bridge.

"Get me a rope. A hundred feet or more," he called to the nearest soldier on the bridge. "Go now!"

The soldier scurried off. Lacdur scanned the land around him, searching. A torch sconce fitted into Walvor's archway, heavy iron, would do nicely for what he had in mind. He threw the torch aside, retrieved his axe, and cut the sconce down with one strike. His dutiful soldier returned a moment later with a heavy coil of rope. Ariel Forn and his guards followed him.

"Captain," the Cortazian king yelled, his dusky face alarmed. "I thought you were staying at the bridge?"

Lacdur laughed, taking the rope and throwing it over his shoulder. "You want me out there. Trust me, Lord Forn. These things aren't the Soul Seekers we're accustomed to fighting. We've already fallen into the trap we were anticipating."

Ariel stiffened in protest, but Lacdur saw understanding in his eyes. "Do what you must, Captain."

Lacdur nodded and picked up the torch sconce where it'd fallen. "I'll see to it." He turned away, but paused. "Find Nidic Waq. He's our only chance if I fail."

He sprinted despite the weight of the rope and sconce. His throat tightened and his lungs screamed for air, but the certainty pumping through him pushed him on. Lacdur skirted the perimeter of the fighting troops, making his way south towards where he hoped the Daravens still waited to relieve the Cortazian cavalry.

This has to work.

At the far southern edge of the Ictarian Army lines, the huddled shape of horses and the black spears of their Daraven riders appeared stark against the night. Lacdur quickened his pace. Vertain would be at the front of their lines, closest to the approaching devourers. When he found the man, Lacdur dropped the rope coil and found an end.

"Captain, you shouldn't be here," Vertain protested. He looked down at Lacdur, scorn glittering in his eyes. "We may have to relieve the Cortazians at any moment, and you risk your life standing here."

Lacdur met Vertain's gaze briefly and returned to the rope, fastening it securely to the heavy sconce. "We don't have a lot of time, Vertain," the Dwarf warrior retorted. "These creatures, these devourers, aren't easily taken down, but I have a plan."

The sconce dropped to the ground, and with a grunt, Lacdur hoisted the rope coil up to the Daraven closest to Vertain. "These things don't attack like the Soul Seekers. They fight. They react and they counter, and with that armor, they aren't easily overcome." He handed the other end of the rope with the sconce attached to the rider. "This might give us the edge we need. Hook this around one of them and pull it down. I'll do the rest."

The Daraven looked uncertainly to Vertain, who looked uncertain, though he didn't break eye contact with Lacdur. "You risk my man, Captain," he said.

Lacdur raised his chin. "You risk all our men if you don't try this. We won't last the night if this slaughter continues."

Vertain sneered, but a glimmer of respect shone through. He smiled and nodded to the man beside him. "We'll give it a try. How much time do you need, Captain?"

Lacdur turned. A devourer tore its way through one of the lines barely fifty yards away. Between them, a clutch of Dwarf soldiers waited to move up into the fray.

"Three minutes to get into place," Lacdur replied, "then send your man. As soon as the devourer falls, drop the rope and get clear."

The Daraven holding the rope nodded in understanding. Lacdur gave a brief salute, unstrapped his axe, and joined the foot soldiers. He found the men he needed within moments, heavily armored Dwarves with maces and axes, men who wouldn't easily let a fallen devourer up.

"If you know who I am, you know you don't have to listen to me," Lacdur shouted, snapping a dozen of them to attention. "I have a plan to take one of these things down, and if it works, we can get the lot of them. We just have to show the rest of the army how to do it."

Several of the soldiers called out, urging Lacdur to continue. The rest remained silent, eyes darting between the captain and the looming threat of the devourer.

"In a minute, a Daraven will come in and tear that thing down," Lacdur yelled. "When it falls, we pin it down. Try to remove its weapon if you can, but the chest plate is its weakness. If we can crack it open, we win, but not until after it blows apart. When you hear the whistle, get out of the way and hit the ground unless you want to be shredded. Do you understand?"

This time almost all of the men called out, their faces burning now with excitement. They had direction. They had a plan. Lacdur grinned in satisfaction. He tightened his grip on his axe and waited.

The devourer moved closer, swinging its weapon wildly. The soldiers of the Ictarian Army attempted to fight while others fled, but no one was safe from the monster's sweeping attack and sturdy armor.

Soon, demon. Soon you'll see real Dwarf ingenuity.

Vertain's Daraven appeared out of the darkness between the fighting and the watch fires, a black bolt in the fiery light.

"Ready yourselves," Lacdur cried. "This is our moment."

The Daraven swung the iron weight of the sconce around his head several times before letting it fly. The sconce flew over the devourer's shoulder, whipped about its chest and tangled the line against the creature's back. The Daraven's mount cried into the night. Then it reared up before turning. The rope drew tight, and the devourer brought up its arm to strike the new threat, but it did so too late. Its arm craned up over its head, and the Daraven pulled it down with a dull thud.

A battle cry escaped Lacdur's throat, hot and filled with confidence. The devourer fell, and Lacdur surged forward, axe lifted high. His men followed him. Their own cries rang in his ears.

Lacdur reached the devourer first, and with a practiced swing, he dropped his axe on the gauntlet holding the sword. The bone armor shattered and whatever connected the devourer to its sword ceased to be. It made no sound, but it heaved upward in an attempt to rise, its other arm thrashing outward to crush Lacdur.

The Dwarf warrior rolled aside, his axe rose high, and he brought it down on the devourer's shoulder. The Dwarf soldiers joined in, and axes and maces hacked away the devourer's other arm and legs. Pinned down beneath his boot, Lacdur spit on the faceless helmet of the devourer.

A laugh erupted from Lacdur's throat, and the axe crashed down a final time. The sharpened blade fell on the devourer's unprotected chest, breaking the plate apart in a wicked arc. The familiar sharp whistle rang into the night, and black smoke flew from the wound like a geyser.

"Get away," Lacdur cried. He left his axe buried in the devourer's chest.

An overeager soldier continued to beat at the devourer, but Lacdur pulled him away, running for whatever cover he could find. Heavy shields would be nice for next time. He screamed to the soldiers around them, urging them to duck down for cover, but his time was up. He flung himself to the ground and covered his head.

The devourer's whistle became fervent before turning into an ear-shattering boom. Pieces of debris scattered across Lacdur's back, but the screams of men not so fortunate echoed around him. Despite the cries, the urgent roar of victory rose overhead.

Lacdur picked himself up and smiled.

"Now let's do this a few more times," he roared over the elated shouts. "Spread the word. Let's take the devourers down."

Chapter Twenty-One

"No one knows how long the Sephirs have been weakening. How long ago did the Devoid first poke a hole through its prison and let loose an Ovid into our world? Ultimately, it doesn't matter. The Four Elements are crumbling around us, losing the balance between them, and that can only happen with the Sephirs teetering on the edge of failure."

~From the personal writings of the Divine, Zander

"Another attack like last night will finish us. We must withdraw now," Blaque Eris shouted. The Dwarf general's voice shook the canvas of their tent.

Lacdur kept all expressions from his face, undaunted by the grizzled general's tirade. Eris spoke words laced not with fear, but with ignorance. He believed the army needed to withdraw to the other side of Walvor Bridge, wait for the Seekers to attack, draw them forward, and collapse the bridge. The tactic might work on an enemy equal to the men of the Ictarian Army, creatures of flesh and blood and not of magic.

"I don't think a withdrawal will help us here," Bru Kiln Tole said. His calm tone belied his size. "The Seekers have proven to be an unpredictable enemy. Every prediction we've made has failed because we continue to think of them as a mortal foe. They have magic at their disposal, and where magic is concerned, anything is possible."

Lacdur folded his arms, tilting his head up to the canvas roof of the tent. Ariel had requested him to be there as an advisor. Vertain and Crusis Jiln stood beside him, present for the cavalries. Blaque Eris and Bru Kiln Tole stood between him and Ariel Forn. The young king watched them all with studied interest. Lacdur glanced over his shoulder and found Norris Dane lingering behind everyone, a reluctant presence, his tactical knowledge lacking.

He'd seen no sign of the prophet since the day before.

161

Crusis Jiln leaned forward, his chin tilted with concentration. "Shouldn't our best option at this point be to pick a position and make a stand? We shouldn't give up here."

Blaque Eris slammed his fist into the palm of his hand. "That's exactly what I am proposing," he bellowed.

Lacdur had known Eris for most of his life. He'd served under the man in his youth before becoming one of Gyrot Dery's guards. Eris usually got his way using the same tactics he used now.

"You are proposing we run from our enemy," Vertain hissed. Lacdur flinched, but he admired Vertain's courage. The Daraven captain kept his slender arms at his sides, his green eyes a sharp contrast to his dark skin.

Blaque Eris's face contorted in rage, and his words lodged in his throat. "You are out of line, Captain," he shouted at last.

"He is merely stating an opinion," Ariel Forn said, coming forward to stand beside the Dwarf general. "We're all tacticians here, and we each have methods that another would frown upon. We're facing an enemy who won't play by our rules. We cannot assume the Seekers will fall for bait if we set it out for them, nor can we assume they're subject to the same laws of nature that we are. Collapsing the bridge might not slow them at all."

"But it is the best option we have," Blaque Eris shot back. "After those abominations attacked us last night, we have little choice left."

Lacdur shook his head. Perhaps fear drove Eris after all. The devourers had destroyed the front lines during their attack, but the plan Lacdur initiated spread swiftly. Once they knew how to fight the creatures, the Ictarian Army took them all down well before the end of the night.

"This fight has been a hard one, General," Lacdur said, keeping his voice lowered. Antagonizing Eris would get him nowhere. "We do have more than one option here. I agree with Crusis and with Lord Forn. The best way to deal with this enemy is to stand and fight against anything they send at us. If they overwhelm us, we'll have another line to fall back to, but only if we stay on this side of the bridge. Once we cross Walvor, our chances to strike back will be nil until we reach Exed, and if Exed is to be our final refuge, it'd be foolish to make our first stand there."

All heads turned back to Blaque Eris, awaiting a response from the general. Arms like tree trunks folded across his chest, barely containing the anger boiling within his heavy frame.

When he lowered his arms, he did so with reluctance. "It's better that we agree, I suppose. I'm deciding with the rest of you. We'll stay."

Ariel met Lacdur's stare and gave a perceptible nod. Lacdur did nothing in response. He still hadn't made up his mind about Ariel Forn.

* * * *

An hour after sundown, Lacdur stood on Walvor Bridge alongside Ariel Forn when the Seeker mists parted. Waves of the familiar Soul Seekers poured forth, an inky spill. The Ictarian Army ranks held firm. The Seekers rolled towards them, a soundless black carpet spreading over the plains.

When the Seekers were a hundred yards from the front lines, red flags rose into the air, a signal issued not by the infantry commanders, but by Captain Rosk of the Cortazian archers. Hidden close by the watch fires that would light their arrows, hundreds of archers stepped out along the flanks of the Ictarian Army. A hail of fiery brands flew into the air, painting a swatch of color across the dark. The arrows found their marks at the front of the Seeker lines, ripping through their robes of black, sending smoke and fire racing through their ranks.

Lacdur folded his arms, his expectations low. An army of mortal men would've faltered at the onslaught, but the Devoid's army came on. The Seekers didn't know fear or hesitation.

The fire archers continued their assault until the Soul

Seekers came within striking distance of the infantry. A battle horn sounded. The Cortazian horsemen and the Daravens swept down out of the surrounding highlands, raking the flanks of their attackers. The cavalry units tore at the flanks, but Bru Kiln Tole and Blaque Eris pulled the infantry forward.

The Soul Seekers met them, a tidal wave meeting a bulwark, swift and unrelenting. The Ictarian soldiers stood their ground, tempered with the faith they faced a beatable enemy. Both sides took losses, but the Seekers took the heavier of the two. Slashing claws were no match against the shields and broadswords of the soldiers. The Ictarian Army inched forward.

"If this keeps up, our troops will reach the mists," Ariel Forn announced beside Lacdur.

The Dwarf warrior grunted. "I wouldn't count on that just yet, my lord. The Seekers are still coming."

After several hours of fighting, the Ictarian troops began to falter. The Seekers' numbers continued to flow from the mists while the Cortazian and Dwarf troops tired, pushing them closer to the highlands and the bridge.

When the Seekers had completely enveloped the front lines, a fresh wave of fire arrows swept into their ranks, from the flanks of the Seeker horde. Under cover of darkness, and with help from the Daravens, the archers had managed to gain nearly fifty yards deep into the Seeker lines from where they launched their assault. Now, two lines of fire lit the battlefield along the Soul Seeker flanks. When the Seekers charged towards them, a second line of archers fired into their midst. In a matter of minutes, no Seekers remained left to burn. The remnants retreated into the mists, pulled away with the swiftness of a sharp breeze.

The battlefield turned quiet once more. For another night at least, the Ictarian Army stood victorious.

* * * *

With two nights of battle under their belts, and no

ground lost, Lacdur walked among the ranks of the Ictarian Army a proud man. They'd fought bravely the last two nights where other men might've run screaming into the night. Overall, the soldiers gathered here were fearless, and despite the casualties they'd taken, hope ran high.

Lacdur snorted. His brief smile tilted into a scowl. Their time grew short.

They faced an enemy who could replenish its numbers no matter how many they destroyed. Worse, the Seekers had no physical form when inside their mists, preventing any kind of counterattack. It might take a few days to rebuild its numbers, but in the end, the minions of the Devoid would come at them again. The Soul Seekers would eventually force them into a retreat.

He passed a unit of Dwarf infantry he recognized, and gave the soldiers an approving salute. Though he didn't lead these men, they looked up to him nonetheless. He remained a direct advisor to Ariel Forn, and with his quick thinking on the night the devourers attacked, he'd become something of a celebrity. He didn't like it, but he saw the effect he had on the men around him. Their morale mattered more than his disdain for attention.

Near the front of the army encampment, where a line of infantry soldiers stood watch over the plains, Bru Kiln Tole conversed with Vertain of the Daravens. He liked Vertain despite the man's cold demeanor. Fierce and intuitive in battle, Vertain's tactical skill was a valuable resource. Of all the Dwarf leaders, Vertain commanded the most respect.

Tole and Vertain stopped talking at Lacdur's approach. Lacdur saluted them both.

"How does the day find you, Captain?" Vertain asked.

"It finds me wishing we had a little more help in this fight. Any word from the Elves?"

Bru Kiln Tole shook his head. "Nothing yet," the Cortazian general replied. "Vertain's Daravens are out patrolling on both sides of the bridge."

"They find anything?" Lacdur asked.

Vertain shifted his body, shaking himself of something

unpleasant. "Not a single Elf, but the news is worse than that, I'm afraid. Two of my riders just returned from the outpost of Vanla." Vertain lowered his eyes. "They found it abandoned."

You can never trust the Elves, Lacdur thought, anger boiling to the surface. He forced his feelings down. Now wasn't the time for his prejudices.

"Something's wrong then," Lacdur said, leaning in close. "Lendor Terwin of the Elves knows the danger we face. He'd never abandon us."

Vertain nodded. "You're probably right, but that leaves us in a difficult position."

Bru Kiln Tole stepped forward, his massive body filling the empty space between the three of them. "We can't hold this side of the bridge forever. Another night or two and we'll be overrun. This smells awfully like some kind of trap."

Lacdur tilted his head up to Vertain's lean face. "Can you spare one of your Daravens?"

A smile wormed its way across Vertain's face. "What do you have in mind?"

"Send the quickest and most reliable horseman you have to Exed," Lacdur advised. "Find the Elves and get them here. Obviously, something has happened that either delayed them or forced them to withdraw. Either way, we must get them here."

Vertain bowed his head. "I'll go immediately. I know the man to send. He'll be quick." Without a backwards glance, the Daraven captain hurried off.

"What could've made the Elves withdraw from Vanla?" Bru Kiln Tole asked, his quiet voice rough.

Lacdur folded his arms across his chest. "I don't know, but it reeks of deception."

"Then let's hope we find out soon," the Cortazian replied. "Before the Seekers attack again."

In the depths of his soul, where fear ran wild, Lacdur knew they wouldn't.

* * * *

An hour after midnight, Lacdur stood on the west side of Walvor Bridge, his fears realized. The Ictarian Army retreated, slowly, but they wouldn't last the night. The Seeker masses poured through the mists at sunset, their numbers stronger than ever. The Ictarians fought hard, but they couldn't match the Seekers' numbers.

The Daravens and the Cortazian cavalry raked the plateau on the east side of the bridge, slowing the Seeker advance so the infantry could retreat. As they did so, Dwarf engineers pulled up six of the eight wenches to initiate the collapse of Walvor Bridge. They would pull the last two once all the Ictarians were across.

"We did the best we could," Ariel Forn said. He sat atop his mount, a necessity in case the retreat came quicker than they anticipated.

Lacdur grunted, but gave the Cortazian King no comfort. Against the Soul Seekers, all they could ever hope to do was slow them, never stop them. Only the Chosen of the Light could do that.

Norris Dane stood with them, shifting uncomfortably, unaccustomed to the battle raging around him. With the bridge collapse eminent, he wanted to be close if anything went wrong. "After this night," Dane said, "a symbol of peace among the races will be destroyed by the darkness consuming the land."

Ariel edged his mount forward a step. "Our unity during this battle will stand as a more poignant symbol than a structure of stone and iron ever could."

Words. Politics. None of it mattered. Only survival mattered. The last of the general infantry soldiers crossed. Bru Kiln Tole remained behind with a handful of seasoned warriors to help support the horsemen. The cavalries kept the Seekers from the bridge, using their speed and precise timing to hold them back. The Seekers raged against them, a wave of black and silver. Eventually, the cavalry wouldn't be able to hold them.

The troops behind Lacdur stirred and moved about,

begging his attention. Even with the poor light and the sounds of battle ringing through the night, it appeared the crowds of soldiers parted. Was someone coming forward? This is a retreat. No one should be coming to the front lines.

The shapes of riders astride horses materialized out of the dark. The tallest one, Lacdur recognized immediately. Nidic Waq.

Ariel rode forward, but his last kingsguard, Roelian, stepped protectively in front of him. Roelian might be a warrior, but he was still green. No threat approached them. The stark white insignia of a shield shone in the darkness. The Elves had arrived at last.

The riders came to a halt, and the front most soldier leapt from his mount and strode forward in one fluid motion. Tall and lean, his body draped in white, an Elf through and through. Though his pointed ears weren't visible, the way he carried himself identified him clearly.

The Elf came within three feet of Ariel and dropped to his knee.

"Lord Ariel Forn," the soldier announced, his head directed downward. "My name is Alman Ohnler. I am the captain of the White Knights."

Ohnler. He'd met the man several years past along with his king. The knight's head came up, and his pale eyes caused Lacdur's breath to catch in his throat. He'd never get used to those eyes.

"My liege," Ohnler began. "Lendor Terwin of the Elves sends his deepest regrets. Someone masquerading as one of Lord Terwin's aides dismissed our troops on these borders over a week ago. Once we discovered the ruse, we came here as quickly as our horses could carry us. We've ridden nearly two days and nights to reach you."

Nidic Waq's tall form materialized beside the white knight, his robes streaked with dust. "I'm sorry I told you nothing about my suspicions," the prophet apologized. "I never believed the Devoid's manipulations could carry this far. I wish I could've brought more, but they were the closest."

Ariel leapt down from his horse and pushed past Roelian. He took Ohnler's hand in greeting, pulling the man to his feet. "No apologies are necessary," he said to both men. "You are here now. How many accompany you?"

"I've brought two hundred White Knights and another five hundred light horsemen."

Seven hundred? The number rang in Lacdur's head like a bell. He wanted to laugh. Such a foolish number to add when they were so hopelessly outnumbered. Alman Ohnler stood rigid, waiting for Ariel to say something.

Norris Dane couldn't hide his shock. "Seven hundred? That's all the Elves can muster?" The Dwarf Elder's face shook.

Alman Ohnler nodded, unfazed. Lacdur came forward, stepping in front of Dane. "The fort city of Vanla is our last option before Exed," he advised. "We'd better get moving."

Ariel Forn continued to stand motionless, eyes glittering. Nidic Waq slid beside him, leaning close, but Lacdur heard him. "The Elves have come at last, Lord Forn. Numbers don't matter as much as the way in which we utilize them."

Ariel's eyes focused. "Seven hundred," the Cortazian king said. A faint smile formed at the corners of his mouth. "I think that will do us well."

An explosion of noise erupted from the far side of Walvor Bridge, bringing cries of pain and shouts of warning. Alman Ohnler's face contorted in confusion, and Nidic Waq vanished like dissipating smoke. The Soul Seekers were coming. Out of the darkness of the bridge, the booming hooves of the cavalry's retreat rang dully against the stone of the bridge. Bru Kiln Tole, who'd been helping direct the retreat, stepped aside to report.

"They finally overwhelmed us, Lord Forn." The Cortazian general's great chest heaved. "Most of the Daravens are still back there, trying to hold the Seekers back until the last two wenches are pulled up, but they won't last long."

Ariel acknowledged him hastily and turned to Norris Dane. "I've already ordered the engineers to work," Dane announced. "We should see the signal at any moment."

Bru Kiln Tole's face remained taut. "We must get you to safety, my lord," he stated, his gruff voice lowered. "The cavalry will need room for their retreat, and if something goes wrong, I can't have you this close to the front lines."

Ariel climbed on his mount, but before riding away, he called down to Lacdur. "Use the White Knights as you must, Captain. Once our men are clear, I want that bridge destroyed."

This time, Lacdur laughed. "I wouldn't have it any other way, Lord Forn."

With his kingsguard and general leading the way, Ariel rode away from the bridge and back to his troops. Lacdur eyed Alman Ohnler, his lean frame a rigid pillar. "Relax, Elf. If you aren't loose when the Seekers attack, they'll tear right through you."

The White Knight followed instructions, though reservedly. The minutes ticked by. The Cortazian cavalry retreated in spurts, pulling away when the opportunity arose. Norris Dane grew more uncomfortable the longer they remained. The battle grew closer to the bridge, and Dane knew nothing about battle.

An hour before dawn, a massive explosion rocked the western side of Walvor Bridge. Casks of oil, set in place several days ago, exploded into the night, a signal to the Daravens the bridge was ready to drop. Scores of Daravens began pouring off the bridge, a river unleashed, and the pounding of hooves on stone roared. One of the horsemen detached himself, coming straight for Lacdur, a long spear strapped to his back. Vertain. Lacdur's stomach lurched.

"Captain," he called, drawing to a halt before the Dwarf warrior. Slashed with wicked claw marks on one cheek, his breathing ragged, Vertain nonetheless looked immutable. "We must order a full retreat. An engineer on the east side of the bridge has fallen."

Lacdur tensed, but he knew where his axe rested. Its handle, newer than the last he'd known, still slipped comfortably into his palm. "We'll send another then." He glanced at Norris Dane. The Elder's eyes opened so wide they could've fallen from his head.

Vertain shook his head. "The Seekers are too close. We must retreat now," he roared.

Lacdur peered through the retreating masses. *How close could the Seekers be?* Before he had a chance to guess, Alman Ohnler cried out, climbed atop his horse, and charged into the retreat. In stunned silence, Lacdur lowered his arm to his side.

"Fool," Vertain swore. "No matter, you must get Elder Dane to safety, my lord."

Lacdur scowled. "He can get away just fine without me. I'm doing as ordered. I'm staying until this bridge falls."

Vertain wheeled about, and Norris Dane followed him. Along with the White Knights, Lacdur waited. Within moments, the pounding hooves of the retreating Daravens faded into the distance. Walvor Bridge stood silent in their wake, except for what sounded like a huffing breath from the opposite end, quiet and lulling. The Seekers, incapable of words, bereft of booted feet, brought only the sound of their black robes whipping through the air. It wouldn't be long.

Lacdur returned his hand to the handle of his axe, tightening his grip. He hoped the White Knights would fight valiantly, the way he'd heard.

The sound of wrenching metal on metal, a deep whine, shook the ground all around Walvor Bridge. Lacdur leaned forward, his gaze riveted on the bridge. The deep whine lasted a moment longer, paused, and then a booming cough erupted from the dark maw along the bridge's length. All but the most fearless of the horses stirred and shied from the noise, preparing to bolt.

In the blackness beyond the plains, at the center of Walvor Bridge, a plume of whiteness rose. The booming explosions shook the land. From out of the black void beneath the bridge, where the Wilamedde River flowed, stone and iron splashed in a cacophony of sound.

"'Aos," Lacdur said. "He did it. He actually did it."

Alman Ohnler rode out of the swirl of dust and noise to meet him. He looked as if nothing spectacular had happened.

His face calm, his body steady and unharmed, but his pale blue Elven eyes betrayed him. They shone with exhilaration.

Ohnler rode to Lacdur. "I hope this makes up for our long absence."

Lacdur breathed heavily, and laughter erupted from his stomach, deep and powerful. "'Aos, yes. Yes, I think your help will be welcome."

Alman Ohnler climbed down from his mount, leaning in close to Lacdur. "There's trouble here, Captain. Something evil stalks this army."

The laughter died. "Speak plainly, Ohnler," Lacdur replied.

Alman Ohnler leaned closer. The Elf clearly sought discretion. "I found the engineer who manned the last wench. The Soul Seekers didn't kill him. The man had been run through with a sword in his back."

Lacdur bowed his head. Nothing was easy in war. "It could've been an accident," he said.

The White Knight arched his brow. "Either that or we have a traitor in our midst."

Chapter Twenty-Two

"Several months ago, Caeranol took action. He summoned his prophet, the man known as Nidic Waq, and sent him to a boy who lived far to the north of here. This boy, Darr, is a Spirit Summoner. I've had the pleasure of meeting the young man, and he is unlike any Spirit Summoner I've ever met. He doesn't just hear the voices of the spirits. He can talk to them. He is a Summoner in the truest sense of the word."

~From the personal writings of the Divine, Zander

Darr's eyes opened. The white fire of the Light, gone now, still left dark spots against the silvery glow of dawn. Time had passed. A small clearing surrounded him, but the long reach of evergreen limbs drooped above him. The ground beneath him, soft with grass and pine needles, indicated he'd left the Arcnorian Line. Jinn slept soundly beside him, curled up in her blankets.

But how did I get here?

The gray morning light outlined Conra's stooped form. The old Elf stood over Darr's head and looked down on him

"We were wondering when you were gonna join us," Conra said with a cracking of his voice. Caution, anxious and quick, stabbed at Darr from the Currents. *What did Conra have to be cautious about?*

Darr considered asking Conra what was going on, but he resisted and sat up from his blankets instead. "Where are we?"

"We're outside Craw, 'bout a mile or so." Conra walked carefully around him, taking a seat beside a small fire. "We had to carry you this entire way."

The Summoner smiled, but quickly stopped himself. Something about the way Conra held himself indicated this wasn't a laughing matter.

Darr sighed deeply and stretched. "I'm sorry you had to do that. I wish I could've regained my senses a little sooner,

173

but it was a small price to pay for our survival."

"Hmph," Conra grunted once and lapsed into silence.

Jinn stirred, followed by a stiff yawn. She tilted her head and looked in Darr's direction, furrowing her brow in confusion when they locked eyes. She hesitated for a moment, then threw aside her blankets and wrapped her arms about her brother, hugging him tight.

"I was so worried about you," she whispered.

Surprised at her fierceness, Darr let her hold him for a while longer before dislodging himself. The look on her face startled him, a mixture of fear and loss suggesting he'd gone somewhere she could never go.

"It's okay," he told her. "I'm fine."

The green of Jinn's eyes held him captive before she turned her gaze towards the fire. The same cautious feeling Conra sent into the Currents flowed from Jinn, but Darr bit his tongue. Even if he didn't actively search their Lights, he intruded on their souls.

Darr slid closer to the fire, letting its warmth sink into his skin. "Where's Feywen?" he asked, attempting to change the subject.

Jinn's eyes remained fixed on the fire, and Conra looked up at him briefly. "He went into Craw yesterday afternoon to find supplies and horses. Feywen thought..."

"Wait," Darr interrupted. "Yesterday?"

The Summoner's gaze darted from Jinn back to Conra. *Were they teasing?* Yesterday afternoon they'd still been in the Arcnorian Line. Jinn's shrunk back, worry lining her face.

"We didn't leave the Arcnorian Line yesterday, did we?" Darr asked.

The silence confirmed his answer.

Darr swallowed. "How long have I been asleep?"

Conra remained firmly in place, but Jinn leaned forward. "We've been here nearly three days. We carried you from the ridge all this way. It took us most of the night, but Feywen wouldn't rest until we were within running distance of Craw. We couldn't risk running into the Soul Seekers with you the way you were."

Darr twisted up his mouth and shook his head. "Why didn't you tell me this? Why did you try to keep this from me?"

"Because we're not exactly sure about you, Boy." Conra's stare burned into him, stern and honest.

Jinn leaned closer and took his hand. Darr let her without resistance, stunned by Conra's words. "What he means is none of us knows what you can do except, well, you. Every time you use your magic, bad things always seem to happen to you. I can't say that you've ever stayed conscious after using it, and who knows what kind of damage that does to you."

Jinn's grip on his hand tightened. The intensity of the emotions radiating from Jinn came not from the Currents, but from her mere physical presence. "We all love you and care about you, Darr. None of us can get to the end of this journey without you, but we can't depend on someone we can't trust, who saves us one moment and fails us the next."

The words were harsh, but Jinn didn't mean them to be so. Besides, the spirits agreed with Jinn, and he couldn't disregard them. Conra eased back in front of the fire, at ease now that Darr heard their concerns.

Darr closed his eyes and took a breath. Understanding washed through him. "I've tried to share the abilities I possess with you, but I've never fully explained the relationship between the Currents and the physical world. It's time you know, so if this happens again, you'll know why."

Jinn and Conra said nothing. They only watched him.

"It all boils down to time," Darr began, "or at least our perception of time. When I go into the Currents fully, time and space don't exist. The spirit world reflects our world, but there's no cohesion to it. I could be everywhere or nowhere at once. The same is true of time."

Conra leaned towards him again, eyes searching. "So time here, in the physical world, stops when you're in the Currents?"

Darr nodded. "Yes. But that's the problem," he continued. "Sometimes my body gets confused by what my soul experiences in the Currents. The first time I went into the Currents, I blacked out after because my body tried to compensate for the time it thought I'd lost. I've found this to be one of the trickiest parts of summoning."

Jinn shifted her body closer. "But I don't understand. Nidic Waq can go to the Currents and summon whatever he needs without passing out. Why is this only affecting you?"

"Because this is all new to me, Jinn," he said in the calmest voice he could muster. "When I started out, I couldn't go into the Currents for a visit without blacking out. Now, I can walk in both worlds at the same time without as much as a headache."

Darr smiled. "It's not easy, but I've gotten better at it." He turned to Jinn. "Do you remember when I told you about how I touched Racall outside the gates of Stern? Do you remember what I said it felt like?"

Jinn bowed her head. "Yes. You said you connected with Racall in the spirit world, but also in the real world."

"That's right," Darr said, turning back to Conra. "Racall showed me it was possible to connect the two worlds, and over time, I learned how to do it myself. The two worlds blend, and the Currents become a true reflection of our world. Every bit of life, every twist of magic, stands fully revealed. That's how I was able to find the laechin yesterday...er, well, a few days ago."

"Wait, wait, wait," Conra barked, shaking his head. "You said time doesn't work the same way in the Currents. How can you be in both places at once?"

Darr stretched his legs out toward the fire. "The Currents exist regardless of time. Even if I step back into the physical world, the Currents continue to flow along while feeding life into the world."

Concern twisted Jinn's features once more. "That's how you summoned that fire in the Arcnorian Line, isn't it?"

The pure white light of his summoning danced before his eyes, a memory born from his sister's words. Darr nodded.

"Nidic Waq told me I needed to master the ability to summon the Light when we were still in the Triker. I've tried before, but I didn't understand it until we were threatened by the laechin."

Conra and Jinn watched him in silence. Darr said nothing, debating inwardly if he should go on.

"Well," Conra said, wide-eyed. "Get on with it."

Darr cracked a smile. "When the laechin came after us, I had to go into the Currents to figure out where it was, and when it attacked, I tried to summon one of the Archons to help us. The Archon refused, saying I had to go to the spirits for help. I knew what he meant. If we were going to survive, I'd have to figure out how to summon the Light."

He folded his hands in his lap. "I had to walk in both worlds, that I knew, but Nidic Waq told me I had to have strength of spirit. I had to be strong, wise, and in control of my own Light. The spirits were supposed to respond to my needs in the physical world, and in the end, they did, but they had to merge with my own Light first."

Jinn put her hand over his. "You told me you couldn't let the spirit do that. They'd make you one of them if you did."

"Yes," Darr replied in a soft breath. "But walking the line between both worlds kept me rooted, and the spirits, when they touched me, they felt my need and they responded by gifting me with the Light. Their magic to counter the magic of the Devoid."

A sharp grunt coughed out of Conra's chest. "I figured that laechin was no ordinary creature. No wonder you slept after all that." He shook his head. "But that doesn't give you an excuse for waiting until now to tell us all this."

"I know," Darr replied. Shame caused his eyes to dart away. When he looked back, he met Conra's stare. "I was afraid you wouldn't understand, and I was wrong for that."

He held Jinn's hand. "I should've told you sooner. Please try not to worry about me now that you know."

A sarcastic grin tweaked the corners of Jinn's mouth. "Impossible, Darr. But I'll try."

* * * *

The day passed by while Darr, Conra, and Jinn waited for Feywen to return. Forgiving of their mistakes and content with each other's company, they waited as friends again. When night fell and Feywen still hadn't returned, Darr offered to take the first watch while Conra and Jinn slept.

He sat before the red glow of the fire, crackling lazily in the middle of the clearing. So close to the city of Craw, Darr didn't believe they'd be in danger of seeing the Soul Seekers, but he kept the fire small anyway. The spirits put him at ease, whispering all was well.

He glanced over at Jinn. He'd shared so many secrets with her today about his summoning. The joining between the physical and spiritual worlds only scratched the surface of what he'd experienced. The Light, the pure white power of life and death, had been at his fingertips. When he sent the Light into the laechin, it only appeared that he'd incinerated it. In reality, he'd shattered the laechin's Light, relegating it to the deepest reaches of the Currents where it could do no more harm. The Light wouldn't work on just anything. He doubted the spirits would gift it for anything other than a creature whose soul had been corrupted or twisted.

A sharp crackling echoed through the dark, far away but easily heard in the quiet. A quick glance into the Currents confirmed Feywen had returned with horses in tow. Weariness and anxiety spilled into the Currents, born from Feywen's approach, but Darr shut his mind away from the spirit realm. He'd intruded on the hearts of others enough for one day.

When he was several paces from the camp and still outside the clearing, Feywen tethered the horses. When he finished, he walked on cats' paws to sit next to Darr beside the fire. Conra and Jinn continued to sleep undisturbed.

"You're awake," Feywen said, concern a soft flicker in his eyes.

Darr smiled, giving a cordial nod. "I am. Did everything go alright?" he whispered.

Feywen shrugged, a hasty action. "I managed to find horses for each of us," he said. "I could only find enough food for a couple of days. Resources are slim in the city. I was fortunate to get what I could. You'll have to forage for a day or two before you get to Plad."

You? Darr wondered, but he hid the surprise from his face.

"It's not good out there," Feywen said, looking into the fire with an expressionless face. "Jacova was attacked from behind. The Seekers came over the cliffs in the back of the city, catching everyone by surprise. The Dwarf Elder Council perished, so did nearly a third of the city's population."

Feywen folded his arms before him, as if the fire didn't warm him. "It's not much better here in Craw. All of the refugees from Jacova came here. They would've begun to starve if supplies hadn't arrived from one of the Ogre tribes south of here."

"Ogres?" Darr couldn't hide the surprise from his voice this time.

Feywen smirked. "They're not all bad, Darr. The Ogres south of here are beginning to pull together, and it makes my heart warm to see them lending help in this time of need."

"I didn't mean anything…"

"It's okay." Feywen gave a dismissive wave. "I'm on edge with everything that's going on. My people are on the verge of starvation, camping in fields under open skies in what will soon be freezing weather. Meanwhile, the Ictarian Army— that's what everyone's calling it now—is in a similar state."

"What about the Soul Seekers?" Darr asked. "Have they reappeared?"

"Yes," Feywen breathed. "A few days ago the mists reappeared, and the Ictarian Army held them in place for almost three days at Walvor Bridge. They had to retreat last night, and from what I've heard, they've converted the Elven fort city of Vanla into a veritable fortress. If the Ictarian Army is cautious, they should last several days. That will give you plenty of time to make your way past them to Plad." Hesitation flashed on Feywen's face, followed by an awkward pause. "How are you doing?" he asked abruptly.

The question startled him, so out of character it sounded for Feywen. Feywen, usually straight and to the point, so obviously avoided whatever bothered him. Darr would give Feywen the benefit of the doubt, but the ruse would end now.

"What's going on?" Darr asked. "I know something's wrong."

Feywen stared back and the smile dropped from his face. His jaw clapped shut.

"I've decided to leave you," he said at last.

A pit opened up in Darr stomach, and his ribs turned to ice. His throat burned, but he tried to talk anyway. "Why?"

Feywen's eyes glazed over. "I have been thinking about this since Navda, since I sent Lacdur ahead to Jacova. I thought I could travel Ictar with you, leaving the care of my people in his hands because what I was doing here with you seemed so much more important. But after spending the last couple of days in Craw, I was reminded of what I once was."

When he looked up, his eyes burned fiercely. "I was the crown prince of the Dwarf King, Gyrot Dery. I spent my life preparing to protect and lead my people, and when the time came, I abandoned them to pursue my own interests. I did so because I believed they wanted change. Now I see I made a grave mistake. The people in Craw and the survivors from Jacova still look to me as their leader. They look to me for guidance and strength because that's what my father provided for them, even if his monarchy no longer stands."

Feywen took a deep breath. "So I will return to them. I will find the Ictarian Army, and if they'll have me, I will help them in any way I can. I owe the Dwarves that much. They have sacrificed so much already, and I must do the same."

When he finished, Feywen hunched up his shoulders and moved close to the fire. His demeanor changed from that of nobility he'd displayed a moment ago into something cooler and more aloof. At last, Feywen had returned to the person Darr remembered.

"You've led us through some difficult times," Darr began, "and you've done it well. We couldn't have done it without you."

A smile danced on Feywen's lips when he looked up. "I don't believe that for a moment, Darr Reintol. I may have shown you the paths you needed to take, but you helped us through the dangers we faced. Even when the Ogres captured you, you escaped their grasp on your own."

The Summoner fought to say something, but the words caught in his throat. Jinn's support, Conra's wisdom, and Feywen's leadership--all had aided and guided him in the use of his power. He never pretended to do it all alone.

Feywen moved closer to him, keeping his gaze focused on the fire. "When I was young, my father insisted I study with the Divine," Feywen said, his voice distant. "Because the Divine played such a crucial role in Ictar's development after the Aeon Wars, I was expected to interact with them. I never did buy into their dogma, but I found their lessons interesting. They taught lessons of virtue, of right and wrong, told against the backdrop of some ancient time when people could harness the powers of the Sephirs at will." He paused and looked briefly at Darr. "Looking back on it, those people could do what you can. They were Spirit Summoners."

Darr remained silent, ears sharp. Feywen continued. "These magic wielders could do magnificent things with their abilities, and the stories told about them ranged from the extraordinary to something akin to omnipotence. The Divine, of course, didn't think highly of these people, for they were flawed, magic-wielders. With these lessons, they sought to advise me of the dangers such power could bring."

Feywen laughed, a soft breath of sound through his nose. "But the men and women portrayed in these stories made use of magic for themselves. The choices were theirs, and against the wishes of my Divine instructors, I developed a belief not widely spread among their order. Even to this day, I don't believe magic in itself is inherently good or evil. The wielder determines that. After watching all you can do, Darr, I know without a doubt it is the wielder who chooses how the magic is used."

Darr stared in shock. Feywen looked over at him, the

smile dropped from his face, and he said, "I suppose what I'm trying to say is it's been an honor to walk beside you, to serve you in any way I could, and to see you do the things you can do."

Sadness and pride simmered in Darr's Light, and his throat released. He would miss Feywen. The days ahead wouldn't be the same. "Thank you," he said. "It's been an honor to know you, too."

* * * *

When dawn arrived at last, Feywen told Conra and Jinn of his intentions to leave them. They took the news well, however both were shocked at the announcement. After hearing his reasoning, neither Jinn nor Conra could discredit Feywen for leaving.

They ate a quick breakfast, the last they'd eat together. Afterwards, Feywen walked into the trees surrounding the camp and retrieved the horses from where he'd tethered them the night before.

He handed the reins to Conra, and said, "You should be able to find a crossing over the Wilamedde River due west of Craw. Once you cross into the Elven lands, keep far to the south of Vanla. If the Ictarian forces are as strong as everyone has been saying they are, you shouldn't be threatened."

The old Elf took the reins from him and shrugged. "I'll keep them safe," he said. "You make sure to do the same for yourself."

Feywen flashed a knowing smile. "I'll be okay. I know a crossing north of Walvor. If I can get around the Seeker mists without a problem, I can be in Vanla by the end of the day."

Jinn came up behind the Dwarf, and tapped him lightly on the shoulder. He turned, and she embraced him, holding him for several moments. "We won't forget what you've done for us," she told him. "We'll miss you."

Darr walked up beside her. She pulled away and added,

"I don't care what you say. We still couldn't have gotten this far without you."

Feywen gave a stiff nod. He started to turn towards his horse, paused, and reached into his tunic. When he turned around, he held a small leather pouch that he set in Jinn's hands.

"This is the last of the coin I carry," he said. "It'll ensure you are outfitted in Plad, and since I assume you'll need to cross the Wilamedde by ferry, it should buy you that service as well."

"Thank you," Darr and Jinn said together.

Satisfied, Feywen mounted his horse, and looked down at the three he'd traveled with over the last few weeks. "Take care of yourselves," he said, his final words to them.

With a sharp whistle and a flick of the reins, Feywen commanded his mount into a trot carrying him away from the clearing and out onto the plains of Borland beyond.

Darr wondered if they'd ever meet a braver man.

Chapter Twenty-Three

"Of course, when I met Darr, he'd been traveling for quiet some time. When Nidic Waq sent Darr away from his home and on his quest to free the Sephirs from the Ovids, the boy had hardly any awareness of his abilities. Interesting that Caeranol would throw such a valuable asset into the lake before knowing if he could swim or not, but then, I presume that Caeranol doesn't know what he is doing, and that can't be right."

~From the personal writings of the Divine, Zander

Amidst the bustling activity within Vanla's inner courtyard, Nidic Waq strolled among the throngs of people. He used the Currents to manipulate the Lights of those around him, temporarily erasing any feelings they might possess of him. It might not be the most ethical use of his abilities, but he didn't want to be bothered. Most of the soldiers and workers within Vanla's walls were mistrustful of him, but now he walked among them, an invisible presence. The damage he risked on the unstable Currents was a small price to pay to relieve some of the fear and suspicion among the Ictarian soldiers.

Nidic Waq left the main courtyard of the city beneath the midday sun, leaving behind the activity and noise of the soldiers, making his way to the barracks. In reality, Vanla wasn't much of a city. Barracks, stables, and high walls surrounded by an enormous courtyard market were all the city had to offer. The Elves had elevated it to city status to increase trade with the rest of Ictar, being that it lay so close to the border.

Vanla had changed since the Ictarian Army arrived, but more so since the events at the Tower Castle over the summer. Engineers reinforced every defense between Exed and the Wilamedde River. Vanla received a massive amount of attention. Soldiers replaced traders and artisans, engineers reinforced the wooden walls with stone and iron, and earthworks scattered the surrounding landscape.

Nidic Waq rounded the main barracks where the marketplace began, but the open grounds now held the bulk of the Ictarian camp. Nidic Waq kept to the fringes, his concentration faltering. Mingling with the soldier held no interest, but something else needed his attention.

The Currents pulled at the corners of his mind, a familiar, but urgent sensation.

Nidic Waq retraced his steps, stepping back into the shadow of an alley between the barracks. He sat down against one of the buildings and dipped his head, hiding it within his cowl. When he was ready, he submersed himself in the spirit realm...

...The swirling brightness of the spirits dispersed before the soft glow of the wisteria lights. Nidic Waq focused. No need to be in the Currents any longer than necessary. He found the tugging sensation easily enough, the presence scratching at his Light. With a thought, he let it pull him where it wished.

The spirits buzzed past him, their voices indistinct, and their collective memories a flash of color and emotion. Soon, even they were gone, and the wisteria glow of the realm turned to a pale blue. Very few Summoners understood the Currents had many levels.

--Prophet--

Caeranol's presence fell on him, powerful, kind, and unflinchingly straightforward. His was a presence that Nidic Waq had come to respect immensely over the years, much like a father.

"Why have you summoned me?"

--Vanla's defenses will be tested soon--The city will not likely survive--

Nidic Waq's trust in Caeranol built on top of his fear. "How soon do we have?"

White light began to filter out of the blue waves of the Currents, bright luminescence that cascaded like water.

--The spirits have anticipated this event--Vanla will be tested, but it will be up to the Ictarian soldiers to determine

whether it falls or not--

Nothing was certain. Even though the spirits anticipated the fall of Vanla, time remained to prevent it.

"Have you learned anything more about the traitor?" Nidic Waq asked.

The cascading light took shape and gained definition. In this part of the Currents, the lights weren't a reflection of the physical world. Caeranol's features took shape. Tall and regal, his dark hair long and tied back, his eyes a soft brown but startlingly bold.

--There is a traitor, of that I am certain--That is all I have been able to learn--Keep your eyes sharp, and your mind close to the Currents--The traitor will not stay hidden much longer, but I fear the damage it reaps will be vast--

A surge of discontent roared through Nidic Waq's Light. Until now, he wasn't completely sure of the legitimacy of a traitor. A traitor meant the Devoid was much closer to freeing itself than even Caeranol had thought.

--The Summoner has been doing well--

If Nidic Waq could've smiled, he would have. Darr Reintol. To think his name gave him hope.

--He is progressing faster than either of us could have anticipated--

"Is it possible he is one of the Chosen? His power is incredible, more so than any Summoner I have ever felt before."

Caeranol shook his head, his face troubled and sad.

--I have searched his Light thoroughly, and the spirits confirm they did not choose him--But I also do not understand the source of his summonings--His power is vast, and the limits to which he sets himself are further than any Summoner since the Continese--Perhaps some other force is at work--

"But who? Who else had the insight to bring forth such a powerful Summoner?"

--The spirits--

The words disturbed him. The spirits almost never interfered with the physical realm. On one of their few *incursions, they'd transformed Caeranol into an Archon, and then they'd done so at the High Elder's prompting. They also would've interfered when sending out the magic that would manifest itself in the Lights of each of the Chosen, but again, they'd done so at Caeranol's request. If they'd somehow given Darr an ability of such incredible power without direction, the implications were terrifying. It meant Darr was a tool of the spirits.*

Caeranol reached out to him, soothing him. --No fear, Prophet--I do not believe the Summoner is a harbinger of doom--Still, there is something about him that we both have missed--

"Keep your eyes open then, as well."

A tremor shook the prophet, and the pale blue light of the Currents faltered. This part of the Currents couldn't stay inhabited for long, at least not by one whose Light remained attached to the physical world.

--Remember--Vanla depends on you--Keep your instincts sharp--

Caeranol's face, so kind yet stern, disintegrated back into pinpricks of light, exploding out across the Currents, returning the light to familiar wisteria in the process. The spirits returned, dancing before him. Given Caeranol's realization, they felt alien, and Nidic Waq left them at once...

...Nidic Waq lifted his head and studied the sky. The sun had nearly set and a thick blanket of clouds had rolled in. Time traveled differently in that part of the Currents. Thankfully, he didn't travel there often.

Nidic Waq rose and stepped out from between the stack houses. Unease trembled in the spirit realm. It would grow with the approach of nightfall. The army leaders were undoubtedly in conference in the upper chambers of the barracks. He must go to them and learn what he could of the dangers Caeranol had warned him about.

Nidic Waq shook off his doubts. Encased in the iron of bravery, he started towards the building where the leaders met. He no longer concerned himself with distorting the

Currents. The icy stares and skeptic minds of the soldiers he passed were the least of his worries, and he passed them without sympathy for their feelings.

At the end of the stack houses, a presence called out to him across the Currents, an unexpected find. A vague presence, one his trained mind nearly shut out. This presence had memory of Darr Reintol, a person no man within the walls of Vanla should know, except for Lacdur, but this was not him.

Without hesitation, Nidic Waq turned from the barracks and followed the presence towards the front gates of the city. Within minutes, he reached the gatehouse along the front walls, a small, rectangular building, an office for the watch soldiers. Within it, he would find who he was looking for.

Outside the building, two Elven guards and their captain stood watch, and their cautious stares didn't change at his approach.

"Halt," the captain cried out, his face worn. "Civilians are not allowed past this point."

Nidic Waq lowered his hood, and the soldiers before him shifted uneasily. "I am no civilian. I am a personal friend and advisor of King Ariel Forn."

The two lesser soldiers shifted uncomfortably, but the captain remained rigid. "Do you have business here?" he asked.

"I'd like to have a word with the man you have detained in the gatehouse," Nidic Waq said.

At once, the Elf shook his head. "I have already sent a messenger to Alman Ohnler regarding this detainee. Until he responds, no one may enter."

"And why is that?" Nidic Waq asked. "Who are you holding?"

The captain's stare froze over. He bit his lower lip and said, "He claims to be Feywen Dery of the Dwarves."

Fascinating. Nidic Waq concealed his emotions, keeping his gaze level on the Elf captain. His emotions cooled within his tall frame. Carefully, he searched the Currents, asking the spirits if the captain spoke the truth. He did.

"I must speak with that man," Nidic Waq said. "I can verify his identity."

The captain remained rooted in place while his soldiers had all but stepped aside. "I cannot allow that," the Elf replied through gritted teeth. "Until Alman Ohnler himself responds to my message, nothing you do or say—"

Through the Currents, Nidic Waq reached into the Elf's Light and pulled on a thread of emotion within him. Instantly, the man's perceptions shifted. Nidic Waq didn't physically change, but to the man before him, he became something so dark and commanding the captain feared for his life.

"I'm sorry," the Elf squeaked. He turned to open the door, fumbling with the latch and swinging the door open before scurrying behind his guards.

Nidic Waq brushed past the guards without a glance and closed the door behind him. Through the dim glow of an oil lamp, a Dwarf sat in a chair not more than a few feet in front of him. Aroused by the sudden movement, the man shifted to meet the prophet's gaze.

"Nidic Waq," Feywen breathed, a smile creasing the edges of his mouth. Relief rippled into the Currents, and something else. Anxiety?

The prophet stepped into the full light of the lamp. "Feywen Dery," he said.

The once-prince remained in his chair. Feywen wasn't afraid of him, but his anxiety grew the longer he sat, becoming something almost tangible in the Currents. Yet, he refused to let whatever it was he felt show.

"You were traveling with Darr Reintol," Nidic Waq said. He said the words softly, but with force born from the Currents. "You guided him on his journey. Why then are you here?"

Guilt and frustration started to boil to the surface of Feywen's Light, but he kept it in check. Feywen had become stronger since he last saw him.

"I left them in Craw," Feywen answered. "The Elf named Conra knows the way north, and he'll guide them well. I left because my place is here, among my people."

Nidic Waq watched him, his eyes boring into the once-prince. Feywen didn't move. *Does he sense my uncertainty?*

"Why do they travel north and not west?" Nidic Waq asked.

Feywen's shoulders sank, and his anxiety lessened. "Conra is leading Darr and Jinn north to the mountain called the Edge," the once-prince replied. "Jinn intends to claim a relic there, one necessary for the fight against the Devoid."

Nidic Waq's mind buzzed. How had Caeranol not mentioned any of this? Unless, of course, he didn't know. Were the Currents really that badly clouded?

The prophet knelt down to meet Feywen's gaze. "How did they learn this?"

"One of the Divine in Arcnor knew," Feywen answered, his tone polite and even. "He told Jinn after Darr secured the Earth Sephir."

Nidic Waq leaned back and straightened, an attempt to distance himself from the emotions threatening to overwhelm him. He concentrated and reminded himself Caeranol put his plans into motion a millennia ago. He did so because when it tried to escape, the Devoid would mask everything with its lies.

Nidic Waq never believed its deceptions would be this pervasive.

"The knowledge possessed by the Divine was kept exclusively within their sect," Nidic Waq added, returning to himself. "Even as Caeranol's own emissary, I am kept ignorant of certain aspects concerning the Chosen of the Light."

"Maybe they were led astray. Is it possible?" Feywen asked. Nidic Waq shook his head.

"Darr would've sensed a deception at once," the prophet replied. "The spirits would've informed him if the Divine was lying."

A short silence stretched between the two men.

"Prophet," Feywen said, bringing Nidic Waq to attention. "Will you take me to Norris Dane?"

Nidic Waq stood up, looking down at Feywen without expression. "What is it you hope to accomplish here?"

Anger swept through Feywen, but he calmed himself quickly, and again, without revealing his emotions physically. "I want to join the ranks of the Ictarian Army," he said. "I may no longer possess the rank and title I once had, but I would still fight alongside my brothers."

A careless smile worked its way up the side of Nidic Waq's mouth. "Norris Dane isn't a suitable tactician and he knows it. He's given up his control of the Dwarves to Ariel Forn and Blaque Eris. With your return, I suspect he'll ask you to take his place."

Fear crept into Feywen's eyes, the first emotion he'd shown. His people had lost their king and most recently, their home. Feywen had left them when they needed him most, and he knew it. Some might consider his return to a position of power a slap in the face to the monarchy and to the Dwarves themselves.

"The best Norris Dane will get from me is a position as captain," Feywen answered, his head tilted. "The Dwarf Elder Council now leads the fate of the Dwarves. I'll support him and provide whatever courage and advice I can lend, but the monarchy died with my father."

The slow smile on Nidic Waq's face froze. "You are truly as noble as your father," he said. "I suspect he, too, would have said something much the same had he been in this position. The Dwarves will be fortunate to have you."

From the moment he'd first met Feywen, he'd seen a fighter. His expertise tracking the Soul Seekers had been invaluable and his help in guiding Darr even more so. That he'd given up his leadership position proved nothing about his character. Now, for the first time, Feywen Dery's importance stood fully revealed.

"Come," Nidic Waq ordered. "The army leaders are in conference. You might as well accompany me. You won't be sent away."

Feywen smiled despite his fear. He stood up and followed Nidic Waq from the gatehouse.

Chapter Twenty-Four

"Early on in his travels, Darr had help from a mutual friend. The Earth Archon, Racall, guided him during his early days, teaching him the extent of his powers as a Spirit Summoner. And though I don't quite know how it was possible, they fought together to reclaim the Sephir of Water. They fought together, as one. Not even during the Aeon Wars was such a thing possible."

~From the personal writings of the Divine, Zander

Following Feywen's departure, Darr, Jinn, and Conra set off for the Wilamedde River beneath an overcast sky. Despite the chill in the air, a feeling of camaraderie among the three warmed them. Nidic Waq, Erec, Lacdur, and Feywen were gone. They could only rely on themselves. Their conversations were infrequent, but when they did talk, it came welcome and comforting.

They rode out of the hill country surrounding Craw onto the boulder-strewn flatlands of Borland. Conra led them with certainty. It'd been nearly thirty years since the old man had passed through this country, but he remembered the important landmarks needed to navigate the land.

By nightfall, they arrived at the eastern banks of the Wilamedde River and a dozen miles south of Walvor Bridge. Conra wanted to stay far away from the conflict with the Soul Seekers. When they stopped for the day, they tended to the horses before settling themselves.

"We'll have to find a crossing in the morning," Conra explained over supper. The last meager light of the day faded to black over their fire. "The Wilamedde is a broad river. Shallows are nearly impossible to find this far south."

Jinn swallowed the piece of bread she chewed on. "Isn't that why Feywen told us to find a ferry?" she asked.

The old Elf nodded, but added nothing. Before them, their fire burned to ash. In the black of the night, the river churned along, a constant thrumming. A memory flashed in

Darr's mind, quick and stabbing.

"Erec met a man who lived along the Wilamedde," Darr said, the words spilling out involuntarily.

Conra watched him without expression, but Jinn nodded, and a bittersweet smile spread across her face. "A trapper, wasn't he?" Jinn asked. "He'd come to Tyfor to hunt for the season."

Darr smiled. "Yeah. He told Erec all about life down here, but Erec was more excited about the man's stories as a soldier. Father was so angry that night..."

Silence followed, but Conra asked, "Why was Hydle so upset?"

Jinn dipped her head. "Father told Erec he'd get himself killed."

Darr folded his arms across his chest, warding off the cold inside him. The memory ached, but it no longer burned with guilt, a sign that perhaps healing had arrived.

"You'd better get to sleep," Conra suggested. "I'll take the first watch."

Darr and Jinn rolled into their blankets without complaint.

The next morning began with a drenching rain. The three ate a hasty breakfast, packed their things, and began riding south along the river. Conra didn't know the south end of the river, but they wouldn't risk traveling toward the Ictarian Army's position. By midmorning, the rain turned to a steady drizzle, but it did nothing to help their moods.

Conra had been right. The Wilamedde's formidable width and depth showed no sign of lessening. Darr contemplated using a summoning to stop the flow of the river or even to stop the rain, but such thoughts burned away quickly. The tenuous balance between the Sephirs wouldn't be able to handle such an abuse of power. The Currents, on the other hand, might shed some insight. Darr closed his eyes, slipping easily into the Currents...

...the wisteria light poured over him. Darr slid in between the spirits an unobtrusive presence. He only came to look.

The Wilamedde River glowed beside him, a shimmering blue sparkle winding into the Currents. Somewhere along its length, life would flourish. He drifted along the sapphire ribbon, finding sparks of animal life, wild and untamed.

He drifted further. More animals appeared, but these were less skittish. They knew humankind. He was close. Soon a cluster of white lights appeared through the wisteria glow, settled on the edge of the Wilamedde...

...Darr anchored himself within the Currents but returned to the physical world. Far out in the rugged landscape south, the white glow of the village pulsed gently.

"There," Darr announced, pointing.

Conra brought he horse around, following the line of Darr's hand. "I don't see anything. What did you find, Boy?"

The Summoner shook his head. "You can't see it yet. I found it in the Currents. There's a village along the river ten, maybe fifteen, miles out."

Conra scoffed at first, a direct result of the cold soaking through his clothes. "You've been right before," he muttered. "No reason to doubt you now."

The three spent the remainder of the day riding south, keeping their thoughts to themselves. In the late afternoon, when the gray light of the day began to die, the lights of the village came into view. It didn't appear to offer much. The buildings were few and hunched down amongst one another surrounding a lone dock. If it had a ferry, it wasn't in service. Still, he couldn't ignore his hope for a warm meal and a fire.

"I think there's an inn," Conra croaked over the pattering of rain. He pointed to a well-lit building. "I know it's money best spent in Plad, but we can't stay out here. Let's go."

When they approached the building, voices grew louder, interspersed with occasional laughter. They tethered their horses outside. If they could, Darr promised himself to come back and find them proper shelter.

"Keep to yourself and follow me," Conra advised, his gaze stern.

He walked up the steps and pushed the door open. Smoke filled Darr's nostrils, accompanied by the angry orange glow from hanging lanterns. At first, the few people gathered around the serving bar seemed bothered by the appearance of the travelers, their faces reflecting a mix of curiosity and skepticism. Mostly they were Dwarves, but a couple Elves and at least one Cortazian sat among them. Conra made his way towards a lone table in the back of the room, but a portly Dwarf woman intercepted him.

"'An I 'elp ya?" she asked, her accent thick. She wheeled about suddenly, and a fat arm stretched out to the men behind her. "Get ba' to yer beers, ya bums. 'uit frighten' the 'ustomers."

The gathered men went back to their drinks, and the old woman's face brightened with a sweet smile. "Now, what 'an do for ya?"

"We're hoping to cross on the ferry in the morning," Conra answered, leaning close. "If it's still running, of course."

A screeching cackle escaped the woman's throat. She reached out and slapped Conra's shoulder. "'Ourse it's still runnin'. 'Aos. Suppose yer be needin' a room as well? I'm the inn'eeper here."

The old Elf nodded with his smile neatly in place. "A stable for our horses and a hot meal, if you have anything left."

The innkeeper's answer was another cackle. She seated them along the bar before scooting behind it. The curiosity of the gathered men drew them close, but a sharp command from the old woman sent them back to their private conversations. Within minutes, she brought out plates heaped with piles of stew and a board with hot bread. Darr worried his eyes might fall out of his head.

"One a my boys took yer 'orses 'round back," she told them, setting the food down. "They'll be safe tonigh'."

During supper, the bar patrons' tongues loosened the more they drank. The Ictarian Army had recruited many of the young men, and even a few women, in the village. The army was desperate for anyone who could help.

One of the men recounted a terrifying story he'd heard

from one of the soldiers. Several days past, the Soul Seekers appeared on the battlefield as monstrous, armor clad giants. The soldiers called them Soul Devourers because these creatures didn't merely seek souls—they sucked them in like a bellows. Many of the Ictarian soldiers had perished that night.

At one point, Conra leaned over towards him, and whispered, "It's strange to hear them talk so casually, isn't it? This part of the world has been seeped in magic since the days of the Aeon Wars. It's a lot different than from where we come from."

As the night wore on, they learned about the stronghold at Vanla. The Elves were finally involved in the fight. A good sign, considering the Seekers invaded the Elves' own lands.

"I wonder if Feywen made it to them," Jinn whispered at Darr's shoulder.

"It's hard to say," he answered. "I'd like to hope he did, but if Walvor Bridge was collapsed, I don't know how he would've made it across."

Eventually, their conversation turned to them. How had two Cortazians ended up traveling with an Elf in the Dwarf territories? Conra concocted a vague story about visiting sick relatives, turning their attention towards some of the sights they'd seen. Most of the villagers had seen nothing of the outside world.

By the end of the night, Darr and his companions had established such a good rapport with the villagers the innkeeper offered them a room free of charge.

* * * *

The following morning, Darr and his companions ate in the inn with the innkeeper, but nothing could repay them for their acts of kindness, however Conra left all the money they could spare tucked under the pillow of his bed for the old woman to find.

Little over an hour later, they boarded the ferry with the horses and crossed the Wilamedde. By midmorning, they were on their way across the Ladornaleah. The landscape changed drastically on the west side of the river. While the plains of Borland had been dry and flat, laden with boulders, the Ladornaleah's hills rolled on, a green ocean studded with trees and interspersed with great stretches of farmland.

Even with the Earth Sephir restored, the seasons had yet to return in full.

"These plains, along with the Norstag Plume to the north, feed all of the Elven Lands," Conra explained while they rode, heading northwest from the banks of the river. "It's a shame they keep it mostly to themselves."

Darr glanced sideways at Jinn, confused. "What does that mean?" he asked.

Conra sighed. "For nearly two decades, Feywen's father worked with the Elves in establishing a fair system of trade. You see, the Elves have all this land, all these resources, but they don't openly trade with any of the other races. I'm not sure why. It's not as if they don't have enough. Anyway, over the last few years, the walls between the two nations began to crack. Slowly, trade opened up, but I fear with Gyrot Dery's death, nothing will come of his work."

Silence followed. Shouldn't both the nations work together naturally, Darr wondered? They shared borders, and each possessed skills the other lacked, but in some way or another, the Aeon Wars still lingered in the hearts of the people.

They camped for the night within a grove of birch with no fire to warm them. Darr slept well enough up until midnight when the rain returned. With only the light protection from the skeletal birch limbs above, he found little rest.

Morning brought no relief. The night's drizzle turned into a raging storm, complete with wind and monstrous claps of thunder. Conra kept their pace steady, taking them further west before angling northward.

"Shouldn't we take it a little slower, Conra?" Jinn called out against the roar of wind and pouring rain.

The old Elf shook his head. "I want as much distance

between us and Vanla as we can get. That means we don't stop until we're far north of that place."

Darr wanted to rest, too, but he agreed with Conra. Danger, hidden and rooted deep, pulsed within the Currents.

Chapter Twenty-Five

"After the Sephir of Water was secured, one of the Divine helped Darr to return it to its altar unnoticed. I believe he was aided by another Covenant Bearer, but it's impossible to know for sure. There are so few of us left, and we have no way to find each other. In this time of union between the races, it's important to remember there are still walls between us that yet need to be broken down."

~From the personal writings of the Divine, Zander

"Now isn't the time to be debating whether this will work or not," Ariel Forn advised, composure intact. "Our defense of this city will last no more than a few days. We knew that coming in."

Nidic Waq stood beside the young king, the faces of the Ictarian leaders grim before them. Despite the reinforcements of the city's defenses, Vanla couldn't withstand a focused attack for long. After only one battle, the Seekers tore through nearly all of their defenses. They were lucky to have stopped the Seekers at the outer walls.

For tonight, the Seekers wouldn't make it up the hill.

"This plan won't work without the prophet," Norris Dane chided. "Are you sure we can count on him?"

"Pretty bold of you to say, Dane, when he's standing right there," Lacdur retorted, compact body rigid.

The electric twinge of a smirk jerked at the corners of Nidic Waq's mouth, but he didn't show it. Distrust followed him wherever he went in Ictar, but some supported him.

Ariel Forn's stare shifted to the Dwarf Councilman. "Nidic Waq has not let us down. He's loyal to us. Put aside any of your doubts in him or the power he wields. There are much more destructive forces at work here."

Norris Dane clamped his mouth shut. Beside him, Vertain slid into view, ominous in his Daraven armor. "I'd like to make one more suggestion regarding our lure."

Ariel nodded. Crusis Jiln, the leader of the Cortazian

Calvary, had fallen during Vanla's first Seeker attack. Now Vertain commanded both the Daravens and the Cortazian horsemen.

"I believe the cavalry would be safer bait," Vertain suggested. "We can walk the horses to the field and lure the Seekers into our trap, then remount and ride away once it is sprung. We'd be able to move much quicker than the infantry."

"We've been through this before, Vertain," Blaque Eris grunted. His bulk rose into the space before Vertain like a dark cloud. "The Seekers are not as mindless as we once thought. Whatever evil drives them will know something is wrong if the cavalry is present instead of the foot soldiers."

Vertain stood firm. "The Seekers are not driven by logic. The Seekers know our next moves because of the traitor."

"If there is a traitor," Nidic Waq said, his voice even and cool. "Right now, we have only a theory. Until we have further proof, the best course of action is to make our decisions based on what we know."

"But what we know right now may be different than what we'll know tomorrow," Vertain snapped back.

"Then we'll adjust our thinking accordingly," Nidic Waq replied.

"Lord Forn, may I say something?" Feywen Dery asked. He stood alongside Alman Ohnler and a few of the other Elf captains. A show of unity perhaps?

Ariel nodded. "You may speak."

Feywen cleared his throat. "I once thought as you did, Vertain, hoping for some kind of uniformity to the Seekers movements. I also thought they were completely mindless, but I've come to respect that's not the case. Their hunger for our souls is what drives them, traitor or no, make no mistake. Because of their hunger, they can sense treachery. They can sense when a trap has been placed between them and their prey, and they will move accordingly."

"So the best way to trap them is with an irresistible lure," Vertain said, his head bowed in defeat. "Still, this plan is overly risky."

"There is risk in everything we do," Feywen countered.

Nidic Waq smiled. Feywen's addition to the army ranks would prove invaluable. He possessed his father's charisma, and the lessons he'd learned over the last few months, made him a crucial piece in the Ictarian defense.

"By your leave, Lord Forn," Feywen Dery stated, "we should take up our positions. The Seekers could attack at any time."

Not a whisper passed among the gathered men, no murmurs of discontent or unease. Even though the once-prince had been back for a short time, they understood the respect he commanded.

Ariel bowed his head. "You are dismissed," he said, but with an edge that cut to the bone. "Be brave and strong. We stand, body and soul, together."

The army leaders dispersed in something short of a minute, even Vertain, who habitually persisted on matters he thought to be right. Feywen lingered, standing at Ariel's side until no one remained but the three of them.

"I saw nothing that would indicate anyone is disloyal to us," Feywen reported, standing close to Ariel and Nidic Waq. "If there is a traitor among us, I don't believe he sits in this circle, my lord."

"Just because you cannot see it doesn't mean it isn't there." Nidic Waq kept his voice smooth and even, his face still hidden within his cowl. "Something dark is at work among us. The Devoid's reach into our world is much more profound than I estimated."

Ariel arched an eyebrow. "You've heard from the spirits then?"

"No," Nidic Waq replied. "I've heard from Caeranol. A traitor is among us, of that he's certain."

"And if we cannot find the traitor, what then?" Ariel asked.

Nidic Waq let the weight of his fears pour through the Currents. Feywen and Ariel needed to understand the danger. "The traitor may very well take down our entire army, but sooner or later, he will make a mistake. We must be looking when that mistake is made."

"We'll maintain our subterfuge then," Feywen said. "There is no traitor."

Nidic Waq said nothing, but he gave a slight nod.

Feywen stood for a moment longer before turning to Ariel. "I'd better return to my men," he said. "I've been gone too long as it is."

Ariel released him with a dismissive wave. Feywen passed Nidic Waq, acknowledging him with a stern bow of his head. The doors to the room opened, and Feywen closed them behind him.

Once he was gone, Nidic Waq lowered his hood. A ragged strand of his fiery hair fell into his face. "If I do tonight what you wish of me, there'll be no more doubt about the power I wield."

"I know," Ariel said. "You will be more of an outcast than ever."

Nidic Waq took a step forward. "I am prepared for that. I've always been prepared. But that doesn't mean the rest of Ictar is."

"We need the power you wield if this trap is to succeed," Ariel replied. "For better or worse, Ictar will have to manage."

"No, my lord, Ictar does not have to manage."

Anger burned in the Currents, but Ariel forced it away. Barely. "What do you propose we do then, Prophet?"

"We must do what we feel is right," Nidic Waq answered. "But as a leader, you must be prepared for the conflict to come."

Nidic Waq lingered a moment. He turned and began to walk to the door leading from the chamber.

"Thank you," Ariel said behind him.

Nidic Waq stopped and replaced his cowl. He didn't look back.

* * * *

Nidic Waq stood behind the Ictarian Army after the last

evening light faded to black. Lines of soldiers stood defiant, the prey set to lure the Seekers. The mists rose out of the flats before the rocky hill country. Beside him, Feywen Dery and Lacdur stood with a small contingent of soldiers, reserves waiting in case trouble arose. Both men were official advisers to Ariel Forn, but for tonight at least, the king needed them to be able to command troops in case trouble arose.

"It's good to have you back," Lacdur said, his voice intentionally low.

Feywen didn't look over at him, but satisfaction ebbed into the Currents anyway.

"I'm right where I belong," Feywen replied.

"What about the boy?" Lacdur asked. Nidic Waq flinched, but he didn't lose his focus.

"No," Feywen answered at last. "My place is here."

The sky overhead thickened with clouds. The only light came from the watch fires scattered along the hills and flats. The Seeker mists rose up, a black wall against the night.

"Do you think this will work?" Lacdur asked.

Feywen glanced up at Nidic Waq, but the prophet pretended not to notice. "It will work," he answered, an edge to his voice.

Lacdur shook his head. "Maugwrith by itself won't do anything. The barrels won't ignite themselves."

Maugwrith. Darr Reintol would recognize it as the same fuel source his village blacksmith sometimes used, the very same fuel that had taken the blame for the firehound attack. A highly flammable, long burning liquid, maugwrith would make quick work of the Soul Seekers, if implemented properly.

A sharp gust of wind, a cold breath exhaled from a corpse, bit hard against the Ictarian Army. The mists began to break apart, and from within, the inky black forms of the Soul Seekers rushed forward silently. Bru Kiln Tole's voice rang out into the night, his command to stand strong. Tension tumbled out of the Currents. The wave of Seekers grew closer.

Without a word, Nidic Waq replaced his cowl and started forward. With long, even strides, he glided down the hill towards the rear Ictarian ranks. An unobtrusive presence, he made his way to the front line, passing between men as if made of air. Fighting hadn't begun yet, but it would soon if he didn't act quickly.

The front lines fell away behind him, and Nidic Waq walked alone into the field between the Ictarian soldiers and the approaching Seekers, a single reed of grass standing tall against a rushing tidal wave. Blood pounded through the veins in Nidic Waq's neck, but he closed his eyes anyway, concentrating.

The Currents tumbled around him, fiercely chaotic. Nidic Waq's stomach churned. He fought away the distortion, rooting himself firmly in both worlds. The power he summoned surged within him, but it wasn't yet time to release it. Around him, the spirits buzzed in discontent. The air grew colder. Unease suffocated him. Still, he held on tight, careful and focused. He wouldn't allow the balance between the Sephirs to break. He would take the barest amount of power the Currents could spare.

Now!

The Soul Seekers tore their way within a hundred yards of the Ictarian frontlines. Nidic Waq spread his arms wide before thrusting them skyward. Golden fire launched into the sky out of his palms, burning the air itself, traveling up into the clouds. Thunder rumbled like a massive beast coming to life. Their bodies illuminated by the golden light, silver claws flashing in the night, the Seekers didn't slow.

Nidic Waq closed his hands, halting the flow of magic from spilling into the physical world. He lifted his head to the sky. The golden light churned within the clouds above, heaving and rumbling. Like a giant taking a deep breath, the clouds sucked in on themselves, a roiling mass. A thunderous clap shook the battlefield and a spear of lightning thrust itself into the ground before the Soul Seekers.

The ground itself heaved upwards at impact, spawning a jagged line of explosions between the Ictarian Army and the approaching Seekers. The maugwrith barrels, buried shallow in the middle of the field, ignited and exploded, shooting flames twenty feet into the air. The explosions expanded, sweeping up and down the battlefield.

The fire sucked in and consumed the first of the Soul Seekers. Hundreds fizzled out in the orange rage. Detecting the obstacle, the remaining Seekers split in an attempt to bypass the fire. Nidic Waq stood tall, his chin tilted up to his attackers.

The continuing eruptions closed up and around the flanks of the Seeker masses. Unable to divert from their course, the Soul Seekers rushed the fires again. Hundreds more of the black shapes disappeared into the red glow. Within a few minutes of the initial strike, the circle of explosions closed. The maugwrith continued to burn, an independent fuel source, shooting flames hot and high. Nearly a thousand more Seekers massed within the burning ring with nowhere for to go except out through the flames.

Nidic Waq knelt down on one knee, focusing once more. Many Ictarian soldiers had seen him walk out on the battlefield. Even more had seen the magic he commanded. Ictar wasn't ready for a revelation like that, and he'd do what he could to minimize such a revelation.

Using the Currents to twist the perceptions of the soldiers behind him, he disappeared into the flames, or so it would seem to them. A few attentive individuals might see him walk away from the battlefield, but they would be only a few in a thousand. Most would remember only the freak thunderstorm and the maugwrith explosions.

The Ictarian Army rejoiced in their victory. The maugwrith fires burned, and the Seekers slowly disappeared into the smoke and ash. Nidic Waq returned to where he'd stood before the battle alongside Feywen Dery and Lacdur.

Though he'd saved them all this night, he hoped the damage done to Ictar wasn't irreparable.

"It seems your ruse may have worked, Prophet," Lacdur grumbled beside him.

Nidic Waq didn't look at him. "We'll see."

"We're still fortunate it worked," Feywen added. "Even if your display of magic opened up new possibilities of fear for the people of Ictar, you still saved us."

Nidic Waq kept his gaze fixed on the burning fires below. The remaining Seekers continued to throw themselves through the flames.

"How much of the maugwrith remains," Feywen asked.

Lacdur snorted. "We used almost everything the Ogres gave us. Several casks remain, but not enough to do this again."

"Quite the display you put on, Prophet," Vertain called behind him. The Daraven captain rode up beside him and dismounted.

Nidic Waq didn't answer.

"Lord Forn requests our presence to discuss our next move," Vertain advised, dark eyes burning with excitement.

"A little early, isn't it, Vertain?" Lacdur retorted, sharpness in his voice. "The Seekers are still down there. It's not likely they're going to break free, but they're full of surprises."

Vertain smiled and shook his head. "Don't kill the messenger, Captain. Bru Kiln Tole will stay on the field in case something happens, but with the battle over so quickly, Lord Forn wants to begin preparation for whatever comes next."

Nidic Waq sighed. More talk.

* * * *

Alman Ohnler, his pale eyes intense, nodded sternly. "I'll send a small number of my White Knights to patrol the cliffs above and below the city."

Nidic Waq folded his arms across his chest. It didn't happen often, but he would need to sleep tonight.

"What about the remaining maugwrith?" Vertain asked, stepping around the close confines of their meeting room to stand before Ariel Forn.

The Cortazian King shook his head. "Right now, our plan

is to use it as a failsafe on the plains west of Vanla. This is the most open area, and it should slow any attempt to flank us."

"That might shield our borders, but will that really protect us?" Feywen turned his head, calmly meeting Nidic Waq's stare.

The prophet breathed lightly, annoyed but complacent. "Our best defense is to stay constantly alert," he answered. "The Seekers will adapt to the move we made tonight. They won't come at us the same way again. Their attack will be unexpected, make no mistake. Our soldiers, in particular, those keeping watch, must report anything no matter how insignificant. That will be our best defense."

"I'll make sure they do so," Blaque Eris agreed. His heavy armor made him look much larger. "I'll advise Bru Kiln Tole, but who should our soldiers report to?"

All heads turned to Ariel Forn, his face reflecting calm. "Reports should be collected by a representative in each unit no more than every fifteen minutes. I want those reports sent directly to Nidic Waq."

Blaque Eris stiffened. "My Lord, with all due respect, the prophet isn't a commanding officer in this battle."

"Then I will make him so."

Nidic Waq didn't alter his stance, but the annoyance building within him crushed against his chest. "Lord Forn, while I appreciate your trust in me, I don't feel comfortable in such a position. Might I suggest someone just as familiar with the workings of the Seekers?"

"Lacdur," Feywen said.

"Yes," Nidic Waq replied. "His knowledge of the Soul Seekers is equal to, if not, superior to my own. He's an infantry captain, proven on this field of battle, and he commands much respect."

It took a moment for the Cortazian King to decide. He met Lacdur's fierce gaze. "Lacdur, I'll reassign your unit, and elevate you to a commander rank. You'll be restricted to move large contingents, but you'll be allowed to move several reserve units in an emergency. Eris, do you agree?"

The Dwarf general bowed his head in agreement.

"Thank you, Lord Forn," Lacdur said, his body held straight. The Dwarf warrior wouldn't easily fail at the task set before him.

"What about you, Nidic Waq?" Alman Ohnler asked, his youthful face masking his skepticism. "Where will you be in the battle ahead?"

Nidic Waq gave him an amused look. "I'll be where I always am, close to Lord Forn. I'll do my best to break through the confusion in the Currents, but I can promise nothing."

Ariel looked over at him. Fear glistened in his dark eyes. The last thing anyone wanted was another tragedy like Jacova. Memories of the massacre flashed through the Currents, born of Ariel Forn's fear. The shiver of fear remained a moment longer, but tempered courage replaced it.

Ariel turned to Vertain, Alman Ohnler, and Blaque Eris. "I'm relying on you three to set your perimeters and begin assigning soldiers to give reports beginning immediately. Anyone you need to assist you is at your disposal."

The three men nodded, and then left the room in single file. The other leaders followed. Ariel stood by himself on the far end of the room, lifting his head slightly.

Nidic Waq regarded him for a moment before following the others from the room.

Chapter Twenty-Six

"Darr knew the next Sephir, the Sephir of Earth, lay a great distance south, further than even his considerable imagination could take him. Joined with his brother, Erec, and his sister, Jinn, Darr believed the task ahead might be possible. His brother knew better, and he led his siblings to an old family friend, a temperamental old Elf by the name of Conra. After speaking briefly with the man, it's clear to me he has ulterior motives for traveling. Something else drives Conra to Darr's side."

~From the personal writings of the Divine, Zander

Darr, Jinn, and Conra lasted another hour in the open before the storm sweeping along the plains south of Vanla forced them to find shelter. Though Conra wished to push on, he knew their safety was in peril. He led them back to a lone walnut tree they'd passed several minutes ago, its aged branches sweeping out in a broad canopy.

"No sense in getting ourselves killed," the Elf called out over the roar of the wind.

Darr dismounted alongside Jinn, and they tied their horses to a low hanging limb of the walnut. They settled down next to Conra, who produced his water skin. He took a sip and passed it on.

Darr shivered, but not from the cold. "Where's Vanla?" he asked.

Conra gestured north. "Another twenty miles. Once this downpour stops, we'll continue west for an hour before heading north. We should avoid any fighting that way."

"Is something bothering you?" Jinn asked, leaning in close.

Darr hunched his shoulders. "Just a feeling. I sense danger in the Currents, like something bad is about to happen, but neither I nor the spirits can identify it."

"Someone's playing tricks on you, Boy," Conra grumbled.

209

"I'm not saying I don't believe you. I'm saying someone or something is trying to pull the wool over your eyes. You let me know if you figure something out."

Darr rubbed his hands together. He'd keep an ear to the Currents, but he believed Conra was right. The danger he felt was a direct result of the masking going on within the spirit realm. Something bad was coming, but not even the spirits were able to find it.

Minutes passed by, then a half hour. The rain began to lessen.

"Time to get moving," Conra advised, pushing himself up from the ground.

The three remounted and continued out across the plains. The remainder of the day drudged on, a slow and steady pace made miserable by wet clothes and piercing wind.

They followed the upper ridge of a canyon northward towards Plad and west of Vanla when dusk approached. They'd begun searching for shelter for the night when Conra called a halt. Darr searched the Currents, sensing his unease, but nothing presented itself. The spirits remained eerily quiet.

Conra dismounted and walked his horse along the ridgeline, looking down into the canyon. He paid no attention to the Reintol siblings trailing after him. Around them, the rain and wind whipped at their bodies.

"What do you think he's looking for?" Jinn asked. Her body hunched up within her cloak.

Darr shook his head. "I don't know. I can't find anything in the Currents, but Conra's bothered by something."

Below them, the canyon broke off into separate directions. One line led north and back onto the plains, while the other led east towards Vanla. Conra froze, sending a pulse of fear across the Currents. Darr leapt from his mount and ran to him.

Conra extended his arm and pointed towards the canyon's eastward fracture. "There. Seeker mists."

Darr couldn't see anything, not with his physical eyes.

He revisited the Currents, paying attention to the feelings and the whispers of the spirits. His perceptions, though numbed, detected the unmistakable cold of the Soul Seekers.

"They're heading to Vanla, aren't they?" Jinn asked of no one in particular.

Darr grimaced and said, "The Currents are unsettled. If Nidic Waq is there, I doubt he knows they're coming."

Jinn and Darr studied each other. The fear in her eyes likely mirrored his own. "We have to help them," Jinn breathed, her voice shaking.

To attempt such a task was beyond risky. It was in direct opposition to what Feywen had told them. They were to avoid any contact with the Soul Seekers.

"I don't think we can go there," the Summoner whispered. "We risk everything if we do."

"And we leave all those people to die," Jinn said through her teeth.

Darr folded his arms in front of his chest. "We endanger everything by going to Vanla. If something happens, then—"

"Then you will protect us," Jinn cut in.

Darr looked to Conra for help, but the old Elf shook his head. "She's right, Boy. That army isn't prepared for this and we all know it. You said yourself that the prophet doesn't know."

"I said I doubt he knows."

"Well, what does it matter if we avoid Vanla?" Jinn barked, angry now. "If the Ictarian Army falls, then Exed falls, and if Exed falls, then all of this is for nothing."

Darr chewed at his bottom lip. Going to Vanla might be the right thing to do, but he had to consider the Chosen of the Light. He couldn't put Jinn in the kind of danger that going to Vanla would bring. He could protect himself much easier than he could protect Conra and Jinn.

"Fine," Darr agreed. "But I'm going alone."

"What's the matter with you, Boy?" Conra spat. "What makes you think you'll have a better chance at this than the three of us?"

Darr stared. "I can protect myself from the Seekers, but

not all of us. You'll have to stay behind with Jinn. It's the only way this will work and leave at least one of us safe."

Jinn and Conra stood rigid. They weren't going to agree with him, but there no time remaining to argue.

Darr whipped aside and climbed back on his horse. In the dying light of the day, through tearing wind and rain, he bolted out along the open ridge. The dull pounding of his horse's hooves matched the beating in his chest.

Because the canyon they followed split in separate directions, they'd have to reach the plains before heading east towards Vanla. The storm didn't help them at all. Once darkness enveloped them completely, the race against time became a sprint at best.

They'd reached the open plains, but their speed increased marginally. The landscape was reduced to shades of violet and black. Far to the east still, the faint orange glow of Vanla's watch fires burned. Darr kept his senses trained on the Currents. With the darkness, he'd lost track of the Seeker mists.

Nearly an hour into their ride, soaking wet from the rain and chilled from the cold, Conra called a halt. Darr looked around and quickly decided he had no idea where they were. The glow from the watch fires still burned on the horizon.

"We're not far," Conra yelled over the rising wind. "I can't tell where the Seekers are. I'm afraid we might ride right into them."

"Can you ask the spirits to tell us where they are?" Jinn asked.

Darr shook his head. "It's difficult to tell anything, but I'll try." He closed his eyes.

...Everything looked the same in the Currents. The bright lights of the spirits danced wildly around, and the Lights of Jinn and Conra burned brightly in the wisteria afterglow.

Appearances deceived in the Currents. It might look the same, but the feel of the spirit realm set Darr on edge. Numbness surrounded him, separating him from the emotions and memories he normally fought to keep at a distance. Even in their own home, incoherent whispers replaced the spirits' normal voice.

One feeling alone remained. Hostility. It filled the Currents with its oppressiveness, a cloud of poison infiltrating every facet of the spirit realm.

Darr attempted to track the source of the feeling, but nothing revealed itself. The dark emotions came from everywhere and everything. Such power! How much hatred did the Devoid possess in order to affect an entire world?

Darr calmed himself, focusing on what he'd come to find. The Soul Seekers had to be close. He'd find a way to locate them. Blindly, the Summoner drifted through the wisteria light, reaching outward with his Light to find the icy feel of the Seekers.

He slowed. The coldness of the magic binding the Soul Seekers together, empty of any life, struck him. Darr drifted closer to them, careful to avoid detection. When he had their feel firmly in his mind, he let his Light return to his body...

...His physical senses crashed in, but Darr caught the briefest glimpse of the Seeker mists when the two worlds merged. Distant still and further to the south, the Soul Seekers wound their way through the canyon. They moved swiftly under the cover of dark. If they didn't get to Vanla soon, the Seekers might beat them there.

"I have to go on alone now," Darr explained. "They're behind us but catching up quickly."

"We're going with you," Jinn added at once.

"No," Darr yelled back, his calm replaced by anger. "Enough discussion. It's bad enough we put everything at risk by doing this. There's no reason to involve us all."

Jinn shrunk back, an emotional response in the Currents. Conra leaned forward in the dark, his face barely visible. "We've been looking out for one another for a long time now, Boy," he explained. "I know you feel like you have something to prove, but this isn't the time or the place. It's too dark, and with the Seekers out there somewhere, you'll need all the help you can get."

"I can track them in the Currents," Darr lied.

"The Currents are disrupted, you said so yourself," Jinn retorted, a sharp edge in her voice.

An almost irresistible urge to reach into the Currents and force his two friends to remain behind occurred to him. Darr stifled the thought. It was one thing to lend courage when fear ran rampant, or lessen anger when it became overwhelming. Turning his friends aside through sheer force of will bordered on malicious, even if he protected them by doing so.

"Let's go then," he said at last.

Darr reined his horse about and laid into its flanks with his heels, setting off into the night. Conra and Jinn caught up with him, riding beside him. The darkness around them deepened, and the storm continued unabated, obscuring even the glow from the watch fires. Conra kept them all together, his Elven senses attuned to each of them, calling out gentle commands to keep them together while Darr led the way.

Their ride continued with no end in sight. The cold of the wind and rain bit at Darr, penetrating his clothing, freezing his face and hands. Nothing was more important than reaching Vanla before the Soul Seekers. Slowly, the glow of the watch fires grew more defined, becoming a false sunrise on the horizon.

When they crested the final rise, a wall of flames sprouted out of the ground a couple hundred yards before them.

Darr slowed his mount, and Conra and Jinn fell behind a few paces. Still a hundred yards out, the first of the watchmen spotted them. Shouts echoed into the night, and weapons raised to greet them. The Summoner led them forward, fearless. A dozen yards from the fires and the waiting soldiers, Darr stopped.

Gently, Darr reached into the Currents, summoning a memory of Nidic Waq, using the prophet's forbidding nature to model his own Light. The men before him, some Cortazian, some Dwarf, detected the change. Several shrank back, but a few weren't intimidated.

When the Summoner called out, his voice rose over the howl of the wind. "My name is Darr Reintol. I've come to issue a warning. The Soul Seekers are coming this way, directly from a canyon to the south and east."

A Dwarf, stocky and pinch-faced, took a step forward. "We don't know your name, Boy," the Dwarf called out. "Leave this place and take your games with you or we'll put you under arrest."

Anger boiled in Darr's throat, but he forced it to calm. "You may not know me, but this is no game. Seekers are headed this way. You have an hour, maybe less. Either way, I've no intention of staying to see if you heed my advice."

The Dwarf didn't move, his scowl deepening. "Why should we believe you?"

Darr turned his mount about, sending a feeling of urgent caution into the Currents and the Dwarf's Light. "Perhaps you shouldn't," Darr called over his shoulder. "Perhaps you shouldn't even report this warning to your commanding officer. But you'll have plenty of time to think about your error once the Seekers arrive."

The Summoner abruptly met with Conra and Jinn, closer behind him than he'd thought.

"That's all you're going to say," Jinn cried, shock lining her features. "We rode out here for that?"

Darr slowed, his brow furrowed. "We've done all that we can, Jinn. We can't get dragged into this battle. We can't risk being arrested. We gave our warning, and now we must leave."

His sister's eyes flared angrily before settling into something bordering on fear. "But they didn't believe you," she protested, desperate now.

Darr shook his head. "Some of them believed me. Word will spread quickly, I think. Someone will report it."

"C'mon, Girl," Conra ordered, gruff and loving at the same time. "There's some things you can't change. Darr's right, there's nothing more we can do here."

Had the Currents been in a better condition, Darr would've lent her some measure of comfort. Perhaps even a promise from the spirits that everything would work out.

No such comforts were possible.

Jinn grudgingly followed after with Conra a few paces behind. Darr glanced over his shoulder a final time at the angry glare of the watch fires. It appeared one or two soldiers had disappeared. Maybe they'd gone to warn their commanding officer, or maybe they'd gone back to warming themselves by the fire.

Either way, the battle for Vanla was out of his hands.

Chapter Twenty-Seven

"Outside the city of Oasis, just north of the Borderlands, Darr learned of a consequence to his abilities. With the balance between the Sephirs slowly breaking apart, the Currents have become sensitive. This sensitivity makes it dangerous for a Summoner with Darr's abilities to even test his power, let alone use it. Outside Oasis, Darr pushed the limits of his abilities too far, and he released an elemental into the world."

~From the personal writings of the Divine, Zander

Nothing much changed for Lacdur with his appointment to a commander of the Ictarian Army. He made his rounds, checking the watch posts around Vanla for anything unusual. Now, he did so with the knowledge he could reorganize select troops if it became necessary. His senses sharpened. Dusk had arrived, and anything could happen. He climbed an east-facing parapet and checked in with a small contingent of Cortazian archers.

"Captain Lacdur," one of the men called out at his approach.

"Commander now," Lacdur replied. "Check in with your superior for confirmation. Do it now." The soldier hesitated, but hurried off the parapet. In the midst of battle, he couldn't have soldiers questioning orders.

The Dwarf warrior leaned against the edge of the parapet. In the distant fields of the Ladornaleah, the Seeker mists built up against the coming dark.

"'Aos, they'll be coming for us tonight," Lacdur grunted to no one in particular. He turned to the remaining archers. "Anything to report?" he asked.

The men shook their heads in unison. Lacdur shifted his stance, leaning in. "Even I don't know what we're looking for, remember that," he confided, his voice low. "After the stunt we pulled a couple days ago, the Seekers will retaliate. They'll try something new, I promise. Just keep your eyes sharp for anything that looks different."

One of the archers folded his arms. "With all due respect, Commander, everything we've done and seen since Jacova is different," he objected. "Everything about this is unusual."

Lacdur gave a sharp laugh but it came out like a grunt. "You've been doing this long enough to know to expect nothing," Lacdur replied. "The Seekers are always gonna try to catch us off guard, to mess with our heads, our fears. We have to catch them in time to fight back. So just keep your eyes sharp and your wits about you."

His words came out vague, but that was the point. He couldn't tell anyone what to expect because he didn't really know. All he could do was attempt to figure out the Seekers' next move before it happened. Lacdur nodded to the other archers and climbed down from the parapet.

When his feet touched the ground, a smattering of raindrops hit his face. A storm approached.

* * * *

Night fell and Lacdur had come up with nothing.

Several hours after sunset, the Seeker mists split wide followed by a familiar wail, and the monstrous armored Devourers erupted onto the field. Two dozen across, the Devourers charged the fort city. Though the attack came suddenly, it wasn't an attack the Dwarf warrior found worrisome.

"This is too easy," Lacdur shouted, his voice booming over the noise of the battle and the howling storm.

Feywen stood beside him. A captain now, the once-prince led a reserve unit of Dwarf soldiers at Vanla's east gate.

"No doubt, those creatures will cause a lot of destruction," Feywen replied, his own voice rising over the battle raging before them.

Lacdur shook his head. "But this is no surprise. We've prepared grapplers for an attack like this. Attacking us with brute force is nothing unexpected from the Seekers."

The Devourers drew close to the frontlines of the Ictarian Army. The soldiers there stood strong, the bait for their latest strategy. As planned, Vertain sent out several units of the Cortazian heavy horse, units held in reserve strictly for this situation. Rather than spears or swords, the horsemen carried heavy grappling hooks attached by ropes to their mounts.

The cavalry swept the flanks and rear of the oncoming Devourers, catching the creatures' cumbersome armor and pulling them to the ground. Axes and heavy maces appeared in the hands of the frontline soldiers, passed up to the front as they'd practiced. The soldiers swarmed the fallen Devourers with their heavy weapons, while more grapplers came forward.

The attack moved swiftly, and though they were prepared, the Ictarians fell back a hundred yards within the first hour. With the pouring rain, footing became unreliable, and the sheer bulk of the charging Devourers pushed the infantry up the hill towards Vanla's perch. The dull white of the bone-armored creatures contrasted starkly to the darkness around them. Powerful maces swung left and right, crashing through the front units of soldiers while booming claps of thunder shook the air.

Feywen leaned close. "This is going to get out of hand."

Lacdur laughed sharply. "Give it a minute."

Vertain's Daravens, absent during the heaviest attacks, swept onto the field with grappling hooks flying into the night. Hooks also began flying from among the infantry ranks, and strong contingents of men pulled the ropes. Casualties were high at first, but within a couple hours, the soldiers developed a methodology. A dance formed, of luring and dodging, of grappling and systematic hacking apart of their enemy.

Lacdur raised his arm to Vertain where he rode in with his cavalry. "It'd be wise to leave one unit of your Daravens behind with the main army. They might need them again."

Vertain nodded, and signaled to one of his captains. A group of Daravens took up watch along the walls. Lacdur pulled Feywen close.

"I don't think this is over," he said. "I'm going to check in with the rest of the camp."

Feywen gave him an encouraging smile and turned his attention back to the battle. A once-prince maybe, Feywen was still a warrior at heart.

Lacdur headed back inside Vanla's walls. He spoke with several of the men along the parapets, working his way towards Vanla's west gate while the storm raged around him. Aside from the unusual nature of their attackers, nothing new presented itself.

He climbed down from the walls beside the west gate, intent on speaking with the men out near the watch fires.

"...not sure. Said his name was Darringtoll or something."

Lacdur froze. The words somehow reached his ears over the wind and pounding rain. He craned his head and caught sight of Vertain walking back from the watch fires with three soldiers trailing him. The soldiers, their faces alight with distress, didn't affect Vertain's distracted mood.

"Must be some local trying to stir this hornet's nest. Please, return to your post," Vertain ordered.

The soldiers saluted and started to turn away, but Lacdur rushed to intercept them. He grabbed the nearest man and spun him about. "Give me your report," he barked.

The soldier's eyes widened, and he swallowed hard. "Three riders came to us at the watch fires on the west wall near the canyon. A boy approached us. His name was Darringtoll, I think, but it was too hard to hear over the rain and wind."

"What did he say?" Lacdur asked, more insistent this time.

The soldier shook his head. "He said the Seekers were coming at us from behind. But they'd already begun attacking at the east wall. I didn't believe him at first, but..."

Lacdur gripped the man gently, pulling him close. "Doesn't matter. 'Aos, you've done well. How long ago did you see this boy?"

"Half an hour."

Chaos, Lacdur thought. "Get back to your post and keep your eyes sharp," he ordered, and the soldiers hurried off.

Lacdur turned and bellowed across the narrow courtyard. "Vertain!"

The Daraven had disappeared amid the barracks, but he reappeared out of the shadows at Lacdur's summons. "Yes, commander," he called, sliding between the soldiers gathered between them.

Lacdur leaned in close. "Get as many units of cavalry to the rear of the city as you can assemble. Report to Lord Forn if you must, but this isn't over."

Vertain didn't argue. He nodded to Lacdur before turning away, shouting orders at the small unit of men he'd gathered around him.

Lacdur paused. His heart raced, but panic only served to hinder them. *A warning from Darr Reintol? Is it truly possible?* The boy must've been traveling west and saw the Seeker mists flanking them. How much time did they have left?

Nidic Waq would know.

Lacdur raced from the west gate to the eastern battlefield. Ariel Forn would be there, with Nidic Waq undoubtedly close by. As he ran, he called out to soldiers standing idle around the barracks, urging them to take up positions at the east wall.

Hurry!

Half a dozen yards from Vanla's east gate, Nidic Waq's forbidding height appeared out of the darkness and rain. Lacdur drew up before him, caught off guard by the prophet's sudden appearance, but not surprised that he'd found him.

"Something's amiss," Nidic Waq called out. "But you already know that, don't you?"

Lacdur nodded, catching his breath. "The watch at the west gate warned me of a possible flanking attack by Seekers. They were warned by a boy named Darr Reintol."

Nidic Waq's face softened within the folds of his cowl. "I

felt him in the Currents, but it was too difficult to tell if he was close or far. I fear he's right, though. The Currents are too badly disrupted after the Devourer attack to believe this night is over."

Lacdur agreed. "Prophet, I need you to speak with Lord Forn and the generals. We can't abandon the eastern field, nor can we ignore an attack from the west." He pointed towards the swirling Seeker mists, still a wall of darkness behind the decimated Devourer ranks. "The mists haven't retreated. Something more is coming."

Nidic Waq sprinted off into the rain without another word. Lacdur made his way back to the west gate, scooping up regiments of foot soldiers on his way. Memories of Feywen flashed in his mind. Feywen was a grown man, but Lacdur would always remember the ten year old boy who'd come to him to learn the way of the sword, utterly unaware of the world he wished to enter. *Nevermind! You can't think on that!*

Lacdur ran on, weighed down by his armor. Units of cavalry soldiers rode past with orders from Vertain. The cavalry would have to do everything in its power to prevent the Seekers from entering the city from the west, while the infantry protected the east from a possible counterattack. There weren't enough reserve soldiers to hold both walls.

Ahead, a group of fifteen or so soldiers huddled under an easement along the walls to find shelter from the storm. "'Aos! C'mon you lazy brood. Follow me or this city will burn."

Lacdur didn't care if the soldiers fell into line behind him or not. They would or they wouldn't, but no matter what they did, they'd likely be leaving Vanla after this fight. The naivety of the soldiers still surprised him. Most thought if they killed enough of the Seekers, they'd simply go away.

Fresh and steady cries echoed through the dark when Lacdur reached the west gate. As expected, the Seekers attacked. The mists rolled out of the western hills, bringing a fresh wave of dark shapes. With the watch perimeter destroyed, if not for Vertain's cavalry, the Seekers would already be inside the walls.

The Dwarf warrior ran with axe in hand, locating an infantry captain.

"Shut the gates, now," Lacdur ordered, his voice cutting through the howling wind.

"But sir, the cavalry..."

Lacdur pulled the captain close. "Give me five minutes, then shut them. Let me worry about Vertain."

The captain ran for the gates in a sprint, disappearing into the wind and rain. Lacdur followed the man, shouting at a regiment of foot soldiers to follow him outside the gates. Without hesitation, the Dwarf warrior leapt into the fray surrounding the cavalry and remaining watchmen. The Seekers had already broken through, tattered black cloaks flowing like blood around the fallen.

With his axe lifted high, Lacdur went out to meet them.

Soul Seekers materialized out of the darkness around him, specters given life. They raked his armor with their claws, but Lacdur's axe flew into them, severing most at the torso, their black robes and silver claws exploding into dust.

Reach Vertain. Warn him. The only thoughts on Lacdur's mind.

The Seekers continued to swirl out of the darkness, but Lacdur tore through them. Even when his face got slashed open and his ear torn off, Lacdur didn't stop. He barely noticed. All he felt was the fervor of the battle.

When he found the Daraven captain, Lacdur didn't pause in his fighting. "Vertain, we must retreat. The gates are closing," he shouted over the battle raging around him.

Vertain looked over in shock. Was he shocked because of the order, or was he really in that bad of shape? Lacdur wondered.

"As you wish," Vertain roared, followed by a furious whistle. "Rear guard, retreat. Watch the foot soldiers!"

Without waiting for the cavalry, Lacdur turned and began fighting his way back towards the gate. Blood poured down his face, sticking around his neck where it pooled against his armor. Little bits of his energy ebbed away. Still, he tore into the Seekers.

Lacdur reached the gate and stumbled inside the walls when one of the Soul Seekers threw itself on top of him. Lacdur howled in rage. The darkness closed about him. The creature pinned him to the ground, but the Dwarf warrior gained his knee and lifted his axe. He tore into the Seeker's robe and let the storm wash over his face.

He blinked.

The Seeker's robe still clung to his body.

Why didn't it turn to ash?

Crushing pressure filled his lungs, sending Lacdur to the ground, his legs useless. He slumped into the mud. Fiery pain rushed into his back, moving to his arms and chest.

"Commander!" a younger soldier cried. He tore off the black cloth tangled about Lacdur's body.

The Dwarf warrior felt along his back, gasping for air. *What in spirits' name was that?* There. Blood, slick and hot. At the source of the pressure, the hard contour of a blade's handle had been wedged into his back, buried somewhere along his spine.

The young soldier knelt at his side, his hands covered in Lacdur's blood. "Commander, I'm sorry," he cried. "The black robe... I thought you were one of the Seekers."

Lacdur almost laughed. He'd killed hundreds of Seekers in the last few months. Logic always told him he'd die by their clawed hands. Instead, one of his own men had brought about his end. Of course, this was no simple accident. The army leaders decided early on to forbid the use of dark cloth for this reason. The traitor, the one he didn't believe existed, truly was among them, manipulating and betraying them.

Warmth filled his throat, and Lacdur coughed blood. "Tell the prophet... The traitor is real..." Lacdur pulled the soldier close. "Tell him, I'll find him in death...if anything happens to Feywen..."

A memory returned soft and sweet, of himself, a young man already in service to Feywen's father. The day was bright, with the pungent smell of evergreen trees in the air. A boy came towards him, small and slender. Blue eyes shone with intelligence.

"Teach me to fight," the boy had said. Feywen had said. "I want to be a warrior like you."

The raindrops fell into his eyes, stinging them raw, Lacdur wondered if they were tears. His breath caught in his throat. At least his soul would belong to the spirits this night, and not to the Seekers.

Chapter Twenty-Eight

"The elemental, born of the Earth Sephir's imbalance, threatened to crush Darr and his friends. According to Darr, a practiced Spirit Summoner might've been able to prevent the elemental's release. At this early stage, Darr could only fight against it. He succeeded, but he explained that he did not truly summon the Archon of Air, only its power. I cannot comprehend the difference, but somehow, it is different, at least to a Spirit Summoner."

~From the personal writings of the Divine, Zander

Darr and Jinn Reintol walked the docks of Plad, content with watching the rough waters of the Orminion Sound and breathing the fresh air blowing from it. The storm from the day before finally headed south, and at Conra's insistence, they decided to look around while he went about gathering supplies. This journey wasn't all about saving Ictar, he told them.

"This sure beats sitting in a saddle for hours on end," Jinn said. Her face tilted up, and Darr followed her gaze to a lone hawk soaring overhead.

Darr grinned. "This beats anything we've done over the last couple days."

He forgot the wind and rain of the past couple days, replaced now by a sky sunny and bright with a smattering of clouds. The wind blew gently on shore, but harder out across the water, where a few brave fishing boats struggled in the distance.

The waterfront district of Plad bustled with activity. Anglers and traders tramped along the heavy planking oblivious to anything and everything around them. Deckhands, young and old, scurried over the docked boats, cleaning and painting, tying lines and stitching sails. Darr and Jinn kept out of their way, staying close to the surrounding buildings.

"Should we get moving?" Jinn asked.

"Give me just another minute."

The ramshackle buildings along the docks with their weathered gray siding reminded Darr of his father's store. These buildings, too, belonged to families. A pang of sadness welled up inside him. He missed Erec and his father so badly his chest ached.

Jinn's hand fell on his shoulder. "I miss them, too," she said.

Tears welled up in Darr's eyes. Uncanny, his sister's ability to read him.

"We should start heading back to the square," she said. "We told Conra we'd meet him at noon."

Darr let his hair fall into his face and wiped away his tears when he brushed it away. He walked with her a short distance along the docks and veered down an alleyway. In moments, they popped out onto a busy side street.

"Do you remember which way?" Jinn asked, pressing against his arm to avoid getting separated in the crowd.

Darr scanned the horizon. A lone, white spire rose above the buildings clustered around them. "There. That's the Vahl. It's sitting in the central square."

Jinn shook her head, shading her eyes with her hand against the sunlight above. "That's a ways off. I didn't realize we came this far."

Darr took her hand, and led her up a side street alongside the flow of Plad's citizens. They'd yet to visit a city like this. Despite its placement within the Elven territories, no one race predominated the streets of Plad. Men and Dwarves alike worked alongside Elves. That such peace could exist between the races encouraged Darr. Ictar might one day forget about the Aeon Wars.

An hour past noon, they arrived at the massive structure that was the Vahl. The building easily dwarfed any other in the city; its exterior decorated with ornate moldings and sculpted figures. A wrought-iron fence stood nearly ten feet in height around its tended grounds. Perhaps this Vahl, like Zander's in Arcnor, held a Covenant, but Darr doubted it. Zander had told them of the uprising among the sect, how the more conservative side had driven the others into banishment or death. As confirmed by Conra, that uprising had begun in the Elven territories. As such, the Elves were their closest followers.

At the base of the Vahl's towering heights, the central square spread out in a hexagonal swath of brick. No shops or vendors lined the square. Still, the number of people amazed Darr. A crossroads for the entire city, traffic swarmed around them in every direction. How would Conra find them in this mess, he thought.

"There are some benches over there," Jinn said, pointed to a line of stone fronting the Vahl.

She led Darr to the benches, angling between the people around them, and sat in the relative quiet beneath the shadow of the Vahl. People passed them by, seemingly unaware of their presence while they went about their business.

"What do you think Zander meant when he said 'beware the termites'?" Darr asked, his mind wandering to the task ahead. Tomorrow they'd begin the trek up to Spirits' Reach to find the Moonstone.

Jinn shook her head with meticulous caution. "He couldn't mean real termites," she presumed. "We're traveling up a mountain. How could termites affect us there?"

"Maybe it isn't the mountain he was talking about? Maybe he was talking about the forest surrounding the mountain."

"No," she said with a shake of her head. "That doesn't make sense either. Conra said the mountain was forbidden because people have mysteriously died there. That can't be a coincidence."

A tremor of fear rippled out into the Currents, Jinn's fear of the events to come. They were making the trek up to Spirits' Reach so Jinn could claim the Moonstone. The mystery of the stone's guardians, and how to claim the artifact would give even the bravest warrior pause. Jinn handled the stress well, but the true test would come in the next couple of days.

Darr continued his thought process aloud. "So, we climb the mountain and somehow evade these termites Zander told us not to go near. Then what?"

Jinn remained silent. Fragments of her memories of Zander flipped through the Currents like some ancient pictograph. "When light leaves you," she said, "reach beyond the Edge towards the peak of dawn."

"Sounds literal," Darr mumbled. "Maybe you just reach over the edge at dawn."

"But he said when light leaves you. Light leaves you at sunset, not sunrise."

"Then maybe you reach in the direction of the sunrise at sunset."

Again, Jinn shook her head. "Zander said the verses in his Covenant were written to confuse the reader if they fell into the wrong hands. Doesn't that mean the saying shouldn't be taken literally?"

"Obviously we don't know enough about where we're going to figure this out," Darr replied. "Maybe we should wait until we get to the mountain. Maybe the spirits will aid us once we get closer. If anyone knows how to figure this out, it'll be them."

"I hate that all we have to work with is 'maybe'," she said, hugging her small frame.

She wanted answers because her destiny rushed to meet her and she had no idea what to expect. Through the wisteria waves of the Currents, Darr sent a feeling of calm to her, but it didn't ease her.

"I thought you might be here."

Conra appeared out of the crowd, a crocked smile on his face.

"You seem to be drawn to the Divine like a swamp rat to fresh meat," he said, followed by a short cackle.

"Not likely," Jinn said, gesturing to Darr. "They'd have him in chains if they knew what he could do."

A joke, but the reality of Jinn's statement burned. Darr flinched inwardly, and Jinn noticed. "I'm sorry," she said. She placed her hand over his. "You know I didn't mean that."

Darr forced a smile. Conra continued unabashed. "I gathered everything we'll need. We even have a little of Feywen's money left, and we'll need it once we reach Qued. Hopefully nothing comes up between here and there."

"Where is everything?" Jinn asked, casting a glance over Conra's shoulder. He carried nothing, nor were the horses with him.

The old Elf waved his hand towards a western side street. "The horses and our supplies are outside the city. I stashed everything inside the tree line around Spirits' Reach so I could come find you." Conra's eyes shifted uncomfortably to the people passing by. "We should get going. I want to reach the base of the mountain by nightfall."

Without waiting or checking to see if they followed, Conra led them into the sparsely populated industrial center. Most of its buildings had fallen into disuse and decay. Some businesses still functioned, but for the most part, Plad's west side looked like a trash heap.

"During the Aeon Wars, Plad was a hub for shipping weapons and supplies for whoever controlled the port at the time," Conra said, keeping his voice low. "Once the war ended, this side of the city became a dead arm waiting to be cut off."

"It doesn't seem like a very good location in any case," Darr said. "There's no wall to protect it, and it's open for pretty much any one to raid or attack."

The old man nodded grimly. "And it was. Many times. But somehow it continued to function."

Since crossing the Wilamedde, Conra become more talkative than usual, specifically about the land around them. He didn't simply inform them about the territory in which they traveled. Conra spoke nostalgically, eager to share about a land in which he was passionate.

The rotting buildings of Plad's west side fell away, and the street they walked upon disappeared into the rolling plains of the Ladornaleah. The dark smudge of the forest around the lone peak of Spirits' Reach lay before them. Darr shivered. Something about that single spire bothered him.

Their walk ended quickly. A few paces inside the tree line they spotted the horses, loaded with gear and saddled. The three mounted up, and for the remainder of the day, they rode through the trees towards the looming bulk of Spirits' Reach, called the Edge by the Dwarves. Darr caught glimpses of the peak through the overhanging branches. According to Conra, somewhere on the high slopes, an overhanging cliff looked out over Orminion Sound, the edge or reach for which the mountain was named.

As night fell, the skies grew cloudy once more. When they stopped for the night, Conra located a spot protected by a slab of rock on one side and a heavy stand of trees on the other. After tending to the horses, they settled for the night beneath the giant slab of rock. Conra started a fire and began preparing a stew. Jinn and Darr sat side by side, looking out at the day winding down to blackness outside their shelter.

"Tell me again about the Divine's prophecy," Conra asked. He feigned disinterest while he worked on their stew.

Jinn stared at the fading light. When she didn't answer, Darr replied. "Zander said the Moonstone was at the top of Spirits' Reach, and it can only be claimed by the Healer of the Light. Watch for the termites for they'll swallow you whole. As light leaves you, reach beyond the Edge towards the peak of dawn."

"What in chaos is a termite?" Conra asked. He leaned back from the fire. "He couldn't have meant the bugs. What kind of a danger would a termite pose?"

Darr shook his head. "What did you say about this mountain, Conra? What makes it taboo?"

The old Elf cleared his throat with a sharp cough. "People who come here have been known to drop dead for no apparent reason. I knew a trapper when I still lived in Qued who claimed to travel here all the time and he never saw anything strange. I don't know if was rumor or not, but enough people died up there for the Elven people to take notice. It didn't take long for the Divine to call it a work of magic and make the place forbidden. I don't imagine anyone's been here in years."

"That doesn't make me feel any easier about our journey tomorrow," Darr said. He glanced sideways at Jinn who'd turned around to join the conversation.

"Do you know how to reach the edge?" she asked.

Conra didn't blink when he answered. "I've traveled enough to know what to look for. From what I've heard, there's a trail leading up, but if it hasn't been used in a while, then it might be rough going. I don't think there'll be any problems, but you'd be wise to keep your eyes open and watching."

"What about you, Darr?" Jinn asked. "Do you sense anything out there? Have the spirits told you anything?"

Darr shook his head. "No warnings of any kind. In fact, the spirits have been almost nonexistent since we arrived. That alone should give us some kind of clue."

"Maybe it's the Seekers," Jinn suggested. She looked back out at the darkness. Darr said nothing in response.

Conra sighed. "Anything's possible, but the mystery surrounding this mountain has been in place since before even I was born. It far outdates the Soul Seekers."

"Maybe this is where they come from," Jinn speculated. "Maybe this is their home."

Darr's breath caught in his throat. He didn't want to talk about it anymore.

* * * *

Conra had them up before sunrise. Once breakfast was finished, they tended to the horses, checking their access to water and food. They would have to leave them behind, so Conra hobbled them to keep them from wandering. Many of their supplies would stay behind also, tucked safely into a nook along the back of the stone slab under where they'd spent the night. Ideally, they'd be back before nightfall. Conra advised them to pack for a couple days anyway.

By Conra's estimation, Spirits' Reach rested about two-thirds of the way up the mountain. "If we can find a workable trail," he said, "we should have no problem reaching the edge by the afternoon."

With the old Elf in the lead, Jinn followed him up the mountainside while Darr trailed behind. Hardly any vegetation grew in the rocky landscape, and few animals lived there, making it difficult to locate a way forward. Darr reminded himself the Barricade Mountains had shared a similar terrain, yet Conra had led them through without any difficulty.

They'd traveled for no more than an hour, and they were working their way along an open ridgeline when Darr called a halt.

"What's the matter?" Conra asked, clearly annoyed that they'd halted their uphill trek.

Darr shook his head. "I can't say. Something's wrong. Give me a minute."

Conra and Jinn walked downhill, gathering around him, giving him temporary shade while they waited.

Darr submerged himself in the Currents. Like taking a hot bath, he kept half of his body anchored in the physical world in case he needed a fast escape. The spirits were almost completely absent on the mountain. A few stray bulbs of light floated in the ether, their whispers confused and indistinct.

After a few moments, he found something both terrible and amazing. The Currents had somehow burrowed their way into the physical world. The openings were small, almost undetectable, but somehow the barrier between the two worlds had broken apart. Like a tiny door or hole, the breaks would allow access to the Currents from the physical world, but Darr feared his natural link to the spirit realm was the only thing keeping him safe. What of his companions?

He scanned past Conra and Jinn, looking up the mountain. The holes were all around them, across their path, above and below it. Navigating a quagmire like this could take days.

Of course, what better hiding spot for a talisman like the Moonstone?

"I think I know what the termites are," Darr said with a

sigh. He freed himself of the Currents in the same breath.

Conra leaned in close, his body tense. "What is it? Where?"

Darr shook the hair from his face and folded his arms in front of him. "They're all around us. They're everywhere, and I have no idea how to get around them."

Chapter Twenty-Nine

"Darr's brother was injured in the attack, and so they entered the city of Oasis to recover, but they weren't alone. Nidic Waq had been tracking them for some time. Caeranol had located the first of the Chosen, and strangely enough, he'd been able to do so because of Darr's actions in securing the Water Sephir. Somehow, Darr's fate is tied to the Chosen, and by merging himself inside our world and the Currents, he revealed his sister to Caeranol as the Healer of the Light."

~From the personal writings of the Divine, Zander

Conra and Jinn stared while Darr hung his head in defeat. The termites, the ones Zander had warned them to watch for, were all around them. He would be safe from them, but neither Conra nor Jinn could touch them without risking their lives. Worse, in the physical world, the termites were both invisible and undetectable.

"What are they?" Jinn asked, looking over her shoulder, searching for something she couldn't see.

"I'm not entirely sure. They're holes leading to the spirit realm, but I've no idea how they got there." Darr looked up again. "I'm protected because my mind is always connected to the Currents, but I think if you two step into one, your Light will be separated from your body. I think that's why so many people have died up here. Their souls were stolen by the air around them."

Conra kicked at a rock. "That makes sense, I suppose," he said. "That's why all those people were found without a mark on them. But how come people have traveled here without falling into one of these holes?"

"Maybe they shared a connection to the Currents like Darr," Jinn offered. "Or maybe it was blind luck." She looked back at Darr and asked, "Can we get past them?"

Darr took a minute to let his mind reconnect with the

Currents. The two worlds merged in his eyes, and he focused on the termites. Little pockets of wisteria light formed on the ground, the sky, and the air itself, all marking the locations of the termites. He scanned his surroundings, looking up the trail ahead. He could pick out a path between them.

"I can get us past," he said and meant it.

Conra continued to guide them, but Darr look the lead, a shield for his companions. If one of the termites crossed their path, Darr could warn the old Elf and his sister before they stepped into it. It seemed the best way to avoid disaster.

They traveled slowly. The day wore on, and the termites grew more frequent, slowing them further. Several times the termites blocked their path completely, forcing them to find a way around them. Occasionally, Jinn or Conra got too close to the termites and experienced a spell of nausea, forcing them to stop for several minutes at a time.

The mountain continued upwards, its terrain of rock and dust barren of life. A few times, they found scatterings of bone across the path, an eerie reminder of the danger around them.

During the hour before sunset, the termites disappeared altogether. About two-thirds of the way up the mountain, Conra found a climbable path leading sharply upwards. The three scurried up it to a narrow chasm on a nearby cliff. Darr passed through the fissure and discovered the sweeping gold light of the sunset dancing on the Orminion Sound.

Spirits' Reach jutted out from the cliff wall, a tremendous shelf of rock stretching a hundred feet out to its sheer edge. From this vantage point, a full view of the Orminion Sound and the land surrounding it spread out, a lifelike tapestry. To the east, the Ladornaleah swept away to the Wilamedde River, while to the north, another range of mountains rose up, shrouded in darkness and snow. Somewhere far to the northeast, across the silver and gold shimmer of the water, a little peninsula held Tyfor.

So caught up in the moment, Darr almost missed the termites.

"Stop," he shouted. "Don't move."

Soul Seekers

He tried to calm himself, but confusion overwhelmed him. The termites surrounded Spirits' Reach, the wisteria lights shining like soldiers lined up before battle, enclosing the entire perimeter of the cliff. How could Jinn go out on the edge to find the Moonstone if doing so would kill her?

"They're everywhere," Darr whispered.

He turned back to tell Jinn and Conra of his discovery.

* * * *

At sunset, Jinn crept to the end of Spirits' Reach, her face pointed to the east. Darr guided her from a step behind, telling her how to move to avoid the termites clustered all around.

"Don't go any further," Darr growled. His eyes fixed on the space around his sister. Another inch or two and Jinn would step into a termite.

"Reach beyond the edge," Jinn said. She stretched her arm out beyond the cliff.

"Careful now."

After several long minutes of waiting, her hand suspended in the air, Jinn gave up. The sun had set and the stars rolled out above them. If they'd interpreted the Divine's riddle, their next chance to claim the Moonstone wouldn't come until dawn.

Darr and Jinn retreated towards Conra and the cliffs around the fissure. The old Elf found a nook out of the wind where they could camp for the night. Still, the cliff sat high enough up on the mountain that they'd need a fire to keep warm. After nearly an hour of scavenging, Conra found some incredibly dense wood from a tree he'd never seen before.

Conra gestured wildly at their unlit campfire. "This stuff's so hard, I can't get it to burn," he said.

Darr edged closer. "Let me try."

Even with their blankets, a long and dangerous night awaited them if they couldn't get a fire going. Darr set himself inside the Currents, calling out to Racall and the Earth Sephir in search of a way to alter the wood to make it burnable. In moments, the Archon responded with a solution.

Darr reached down and touched the hardwood with a greenish spark. The light settled over it like dust and disappeared.

"Try it now," Darr said, scooting back. "It should be less dense now, enough that it'll burn."

Conra's kindling ignited immediately. The old Elf laughed and shook his head.

Once lit, the fire burned hot and through a good portion of the night. Tucked into their nook, they passed around an ale skin and finished a light supper. Together, they gazed out at the black beyond Spirits' Reach.

"It's strange," Conra's course voice cut the silence. "I've slept under the stars probably a thousand times in my life, but not once have I ever felt this secure."

Darr finished a long pull from his ale skin and said, "Because you're home again."

"How long has it been since you left?" Jinn asked and tilted her head towards the old Elf.

Conra's gaze fixed on the glow of the fire as if he searched for the answer there. "I don't remember exactly, but it's been over thirty years at least. I wonder if anyone there even remembers my name."

"But your family," Jinn started, "your friends. Surely, not everyone forgot about you."

Conra shook his head. "It's hard to say who forgot, especially since we aren't there. A lot can happen in the number of years I was away, and I really don't think it matters anymore."

Darr disagreed, but he didn't say so. In the Currents, he'd seen the connection between memories and emotions. Each influenced the other in startling ways. Someone couldn't simply forget about another person and move on unchanged. Someone in Qued would remember Conra no matter how long he'd been away.

"What're we going to do tomorrow?" Jinn asked the question nobody could answer.

"Have you heard anything from the spirits?" Conra asked without looking up.

Darr's shoulders sagged and he dropped his hands into his lap. "The spirits aren't around to say anything. On this mountain, on this ledge in particular, the spirits simply aren't here. It must have something to do with the termites."

Conra used a stick to write in the dust before him. "When light leaves you," he began, "reach beyond the edge towards the peak of dawn." He studied the words for a moment before tossing the stick into the fire. "It doesn't make any sense. How can light leave you at dawn? Moonlight? Starlight? How can you reach beyond the edge when those termites are all over the place?"

The questions hung in the air. Darr's only idea was to wake before dawn so Jinn could try again to claim the Moonstone. Perhaps the translation given to them by Zander was missing something. Perhaps all the translations were missing something, and the Chosen of the Light were nothing but a tumbling of dust on the wind.

"For all we know, we aren't even in the right place," Jinn muttered.

She could be right, Darr thought, but she wasn't. This was the right place. Darr hunched up his shoulders and folded his arms together inside his blanket. He wished he had an answer. With a heavy sigh, he closed his eyes and bowed his head.

* * * *

Darr opened his eyes. He slept, but he was awake.

He stood in a building, at a meeting of two corridors. Strange lights, embedded in the walls, glowed eerily but bright, illuminating every facet of the building's interior. Tapestries lined the walls, a variety of sizes and colors depicting unrecognizable objects. Men and women, robed and hooded, walked over polished floors, caught up in their separate tasks. They ignored Darr. To them, he'd become a mote of dust floating past their eyes.

Instinctively, Darr knew where he stood, though he'd never been here before. This was the Tower Castle, brought out of the time of the Ancient Ictarians. *But why?*

The presence of the people around him flooded into him, sharing their passions with him. These men and women, they worked relentlessly, studying and reading and experimenting. The Tower Castle wasn't a meeting place for the Elders of lost Contin. This was their home, their sanctuary. The Tower Castle was an institute for furthering one's knowledge and understanding.

Unease shuttered through Darr, coiling within him. Someone approached, someone he'd felt before. Darr turned down one of the corridors, away from the presence that might find him. Voices grew loud and fiercely emotional, echoing off the castle walls. Along one of the narrow corridors, a cluster of robed figures appeared. Some shouted, but mostly they cowered. The other elders, the ones who'd been so caught up in their earlier tasks, stopped and turned. Darr didn't move.

The man in black appeared amid the cluster of Elders, the same man who'd stalked Darr in his dreams. Was this truly Symdus, the man who'd one day become the Devoid? The tall figure passed through the crowd the way a reed stands strong against a rushing wave. No one opposed him, no one stood in his way. They let him pass, watching with burning eyes, their shouts loud but veiled. They, too, feared this man. They hated his ideals, but not enough to stand against him.

The man in black passed by them, crossed the foyer to the massive double doors leading from the castle, and pushed them open to the bright daylight beyond. The crowd followed after, dragging spectators along with them.

The castle became a crypt. It took a moment for Darr to find the courage to move. Once before, the man in black had found him after Darr thought he'd gone. He didn't want it happening again. This might be a dream, but that would mean little to the man who would become the Devoid.

He summoned the courage to move again. Darr started

moving down one of the long corridors. His intuition guided him. Or was it his Light that guided him?

He passed down the first bank of corridors. Doors opened up along the wall, leading into small rooms. Some had desks with books and papers strewn about, others contained strange glowing cubes. A few contained long tables with glass vials set neatly along their surface, filled with odd colored liquids. What kind of studies did the Continese indulge in? A mix of magic and science, Nidic Waq once told him. What exactly was science?

Eventually, the corridor ended at a large commons where a grand stairway stretched up into the tower. Somewhere above, the Great Library, the storehouse of knowledge possessed by the Ancients, waited. Desire filled Darr, urging him to climb the steps. His instincts told him otherwise. He needed to find something else, something close by.

Couches, chairs, and tables filled the commons, scattered with more books and papers, and the strange glowing cubes. Darr worked his way from table to table, searching for the lure calling to him. The language of the Ancients was foreign to him though, and he couldn't make sense of the books they studied.

Light glittered to his left and Darr turned. Finding nothing, but intrigued, he walked towards the wall that had emitted the strange light. His intuition screamed at him. This was the reason he'd been brought here.

A large map of the land hung on the wall, but this was no ordinary map. The cartographer had drawn the mountains and rivers perfectly. No, not a cartographer. Some master painter had floated into the sky and painted exactly what he saw. Darr had seen a few roughly drawn maps of Ictar before, but nothing like this.

The resemblance between his world and the land of the Ancients looked quite similar. They should, even though thousands of years separated them. He recognized some of the larger land figures, labeled in the unknown language of the Continese. The Dwarf Border Lands, the Orminion

Sound, the Arcnorian Line, and the Wilamedde River. What had the Ancients called these places?

Darr traced his finger to the shores of the Orminion Sound and ran it west to the lonely mountain carrying Spirits' Reach. The name scrolled unintelligibly next to it, but something else caught his eye. Another range of mountains rose to the north, the dark, snowy mass he'd seen when they first arrived at Spirits' Reach. Conra had called them the Forgotten Mountains, but some ancient name scrawled next to the drawing popped into his head as he studied it.

Dahnis Mountain, of the Elves.

"Have you found something useful, Darr?"

Darr jerked awake. The Currents receded into the back of his mind, the wisteria light replaced by the glowing flame of the fire. The transition happened seamlessly. Conra looked over at him, concern deepening the lines of his face.

"You okay?" he asked, his voice low.

Darr sat up and stared into the fire. His body trembled. There'd been a voice before he'd woken, gentle and kind. Whoever it'd been, it wasn't the man in black.

"Just a dream," he answered, lying.

Darr rolled back into his blanket and lay back on the ground. In the dirt beside him, he used his fingernail to write the name of the mountain from his dream. Dahnis Mountain. Elves. He'd figure out what it meant in the morning when his eyes weren't so heavy.

Chapter Thirty

"What bothers me most regarding the Chosen of the Light is their inability to be found. In my mind, Caeranol should've had the foresight to know the Devoid would be able to disrupt the Currents sufficiently to hide the Chosen. That being said, I don't believe Caeranol failed to see this. I believe the Devoid has grown much stronger than Caeranol ever believed possible. That in itself could be a fatal oversight and a terrifying one."

~From the personal writings of the Divine, Zander

Jinn Reintol closed her eyes and raised her arm.

She only wanted one thing, one simple thing. The Moonstone, her birthright, the relic that would officially make her the Healer of the Light. If she claimed it, maybe she'd stand a chance against the monster called the Devoid. Maybe there really were other Chosen out there, and together, they'd be able to free Ictar from the death closing around it.

First, she had to claim the Moonstone.

The first rays of dawn warmed her face. Jinn opened her eyes and looked down at the tips of her boots, hanging slightly over the edge of the cliff. At Darr's instruction, she could move no further, not even an inch, without touching a termite.

"There's about a foot on either side of your arm," Darr said. His breath brushed her ear.

She swept her fingers towards the rising sun, then back to the west, daring herself not to move too far. Again, she found nothing.

"Nothing?" Darr asked.

Jinn shook her head. "Not even a tingle."

A real possibility existed that they'd have to go on without the Moonstone. The Sephirs couldn't wait for them much longer. Perhaps once the Sephirs were secure they could find Nidic Waq. Perhaps he'd know how to find it.

Darr stepped away, directing her on how to walk to avoid touching the termites. She stepped where he told her to, ducked when he asked. Once she'd reached the relative safety of the broad cliff, Jinn hung her head.

"I don't want to leave," Jinn said, "but I understand if we have to. The Sephirs are our first priority. Once they're secure, we can come back."

Conra stamped his foot. "Our travels will end in Mord far to the north of here. It'd be best if we didn't have to make the trip back here. We're talking a couple weeks' worth of travel to do so."

"Who's to say we won't do that anyway?" Jinn snapped. "Once the Sephirs are restored, we've no idea where to go next. We might very well have to walk all the way back to Tyfor."

Jinn folder her arms in front of her while her anger simmered. She didn't want to leave the mountain without the Moonstone.

"What if the light that leaves you is not natural light of any kind," Darr said. Jinn's anger drained away, replaced by confusion. "What if the Light that leaves you is your own?"

Jinn shrugged. "If my Light leaves me, won't I die?"

Conra spat. "What're you getting at, Boy?"

Darr stared into space. "I think the termites are here to prevent just anyone from taking the Moonstone," he said at last. "This is exactly the kind of puzzle someone would use to hide something important. It's like a needle in a haystack, except the needle here is the Moonstone and the haystack is the termites."

Jinn lowered her arms, thinking it over. "So even if that's true," she asked, "how would you know which haystack to look in?"

Excited fire lit Darr's eyes, and he muttered something unintelligible. He scurried over to the nook they'd slept in the night before, looking around the spot on the ground where they'd slept. Jinn furrowed her brow, and then followed Conra over to him.

"Here it is," Darr said, his face bright with excitement.

"Last night, I had a dream. I was in the Tower Castle, and I found a map of our world as the Continese saw it." Her brother stretched out his arm, pointing to a far off mountain range capped in snow. "They called that mountain, Dahnis."

"Dahnis?" Conra said. He crinkled his nose. "Those are the Forgotten Mountains. That's the only name they've ever gone by."

"No, the Ancients called the one with the tallest mountain Dahnis," Darr replied, shaking his head. "Dahnis and dawn, they must be the same, a bad translation. Zander said the Divine passed down their Covenants orally for years, centuries before recording them."

Darr brushed past them, striding out towards the end of Spirits' Reach, stopping a foot from the cliff. "Reach towards the peak of Dahnis--that's how the Covenant should've read. I can even see it now. If you stand right here, there's a termite directly in line with those mountains."

Jinn's stomach dropped. Darr made some sense, except for one important part. "What you're saying is I have to step into a termite to claim the Moonstone. When my Light leaves me, I reach beyond the Edge towards the peak of Dahnis." Her breath caught in her throat. "Is this going to kill me, Darr?"

Darr's excitement drained away, but his eyes burned with certainty. "I'm right, Jinn. This is how you claim the Moonstone, I know it."

She breathed in deep through her nose. She'd always had tremendous faith in her brother. *Why stop now?* "Then I suppose I should go."

Jinn's feet lifted heavily. She walked across the barren cliff of the edge. Darr waited for her, a confident smile plastered on his upturned head. A great number of thoughts rolled through her head. She thought about her father and her friends back in Tyfor. She thought about Erec and the sacrifice he'd made, and her mother, whose love and kindness lived on in her.

About halfway to the end of the cliff, Conra stopped and let her go on her own. "Be careful, Girl," he called.

She didn't reply or look back. Since they'd arrived on the mountain, they'd been avoiding the termites. Now the termites offered their only chance of getting what they'd come for.

The sun crested the horizon before her, the golden light cascading over her and warming her body. The warmth strengthened her and gave her fresh resolve.

"You'll be fine," Darr said from a couple feet away. He slid aside, pointing down at the narrow strip of rock he'd occupied moments ago. Jinn stepped onto the spot.

She shivered once. She stretched her arm out over the open edge.

A wave of nausea washed through her. Her head buzzed, and her body weakened, but somehow she remained upright. The light around her changed. The blue of the sky and sea, the gold of the sun, they all washed out, overtaken by a strange lavender hue. Tiny fireflies of white sparkle danced before her eyes. Without thinking, she reached out to touch them.

--No, Jinn. Reach towards the peak of Dahnis. Reach only there--

The voice belonged to Darr, but he sounded like he spoke to her through an empty barrel. She did what he told her, moving her outstretched arm to the dark smudge on the horizon. Her fingers snaked out to the peak of the tallest lonely mountain.

Heat flooded into her palm, but it didn't burn. It felt right. She let the heat rise for a moment, letting it stretch outward into her wrist and fingertips.

Then she closed her fist to trap it.

A pair of hands grabbed her from behind, wrapping about her arm and waist and ripping her backwards. Jinn's eyes drooped lazily, and her mouth struggled to work. The strange light disappeared and the nausea rushed through her again. Her palm burned, but when she tried to open her fist, she couldn't.

A squeak tore at her throat and her mouth opened wide. Then blackness covered her, and everything stopped.

When she woke, afternoon had settled over them. She lay on the ground in the nook they'd camped in, a small fire crackling before her. Gingerly, she sat up.

Darr and Conra watched her from the other side of the fire, concern draining from their faces.

"What happened?" she asked.

"You almost fell off the end of the cliff," Conra said. His eyes revealed the fear he'd experienced in that moment. "Darr saved you."

His face framed by his lanky hair, Darr smiled at her from beside the fire. "Thank you," she said.

Conra cleared his throat. "So, what's in your hand, Girl? We've been waiting."

Jinn's hand knotted into a tight fist. The warmth she'd felt earlier had vanished, replaced by something heavy and hard. She brought up her fist, her fingers lifting one by one.

A smooth round stone, about the size of a robin's egg lay nested in the soft folds of her palm, its surface flawless and glossy and milky white.

A warm feeling boiled within her, and Jinn smiled.

"I thought it was supposed to be green," she said.

Chapter Thirty-One

"Despite whatever reasons led to Jinn's identity, or her lack thereof, she carries the mantel of her position as the Healer of the Light with extreme seriousness. Having met her myself, I saw the qualities I always believed I would see in the Chosen. Bravery, but reserved with some fear. Curiosity, balanced with both skepticism and openness. And perhaps most important of all, acceptance."

~From the personal writings of the Divine, Zander

With the Moonstone in Jinn's possession, Darr led the way back down the mountain using Conra's directions. The termites persisted. They must be native to the mountain rather than simply a guardian for the Moonstone. Racall told him the Ancients had been able to create objects both inside and outside the Currents, the altars of the Sephirs being the most obvious example. Perhaps the termites were something a similar.

The journey down the mountain took far less time. Between Darr's connection to the Currents and Conra's tracking skills, they retraced their original path with ease. A couple hours before nightfall, they reached the base of the mountain intact.

Jinn knelt on the forest floor beside the horses. "I never want to go there again," she said, blinking her eyes as she looked up through the canopy of trees.

Conra grunted. "Agreed. I think it'd be wise to spend the night away from the mountain."

No one complained.

They retrieved their gear and horses, and with the old Elf in the lead, set off in a westerly direction. They rode in silence. Conra kept his attention focused on where they were going, and Jinn hadn't said much of anything since claiming the Moonstone.

Darr glanced over his shoulder. Jinn looked off into the trees, staring into the light and shadow. The Moonstone hung about her neck, bound and tied with a leather cord, its white surface glistening softly in the light. With her talisman claimed, Jinn had become the Healer of the Light. He smiled before turning around again, pride welling up within him.

An hour past sunset, Conra made their camp on a small rise on the fringes of the forest. After a quick supper, they sat before a fire, looking out at the boulder-strewn plains of the Norstag Plume, a stark contrast to the gentle, rolling hills of the Ladornaleah.

"I think we can make it across the Plume in about four days, then we'll be well on our way to Qued," Conra said. He kept his head down, working on a rough map of the region in the dirt. "We'll have to cross the Gethma River, but I know a crossing that'll put us out about half a day. I'm also counting on there not being any trouble around Exed. I guess that all depends on how well our warning at Vanla was received."

Darr shot a glance at Jinn. Though she looked down at the map, her eyes glazed over with some hidden thought. Conra continued.

"So, in about four days, I should think we can reach the Greenfhyre surrounding Mount Terlak. Then it's a simple matter of navigating the trees and the mountain, and that should take us no more than a couple of days. I'd say a week will put us within reach of the Air Sephir."

"What's the Greenfhyre?" Jinn asked. Her eyelids drooped lazily, but she waited patiently for an answer.

Conra watched her for a moment before answering. "The Greenfhyre is a jungle of sorts, wild and tangled, like the Barricades except with trees. It surrounds Mount Terlak in every direction. Qued is the original city of the Elves, the place from which they emerged prior to the beginning of the Aeon Wars. For many centuries, Mount Terlak was our homeland, and the Greenfhyre was the wall protecting it. Only the Elves know how to navigate it, and lucky for you two, I know the Greenfhyre like the back of my hand."

"But how can a city sustain itself all the way up in the mountains like that, cut off from the rest of Ictar?" Darr asked.

The old Elf looked up at the sky, searching for answers in the stars. "Qued is a mysterious land, even to the Elves who live there, but its soil is fertile, finding water is never a problem, and a variety of animals make their home in those upper peaks. The main trick to living there is to respect the balance in nature. That was one of the reasons the capital relocated to Exed. The Elven nation grew too big to keep Qued's balance intact."

Darr's mouth hung open in bewilderment. "So they moved an entire nation?"

With a laugh, Conra nodded his head. "It didn't happen all at once, Boy. It took the Elves nearly a hundred years to make the transition completely, mind you. They were fighting a war at the time."

The Summoner smiled in awe and shot a glance at Jinn. His sister leaned back on her elbows, her green eyes directed at the fire, dazed. If she'd been listening to the answer of her own question, it didn't impress her. Darr's smile faded.

"Give her time, Darr," Conra whispered, catching his eye with a flick of his finger. "An enormous responsibility rests on her shoulders. She'll come around once she makes sense of it."

Darr leaned forward and turned away, but his hopes weren't very high. With the Moonstone claimed, Jinn slipped away from him, entering into a destiny in which he wouldn't be a part.

Darr offered to take the first watch. His mind worked relentlessly, fighting off sleep even in light of all he'd endured over the last few days. The mysteries surrounding the Chosen of the Light became a scab he couldn't stop picking.

They'd traveled over halfway across Ictar, and so far he'd only found the Healer of the Light. With half of his quest completed, and one of the Chosen found, time slipped away from him. Was he supposed to travel everywhere in Ictar, conducting summonings in front of everyone he met? He doubted it.

Could the other Chosen be looking for him? The thought

gave him pause. Could someone else know about Caeranol's promise and resolve to find the other Chosen? Darr smiled, laughing to himself. To his knowledge, only Zander knew of the Chosen, and he kept it a closely guarded secret. Jinn didn't even know she was one of the Chosen until after Nidic Waq had identified her. Nothing Darr could think of could convince him the other three Chosen knew who they were.

* * * *

Darr and his companions traveled in a southwest direction across the Norstag Plume over the next four days. The skies remained mostly clear, but cold, bringing them rain in occasional fits. Conra kept them at a quick pace over the rocky terrain, but not hurried.

At the beginning of their second day, prior to their crossing of the Gethma River, Jinn began talking again. At first, Darr and Conra didn't know how to react.

"You haven't exactly been talkative the last couple days," Darr told her.

Conra laughed, happy to have her talking again. "What were you thinking about all this time?"

Jinn bowed her head, but she didn't look ashamed, only thoughtful. "I don't believe I thought much about anything," she answered, lifting the Moonstone by its leather cord. "I was stunned more than anything. This little stone is so small. To think something I could just flick away can save us."

"I don't think you'll be able to do that," Conra said, leaning forward.

Jinn arched an eyebrow. "No doubt. Something happened to me when I touched the Moonstone. It bonded with me, almost like it was alive." She turned to Darr, and their eyes locked. "The light I saw up on Spirits' Reach...was that the Currents?"

Darr shrugged, but hesitated. "I don't know for sure what you saw," he replied. "The termites led into the Currents though. It seems obvious that you reached into the spirit realm. What I can't understand is how you brought the

Moonstone, something tangible, out of a world of illusion."

The fire cracked and spit in the darkness. Darr lay back, resting on his elbows. Stars unfolded over the night sky, a blanket of white sparkle much like the spirits of the Currents.

* * * *

The following day, they crossed the Gethma River at a shallows north of Exed, spending the remainder of the afternoon climbing the foothills of the Norstag Plume. As evening approached, a break in the mountain chain allowed them to see the great Elven city. Nestled between the rocky folds of the low mountains, Exed sat like a sleeping child in the arms of its mother, content and unobtrusive.

"I thought Stern was a big city," Darr said. He shielded his eyes from the setting sun.

Conra laughed. "Exed would fit three Sterns within its walls." The old Elf rode close to him. "It's a gorgeous city. You'll have to come back one day and see for yourself."

By the end of the third day, they crested a rise along the Norstag Plume. The highland plains trickled down into a vast hill country leading to the dark smudge of the Greenfhyre. At its center, the spire of Mount Terlak rose up against the coming night.

A twinge of sadness stabbed at Darr from the Currents. Conra, he realized, held great sadness and regret while looking down at the city. Respectful of the old Elf's feelings, Darr focused on other things.

The following day, with the weather beginning to turn colder and wetter, Darr and his companions were grateful to be within the protective confines of the Greenfhyre. The forest reminded Darr of those surrounding Tyfor, a mix of conifer and deciduous trees interspersed by rocky hills and meandering streams. The woods around Tyfor were small and easily navigable though.

"This is strange," Conra said, his face stricken. "This forest should be half stripped of greenery with all the leaf trees around."

"It's the unbalance in the Sephirs," Darr reminded him. "Until they're all restored, nothing will be normal."

"This winter hasn't been right since we left Tyfor," Jinn said, her green eyes imploring.

At nightfall, Conra left Jinn to prepare supper, making himself useful by constructing a lean-to with Darr's help. Though Darr couldn't tell from the skies overhead, Conra anticipated rain soon. They needed a shelter, something other than the canopy of trees above. After sunset, the rain began to fall, and the three sat beneath the lean-to, warm and dry, watching the falling rain. Even the horses, protected only by a copse of birch, seemed content in the warm glow of the fire.

"How did you learn to build these things?" Jinn asked, pointing to the lean-to above their heads.

Conra clasped his hands behind his head. "Every good woodsman should know how, but I learned back when I was young. I was a forager."

"Was that your trade?" Darr asked, keeping his voice low.

Conra sighed. "Yes, my brother and I, we both were inducted to the foragers at young ages. It was a great honor for my family."

Darr scrunched up his face. "Why was it so important?"

The old Elf's brown eyes grew wide with surprise. "During the winter, everything turns to snow and ice up there. If it weren't for the foragers, the people of Qued wouldn't make it through an entire year without aid from the outside. In order to be fully independent, the foragers need to find other sources of water, native plants, fruits, and vegetables. They also keep an eye on the local animal populations."

"And you left because of your brother?" Jinn asked. The pain Conra felt at the question struck Darr through the Currents.

The old Elf shifted his body away from the light. "Yes, my brother, Belmon. We weren't even out for the foragers. We were hiking the ridges to see if there was something new to find. Then out of nowhere, this strange light appeared and took him away."

"And no one believed you." Jinn made it a statement rather than a question.

Conra shook his head. "The Divine were ready to hang me. They believed either I killed Belmon, or I was experimenting with magic. I didn't want to stick around and see what they decided."

"Nobody stood by you?" Jinn asked, worry lacing her features. "No one cared enough to stand up for you?"

Conra paused, his gaze losing focus. A sad smile crept onto his face. "My family tried to stand up for me, but no one would hear them, as I'm sure my wife did as well, but..."

"Your wife?" Darr asked, leaning forward, his mouth hung open in disbelief.

"Yes, my wife," the old Elf replied. "I'm sure she's the only one who believed me. She alone understood why I left. The last thing she wanted was to see me imprisoned or worse, executed, for something we both knew I didn't do."

"So, all these years alone out there in the lowlands and you were married the whole time?" Jinn asked with something close to awe. "You never said anything about it before. Did father even know?"

Conra nodded. "Hydle suspected, of that I'm sure, but he never brought it up. Besides, I'm sure she's moved on. I told her I never planned to come back here. I guess that's why I never mentioned it. I never expected it to be an issue."

All his life, Darr thought Conra a lonely hermit, a man with no desire for family. Even his father, Conra's closest friend, believed him so. Now it seemed Conra's desire for family is what drove him away in the first place. He'd given up everything so he could leave those he loved with a feeling of normalcy.

Darr stretched his legs towards the fire, touching a log and sending up a fresh wall of sparks. "So you never found out what happened to your brother, did you?"

Conra's eyes hardened. "No. Never. But, after everything I've seen traveling with you, I believe it was an Ovid. The light we saw came from the Spire, the tower where the Air Sephir is kept."

"But, Conra," Jinn objected, "I don't think the Ovids have been around that long. Weren't the Soul Seekers the ones to summon them?"

Jinn and Conra both turned to Darr, the resident expert of everything related to the Currents. "The Devoid is the one who summoned the Ovids," he answered. "Even still, what happened to your brother took place nearly thirty years ago. You'd think Caeranol or Nidic Waq would've done something to stop all this if it'd been going on that long."

"Well, I'm sticking to my theory," Conra announced. "I don't care if the Ovid has been there for a hundred years."

A disturbing notion, Darr thought with a shake of his head. If the Ovids had been in Ictar for thirty or more years, the damage done to the Currents by now must be serious indeed. Why hadn't Caeranol done anything to stop it until now? Perhaps Nidic Waq had been too young to be the servant Caeranol wanted him to be. Perhaps there really wasn't anyone besides himself and the prophet.

"We shouldn't let the fire burn tonight," Conra said. "Best not to draw attention to ourselves."

"I'll take the first watch," Jinn replied.

No one argued.

Chapter Thirty-Two

"Alongside Nidic Waq, Darr and his friends traveled south on their way towards the Sephir of Earth. Nidic Waq arranged for Darr to be taken south by Feywen Dery and his mentor, Lacdur. Nothing could've prepared them all for what they found on their way. The Soul Seekers had destroyed the village of the Crossroads, killing most of its inhabitants in the process. Navda was next in their sights, and as such, Darr's plans had to change."

~From the personal writings of the Divine, Zander

When morning came, the three ate a quick breakfast and tended to the horses before packing their gear. Conra left the lean-to in place, saying it would aid some other traveler in their journey someday.

"If it doesn't disturb the local wildlife," Conra said, "it's customary for the foragers to leave structures like this in case of emergencies."

Darr looked up from his pack. "It's strange hearing you talk about the foragers, Conra. You haven't said a word about them before."

The old Elf shrugged. "Hmph. Guess I'm getting nostalgic."

With their horses in tow, the three started into the Greenfhyre. The forest grew in a tangle, bereft of any trails or identifying passages, and the canopy of evergreens overhead blocked out any indication of where they were. No wonder the Greenfhyre provided Qued's first line of defense. If they didn't have Conra with them, Darr would've been lost within the first half mile.

The morning waned to afternoon, marked by the thin streamers of light breaking through the trees. Conra shared more tales concerning his past, talking almost nonstop since they left their camp. Most of his stories revolved around his brother and the life they led with the foragers.

While he neared his homeland, the memories Conra

thought buried resurfaced. They echoed through the Currents, mixed with sadness and guilt, excitement and pride. An odd combination of feelings, for sure, but they were Conra's nonetheless. Now and again, when they stopped briefly to rest, and if their surroundings were quiet, Conra would think of his wife, Tamber.

Darr tried to ignore the whispers from the Currents, but failed. "You miss her," he said to the old Elf. He didn't want to attract Jinn's attention.

"Who?" Jinn asked.

A flash of anger burned on Conra's face before softening. "My wife, Tamber. How did you know?"

Darr smiled, keeping his gaze locked on Conra. "The spirits. Whenever we stop like this, you think about her. Your memories are strong. They bleed into the Currents, and I can't shut them out right away."

Conra breathed deep, tilting his head up. He didn't reply.

They forged ahead into the afternoon, and somewhere before them, Mount Terlak grew closer. As it did, the ground became more solid, hunching into an upward grade. Even when the massive peak of Mount Terlak appeared through a break in the trees, a behemoth in defiance of the sky, the Greenfhyre refused to break apart.

"This place is less a forest and more like the jungles Father told us about," Jinn announced at one point.

"No mistake about that," Conra said, looking over his shoulder. "Old Hydle never traveled that far south, but he heard about them from me. And yes, you're right. As the Greenfhyre stretches south and west, it turns into the jungles you heard about."

When the Greenfhyre finally broke apart and the trail leading up to Qued stood revealed, no doubt remained how the Elven city had survived war for so long. The mountain trail cut upwards at a shallow angle, leading up narrow and smooth, but it appeared to end at a sheer cliff stretching to Terlak's top.

"Conra, how are we supposed to climb this thing? We need our horses if we're going to make time," Darr pleaded.

Conra laughed and dismounted. "The horses will come with us, don't you worry, but you won't find out until morning." The old Elf explained no further. He began setting up camp for the night.

In the morning, they made the climb up the trail easily enough, though with the horses, it took them nearly an hour to reach the sheer cliff wall. As they crested the rise, a break formed in the wall, revealing a tunnel hidden from the forest below.

Darr stopped walking, frozen by the unnatural appearance of the tunnel. Nearly twenty feet tall and double across, the tunnel burrowed upwards into Mount Terlak, its sides smoothed to a precision Darr couldn't fathom. Even the Dwarves, with their entire engineering prowess, couldn't have carved something so perfectly.

"What made this?" Jinn asked, her eyes wide in awe.

"No one knows how it got here," Conra began, "but almost everyone thinks it was the Ancients. There's more once we get inside."

The old Elf led the way forward, fearless and accustomed to the massiveness of the tunnel. With a stern urging to his horse, Conra started into the tunnel with an echoing clip-clop of hooves.

"Won't we need torches?" Darr called after. Conra either didn't hear him or ignored him.

Darr glanced over at Jinn, her brow furrowed in doubt.

"How does it not collapse in on itself?" Jinn asked quietly, shaking her head.

"Conra seems pretty sure of himself," the Summoner replied.

With little choice left to them, they urged their horses forward into the giant opening. Surprisingly, the dark Darr anticipated never came. About thirty or so feet into the tunnel, strange lights appeared along the ceiling, long and narrow. The lights glowed steadily from flat plates fixed into the stone, turning on when they approached and going out when they passed. Darr had seen lights like this before, from his dream of the Tower Castle. Perhaps the Ancients had constructed this tunnel after all.

Conra slowed his pace to match theirs. "Guess there's no reason to lead anymore. There's pretty much only one way out of here."

The tunnel, while an engineering marvel, was plain and uninspiring. Its floors, walls, and ceiling were all bare and plain except for the lights.

"So what do you think the Ancients used this tunnel for?" Jinn asked. She eyed the tunnel warily, as if she expected the roof to fall on her at any moment.

Conra smiled. "No one knows," he replied. "When the Elves first discovered it, the valley above was empty. It took many years for them to cultivate the soil and stimulate the land for growth. It was an excellent hiding spot, though. Wherever this tunnel led for the Ancients, it must've been important."

Conra made an effort to keep them all talking by asking questions or telling stories. He explained how the monotony of the tunnel got to many people, but the best way to deal with boredom was to talk.

The three climbed higher along Mount Terlak, though it was impossible to tell for sure how long they'd been traveling. The tunnel was graded, but not so bad it was hard on the horses. Even still, every so often, Conra instructed them to dismount and walk the animals for a while.

"There's no water until we reach the top," the old Elf explained. "Best not to overwork the horses."

They took a quick break for lunch after a few hours or a few days, Darr couldn't be sure. Conra took note of his confusion.

"I know it's difficult to tell time here, Boy, but we don't have much further to go."

How he could know that baffled Darr further? Perhaps there were other signs, signs the Elves knew indicating how far they'd come.

They resumed their trek, but their conversations grew farther apart. Darr's mind wandered during the empty spaces. Daydreams of his home and his father combined with memories of the past. What would it be like to tell his father about Erec's death? How could he even begin to explain? Darr leaned forward on his horse. Nausea overtook him. He needed to think of something else.

The hours dragged on, but gradually, a faint natural light began to shine on the walls where they wound around the corner. The three quickened their pace. Light flashed brightly, and Darr shielded his eyes, letting them adjust, while he breathed in the cool air outside the tunnel.

They stood on a ridgeline, its edges sweeping smoothly down to the valley floor. Above them, the looming white peaks of Mount Terlak towered to incalculable heights, the massive crests blocking out what might've been a midafternoon sun. Below, the valley spread out like a round plate of earth in the growing dark. Trees and fields gathered in clumps, creating a kaleidoscope of color. Warm lights shimmered, far off in the distance, on the opposite side of the valley.

"Is that Qued?" Jinn asked quietly, pointing to the lights. "It's a lot brighter than I would've expected."

Conra nodded grimly. "That's new," he said.

The old Elf cleared his throat and scanned the skies above. "It's barely late afternoon, but we won't have more than an hour before dark. Light doesn't last long up here. It's gonna get cold, too, Sephirs failing or not, so we better find shelter."

Without another word, Conra rode to the north along the ridge, keeping his horse close to the wall of mountains. Darkness fell much quicker than Darr expected. So did the anticipated cold.

"There's a cave nearby with water," Conra announced. "It's sort of a way station for travelers."

After several minutes, they dismounted and walked the horses to a heavily wooded area that spread out to the rock wall of the mountains. Within a gathering of cedar, a cave popped into view. A small waterfall fell nearby, and while Darr took the horses for a drink, Conra and Jinn set up a fire and began preparations for supper.

Within the hour, the three sat quietly inside the little cave. Outside, the horses whinnied softly, protesting the cold. Darr covered them with blankets and cut some cedar branches to insulate the ground, but no matter what he did, they all would be cold. He expected to see a thick coating of frost by morning. At least they had a fire to keep themselves warm.

After a quick meal, Conra took out his pipe and packed it full of tobacco. In short, slow bursts, he smoked, a habit Darr hadn't seen him practice since they left his cabin. The old Elf took in a deep breath of smoke. The bowl of his pipe glowed red hot, and he exhaled in a steady stream.

"It always did calm my nerves," he said with a chuckle. Jinn, wrapped in a single blanket, already slept beside him.

"You're nervous to be home after all these years," Darr stated. The spirits told him so.

Conra breathed in more of the smoke, and nodded his gray head. "I think... I think I'd like to go find my family tomorrow," he said without making eye contact.

Darr smiled, keeping his gaze focused on the fire. "I think that would be a good idea."

The old Elf shifted, but his gaze remained focused on the fire. "The Pathenine is where you should head tomorrow, that's the home of the Minister of Qued. I'll go take care of my business while you do that. It'll probably take some trickery if you want to get to the Sephir of Air."

"While I do that, maybe Jinn could go with you," Darr suggested.

"Well, I don't want you going off fighting shades unless I'm around," he snapped.

"We don't even know if the Sephir is missing or not," Darr soothed. "Besides, it might take a while to get permission to even see it."

Conra shook his head leisurely, and breathed out a cloud of the sweet smelling smoke. "I want to see that thing. I want to know if that's what killed Belmon."

When it came time for bed, Conra told Darr to get some sleep even though he'd volunteered for the first watch.

Reluctantly, the Summoner rolled into his blankets.

He shut his eyes, but sleep would not come. Conra's tension tightened like a noose through the Currents.

Chapter Thirty-Three

"As they traveled to Navda, Darr told me briefly of a dilemma he often has. The Currents allow him to see much more than any normal man can see. In the world around him, he can see how the elements connect one thing to the next, but in the people around him, he can feel what they feel and the memories connected to those emotions. He cannot always shut out this aspect of his life. He's constantly burdened with the emotions and memories he absorbs, but more so, Darr is burdened with the decision of whether to act on what he sees."

~From the personal writings of the Divine, Zander

By midmorning of the following day, after nearly a week of travel from Spirits' Reach, Conra led Jinn and Darr into the city of Qued.

It's as if I've come home, Jinn thought. This place could pass for Tyfor.

They followed a dirt road leading from the trees below the ridge, walking the horses at Conra's insistence. Farmhouses and barns spread out around them, staggered throughout the fields. Harvesting had already taken place, but farmers and their workers still labored around or in their fields. The locals looked up from their work and waved.

"I would think people wouldn't be accustomed to visitors," Darr said, waving back to the Elves.

Jinn turned to Conra. He gave a distracted nod. "The Elves of Qued are always open to new faces. If you got here, you only did it because you're a friend."

As they came out of the surrounding farmland, a paved road met them. More locals appeared, all Elves and all incredibly friendly. The smile stretching across Jinn's face warmed her.

"It's good to see you smiling again, Girl," the old Elf called.

The smile dropped away, but the warmth remained. "Of

all the places we've traveled, I didn't expect this kind of reception," Jinn replied. "It feels like home."

An elderly couple stopped them to ask their names. Conra gave their names, stammering, but the couple wished them well and went on their way. If they recognized Conra, they didn't show it.

They continued down the road. Houses and buildings gathered close, becoming less a town like Tyfor and more like something Jinn had never seen before.

"Darr, look how the city runs around everything," Jinn called out. She pointed to a series of houses built between a thicket and a creek.

The Summoner leaned close to her. "Even the road works itself around the landscape. It doesn't plow through it like everywhere else we've seen."

Conra grit his teeth in an apparent attempt to smile. "The Elves of Qued live in harmony with this mountain, maintaining the balance like nowhere else in Ictar. If the mountain resources fail, then everything up here will die."

"What's going on with the torches?" Darr asked.

Set into stanchions of metal and wood, torches burned in front of houses and barns alike. In broad daylight, the purpose of the torches didn't make much sense. Conra shrugged and shook his head, but Jinn continued to watch the flames dance in the open air. *What a strange custom.*

At noon, they reached Qued's bustling central square, filled with Elves of all ages and sizes. Conra led them to a low brick wall at the edge of the lake separating the city from the Pathenine.

"This lake is fed by a natural spring that bubbles up from within Mount Terlak," Conra explained. He grimaced and took a shallow breath as he looked out at the placid smoothness of the lake. "Glacial waters feed it as well, but rarely in the winter."

Conra pointed across the lake to a gathering of buildings, beyond which rose a mansion. "That estate is the Pathenine, home to the Minister of Qued. Above it is the Spire." A faint sparkle of yellow peeked out from the rock formation jutting out of the mountain itself. "You should go to the Pathenine first," he said, turning to Darr. "And don't you dare go looking for trouble without finding me first."

Darr smiled. "I know."

The Summoner clasped Conra's hand, and wished him luck. "You can ride now," Conra added. "We didn't need to walk. I just wanted to take my time...you know..."

"You don't have to explain it to me, Conra," Darr replied.

Jinn reached out and hugged her brother close. "Be careful," she said into his shoulder.

"I will."

Darr climbed atop his horse. With a wave, he turned and began the ride around the lake towards the Pathenine. Conra knotted his hands together, and Jinn smiled beside him. She wasn't used to seeing him so distracted.

"Shall we get moving, Girl?" he asked with no intention of getting an answer.

Jinn nodded. They led the horses back through the square, moving easily between the buildings and houses. The Elves of Qued paid them little attention except occasional glances at Jinn. They probably weren't used to seeing Cortazians.

"Thank you for coming with me," Conra said. "This is hard, but it's reassuring having you with me."

"It's okay," Jinn replied with a weak grin. "Besides, I want to meet your family."

Conra exhaled sharply. "Don't get my hopes up, or yours for that matter. I don't know if they're even around anymore. I don't know if they'll even have me back."

Jinn kept close to Conra's side as they made their way through the square. Several times, Conra paused and stared, sweat beading on his forehead. At one point, Jinn reached over and rested her hand on his shoulder. He flinched, fear evident in his face.

"It's alright, Conra," Jinn soothed.

The old Elf took a ragged breath and drooped his chin to his chest. "I'm okay. My old house, the house I shared with Tamber, sits on the west end of the city, away from the noise.

Not much further now."

He started forward again, and Jinn followed after. The larger buildings of the city receded, replaced by a gathering of homes along a narrow lane.

"These homes all belong to foragers and their families," Conra explained, the fear dropping out of his voice. "The Minister of Qued pays for them, making them property of the crown, but it's a fair price for the work the foragers do. Almost everything is provided. They do the same thing in Vanla...."

Conra's breath caught in his throat, and he stopped walking. A stone cottage appeared through a copse of trees off the lane ahead. Jinn waited, her own tension rising up to match Conra's, but for different reasons.

"This is my old house," Conra said at last. "Tamber would've been moved after I left. I'll go find out."

"I'll be right here," Jinn replied, but Conra mechanically passed the reins to his horse, and started away.

He walked up the narrow path leading to house as if in a daze. He knocked on the door, and a small Elven woman answered. After a moment, the woman leaned out of the doorway and pointed down the road. Conra hesitated, nodded, and returned hastily to Jinn.

The woman called after him, but Conra kept walking, retrieving his horse's reins from Jinn. "I don't know why, but Tamber still lives in the forager community," he muttered. "It's this way."

Conra walked his horse down the lane without waiting.

"What happened?" Jinn asked. "Why are you so upset?"

Conra ignored her. The lane rounded a corner, and a long pole fence ran along the side. At the end of the fence sat another stone cottage, nestled amidst gardens of flowers and vegetables.

"That's it," Conra said, coming to a halt once more.

Jinn's hand fell upon his shoulder, her grip solid. "Perhaps we should go see if anyone's home," she said. "Together, this time."

Conra smiled lightly. They tied their horses to the fence,

and Jinn took his hand. Together, they walked up the path towards the house, climbing the front steps. Jinn let his hand go. Conra's breathing turned quick and shallow.

"Easy, Conra," Jinn said behind him. "It's going to be just..."

The front door opened, and an old woman stepped out, one hand clutching a basket, the other holding the hand of a small girl.

"Come on now, Alacia. We don't want to..."

The old woman paused, her round face, framed with curly, white hair, slackened. But her startling blue eyes sparkled.

"Grandmother," the little girl asked, "who is that?"

Conra and the woman stared at each other, their mouths and throats working to speak. Tears welled up in Conra's eyes.

A laugh bubbled in Jinn's throat, and she asked, "Tamber?"

It was enough to bring them both back to themselves.

"Conra," Tamber breathed, her voice cracking.

Her basket fell to the floor and she released the little girl's hand. The space between Conra and Tamber disappeared, and they embraced fiercely.

"I'm so glad you're home."

"I am, too," Conra whispered into her ear.

Chapter Thirty-Four

"When they arrived at Navda, Darr and his company were met by a defenseless city. The leaders of Navda did not believe in the Soul Seeker threat, and so they were grossly unprepared for what was coming for them. Feywen Dery set them straight, but not without help from Darr. How much power does that boy have that he can so easily show people the wrongness of their actions?"

~From the personal writings of the Divine, Zander

Six days.

Nidic Waq breathed slowly, ignoring the aches raging throughout his body, begging him to stop. His brow weighed heavily on his eyelids, but he refused the urge to sleep. His mount's suffering was equal, if not greater than his own was, trudging over the grass of the Ladornaleah crushed flat by the Ictarian Army ahead of him.

Six days gone from Vanla. Six days of sleep mingled with fighting and inevitable retreat.

"It's close now," Feywen said at his side. The once-prince rode alongside him wearing a solemn face, the same face he'd worn since Vanla.

Exed lay ahead of them, another hour or two. The Elven capital, the crux of all their efforts in the war against the Soul Seekers, would be their salvation or their doom. Once they climbed inside the walls of the city, they could retreat no longer.

Nidic Waq observed the slow arch of the sun moving into the west. "We won't make Exed's walls tonight. Another night in the open won't do," he replied, an edge to his voice.

Feywen nodded. Cumulatively, they'd lost half their numbers since Jacova, and more soldiers fell every day from sickness or their wounds, from the Soul Seekers, and in some cases, starvation. With their food and water used up, they'd lived off the land for the last couple of days. For an army of over three-thousand troops, this proved a difficult task.

When the low mountains surrounding Exed came into view, the pace of the infantry soldiers increased. If the Elves were prepared to receive them, as Alman Ohnler promised they would, the Dwarves and Cortazians would finally have rest after their flight across the Ladornaleah.

Nidic Waq turned to face Feywen. "I want to be closer to Ariel Forn now that we're within reach of the city," he said. Feywen kept his gaze on the ground in front of him. "I want you to come with me."

After a long pause, Feywen's shoulders sagged in apparent defeat. Since Lacdur's death at Vanla, the once-prince had grown increasingly withdrawn. Nidic Waq was one of the only people he spoke with, and then, infrequently. His pursuit of the traitor plaguing the Ictarian Army consumed him.

Nidic Waq led him towards the front lines where Ariel rode, protected by Vertain's Daravens. The horsemen let Nidic Waq and Feywen pass, familiar company for Ariel Forn.

They rode up alongside the Cortazian King. Ariel's dark gaze revealed no new hope. "Whoever said the Seekers don't strategize never fought them in the open like this," Ariel cursed.

Nidic Waq kept his face expressionless. "The Seekers are directed. They are a weapon aimed wherever their master commands."

Ariel took a sharp breath. "Vertain just informed me the Seeker mists are converging to our south, perhaps to cut us off."

"They're doing what any predator would do and cutting off the weakest of the herd from the rest of the pack," Feywen retorted, disinterested.

Ariel cast a dangerous glance before turning to one of his messengers. "Find General Tole and General Eris. Get everyone moving."

When Ariel turned back, his face softened. "Feywen, will you ride to the rearguard? Tell Vertain to mobilize the cavalry, and bring them to the south so they can cover us in case the Seekers decide to strike early."

Feywen gave a solemn acknowledgement and rode away without a word.

"Once we reach Exed, I want Feywen to take Lacdur's place as my eyes and ears in the field," Ariel confided. "He's best suited for the task given his history with the Soul Seekers."

Nidic Waq tilted up his chin. "He is quite knowledgeable. However, his obsession with the traitor distracts him."

"That's exactly why we need him watching," Ariel replied. "I don't know if there is a traitor, but I can't have him out leading a group of infantry soldiers hoping he catches something. He needs to have the latitude to go where he must. He must be able to see and hear what he decides will help us."

The Cortazian King had a point. Like Lacdur, Feywen possessed knowledge of the Seekers and their methods that no one else did. Of course, their traitor was no simple Soul Seeker. The traitor was human, or at least more calculating than a Soul Seeker. On the surface, it appeared Lacdur's death was by accident, but like Feywen, Nidic Waq knew that to be false. Someone wanted Lacdur out of the way.

Either way, Feywen Dery, driven by revenge and experience taught to him by his lost mentor, would be best suited to catch their traitor.

Nidic Waq bowed his head, glancing at Ariel. "I think choosing Feywen would be an excellent choice, my lord."

They rode together in silence for a time, their pace even and steady, keeping in rhythm with the infantry soldiers in front of them. The sun touched down on the distant mountains to the west, bathing the Ladornaleah in red.

"We aren't going to make Exed before nightfall," Ariel said.

Cold seeped from the Currents. Nidic Waq lifted his head. "That's the least of our worries. Look."

From the hill country south of the Gethma River, the Seeker mists boiled out onto the plains separating the Ictarian Army from the Angleire, the passage leading up to

Exed's walls. They wouldn't be able to avoid a confrontation. The infantry would have to fight. Sapped of their strength, they wouldn't stand much of a chance.

Ariel shouted orders, urging his messengers to warn the generals and halt the procession. They had to stand and fight. They couldn't retreat again and survive the night.

Nidic Waq closed his eyes. The Currents opened up to him, a mass of confusion, fear, and rage. A summoning would take time, but he could do it, though not without risk. Until Darr restored all four Sephirs, the balance holding the Devoid in check was tenuous.

The prophet paused. No. Something approached. Lights grew stronger in the Currents, sucking away the cold of the Soul Seekers.

"There, my lord," Ariel's lone kingsguard shouted.

On the eastern horizon, caught in the glow of the setting sun, a line of horsemen and foot soldiers rapidly approached. Nidic Waq smiled. The Elves were watching after all. The remainder of the White Knights rode to their rescue. The foot soldiers were something new, unexpected. They were tall, hulking figures, heavily armored against their flesh of green and blue.

"Are those Ogres?" Ariel asked aloud. Nidic Waq stared ahead and said nothing. They were.

Ariel ordered flags for retreat to fly, directing them toward the approaching envoy of soldiers. Not far to the north, the Seeker mists broke apart. The dark creatures swept into the dying light of day, tattered black robes a wave of silver-tipped death against the horizon.

Ariel spurred his mount and rode ahead of the infantry soldiers. Nidic Waq followed, curious. *How had the White Knights come to ride with Ogres at their side?* A large Ogre stood at the forefront of the group. Ariel, atop his mount, met the Ogre's gaze without looking down.

"Greetings, Lord of Cortaz," the Ogre shouted. He spoke the common language shared between the other races, though with an unfamiliar accent.

"I am Ariel Forn," the young king replied. "You've come

to cover our retreat, I hope."

The Ogre's face twisted into a devilish smile. "You'd be correct to say so. My name is Tella Shaw of Oglorn. I'm here at the request of the Elf Lord to bring you to safety."

Ogres allied with the Elves. Nidic Waq tightened the grip on his reins, fighting back the urge to smile. For centuries, the races of Ictar had fought among each other, but something good and unexpected would come from the Soul Seekers.

"Thank you, Tella Shaw," Ariel said with a curt nod. "We're in your debt."

The Ogre shook his head fiercely and with a quick laugh, he raised his longsword high into the air. "We fight!"

Together, Elven White Knights and Ogre foot soldiers turned and charged towards the Seeker mists. To the south, Vertain and his Daravens spread out along the Army's exposed flanks.

"Just in time," Ariel said. He glanced up at Nidic Waq. "Did you ever think you'd see the Ogres fighting with us?"

Nidic Waq said nothing. Even with the Ogres at their side, the Ictarian Army faced a difficult battle ahead of them.

* * * *

Within the monstrous belly of the Elven Ministry, Nidic Waq watched and waited from the shadows of the auditorium. Spread out at the long table normally occupied by the Elven ministers, the leaders of the Ictarian Army talked in turn, making decisions that would affect the rest of Ictar for years to come.

Lendor Terwin took responsibility for the Ictarian Army, merging the Elven light foot with the Dwarf and Cortazian infantry. Ariel Forn accepted command of the new infantry, with Bru Kiln Tole and Blaque Eris as joint commanders. Norris Dane would remain in the war council, an advisor only.

The White Knights and Cortazian cavalry merged under the command of Alman Ohnler, and the Daravens, under

Vertain, would become a rearguard alongside the Elven rangers. The Ogres of Oglorn would remain under the control of Tella Shaw, and the Cortazian bowmen, who'd been useless since Vanla, joined ranks with the Elven archers, the finest unit in all of Ictar.

Some of the Elven ministers grumbled at the lack of control assumed by their King, but Lendor and Alman Ohnler both spoke highly of Ariel Forn's leadership, quelling the dissent.

The new Ictarian Army merged four of the races of Ictar, bonding them shoulder to shoulder against an enemy they could never defend against alone. Since the advent of the Aeon Wars, no such union had ever taken place. As a historian, Nidic Waq respected the gravity of what was happening before him.

With the politics out of the way, the leaders talked more seriously about strategy. Nidic Waq stepped from the shadows, staying close to the perimeter of the table, still out of awareness for most of the men.

"Forty barrels of maugwrith came with us," Tella Shaw announced, his composure cool despite being the largest man there. "Another eighty will be here in a few days once our supply run is complete."

"As we saw at Vanla," Feywen said, "maugwrith can halt the Seekers advance completely, if we use it strategically." As promised, Ariel made Feywen a strategist in the field, his eyes and ears seeking any holes in their defense.

"It's a powerful weapon," Vertain agreed, sitting across from the once-prince. "The Seekers don't sense the flames. They walk into them and they're consumed."

Lendor Terwin thanked him. Tall and regal-looking, with blond hair and a beard, Lendor acted much different since they first arrived in Exed. Earlier, he'd been cheerful and easygoing. Now, his disposition turned hard as iron.

In the following silence, Ariel Forn stood. "Maugwrith or no, we must choose where to make our stand. Since the Seeker mists have not reappeared, I suggest we establish lines well beyond the base of the Angleire."

"What of the earthworks that have been placed there over the last several weeks? We risk falling into our own traps," one of the Elven ministers asked in a skeptical tone.

"The traps will have to be marked," Ariel replied. "The Seekers will not detect any signs if we do. As Vertain said earlier, they'll only follow the living."

A slow hissing, probably a laugh, slid from Tella Shaw's lips. "The maugwrith will aide us well then. We can push them back and forth for weeks."

Do not underestimate them, Nidic Waq thought. Lendor Terwin thought the same. "The Soul Seekers might appear mindless, Tella, but that wouldn't be a correct assumption," the Elf King said. "I mean no disrespect to you, for I know you've fought them a long time yourself, but they will not stop until we're destroyed."

Tella nodded his bald head solemnly. "We'll have to be careful then."

The conversation wore on, and Nidic Waq listened halfheartedly. If they lost the base of the Angleire, then the slopes, and finally, the outer and inner walls, their last stand would be within the city itself. Escape would be possible through the mountains west, but for an army of this size, not to mention the general population of the city, the battle would end in a bloodbath.

Not that it would mean anything by then, Nidic Waq thought darkly. If the Seekers breached Exed's walls, they'd have accumulated enough of the Light for the Devoid to free itself.

The matter of the traitor had yet to be resolved. During the flight from Vanla, Nidic Waq and Feywen both worked hard to ferret out the renegade who'd caused Lacdur's death, but to no avail. They found nothing. The longer the traitor remained in the field though, the less chance they had to survive.

The prophet watched the men at the long table, letting his Light touch theirs through the Currents. It'd long been a suspicion of his that the traitor was one of the army leaders. Of course, such a person must have some connection to the

Currents. There'd be no other way for the Devoid to contact its servant. If not, he wondered if it was possible that someone used the situation to achieve some insidious agenda? Who would gain from the destruction of all life? No one living.

His sweep turned up nothing. Nidic Waq's thoughts slipped away from the Currents, but something brushed against the periphery of his senses, something insidious and cunning. The feeling, almost undetectable, was like someone opening a door on the opposite end of a long hallway. He didn't see the door open, but he felt the slight shift in the air. Nidic Waq thrust himself fully into the wisteria light, but he found himself alone, in the presence of the spirits.

Though the sensation hit him briefly, Nidic Waq received his first clue. Only one kind of person on Ictar could make that kind of connection to the Currents. Somewhere close by, another Spirit Summoner had learned how to access the Currents. They did so purposely and deceitfully.

Worse, it was the traitor to the Ictarian Army.

Chapter Thirty-Five

"Though Navda stood defenseless, Darr and his companions were able to build a strategy to withstand the coming horde of Soul Seekers. Their chances of success were small, but they held a pair of dice that might yield any number. Navda, a city of Spirit Summoners, held vast potential, and Darr planned to exploit that potential by pulling a number of his fellow Spirit Summoners into the Currents. There, they could all summon the Fire Archon's magic and wash away the Seekers from Navda. His plan didn't go as expected."

~From the personal writings of the Divine, Zander

After parting ways with Conra and Jinn, Darr rode leisurely around the lake between Qued's city proper and the Pathenine. The buildings of the town fell away in exchange for small homes and businesses, taking the bustle of the city with them. Eventually the smaller homes disappeared, and the road stretched forward alone towards the Pathenine.

Standing on a gentle hill fronting the lake, the Pathenine held itself tall and regal. The main structure easily stretched three stories high, and each adjoining wing spread out like the arms of a greedy child. Sweeping grounds surrounded the brick building, some farmland, some pasture, while vineyards hugged it tightly along its sides. Conra said Qued was once home to the Elven Kings, and the Pathenine confirmed it.

Several hundred yards from the gate leading up to the mansion, it occurred to Darr he had no idea how he would gain access to the Sephir of Air. It would be under guard, most likely by the Divine, but unlike the others, no one appeared distressed about its current state. *Will I only need to ask to see it?*

In Stern and Arcnor, the Divine had come to his aid. Perhaps they could help him here. Darr shook the hair from his face. Conra told him the Elves were particularly stout in their faith of the Divine. Unless the Divine came to him, he wouldn't likely find them an ally.

His remaining option was to send his influence into the Currents. He could manipulate the Lights of any guards or Divine he crossed paths with and trick them into letting him pass. He hated using the spirit realm for such a thing, especially considering the delicate balance in the Currents, but he might not have an option.

No, I'll use that as a last resort, he told himself. *I'll be direct. Perhaps they'll let me right in.*

A group of Elven soldiers waited patiently at the gate leading up to the mansion. They held no weapons, but tension strung through the Currents gave Darr the impression unannounced visitors weren't necessarily welcome.

"Please dismount, my friend," one of the soldiers called. The Elf sounded pleasant enough, but his stern face showed otherwise.

Darr hid the rising anxiety he felt and leapt down from his horse, keeping a firm hold on the reins once his feet touched the ground. Across from him, another soldier stood defiantly. Elves tended to be taller than Cortazians, but standing before these two men was like standing in the presence of Nidic Waq.

"Please, state your name and business here," the stern-faced soldier asked.

"My name is Darr Reintol," he answered. "I've traveled a long ways, and I'm here to pay my respects to the Sephir."

Faint smiles spread across the soldiers' faces, and they glanced at one another. When the stern soldier looked back, his smile vanished. "Where've you come from, Boy?"

"A village called Tyfor in the Cortazian territories."

"That's quite a long journey." The soldier shook his head. "I'm sorry, but no one except the Divine are allowed to view the Sephir. You may certainly offer your prayers here. The Sephir will hear it, I assure you."

"Would it be possible to appeal to the Divine then?" Darr asked without hesitation.

The soldier took a step forward, his gaze steady. "I'm afraid not. You'll have to leave now."

The soldier turned his back and started away, but Darr refused to back down. "What about a commanding officer?" he pleaded. "Is there someone else I could speak with?"

This time, when the stern-looking Elf turned around, he'd reached the end of his patience. He bent down so his eyes were level with Darr's.

"Now, I've been more accommodating with you than with most," the soldier said, his voice coming out in a hiss. "You're going to have to leave now. If you persist, I won't hesitate to arrest you for disrupting the peace here."

Darr acknowledged the soldier's comment with a stubborn nod, but he wasn't ready to give up. He'd tried everything he could think of to persuade the man. Backed into a corner, one way out remained.

The whispers of the spirits buzzed in Darr's ears. "I think you should bring your commanding officer," he ordered, simultaneously through the Currents. His words bore his confidence into the Lights of the soldiers.

The Elf stood before him, his stern face lined with anger and some mild shock. The Currents roared with the man's confusion, fighting hard against Darr's certainty. His face slackened. His mouth worked to find words, and he rose back to full height.

"Wait here," he commanded. "I'll bring the captain."

Without another word, the soldier turned and started for the Pathenine.

* * * *

The sun held itself high at noon when the captain of the guard arrived.

Relief surged through Darr when the captain appeared. Honesty and a strong sense of duty radiated from the man. Shorter and lighter of build than his guards were, the captain stood taller somehow. The goodness of his nature radiated through his bones.

"I apologize for keeping you," the captain said in a soft voice, blue eyes shining with warmth. When he smiled, he did so to initiate trust, not out of habit or obligation. He offered his hand in greeting, the same way Zander had in Arcnor.

"Thank you for meeting with me," Darr said, taking his hand and shaking hesitantly.

The captain smiled brightly, amused by some private joke. "My name is Kwik Pantheo. My father is Serin Pantheo."

Darr nodded because it felt expected, but Kwik's face drooped slightly. "Serin Pantheo," he repeated. "The Minister of Qued."

"Your father is the Minister?"

Kwik arched an eyebrow. "Yes."

"And you know why I'm here?" Darr asked.

A brilliant smile spread across the Elf captain's youthful face. "I do know," he said. "I suppose you'd like to speak somewhere more private. If you come with me, my guards will stable your horse for you at the Pathenine."

Darr handed the reins to the stern-looking soldier who'd come back alongside his captain. Kwik turned sharply, starting up the gravel path leading to the mansion. Darr followed after. Kwik talked incessantly about current events taking place in the Elven lands. Exed would soon be under siege, bringing together all of Ictar against the coming threat of the Soul Seekers.

Darr listened, but he had a hard time, so powerful were the voices of the spirits. They'd come out of nowhere, their urgings fierce but not threatening. He attempted to decipher what they were saying, but every time he focused on one voice, it faded. Frustrated, Darr shut them away. He sensed no danger in whatever they were attempting to tell him.

Within a few minutes, they reached the vineyards of the Pathenine and walked the perimeter to the east wing porch. All around the mansion, torches sat in stanchions, their flames burning bright in midday, an oddity the citizens of Qued placed everywhere. Kwik directed them to sit at a small table before disappearing into the mansion. He reappeared a moment later without his weapons, casual and more relaxed.

"I let my wife, Aryana, know we have a guest. She'll join us shortly." Kwik's face drooped. "This isn't a problem, is it?"

A twinge of panic raced up the back of Darr's neck. Why was this man being so cooperative? Had he somehow affected everyone in the Currents when he manipulated the Light of the soldier at the gate?

Kwik's silence grew deafening. Darr nodded along with the Elf's question because he expected an answer.

"She'll be delighted to sit with us," Kwik replied, smiling broadly. "Now, what is it you wished to speak with my father about?"

Darr stared for a moment, unsure of how to proceed. He barely knew this man, but he already trusted him.

The Summoner cleared his throat. "To start with, I should let you know I'm a Spirit Summoner. I'm on a quest to bless the Sephirs."

Kwik sighed, some of the cheer fading from his face. "I thank you for coming all this way, but I'm afraid the Sephir is kept under vigilant guard by the Divine. No one is allowed near it. The Divine are very strict about this."

"I understand, but there must be a way to arrange a viewing," Darr pleaded. "I need only a few moments and I'll be on my way. No harm will come to the Sephir, you have my word."

Tense moments of silence passed while Kwik watched him. Darr sat quietly, patiently. A woman appeared in the doorway of the Pathenine, easily the most beautiful woman Darr had ever seen. Long, curly locks of blond hair framed her face and sharp, angular features. Tremendous wisdom radiated from her both in the physical world and in the Currents.

"Aryana," Kwik announced, leaping to his feet. "You're a much better tactician than I am when it comes to the Divine. You might be able to help our friend here. His name is Darr. He's a Spirit Summoner."

The Elven woman walked to the table, her movements

fluid. She seated herself across from Darr. The Summoner smiled weakly, unable to think of anything better to do.

"Our friend would like to view the Sephir of Air," Kwik said, his voice clear but guarded. "Have you any idea how we could make such a thing happen?"

Aryana's heavy gaze fell on him. Like a face appearing through fogged glass, startling and eerie, Aryana's presence appeared gently in the Currents. She couldn't submerge herself in the spirit world, but Aryana Pantheo was a Spirit Summoner. Like Aratan Vanheila in Navda, she had limited access to the Currents, and her presence there gave him pause.

"Why do you wish to see the Sephir?" she asked with an inquisitive face.

Darr answered without hesitation. "I'm on a pilgrimage to bless all four of the Sephirs. Two have already been visited."

Aryana smiled patiently. "Tell me why you truly wish to see the Sephir."

Aryana had some awareness of her abilities after all. She could read the truth in the Currents. *Does she do so knowingly or merely on instinct?*

Kwik leaned forward and said, "Please, don't think we're baiting you, but we both know you have ulterior motives for being here. That's obvious simply by your being here. But you wouldn't be here now if I didn't want to help you."

Kwik sat back and placed his hand gently over his wife's hand. "Aryana is a Spirit Summoner, and she's able to sense certain things. It's a gift from the spirits. When the guards notified me of your appearance, I went to her first. She told me you were who you said you were and that you meant no harm, but you were holding truths back in order to gain something. So again, why do you wish to see the Sephir of Air?"

No wonder Kwik had been so accommodating. The Elf said he wasn't baiting him, but in reality, Darr had already taken the bait. Now he struggled on the line. The Summoner straightened himself and cleared his throat. How much could he divulge to Kwik and Aryana? He'd have to trust the spirits to guide him.

"I'm sure you've heard there's an unbalance in the Sephirs," Darr stated. Both Elves nodded. "This unbalance is happening because of a creature called the Devoid, the mastermind behind the Soul Seeker advance. The Devoid has summoned the Ovids of the Four Archons, and these Ovids are draining the Sephirs of their Light. I'm here to stop the Ovid of Air."

Aryana sat unmoving. Kwik eyed him seriously and asked, "How do you intend to stop this Ovid? Magic?"

Unease rippled across the Currents from Kwik and Aryana. Darr shielded his presence in the Currents for Aryana might be able to see what he could do. Would that even protect him from what he was about to say?

"It's not magic, not exactly," Darr said, meeting Kwik's gaze. "I can summon the Archon of Fire through the Currents, and its balancing power will destroy the Ovid."

"That sounds a lot like magic," Kwik said. "I'm sure the Divine will see it the same way."

Aryana leaned over and whispered something to her husband. Darr remained calm though he wanted to bolt. A flicker of a smile appeared on the corner of Kwik's mouth, and a small measure of Darr's tension drained away.

"I cannot be certain of what you can do, so there's no reason to say anything to the Divine," Kwik explained. "I'll do what I can to arrange a viewing, but on one condition."

"What's that?" Darr asked.

A smile spread across Kwik's face. "You must take me with you."

Chapter Thirty-Six

"Darr's brother, Erec, died during the Soul Seeker attack on Navda. When Darr sensed this, he retaliated out of anger, ripping the Fire Sephir's magic away from its Archon. Not only did he wield this wild and reckless power, he nearly broke the balance between the Sephirs. He saved the city of Navda from the Soul Seekers, but at a cost so high only time will tell if he can repay it."

~From the personal writings of the Divine, Zander

It took only a few minutes for Kwik to gain approval from the Divine to view the Air Sephir. Apparently, he'd also kept things from Darr. Kwik came from the Pantheo line, one of the oldest and most respected families in Qued. There was precious little Kwik couldn't arrange, however the viewing would have to wait until dusk.

"The Divine have to perform rites to ensure the Sephir's protection," Kwik announced, swiftly reclaiming his seat at the table. He gave a short nod to Aryana. "We'll have plenty of time to talk while we wait."

Servants of the Pathenine brought out a light lunch, and for several hours, Darr sat with Aryana and Kwik Pantheo on the porch, eating and talking. Aryana complimented Kwik, a natural conversationalist, by asking intuitive questions and making insightful remarks. Oddly, she didn't see the connection between her abilities and her being a Spirit Summoner. She'd learned early on how to control the voices of the spirits, and like most Summoners in Ictar, she believed that to be the extent of her abilities. While Darr knew her power of intuition came directly from the Currents, Aryana believed it to be a condition of her being. In a way, Darr supposed it was.

As the afternoon wore away into evening, Kwik dismissed himself to tend to his guard captain duties. Dusk approached, and with it, the promise of a confrontation with the Ovid. Unease swelled within Darr's body. He fidgeted, searching for a place to put his hands.

"You're troubled," Aryana said, catching Darr off guard.

"No," Darr replied. Aryana's gaze held him fast, willing the truth from him. He shook his head. "Sorry. Yes, I am troubled. I'm so used to keeping these kinds of things to myself."

Aryana tilted her head inquisitively. "What kinds of things?"

Where do I begin? "Well, because of what I can do as a Spirit Summoner, I guess."

"There's nothing wrong with what we can do, Darr." Aryana tone suggested fierce rigidity. "Our birthright links us to the voices of the spirits. There is no other way for us to be, so we can never be in the wrong. Not unless the Creator is wrong."

Aryana felt the Currents in a way unlike most Spirit Summoners, but she lived a whole world away from understanding what Darr could do. He could literally dive into the Currents and call forth the Archons there. They could wield their magic through his body. Aryana believed in the teachings of the Divine, and the Divine forbade the use of magic. How could she possibly understand what he could do?

"I wouldn't worry too much about the Divine," the Elven woman said, a sly smile appearing on her face. "Kwik and I both think freely. Our beliefs only happen to coincide with many of the Divine's."

Darr narrowed his eyes. "Did you just read my thoughts?"

Aryana's smile brightened. "No, but I am very perceptive. For instance, I can tell you're troubled by something the Divine might do. Another source of trouble lies with my husband and I. You fear we might do something to hinder you."

Darr accepted her comments with a weak nod. "You're right. I am afraid. You've no idea what I can do, what I must do, to save the Sephir."

"Why have you come all this way, Darr Reintol?"

The question stabbed at him, a strange surprise both expected and not. Darr shook off his confusion and answered her question. "I wanted to learn more about my world and myself, and if traveling around Ictar and restoring the Sephirs could do that, I decided I should go."

"And did that ever seem wrong to you?"

Darr furrowed his brow. "I left my father ill at home, and I lost my brother to the Soul Seekers along the way. Knowing the damage my actions have caused, yes, it seems wrong."

"But you have done much good," Aryana said, leaning close. "You've done good that couldn't have been accomplished otherwise."

"Yes. I've saved two of the Sephirs. I suppose that counts for something."

Aryana laughed gently. "Of course it does," she said. "But did saving those Sephirs ever feel wrong?"

Darr shook his head.

"And did you ever get into trouble with the Divine when you saved those Sephirs?"

Again, Darr shook his head and replied, "Most of the Divine didn't even know what I was doing."

"Then I suppose the Divine here won't need to know either."

The pieces of Aryana's narrative came into focus, and Darr smiled in response. Between the lines, she told him as long as some good came of his actions, whatever he needed to do would be okay. Aryana reached over and patted his hand. She started to rise, but Darr stopped her.

"You seem awfully sure of me," he said, keeping his gaze level with hers. "Even if you can tell I'm not lying, you have a lot faith in me, and that's not something you normally pick up after one conversation. Why is that?"

Aryana laughed and stood. "Because sometimes I can hear what the spirits are saying. It's difficult to make out, but now and again, their words ring through to me. When I met you, I could hear them, and they told me to give you whatever you needed. They said you were here to set things right after all these years."

She could hear the spirits after all, Darr thought. He froze, shaking his head. "Wait. What do you mean 'years'?"

"We've known about the Ovid for many years," Kwik replied, his face somber as he stepped from the door leading into the Pathenine. He must have been listening to them. "For a long time, we thought it all coincidence, but we've long since admitted to ourselves an Ovid was among us."

"So the Sephir has been missing for years? How long?" Darr asked incredulously.

"Oh, no." Kwik shook his head. "The Sephir has never once left the Spire. In fact, that's been our greatest problem trying to fight it. The Ovid has never manifested itself. It's intangible, like the air itself."

"So how do you know it's really here?" Darr asked, narrowing his eyes.

Kwik frowned. "I suppose I don't really know. Strange things happen, and we blame the Ovid. That's the reason for these torches. It's become a charm to ward away evil."

Could a simple torch really keep away the Ovid? Fire counterbalanced the Element of Air, so Darr supposed a torch might restrict the Ovid's movement. What worried him more was the Ovid had been in Qued for years. During all that time, the Light from the Air Sephir had been ebbed away, and no one, not even Nidic Waq, had put a stop to it. *Why must this all come to a head now? Why am I at the center of this quest?*

From inside the Pathenine, an Elf appeared and whispered something to Kwik. The Elf captain thanked and dismissed the man before rising to his feet. "The Divine have prepared the Spire. We can leave at any time. They won't be accompanying us." Kwik glanced to his wife. "Would you care to come along?"

Aryana's eyes were distant when she answered. "I think it'd be best if I remained here."

For a moment, Kwik Pantheo looked like he might say something more, but he replaced it with a cheerful smile. "Well then, Darr. We should be off."

Aryana leaned in close when she stood. "Be on your

guard, Summoner. As myself, I don't think Kwik fully understands what you're about to face."

Darr gave her a curt nod. "He doesn't. But I'll be on guard for us both."

* * * *

Kwik led Darr around to the back of the Pathenine along a narrow path lined with small shrubbery and the adjacent vineyards. On the other side of the back lawn, a small orchard led to the cliff wall of Mount Terlak.

From out of the rock of the mountain, a single stone spire jutted outward like a knife blade that might crash into the city below. It rose easily five hundred feet in the air. Darr's legs began to ache at the thought of how many stairs they'd have to climb to get there.

Within a few minutes, they crossed the orchard, reaching an aperture in the wall of the mountain, surrounded by a perimeter of torches. Kwik took one of the brands and ushered Darr inside.

"No guards?" Darr asked before stepping into the dark.

Kwik smiled. "Elven rangers scout the perimeter of the mansion and these surrounding grounds. I assure you, nothing gets in unseen. And if it is something less tangible you are worried about, the Divine have set these torches to ward off any malevolent forces."

Kwik led the way through the foyer, his torch lighting the way forward. Darr shivered. The stone staircase hugged the insides of the Spire, an endless stone ribbon disappearing somewhere into the darkness above. Darr followed Kwik up the staircase, his body resisting the coming climb. Strangely, after several minutes of climbing, Darr found he wasn't winded, let alone tired.

Kwik looked back at him and smiled. "You look surprised, Darr. Could it be you expected the climb to be more difficult? The Divine believe it has something to do with the Air Sephir," Kwik explained. "Myself, I'm not sure. I only know I feel lighter when I climb the Spire, almost as if I am walking downward rather than up."

As they neared the top of the Spire, Kwik's torch was no longer needed. Small cuts carved into the rock of the Spire allowed threads of daylight to crisscross their way downward, illuminating the steps ahead.

With the Air Sephir growing nearer, Darr prepared himself for the inevitable battle ahead. He quieted his mind, exploring the Currents, searching for any traps the Air Ovid might've left. He found nothing, but the warnings issued by the spirits confirmed some sort of danger lay ahead.

After an hour of climbing, the stairs ended at a broad, long hallway, stretching up at a slight angle, ending at a double door, its oak surface gleaming with varnish. Kwik gestured abruptly to small berths carved into the rock on the Spire along the hallway.

"Normally, the Divine sleep here," he explained. "Had I not dismissed them, they'd be here now." The Elf's blue eyes hardened. "Danger lies ahead, does it not?"

Darr nodded.

"Then I hope you're as skilled as I think you are."

Once, Darr had believed Kwik to be a clownish character. Now he saw another side to the man. In a moment's passing, Kwik traded his jovial outlook for the cold professionalism of a seasoned soldier. His eyes, now forged in steel, looked down at the handle of the door. One hand dropped to the hilt of his sword with precise fluidity, while the other reached for the handle. Kwik reminded him suddenly of Feywen Dery, of the way the once-prince could so quickly step into the role of a warrior.

Darr let his awareness merge further into the Currents, prepared to seek help from the Fire Archon at the first sign of danger. He'd gone through this twice now, and he knew what to expect. Darr steadied himself, keeping his fear in check. When he was ready, he nodded grimly to Kwik.

The oak doors opened. Golden light flashed into his eyes, and the Sephir of Air stood revealed on its altar, untouched and unharmed.

Chapter Thirty-Seven

"In the days that followed, Darr struggled with the loss of his brother, unaware that he nearly destroyed the balanced between the Sephirs. His despair opened him up to something I didn't think was possible. The Devoid found him. Using an Ogre Spirit Summoner as its puppet, the Devoid attempted to figure out how Darr was able to wield such power. I fear something much more sinister was at work though. I fear the Devoid sought only to upset Darr and then unleash his anger into the already fragile Currents. We're all fortunate that didn't happen."

~From the personal writings of the Divine, Zander

After an eternity, Conra dropped his arms from around Tamber's shoulders. They stepped back from one another, still touching as if no time had passed between them. The warmth rising within Jinn's chest began to cool.

"Grandmother, who is that?" the girl, Alacia, asked again at Tamber's side.

Tamber blinked. "Oh, Alacia, I'm sorry," she breathed. "This is...this is an old friend."

Conra laughed gently and waved. Tamber's granddaughter. Her little eyes sparkled the same way as her grandmother's.

Tamber's eyes darted to Conra, then to Jinn. "Would you and your friend...oh my, I don't even know your name, dear."

Conra cleared his throat and took a step back. Jinn smiled, leaning forward. "I'm sorry. Tamber, this is Jinn Reintol," Conra said. "I've been traveling with her and her brother for many weeks now. In fact, I don't know that I'd be here if it not for them."

A warm smile lifted Tamber's cheeks. "It's a pleasure to meet you, Jinn. We don't see many from your lands up here." She reached for Jinn's hand and led her to the doorway. "Come in, the both of you. I'll make some tea."

A knot formed in Jinn's throat as she stepped through the doorway. She'd been in this house before. Not this exact house, but a house just like it. Tamber's house looked much the same as Conra's cabin outside Deron. His cozy, little home contained trinkets and artifacts from who-knew where. Like Conra, Tamber collected ordinary things in much the same way.

Conra took a seat beside Jinn at a small table, and in silence, they watched Tamber go about making tea. After setting the water to boil, Tamber walked to the sitting room and preened over Alacia. She whispered into the little girl's ear, running her hand along the back of her head. After several minutes, Tamber dropped her hands into her lap, and Alacia hopped up. She walked with confidence to Conra and Jinn.

"I have to go outside and play. Grandmother says." Alacia gave a little bow. "It was nice to meet you both."

Joy welled up within Jinn at the girl's display. "It was nice to meet you, too, Alacia."

With a whirl of her little sundress and coat, Alacia ran for the door and disappeared into the daylight beyond, shutting the door softly behind her.

Tamber smiled warmly before going back to the business of preparing tea. No one said anything. Jinn suspected she didn't want to talk about anything unless she could look Conra in the eye. After a few minutes, Tamber set hot cups of tea on the table in front of them, along with a plate of small cakes. Tamber seated herself next to Conra, turning her chair to face him. Jinn took a sip of tea, staring past the steam rising around her face.

"I suppose the obvious question would be what've you been doing all these years?" Tamber's gaze turned somewhat fierce.

Conra cleared his throat. "After I left Qued, I traveled north for a time, thinking I might live in Mord, but even there, I still felt too close to what'd happened to Belmon. I wanted to get far away from what happened. Over the next three or four years, I wandered all over Ictar, bouncing from one town to the next, surviving by using my skills as a forager. I worked some odd jobs here and there when I wanted a bed to sleep in or some real food, but for the most part, I looked for a spot as far from Qued as I could."

Tamber listened to him talk without saying a word, her gaze locked on Conra's.

"After a time, I settled briefly in a city called Mertz," Conra continued. "It's far north of the Dwarf Borderlands, populated by Cortazians, but I found work as a carpenter. For a while, I thought it might be my new home, but I kept having nightmares of Belmon. I took that as a sign to leave again, and that's when I met Jinn's father, Hydle."

Without thinking, Conra turned and smiled at her. Jinn smiled back, and he quickly returned his attention to Tamber. "Hydle was traveling as well, and he told me of a place so quiet and secluded I'd never be bothered—the Lowlands of Deron. Hydle helped me locate there. He even helped me build the cabin I lived in all these years."

Tamber's face lost some color. For a moment, her mouth worked, but no words came out. When she finally spoke, her words came out broken and soft. "Conra, I never should've let you leave. I never should've supported your decision."

With a gnarled hand, Conra reached out and covered Tamber's hand where it curled around her cup. "I know," he said. "I wish it could have been otherwise, but to stay would've ruined our whole family."

Tamber shook her head. Conra wasn't seeing the despair in her face. "That's just it, Conra. Your leaving ruined us. It was hard enough losing Belmon, but with you gone, too, there was no one except your parents to turn to. They were kind, but they were old as well, and when our son came along, there was no support."

Jinn started, and her tea cup nearly tumbled from her fingers.

"Your son? Conra's son?" she asked, unable to help her words from tumbling out. Conra sat in frozen silence.

Tamber's lips curled. "Yes. Trent, I named him, after your father. And little Alacia is your granddaughter."

Jinn glanced at the closed door, wondering. Somewhere outside, Conra's granddaughter played in the sun.

"I have a son," Conra said, choking on the words. Tears sprung to his eyes. "A grand..."

Tamber reached out and took his hands in hers. "Trent married a lovely girl a few years ago. They're both foragers. I wish they were here to meet you."

"So you never remarried?" Conra asked, his voice barely audible.

"Of course not," Tamber rasped, taken aback by the question. "I was the one who convinced you to leave. How could you think I would betray you?"

Conra smiled. "I didn't think you would betray me. I figured you would've moved on."

"No, Conra, I could never move on after you." Tamber's face hardened. "Every morning I woke, I wondered if today you would come home. I willed it to happen."

Tamber leaned towards him and touched his face. "Even this morning," she whispered.

* * * *

Jinn, Conra, and Tamber talked through the afternoon. Tamber prepared lunch for them, inviting Alacia to come inside. Jinn watched Conra and the little girl while she ate, wondering what having Conra as a grandfather would be like. He'd been a recluse for so long, yet, watching them now, and knowing what kind of man he was, she had no doubts.

After lunch, Alacia went outside again to play. Jinn cleared the table and cleaned the dishes while Conra and Tamber spoke quietly at the table. Had she thought better of it, Jinn would've gone outside with Alacia. Maybe she would, after she finished the dishes.

In something short of a couple hours, Conra had turned into someone almost completely different. The loneliness and harshness Jinn had known all her life had turned to something soft and almost charming. After hearing Tamber and Conra talk, she doubted the old Elf would want to spend even another second without her. A knot formed in Jinn's throat at the realization. She doubted Conra would travel much further than Qued.

Conra smacked his arm down on the table, breaking the quiet intimacy shared between him and his wife. "You mean they gave up?" he asked, his voice rising in pitch. Jinn turned her head.

Tamber nodded, her eyes sad. "Yes. The Divine had nothing to go on. They didn't even try to figure out what really happened to Belmon." Tamber bowed her head, while Conra stared, open-mouthed.

I was a fool for leaving," Conra whispered.

Tears shimmered in Tamber's eyes. "No," she replied. "You were brave to do what you did. If you stayed, the Divine would've had you tried for using magic whether they had proof or not." She reached out and took his hand. "You know, Belmon wasn't the only one."

Jinn set the plate she was drying on the counter and turned around. *More people had died like Belmon had?*

Conra cocked his head. "What do you mean Belmon wasn't the only one? You mean others disappeared, too?"

Tamber shrugged. "At least two dozen people vanished within a couple of years after Belmon."

"Two dozen," Conra rasped, startled. He flicked a look at Jinn, then back to Tamber. "All the same as Belmon?"

Tamber leaned forward. "That's why the charges against you were dropped. The Divine declared there was a weakening in the Air Sephir. They called it an Ovid, and the only way to counter the problem was with the Fire Element."

"The torches," Jinn breathed. Tamber nodded.

Conra craned his head towards the front window, and Jinn followed his stare. At the base of Tamber's front steps, a single torch burned fast atop a metal stanchion. He stood up and walked to the window.

"Tamber, do the torches actually work?" Conra asked, turning back from the window.

"I suppose," she replied. "There hasn't been a disappearance in probably twenty years."

Conra stared down at the floor. "So the Divine ordered torches lit outside of homes and buildings and the disappearances stopped. What about the foragers? Did any of them vanish?"

"Not a single one in many years," Tamber answered. Worry flared in her face. "The foragers carry torches no matter what time of day. Trent tells me the Divine require them to set up perimeters using the torches."

Jinn stepped around the table and stood at Conra's side. She leaned in close. "This is connected to the Ovid, isn't it?" she asked.

Conra swallowed hard. "The Divine were always unwilling to face the truth right before their eyes. Just because you forbid something doesn't mean it vanishes."

He looked down into Jinn's eyes. "They hid the problem, but they never tried to fix it," he whispered harshly. "The Ovid hides in plain sight, somewhere, waiting for the perfect opportunity to strike. All this time, it's been waiting to strike, just like it did to Belmon. Just like it'll do to..."

Darr. Cold rushed into Jinn's chest, freezing the warmth.

"What's the matter?" Tamber asked, her face stricken. She rose to her feet.

Conra's gaze shot up and he reached out for his wife's hands. "I have to go to the Spire. I have to stop Jinn's brother."

Tamber shook her head. "But why?"

"Because he's in danger," he howled. "That Ovid never left Qued. It killed Belmon, and now it's going to kill Darr if I don't do something."

"But what can you possibly do?"

Conra looked down at Jinn. He saw something in her eyes, something that made him afraid, but a spark of recognition flared, too.

"I was the closest to the fire," Conra murmured, turning back to Tamber. "The Ovid attacked us both, but Belmon was further away and not shielded by the fire."

He reached up to Tamber's shoulder. "I know how to

bring out the Ovid. I know where it's hiding, and I know how to reveal it. I'm sorry, but I have to go. I have to face this."

Tamber held his gaze. "I understand," she breathed. "Just be safe. There is still much to be said between us, Conra." The old Elf smiled.

Conra bent down and kissed her softly on the mouth.

Chapter Thirty-Eight

"When Racall first came to me in Arcnor, before the arrival of Darr and Jinn, he did so in a dream. I'd dreamed of the Earth Archon several times over the years, so it was nothing new to me. He told me where he was going and why, as well as what to expect in the days ahead. I've always valued Racall's help. He owes me nothing, and yet he has given me the world in guidance. If the rest of Ictar knew how valuable the Archons are, they might just listen harder to the Spirit Summoners."

~From the personal writings of the Divine, Zander

At the top of the Spire, the Sephir of Air shone a pale gold against the darkening skies. Inside the oak doors, the altar room opened to the outside world, the rock cut away to screen out anything but the sky. The Sephir sat on its obelisk-like altar at the center of the room, its elongated, symmetrical body glittering with a deep amber color.

"It doesn't appear anything's wrong with it," Kwik said, sheathing his sword.

Darr couldn't agree. Tension filled every facet of the room, its source hidden, foreign. The spirits roared. Their whispers became the raging howl of a waterfall, unintelligible, but urgent and desperate. The Ovid had somehow disguised itself so well the spirits couldn't find it, but its feel, malevolent and chaotic, burned in the air.

Kwik Pantheo took a short step forward. "The Sephir is safe," he said, breathing a short sigh.

"No, it's not," Darr replied. He sifted through the energies and emotions swirling around him. "The Ovid is near."

Kwik's hand lowered to his sword again. "Do you know where?"

"No."

Nothing changed. The spirits continued their tirade of unease, and the unbalance in the connecting forces of the elements persisted, but nothing indicated its source.

Above their heads, the sun sank into the eastern horizon.

"Darr." Kwik broke the silence. "Is it possible we're in the wrong place? Could the Ovid be hiding somewhere else? The Ovid has been seen all over this valley." The Elf captain lowered his head and his despair echoed through the Currents. "This might not be the place it will appear."

How could that be? Darr thought. Every other time he'd fought one of the Ovids, he found it close to its Sephir. No, not close, in possession of it. The Ovids relied on the Sephir for sustenance.

His confidence rattled, and his firm roots in the Currents unraveled. The spirit realm shuttered and changed. A storm of malevolence roared its way to the surface of Darr's mind. In the distant sky, a single crow cawed into the coming night, angry. Another cry sounded, separate, overlapping the first. More cries joined in until an entire murder of cawing screams filled the sky, moving closer to the top of the Spire.

Darr plunged himself back into the Currents, but something prevented him from doing so. Confusion and rage swirled into complete upheaval. Emotions and memories ran rampant, and not just from people close by. They came from everywhere. The sensation numbed Darr. Not once had the Currents been so badly distorted that they forced his retreat.

The caws of the approaching crows became deafening. In an explosion of sound and light, they exploded up over the rim of the Sephir's altar room. Their bodies radiated the gold color of the Air Sephir. Cold blue eyes, burning beside razor sharp beaks, stared down at them, ravenous and bloodthirsty.

Kwik's sword came up, and the murder descended upon them. Robbed of his Summoning abilities, Darr drew the long knife he'd carried from home and held it defensively before him. He gritted his teeth and braced for the attack.

In a funnel of swirling gold, the crows dropped from the sky in a spiral. Kwik backed up against Darr. The crows tore into them like a hail of arrows, their weapons useless. Together, they ducked. Kwik fell over Darr, shielded him while trying to cover his own head. He wore light chainmail beneath his tunic, but that wouldn't save his hands and head. The murder screamed in rage, tearing through the room in a whirlwind of flapping wings. Their beaks ripped through clothing and flesh, cawing incessantly.

When at last the murder lifted back into the sky, circling overhead like vultures, Darr raised his head to assess the damage. He'd suffered a few cuts on the backs of his hand. Kwik had shielded him from the worst of it. At least a dozen slashes crisscrossed Kwik's head and arms.

"We have to get back to the tunnel," Kwik yelled. Blood smeared down the side of his face.

Darr needed no further direction. With his connection to the Currents temporarily severed and no weapons in which to fight, they needed another plan. In a huddle, they made a dash for the door, but the murder descended upon them like lightning, first blocking off the door, then beating them back towards the Sephir.

"Can't you do something?" Kwik screamed, his breath hot.

Darr calmed himself, submerging himself...

...the Currents closed fully around Darr.

Time stopped.

The crows, the Ovid, did not.

Even here, in the world of spirits and memory and illusion, the murderous crows held him tight. Reduced to shimmering flashes of amber, the crows surrounded him on all sides, their rage keeping the spirits away and Darr locked in place.

--Go back where you came from-- Darr commanded, but the Ovid ignored him, and rejected him from the Currents...

"Nothing," Darr cried, defeated. His head burned. He reached up and touched the wet, matted hair, bringing his fingers back dabbed with blood.

Kwik placed his hand on the Summoner's shoulder and leaned in close. "If this keeps up, there'll be nothing left of us. If anything, we'll bleed to death."

Darr's mind raced, and the murder dove at them a third time. Some of the birds crashed into the stone of the wall, but others met their target and flew away. Darr covered his head. Kwik howled in agony beside him, and Darr parted his fingers to see if he could help.

One of the crows had ripped off part of Kwik's ear.

The Elf tore the sleeve from his tunic and tied it haphazardly around his head. "We have to try for the door again," Kwik rasped.

The crows now spiraled around the room, no longer limited to the sky. Even if they made it to the doors, he didn't think a mile of stairs would deter the murder from following.

Darr breathed in and stood with Kwik at his side, their arms placed protectively before their faces. In a flurry of gold, the crows whipped past them and into them. Darr's hope fell away. In defeat, he collapsed on the floor.

Through the gaps in his fingers, the Sephir glowed furiously. If he could reach it, perhaps he could stop the birds. Serious injury, possibly death awaited him if he did, but what other options did he have?

A new presence exploded into the room, bursting through the double oak doors.

Conra?

Standing in the open doorway, Conra held two torches, one in each hand, blazing amid the maelstrom of crows. The disruption in the Currents faltered, and howls of dismay rose up from the returned spirits. Darr cried out to Conra to stop.

With his torches held before him like a shield, the old Elf charged through the crows, making his way to the Sephir. The birds, the Ovid, tore at Conra's exposed head, neck, and arms, lifting away in brilliant sprays of red. Blood streamed down his face, but he charged forward, undeterred.

"Conra! Stop!"

Jinn? No, get away!

When Conra reached the Sephir of Air, Darr stood up. The old Elf thrust his torches into it, and like dry kindling, the Sephir burst into flames.

Everything changed. The light itself changed as Conra

dropped to the floor. Around him, the crows faltered. The cries of the murder silenced together, and the crows lost shape, swirling around the room like falling leaves. The tattered golden lights drifted together into a single mass before the Sephir.

Too late. Darr's connection to the Currents fell into place, and he summoned the Archon of Fire. The Archon merged with him, drawn into the physical world at his command. Darr's open hands lit up like torches. He stepped forward, undaunted by the intimidating figure coalescing before him.

Wind and lightning erupted from out of the mass of golden light and a winged creature burst into view, its yellow eyes burning with madness. It screamed once in hatred, its leathery wings beating wildly at the Summoner.

Darr craned his head, unafraid, and thrust his flaming hands forward. Twin pillars of fire exploded into the Ovid, picking it up and slamming it back against the wall of the Spire, holding it firmly in place. The fire tore into the Ovid, banishing it back into the darkness of the Currents as it screamed in a furious struggle.

The magic surged through Darr, heat that pumped in tune with his heartbeat. The Archon of Fire guided him, and with his emotions firmly held in check, Darr focused his attack into one swift strike. Never had he been so receptive to the will of his Archon and in complete control of his summoning.

The Ovid pushed back from the wall, screaming in an attempt to break away, but Darr's magic enveloped it. An eerie shriek burst outward before the fire died away. Not a trace of ash wafted through the air. The Element of Fire had consumed the Air Ovid completely.

At the center of the room, the Sephir of Air burned bright amber. Its Light reconnected to its altar. Darr's connection to the Currents fell away, but he didn't lose consciousness. The merging of his experiences and memories with his thoughts and emotions had kept him secure. A sense of elation filled him.

His gaze lowered to Conra.

Conra lay on his back at the foot of the altar, his bloodied face staring upward. Deep cuts covered his entire body, the worst of it around his face and neck. Blood leaked everywhere. Through the Currents, the old Elf's Light slipped away from the physical world.

Darr dropped to his knees. Others gathered around him. *Jinn? Kwik and Aryana? Elven soldiers?* It didn't matter. He cradled Conra's head, bringing him close. The old Elf's eyes flickered open, and Darr couldn't believe what he saw, what the Currents confirmed.

Conra was happy.

"I'm sorry, Boy," the old Elf whispered, his throat thick with fluid. "I guess I should've brought...a shield..." He laughed gently, followed by several racking coughs that shook his fragile body.

Darr shook his head. "We can bind your wounds. We can get you down to a healer."

Conra coughed again, but it sounded more like a gruff laugh. "You know better than anyone. I'm not here for much longer. At least...my soul will be safe."

Frustration shook Darr's body. Jinn hovered close, her eyes blurred by tears. She couldn't help.

No one could help.

Conra coughed hard, and he raised his hand enough to motion Darr closer. "I did that for Belmon..." he whispered hoarsely. "I spent all those years running when I should've been here...standing up for what I always knew was right. Now I can say...I've done just that." A smile crossed his lips. "Remember what I said. Don't run away from what you believe, Boy. Face it...head on."

Darr smiled despite the tears blinding him. Those same words, uttered to him once before by his mother, empowered him.

Conra's grip slipped and his breathing slowed. A long time passed before his eyes opened again, but when they did, his smile faded.

"Thanks for bringing me back, Darr. Tell Tamber..."

His breathing stopped. In a beautiful rush, Conra's Light scattered into the Currents, returning his life and memories to the spirits.

Chapter Thirty-Nine

"Racall eventually led Darr and his companions to Arcnor and to me. I was delighted, almost giddy, to meet them all, especially Jinn. Every Covenant Bearer has spent their lives reading about the Chosen of the Light, never knowing when the time might come when they would be revealed. To have met Jinn Reintol is an honor, not only for myself, but for all the Covenant Bearers who came before me."

~From the personal writings of the Divine, Zander

The Seeker mists stretched wide across the western side of the Ladornaleah, holding a firm grasp over the night. A solid wall of gray, the mists swirled softly, undisturbed by even the slightest breeze in the air.

From the base of the Angleire leading up to Exed, Feywen braced himself for the inevitable attack. As a commander now, he'd be able to search out and fill any voids in their defense, a position once held by Lacdur. Will my fate be the same, Feywen wondered.

The mists split apart, and the Soul Seekers bled into the night, a blot of blackness against the already darkened landscape. The Soul Seekers swept across the plains towards the Ictarian infantry. Dwarf, Cortazian, Elf, and Ogre--they stood defiant against the staggering odds before them, defending the plains fronting Exed.

"Stand your ground," the voice of Bru Kiln Tole rang out, rattling the air itself. "Do not let them pass."

The two forces met. Jagged metal scraped across wood and iron, a shriek coupled with the screams of dying men. The Ictarians did not falter. The shock of the initial attack reverberated across the battlefield, but the soldiers resisted it and fought their way forward. The Seekers pressed against the Ictarians, their sheer numbers a threat. A weaker force would've fallen back.

The pulse of the army stopped, halted by confusion.

Feywen straightened atop his mount. On the northern flank, something caused the infantry soldiers to lose ground. Somehow, they died where they stood. They'd lost the ability to fight.

The heavy cavalry led by Alman Ohnler rushed in, and Feywen whistled sharply to his mount and followed. *What trickery are the Soul Seekers using this night?*

At the north flank, soldiers cleared away from their fallen brethren. The Seekers filled in around them. *Why? Why do we abandon our own men?* Feywen lifted his head, peering pass the surge of Seekers in the near dark. He grabbed a torch from one of the nearby captains and threw it into the Seeker horde. The orange light spread for a minute, illuminating enough of the situation for Feywen to pause in disbelief.

In the middle of the Ladornaleah, the most fertile soil in all of Ictar, a sinkhole had opened up, binding the infantry and making them easy prey for the Seekers. Even some of Ohnler's heavy horse caught themselves, unable to avoid the massive width and depth of the hole.

Feywen backed off. The Soul Seekers bore down on them. They sensed a weakness. The front lines could fall apart at any moment.

Feywen raced for the Angleire, searching for anyone who could help.

"Vertain," he cried, catching sight of the Daraven captain alongside a regiment of archers.

"What's going on out there?" Vertain asked, frustration lining his face.

Feywen shook his head. "A sink hole. I don't know how or why, but almost two hundred soldiers are trapped. Deploy the fire archers. We have to break up the Seekers so we can get them out."

Vertain hesitated and looked up to the heights of the Angleire, as if he might find an answer there. When he turned back, his eyes brightened. "I don't think you'll need us, Commander."

Out of the darkness, the gangly forms of the Ogres

poured onto the battlefield. Led by Tella Shaw, his wicked sword flying from left to right, the Ogres cut into the Seeker ranks ahead of the heavy cavalry. The Ogres tore into the Seekers, pushing them past the failing infantry soldiers while the cavalry covered their retreat.

"They came just in time," Vertain said, sagging back into the saddle.

Feywen frowned. "We're lucky tonight. That's all."

Vertain said nothing. Together they watched the rest of the battle unfold, but the Ogres had already won the battle for them. Well before sunrise, the Ictarian Army cleared the battlefield almost two hundred yards further from Exed than they'd begun the night. Cheers and cries of triumph exploded from the throats of the soldiers. The night became the sweetest of victories, one long overdue.

Vertain leaned close to Feywen, his voice low. "Our men needed this, Feywen Dery. We should be happy any time we walk away from a battlefield."

Feywen breathed out sharply. "It was no coincidence we won."

All expression dropped from Vertain's face. "You're talking about the traitor."

Feywen didn't reply.

For a long moment, Vertain stared at him before letting out a slow breath. His shoulders sagged. "You've been under a lot of pressure," he said, moving close. "After what happened to your family, your city, and now your closest friend, you're a wounded man. We've all been defeated by what the Seekers have done. Some of us have grown weary, and some have given up completely. Some, like you, have had lapses in judgment."

Feywen furrowed his brow in confusion. A spark of anger flared. "Judgment? Do you think I'm making this up?"

Vertain lowered his gaze and swallowed hard. "Think about what happened during the Aeon Wars, Feywen," he pleaded. "In the face of the power released during the wars, many soldiers lost faith in themselves and their army. They began to see things that weren't there, things that would explain their loss of faith. Things like traitors who hampered their efforts at every turn."

Feywen turned back to the battlefield, steadying himself. He breathed deeply in an effort to quell the anger smoldering inside him.

"I personally scouted these regions yesterday afternoon," Feywen said, his hands drawn tight against his mount's reins. "Not me, nor my men, found any sign of a sinkhole. This is stable, fertile ground. A sinkhole forming in the midst of this battle is nothing short of power unleashed by something other than the Soul Seekers. Something else is at work here."

Vertain looked around, as if checking to see if anyone else had heard.

Feywen leaned closer to him. "I heard what happened at Walvor Bridge. The structure almost didn't collapse because one of the engineers was killed from behind. We almost lost that battle."

"That engineer was caught in the middle of a massive retreat coupled with a surge of fighting," Vertain rasped, whipping his head back around. "Please, Feywen, listen to yourself. You weren't even there to witness what happened at Walvor. This traitor of yours is turning into an obsession."

Feywen straightened. No one save Nidic Waq believed him about the traitor. It was pointless to try.

He returned the Daraven's gaze. "I hope you're right, Vertain. I hope it's only the Soul Seekers we fight. But that won't stop me from looking."

"Then there's nothing I can do for you, my prince," Vertain said, holding his head high.

Feywen gave a low whistle, turning his mount around. Steadily, he rode away from Vertain, away from the Angleire, out to the darkness away from the light of the watch fires.

If Lacdur still lived, he'd have helped him, believed him. Feywen laughed quietly. That wasn't possible, of course. He'd have to draw out the traitor alone. If Vertain felt this strongly, the other leaders would likely feel much the same.

Vertain was right about one thing though.

Feywen did need some faith. He needed faith he could find the traitor before it destroyed any chance of halting the Soul Seeker advance.

Chapter Forty

"As soon as they arrived in Arcnor, Darr met the Earth Ovid head on. Though much of the battle was hidden from the others and myself, Darr related a difficult fight. It wasn't until he fully summoned the Air Archon, merging its body with his own, that Darr was able to reclaim the Sephir of Earth. Again, I cannot comprehend how he does it. I fear for the day when the Divine sect learns of such power. They won't likely stand for Spirit Summoners to be around."

~From the personal writings of the Divine, Zander

With their victory secured, the Ictarian soldiers went about preparing for another night's battle. They won last night, but the Seekers proved repeatedly with any victory, a crushing defeat would follow. Spirits ran high among the troops, but their fears twisted the Currents nonetheless.

Nidic Waq folded his arms, pulling his robes tight against his body. Overhead, the steely gray sky threatened rain, perhaps even snow. From where he stood along the upper slope of the Angleire, a thick coating of frost crusted the grass of the Ladornaleah.

"The Elements return to us," Feywen Dery called behind him. Nidic Waq felt his Light when he was still a hundred yards away. He continued to watch the activity along the grasslands.

"Three of the four Sephirs have now been restored," he said. He breathed deeply, reminding himself of the Air Sephir's return. "The unbalance blighting the seasons is finally beginning to fade."

Feywen cleared his throat, hesitant before he spoke. "Once Darr restores the Fire Sephir, the Soul Seekers will be banished from the land, will they not?"

Nidic Waq didn't answer right away. Below them, a group of soldiers began unloading barrels from a cart. "The unbalance between the Sephirs allowed the Devoid to summon the Soul Seekers," he answered. "A full restoration of the Sephirs will reseal the Devoid's prison, and the summoning that brings the Soul Seekers will come to an end."

"But..." Feywen said.

A sardonic smile tilted the prophet's mouth, the purpose of Feywen's visit revealed. "The Devoid has demonstrated itself capable of acts well beyond sending messages out of its prison," Nidic Waq answered. "It can manipulate Lights in the physical world, sending not only its magic across the Currents and into Ictar, but also its presence. So long as its presence persists here in the physical world, the restoration of the Sephirs won't save us."

He turned his head. Feywen's stare locked on his own. "This is what you've come to ask me about, isn't it? The traitor you cannot seem to find. The one who eludes us both."

Feywen gritted his teeth, turning his gaze away in frustration. "I spoke with Blaque Eris about the presence of a traitor this morning. He sent me away. He doesn't believe it possible."

"Lucky for us, Blaque Eris doesn't command this military," the prophet replied. "Come. Walk with me. It's time our leaders know what we face."

He lowered his arms and started away, climbing the trails and ramps of the Angleire. Feywen followed closely beside him, eager, but doubtful. Feywen believed what he believed. He couldn't understand it, though. The Devoid manipulated a body within their army, creating a traitor bent on destroying the resistance against the Soul Seekers. Perhaps this person betrayed them willingly, or perhaps he'd merely become a victim of the Devoid's manipulations. Either way, the leadership of the Ictarians must realize the danger inherent in such a person.

At the top of the Angleire, well before the gates of the city, the leaders' encampment stretched out in a mass of tents, ringed by earthworks to deter their enemy.

A pair of guards greeted them. "Good afternoon,

Prophet, Commander Dery," one of the men called out. "Lord Forn and Lord Terwin expected to see you today. They're waiting in the long tent over there."

Nidic Waq smiled lopsidedly. "Thank you."

The guard let them pass, and together they walked towards the long tent where the kings held strategy meetings with the other leaders.

"What are you going to do, Prophet?" Feywen asked, his voice low. "They already know we suspect a traitor, but no one yet has given it any consideration."

Nidic Waq lifted his head. "Then we will put our suspicions to an end. Just follow my lead."

When they reached the long tent, another pair of guards allowed them to pass. Inside, Lendor Terwin and Ariel Forn stood at a table with a number of their aids, taking notes over a set of maps.

Lendor's blond hair and beard glowed gold from the light of the oil lamps. "Nidic Waq. Commander Dery. I'm glad you could come."

The prophet nodded briskly. "We came to inform you we have found the traitor. He won't be meddling with our plans any longer."

Every gaze in the room turned on them. Ariel Forn, the guards, the messengers, and aids. Feywen Dery stiffened at his side, but Nidic Waq sensed no distress from him.

Ariel straightened and dismissed the aids around him. A fire burned behind his stare. "Please give us a moment to clear the room."

The guards and aids scurried away. Lendor and Ariel stood rigid while the room emptied, shock and anger flowing out from them. When the room was empty, Lendor stepped forward, his sharp Elven features uncharacteristically arrogant.

"Nidic Waq," Lendor called out. "I believe I speak for both Lord Forn and myself when I say matters such as these would best be kept quiet."

"Lord Terwin. Lord Forn," he said and bowed before them. "Please forgive my indiscretion."

Lendor Terwin shrugged, waving his hand. "There's no need for that, Prophet. Please, tell us what you've found."

Nidic Waq stepped forward, leaving Feywen in his shadow. "As Feywen and I have long suspected, there was a traitor among the ranks of the Ictarian Army," he declared. He held his tall frame at full height. "But no more. The traitor has been discovered, and he will trouble us no more."

Ariel and Lendor exchanged a glance before returning their looks of confusion. "Please, Nidic Waq. Tell us more," Ariel asked, his voice a sharp knife cutting through the tension.

The prophet frowned, letting his confidence flow through the Currents and into the two kings. "The traitor was an infantry soldier from Jacova. He was a Spirit Summoner, though he never knew his power. His connection to the Currents allowed the Devoid to reach him and corrupt him. The Devoid has been hiding him like a prize ever since."

Nidic Waq folded his arms before him, turning his head back towards Feywen. "The Commander and I discovered our traitor tampering with barrels they were wheeling out to the fields today. I confronted him and discovered the Devoid's presence. When I attempted to hold the man, the Devoid killed him, incinerated him actually."

"Is this true?" Lendor asked, stepping closer, his voice shaken. "Has there really been a traitor all this time?"

Feywen straightened. He hesitated, but he answered, "Yes, my lord."

Lendor stared at him for a long moment, perhaps judging him, perhaps fearing him for sensing something he couldn't. He breathed a sigh and returned his gaze to Nidic Waq.

"Then whatever accidents have befallen us should be put to rest," Lendor said.

"With this man's death, the Devoid has lost its ability to manipulate our forces," Ariel added, now standing beside the Elf King.

Nidic Waq nodded. "It is over. For now. This doesn't mean the Devoid will end its meddling. Your men should be extra vigilant now, for the Devoid may grow desperate."

The two kings nodded in unison. Nidic Waq bowed his head. "If it's acceptable, I'd like to return to the field with Feywen. Even with the traitor gone, there may still be holes in our defense."

"Yes," Lendor breathed. "Yes, please, go at once. And thank you."

The prophet smirked and turned away quickly. Feywen fell in beside him. The tent flaps fell away, greeting him with the cold of the late afternoon. When they were away from the encampment, Feywen ran in front of him, bringing him to a halt.

"What was that?" he asked, flinging his arms, gesturing towards the camp. "Some might consider what we just did treason. Unless, of course, you really did figure out who the traitor is."

Nidic Waq put a finger to his lips. He knelt down beside Feywen, tilting his head toward the men passing them by. "Do you hear it?" he whispered.

Feywen glared at him. "What? Do I hear what?"

"Can't you hear them talking?" the prophet replied, closing his eyes. "Ten minutes ago, no one believed there was a traitor. Now, the word spreads of the traitor's death."

He touched Feywen's shoulder, lending him a small taste of his senses through the Currents. As one, they heard the whispers of the men around them, echoing through the spirit realm. Feywen listened with him a moment, then shook his body away.

"What's the point of this? What does it matter if they believe now?" he asked.

Nidic Waq kept his eyes closed. "Word will spread. Eventually, it'll reach the ears of the real traitor. With the Currents clouded, he won't be able to distinguish the truth of things. He will believe he's safe to do whatever he plans to do next."

Feywen's eyes narrowed. "And what does he plan to do next?"

His eyes opened. "Destroy us." Nidic Waq smiled when

he turned his gaze on Feywen. "This time we have to be looking when he tries."

* * * *

Before sunset, the army leaders met within the seclusion of their well-guarded tent. As expected, the Seeker mists had not completely reformed. After a thorough sweep of the region by Feywen Dery and Alman Ohnler's horsemen, no one expected a flanking maneuver either. For another night, the Ladornaleah would be safe.

Nidic Waq stood away from the leaders congregating about the tent, his thoughts cynical while strategies formed before him.

"My men buried almost two hundred barrels of maugwrith today," Bru Kiln Tole announced. His barrel-shaped body leaned heavily against the table before him. "We'll complete work tomorrow by midmorning."

"And you're sure this will work?" Lendor asked, a regal beacon.

A wicked smile twisting Bru Kiln Tole's feature. "Nothing is certain, my lord," he said. "This plan worked at Vanla on a much smaller scale, but I can't guarantee anything here."

Lendor's features didn't change.

"General Tole is correct," Blaque Eris agreed, his voice grating the silence. "Where the Seekers are concerned, we've faced more than one surprise. Our strategy is sound though. Once the Seekers are drawn to the Angleire, we'll ignite the first line of maugwrith and cut them off. As the Ogres and Daravens secure the flanks, the second line, two hundred yards out into the Ladornaleah, will be ignited as well."

Bru Kiln Tole grunted. "Once that work is completed, of course."

Eris ignored him. "Once the Daravens and Ogres pull from the flanks, the remaining barrels will be ignited, cutting the Seekers off on all sides."

"And what if the Devourers show?" Ariel asked. His dark eyes glittered.

"The maugwrith plan will be put on hold then," Eris stated. "With our numbers and the strategies we've implemented, I don't believe the Devourers will pose the danger they once did. But if the Soul Seekers show, then we'll burn them all to ash."

Despite the cheers that followed, Lendor and Ariel remained skeptical. Good, Nidic Waq thought. Someone needed to stay sharp. General Eris grew too confident, and the other leaders appeared to have followed.

"This won't work the way Eris expects it to, will it?" Feywen asked, materializing out of the commotion.

Nidic Waq closed his eyes. A piece to Eris's plan remained vulnerable, corruptible.

"There are many points in which this plan might fail, but the flanks pose the greatest weakness," he replied.

"Then we'll have to be watching carefully," Feywen agreed.

Chapter Forty-One

"I met with Darr and Jinn after the confrontation with the Earth Ovid for I knew secrets about the Chosen of the Light that I must share with them. As a Covenant Bearer, I'm privy to knowledge specific to their journey ahead, and I told them what I could. In turn, they shared with me what they'd been through. I suspect they have left out details, just as I have, but I've gained much respect for these two young people. They've been through much, and they'll go through more, but they will do so with the strength they've shown."

~From the personal writings of the Divine, Zander

Sunrise over the Spire spilt warm sunlight over Darr's face, but it did nothing to ease the cold. A weight rested on his chest, causing his breaths to come in shallow but even stretches. He couldn't relax. He couldn't focus on anything except the crypt.

To the side of the Spire, a black hole opened into the mountain, marked by columns on either side of the entrance. A small gathering of men and women, Darr and Jinn included, stood at the entrance and waited. Blood pounded in Darr's ears.

Kwik told him the crypt normally held the bodies of dead royalty and leaders, but today, it would hold the body of a true hero of the Elven nation. Conra's sacrifice deserved no less.

A procession of Divine appeared through the vineyards surrounding the Pathenine, a ghostly trail. The blood pounded in Darr's ears, an echo of his heart. Jinn's shoulder touched his, her body rigid, her head held even.

When the bier appeared between the white-robed Divine, Jinn cried softly. Darr held her close, but the cold inside still didn't loosen. Even when Conra's body passed, his aged face cleaned from the damage he'd sustained from the Ovid, the cold left Darr numb.

The Divine continued towards the opening of the crypt. It stopped briefly before an old woman and a young girl. Tamber and Alacia. He'd never met them, but he recognized them from Conra's memories before they scattered into the Currents. Tamber bent close. Her hand fell on Conra's chest, and her gray hair hung like a veil over her face.

When Tamber finally pulled away, she dropped to her knees. Her granddaughter hugged her, and together, they disappeared behind the Divine procession.

Kwik Pantheo and Aryana fell into line behind the bier. As members of the Elven royal family, they alone could enter the crypt along with the Divine. Darr blinked, and the entire procession disappeared into the blackness of the mountain.

Tamber and Alacia knelt on the ground outside the crypt. The old woman lifted her head and met his gaze. *What draws me to her? Is it you, Conra? Your Light touched mine when you died. Does Tamber see that now?*

Tamber stood up, straightened her dress, and took Alacia's hand in her own. Darr let his arm fall from around his sister's shoulders. "Please wait here. I'll be right back," he soothed. Jinn nodded and turned away.

The pounding in Darr's ears deafened him while he walked through the grass. Sunlight poured into his face, contrasting the cold air outside his body, matching the cold within. His gaze locked with Tamber's. He drew close to her.

For an instant, her age melted away. He saw her as Conra saw her, so stunningly beautiful he'd never forget her face.

"He never got to tell you how much he loved you," Darr said. "In all the years he was gone, he never for a moment forgot about you."

Tamber's eyes sparkled, and the smile that followed jarred something within. "I never forgot him either," she replied.

With the little girl's hand tightly caught in her own, Tamber turned and began walking back through the grass towards the city. She didn't look back.

Warmth welled up within Darr. He crossed his arms

protectively, allowing the cold to break free.

* * * *

Darr spent the rest of the day walking the grounds of the Pathenine. Jinn walked with him for a time, but eventually she understood his need to be alone and left him. Two lives were now lost in the name of his quest, a quest he believed early on to be a light-hearted journey of discovery. What he wanted more than anything was to go home. With one more Sephir left and three Chosen still missing, his wish would go unanswered. He would forge ahead. Erec and Conra's deaths would not be in vain.

The branches of a willow, its limbs drooping low, brushed against his face. Darr jerked away. The wings of the crows, the body of the Ovid, felt much the same. The treated wounds on his cheek and neck pulsed, a gentle reminder of their conflict.

The bottoms of Darr's feet ached. He'd been walking for a while now, and he hadn't slept since he confronted the Ovid the night before. Tomorrow, he'd be leaving Qued with Jinn on the last leg of their journey. The shade offered by the willow called to him, urging him to take shelter beneath its boughs.

Darr collapsed against the trunk of the willow. His muscles relaxed, and his breath steamed the air before his face in flowery clouds. He leaned his head against the trunk, pulled his arms tight against his body, and closed his eyes...

...and opened them.

The Tower Castle rose up in front of him. He no longer questioned it. He'd never gazed up at the ivy-covered walls in the physical world. Still, he dreamt of a place he'd never been. He'd heard the castle described to him in fireside tales and by Feywen Dery, but never in this detail.

This was no ordinary dream, of course. His body slept, but his mind traveled to the Currents, marked by the distant swirling lights of the spirits. A pale blue light replaced the familiar wisteria glow, but the feel of the spirit realm remained. *This dream was a summons.*

Carefree, Darr's footfalls crunched on the gravel path as he made his way towards the castle. In previous visits, the garden bustled with activity, but no Elders walked the paths this day. Alone, Darr admired the beauty of the gardens, breathing in their life. The air, sweet and warm, filled his lungs.

Had he not lost another of his friends, he'd be happy right now.

"I apologize for all that you and your friends have gone through," a voice said behind him, gentle and familiar.

The presence of the man behind him didn't startle him, even though he appeared out of the ether of the Currents. On his last visit, before Jinn claimed the Moonstone, he'd been unsure of this man's presence, but this time, he expected it.

"Caeranol," Darr breathed.

Darr turned. Greater in height and build than Nidic Waq, Caeranol didn't possess the prophet's forbidding aura. His weathered face, framed by shoulder length hair, held great warmth and kindness. In life, this is how Caeranol must have appeared to others. As an Archon, he could only mimic what he'd once been.

The High Elder smiled, his dark eyes gentle, and guided Darr to a bench. Darr followed because it was his purpose to do so. Together they sat in silence, watching the beauty of the garden and the wind dancing through the trees. The sweet smell of flowers and soil wafted through the air.

"Your brother and your friend fought valiantly for you," Caeranol said. His voice tuned finely to the tranquility of the moment. "You couldn't have been surrounded by better company. It's hard to see it now, after all you've been through, but you're close to completing the journey Nidic Waq set you on."

Darr smiled. The truth in this place rang through the air.

"Do you know why I have brought you here?" Caeranol asked.

A shiver froze Darr's body. He continued to watch his surroundings. Caeranol leaned close.

"You have found another of the Chosen of the Light."

Darr closed his eyes. The words struck him one syllable at a time, happy and sad at the same time. When he opened his eyes, the Archon smiled at him. "Who is it?" Darr asked.

"Kwik Pantheo is the Guardian of the Light."

It made sense, Darr thought. When he'd first met Kwik, he felt a connection to him, something odd and unreachable. He assumed the feeling came from Aryana, a Spirit Summoner herself.

"He is to carry the Vedin Kael," Darr stated. Nidic Waq's story remained fresh in his mind. "I know nothing about it or where to find it."

Caeranol laughed gently. "Kwik will know how to find it. Trust him. Let him lead the way forward, and he will find it."

Had he been in the physical world, Darr would've been adrift in questions, yet here, he drifted. His questions here were small and inconsequential. He knew what Caeranol would say before the words left his lips, but the question of how he'd explain to Kwik continued to rise to the surface.

Again, Caeranol laughed. "You will find a way to convince him, Darr. It is your purpose to do so."

Darr met Caeranol's gaze. "What should I tell him?"

"Tell him anything you wish," Caeranol replied, shaking his head. "I suspect you will tell him everything you know. His trust in you will be earned when you trust in him. His beliefs are different, but when you break them down, they are not unlike your own."

The two sat in silence. This space in the Currents was a sanctuary, a place of solitude and reflection.

How were the Chosen of the Light drawn to him? Was it simple chance that his sister had accompanied him on a journey across Ictar? Was it coincidence that took Serin Pantheo away from Qued, leaving his son, Kwik, to meet Darr? Would the other Chosen find him the same way Kwik and Jinn had found him? Were they looking for him now?

"When I set my plans into motion for the Chosen of the Light, I saw only the end result," Caeranol said. Concern lined his face. "I left all control on who and where and when to the spirits. Perhaps I planned poorly. Perhaps it never mattered because my faith in the spirits is so strong."

Caeranol shifted his body, holding his head even with the horizon. "I wish I knew the Chosen so I could protect them, but I believe the spirits have already acquiesced to my wish. They guide you, Summoner. They have shaped time and fate, to bring you and the Chosen together. You are the emissary of the Chosen, and their protector."

The words sunk into his body like the warmth of a fire, comforting words. Early on in his journey, Darr had wished to know his place as a Spirit Summoner. Now he understood.

Darr furrowed his brow. "If I truly am being guided to find the Chosen and protect the Sephirs, it means my actions are out of my control. Should I forgive myself for all the mistakes I've made along the way? I don't think I can."

"I wouldn't expect you to," Caeranol soothed. "Just because the spirits guide you to the Chosen, doesn't absolve you from the choices you make. It's good you understand that. It's important. But you also must realize others make choices as well."

Caeranol stood, his body blocking out the sunlight. The surrounding images of trees and sky began to break apart and fade. The textures and smells of the garden melted into the blue light of the Currents around them. After a moment, nothing remained to look at except the pinpricks of luminescence that made up his own Light.

From the ether, Caeranol's voice echoed clearly. "I meant what I said, Darr. I apologize for all that has happened to you. You are strong and brave. I am proud of the journey you've made...

...When Darr opened his eyes, night had fallen.

The air had grown so cold his checks were numb. He brought his hands to his face in an attempt to warm them. Above his head, a scattering of stars twinkled through the hanging willow branches. After a moment, he rose and walked back towards the Pathenine. His thoughts lingered on Conra and his brother, but his heart pounded anxiously for the living around him. Jinn would be worried about him. So would Kwik and Aryana.

When he found them, he would explain everything. Kwik would find it difficult to accept. He might become angry, but not likely. Kwik understood the difference between what was right and what was lawful. His actions atop the Spire yesterday proved that.

By morning, Jinn and he would leave for the northern Elven territories in search of the Fire Sephir, and Kwik Pantheo would be at their side.

Chapter Forty-Two

"I couldn't tell them everything. The Covenant doesn't allow it. By interfering too heavily, I might disrupt the path the spirits had chosen for them, even as muddled as it is. I could only guide them to the places the Divine knew, and then, I could only give the faintest indication. In some ways, I feel that I betrayed them, that I left them blind as they headed into the storm, but I know that's not the way of things. Like them, I am also a pawn of Caeranol and of the spirits."

~From the personal writings of the Divine, Zander

"Darr," Jinn rasped, her voice a near whisper.

She peeked around the corner of the sitting room he'd occupied with Kwik moments ago. With the Elf's departure, she revealed her presence. Darr smiled and walked towards her. Jinn's slender arms closed about him in an embrace. His insides warmed, closing over the wound Conra's death had left on him, allowing him to heal.

"Where have you been all day?" she asked, her head resting on his shoulder.

"I fell asleep in the orchard," he answered. "When I woke, I came back to talk to Kwik.

Jinn pulled away, and a twinge of deceit rippled through the Currents. "You know something," he said. His gaze held her steady.

Jinn hesitated. "I overheard you talking to Kwik."

Darr waited a moment then smiled. "Did you think I would be upset? Why try to hide it?"

"I thought you'd be upset. I was blatantly spying on you," she replied, her words stressed. "You kept to yourself all day. I figured you wanted to keep private whatever you discussed with Kwik."

He'd kept to himself in order to sort through his emotions, weighing the rights and wrongs of what he hoped to accomplish and looking back on all it had cost him.

"I needed some time to myself," he said. He leaned towards her. "So how much did you hear?"

Jinn scrunched her nose, resisting the answer. "Enough to know Kwik is one of the Chosen. Is he going to join us?"

"I'm not sure," Darr said, lowering his gaze. "We'll have to give him some time. I don't think he knows yet."

Jinn stepped back, folding her arms before her. "I still don't understand how you keep finding us."

Darr shook his head. "I think this is all much more than simple coincidence. It's not like Caeranol's magic is randomly selecting the Chosen and we're bumping into them. Caeranol set all this in place thousands of years ago, leaving the spirits to guide it, and even though the Devoid has confused the spirits, it no longer matters. Whatever their plans, they set them in motions long ago. They've been able to manipulate time so the Chosen find each other through me."

Jinn shrugged. She rarely saw purpose in puzzling through something she couldn't understand.

"So are we still leaving in the morning?" she asked.

"I don't know. We must wait to hear from Kwik."

Kwik had been receptive to most everything he'd said. He'd barely flinched at the story of the Chosen, let alone the admission that he was the Guardian of the Light. He accepted the title with honor. However, it bothered Kwik that he'd have to leave Qued on a journey from which he might never return.

"I think he'll come," Darr said at last. "He needs time to sort everything out."

"Hopefully," Jinn whispered.

Darr suggested they get some sleep. Morning would come quickly. They must be prepared to leave when required to. He gave Jinn another hug, holding her close, grateful for her presence. When they released each other, they walked in silence towards their rooms.

* * * *

Darr tumbled through the warm darkness of his dreams, a dance of eerie light and sound. He fell without rhythm, bouncing from one idea to another, content with not knowing his final destination.

It all ended with a knock.

His eyes fluttered open. Darr sat up in his bed, unhindered by lingering sleep. The knock came again without urgency, but Darr threw off the covers and quickly dressed. He opened the door to Kwik and Aryana Pantheo.

"Good morning, Darr," Aryana greeted, her blond hair neatly framing her face.

The Summoner grinned and started to reply, but Kwik cut him off. "We'd like to talk with you for a moment," he said.

Darr pressed his lips together, ending his grin. He'd seen Kwik the night before, but he flinched anyway. The cuts shrouding Kwik's face stood out in the morning light. The stark white of a bandage, partially covered by the toque he wore, covered his torn ear. The Air Ovid had left its mark on Kwik.

He opened the door wide, beckoning them to sit at a small table in his room. Kwik and Aryana entered, closing the door behind them. They each took a seat, and in silence, watched each other across the table. Within moments, Aryana became present in the Currents, her Light ringing out. Darr smiled, aware of her intentions.

"I wanted to speak with you myself," she said, her brow furrowed. "I want to be sure what you have told Kwik is the truth."

Darr shot a glance at Kwik. Trust between two strangers was often difficult. He smiled weakly, and Kwik returned his gesture with a curt nod.

"Kwik is the Guardian of the Light," he said to Aryana. The truth of his words rang across the Currents. "I was told this by Caeranol himself. He summoned me in my sleep, drawing me to his place within the Currents where he watches over Ictar."

Aryana remained motionless, her stare intimidating.

Darr kept his emotions firmly in check.

"Is it true your sister is also one of the Chosen?" she asked.

Darr nodded in agreement.

"And it is also true she carries a talisman that will help destroy the Devoid?"

"Yes."

"Kwik, too, is destined to carry a talisman into battle?"

"Yes."

"Will you be able to protect my husband on this journey?"

Aryana's eyes glistened. Darr's breath caught in his chest. He locked his gaze with Aryana. "If necessary," he replied, "I'll sacrifice myself for the Chosen of the Light. I'll follow in Conra's and my brother's footsteps, and give my life for them. They will be the ones who save all of Ictar, not me."

The words were out before he realized how truthful they were. The room turned crypt silent. Aryana's iron shell melted, and relief shone on her face. She reached out for Kwik's hand and held it firmly.

"You will be safe," she said.

Kwik's solid features relaxed. His familiar smile returned. "Thank you, my love," he said. "You'll be with my soul every step of the way until I'm returned to you."

Aryana smiled back. "As you'll be with mine."

Darr fidgeted in his chair. Kwik and Aryana let their hands drop away, and they stood up from the table. Darr stood with them.

"Thank you for speaking with us," Kwik said. "I hope you realize this wasn't about trust. It was about confirmation."

"I know," Darr answered.

Kwik straightened and gestured to the door. "Breakfast is prepared in the main hall. Our supplies have been gathered and packed. We'll leave within the hour."

Anxious surprise flooded Darr's veins. He didn't bother hiding it. "I knew we'd leave today, but why so hastily?"

Kwik arched his eyebrow. "You haven't had a chance to look outside, have you?"

Darr turned about and pulled back the curtains on his window. Outside, a blanket of snow stretched unending across the valley.

Chapter Forty-Three

"Darr and his sister travel alongside their friends towards the city of Qued and the Sephir of Air. I cannot fathom the journey ahead of them, although I can guess. Somewhere between here and there, they will find the rest of the Chosen, as well as the relics they'll need to defeat the Devoid. I wish them all the best, and though I know the road ahead will be heavy with danger, I believe they'll succeed."

~From the personal writings of the Divine, Zander

Something changed in the air. Feywen pulled his heavy cloak close around his neck. A day ago, the elements had left behind the season of winter, but this evening it returned with biting cold winds and a steely gray sky that foretold snow.

From the base of the Angleire, Feywen watched the Seeker mists gather on the fields before the Ictarian Army. What did all this mean? Was the return of winter a blessing or a punishment? Was this a return to normalcy or was it the end?

Feywen let the thought drift away on the chill wind. The only thing that mattered had nothing to do with the weather. In the two days since Nidic Waq falsely declared the discovery of the traitor, neither of them was any closer to discovering the real traitor's presence. Perhaps the prophet's announcement hurt more than it helped. Perhaps it was time to come clean to Ariel Forn and Lendor Terwin.

Feywen shivered, but not from the cold. Confessing the truth would help no one. He and Nidic Waq had been the only two people looking for a traitor since Vanla. If he confessed now, the kings would lock them up. Then no one would be looking for the traitor.

Laughter roared out from the men behind him. Feywen turned. Flames danced around a campfire, warming the soldiers' bodies. They must know an attack was coming. Strange to hear laughter at a time of so much apprehension.

Laugh it away. Pretend no harm would come. Fight later.

Feywen returned his gaze to the Seeker mists. During the calm hours before battle, he did what Lacdur taught him. Emotions often blurred during battle. So did the mind. In hindsight, one would remember a hundred things forgotten to do. Feywen smiled to himself. Those were the things he loved to fish out of his mind before going into battle. What would he forget? What would he remember?

Feywen made mental notes to himself while the day faded to dusk. He examined the Ictarian Generals' plan to trap the Seekers with maugwrith fire. He followed the lines of their expectations. He cross-examined all the minor details, particulars the generals might've glossed over.

The details he felt strongest about were the flanks of the Seeker masses. The Ogres would be responsible for securing the flanks going into battle, but he didn't worry about them. The cavalries, the Daravens and White Knights, would be covering the flanks during their withdrawal. There'd be no vanguard for them, and if anything happened to either side, the Soul Seekers would slip through the noose.

Where would the cavalry fall if they failed? Would it be an attack from within or without? Would it come slowly or quickly, with overwhelming force or a subtle assault?

Feywen took note of his questions, making a mental checklist. He hoped his assumptions were wrong.

At sunset, Feywen mounted his horse. Holding his head high, he rode out from the Angleire. Rise or fall, he'd find the traitor this night.

He would find him and bring him down.

* * * *

The first of the maugwrith fires rose hot and angry against the night. Behind the wall of fire, separating himself from the Soul Seekers, Feywen Dery sought out anyone or anything out of the ordinary. Deep in his veins, where his instincts burned hot, something threatened. He had to get closer to the fighting.

Behind him, his reserve unit waited patiently. Intent to move into the fray whenever he signaled them to do so, they watched the maugwrith fires.

Feywen dismounted and came up beside Trent, a soldier he'd fought alongside since Vanla. "I need a favor from you, but you need to tell me if you can't comply."

Trent's brow creased, but he nodded.

"I intend to leave you in command," Feywen explained, holding Trent's gaze steady. "I have to move closer to the fighting, but I can't risk the entire unit. If you receive orders from Blaque Eris or anyone higher, you must comply at once, but until then, do not break formation. Can you do this?"

Trent gave a compliant grunt. "Whatever you have planned, I have faith in you, Commander."

Feywen smiled. "Pray that your faith isn't misplaced, Trent."

He signaled to Colt and Briggan, the Dwarves he'd selected before the fighting began, soldiers he trusted implicitly. They wouldn't betray him.

Feywen led his Dwarf soldiers through the ranks of infantry between his reserve unit and the fires. Feywen held his frame straight and his jaw set. No one questioned him.

They arrived at the eastern edge of the maugwrith fires in time to see the second line of fires explode into the crisp air. Between the two walls of fire, the Soul Seekers milled around like a boiling cauldron of blackness, their silver claws ripping outwards towards its east and west flanks.

The Ogres began to withdraw from the western flank, and the White Knights swept down to cover them. On the eastern flank, the Daravens cut off the Seekers' assault.

Feywen held his breath.

The air exploded on the western flank when the maugwrith finally ignited. The White Knights withdrew. The noose tightened.

On the eastern flank, nothing happened. Feywen tightened his fists into knots. The Daravens fought to keep the Seekers at bay, but with the Ogres in retreat, they wouldn't last long. Minutes ticked by. No maugwrith explosion came.

Feywen's insides churned. Turning quickly to Briggan, he shouted over the cries of battle. "Find Nidic Waq and bring him here quickly. The traitor is here on the east flank. Go now!"

The burly Dwarf nodded and rushed away. Colt stood rigid, his lean face set in stone. His eyes said everything. Whatever you wish of me, Commander. Feywen smiled bravely at him. Together they ran along the wall of maugwrith fire towards the east flank.

With three escape routes now closed off to them, hundreds of Soul Seekers rushed for the opening on the eastern flank of the maugwrith fires. The opening, while narrow, was too wide for the Daravens to close. Many Dwarf horsemen leapt from their mounts, spears discarded for short swords. The Daravens weren't equipped to remain on the field for a prolonged period. Their numbers were too small. They'd have been able to hold the flank long enough to ignite the last of the maugwrith, but that wouldn't be happening any time soon.

The Daravens needed support, but it would take time to reposition the infantry or the Ogres. Feywen gritted his teeth. The only way to save the Daravens was to ignite the maugwrith himself.

His death was likely close at hand, but death would not deter him.

With Colt in tow, Feywen sprinted around the fighting Daravens, his brief deliberations put to an end. He cut away from the fiercest of the fighting before bolting through the ranks of the cavalry trying to back up the rest of their unit. Beyond them, yet unseen, the unlit pyre that would ignite the maugwrith stood. A plan formed in Feywen's mind. All he needed was to snatch up a brand from the pyre, light it, and...

Feywen skidded to a halt when the heaviest fighting fell behind him.

"What in spirit's name is he doing?" Colt hissed at his side.

Vertain stood before the unlit pyre, defending it from his own men. The Daraven captain had discarded his horse, yet with his intimidating height, he wielded his spear with murderous efficiency. Several of his men came at him, some on horseback, some on foot, but Vertain took them all down, a manifestation of terror with his spear whipping through the air. The spear's twenty-inch blade found mark after mark, halting the oncoming Daravens, leaving them dead or incapacitated to await certain death.

Anger burned hot through Feywen's veins. He threw off his cloak and drew his sword.

"Colt," Feywen rasped. He brought the Dwarf soldier to his shoulder. "I'll draw him off. Find a brand and ignite that pyre. We must get it lit or it won't matter that we found our traitor."

Without question, Colt hurried toward a mob of Daravens and Soul Seekers that would bring him up behind the pyre. Feywen's eyes focused. He drew a shallow breath. A brief image of Lacdur flashed in his mind. *'Aos, don't muck around out there!*

He let his arms hang loose. Spotting an opening, Feywen rushed for Vertain. To the Daraven captain, he was another body in need of disposing. For a moment, his presence didn't register on Vertain's face. Feywen dodged in between two attacking Daravens, rolled to the ground. Vertain's spear tore overhead. As Feywen rose to his feet, he slammed into Vertain with such force it sent his spear flying.

Separated from his weapon and shocked by the stealth attack, Vertain brought his elbow up. Feywen drove his sword toward the traitor's unprotected middle.

As Feywen rose up, Vertain pulled a short sword free and slashed upwards. Feywen flinched away, but the blade burned hot when it slashed across his jaw. He rolled away in time to miss the sword's downward motion, but two more of the oncoming Daravens weren't so lucky. Vertain cut them down without expression, one from the side and one head on. He'd known they were there. He fought as if he knew everything happening around him.

Feywen's head buzzed. Somewhere distant, he heard Lacdur yelling. *Shake it off and focus!*

Feywen snapped back to attention and rolled to his feet, regaining his wits. He danced away from Vertain. The Daraven captain's stare quietly raged. With his sword held rigid beside him, Vertain bolted away from the pyre.

Feywen blinked, hesitant. Colt appeared from the fray of Daravens beside Vertain with a blazing torch held high. Vertain's eyes widened in shock, his first genuine emotion. He wheeled about, sword raised towards Colt.

Feywen howled. Vertain cut Colt down without compassion, his face a mask of brutality. The bloodied torch tumbled from Colt's lifeless fingers and into the pyre. The dry wood ignited with a high-pitched crackle. Feywen scrambled to his feet, screaming to everyone around him to retreat.

His eyes burned with the light from the pyre, followed by the deafening explosion of the maugwrith. The blast threw him backwards. Vertain's hideous face, along with several dozen Daravens and the Soul Seeker horde, disappeared into the conflagration.

Chapter Forty-Four

"After everything I've examined, I have found myself no closer to the answer to my question. Will the Chosen of the Light be able to overcome the evil before them? I do not know. The odds are stacked so high against them. Logic tells me they will not. But hope... Hope tells me they will find a way."

~From the personal writings of the Divine, Zander

The icy blackness of the night captured Feywen. Wind rushed past his ears and his breath left his lungs. When the ground came up beneath him, it smacked him hard. His head bounced up. Pain raced through his limbs. He struggled for air while lights mixed with the dark and danced before his eyes.

When his chest allowed him to take in a breath, he did so with great effort. The lights danced away. Out of the corner of his eye, a black shadow rose up, obstructing the angry glow from the fire. Feywen rolled to his side, grasping blindly for his sword.

Vertain rose up out of the maugwrith flames like a Seeker himself, blackened and tattered, a bringer of death. Fists knotted at his side, Vertain came at him. Death masked his face, and he kicked Feywen hard in the ribs. The air left his lungs again along with a cracking that meant some ribs were broken.

"Meddling fool," Vertain hissed. His voice sounded odd, as if another spoke in tandem with him. Feywen crawled to his knees and fought for another breath.

"Tonight was to herald the end of this city," Vertain said, crouching down beside him. With a fistful of Feywen's hair, Vertain pulled him up. "The Seekers should've torn through half of this army tonight. All this fighting could've been brought to an end with my master's return."

Feywen splayed his fingers, in search of anything that would protect him while Vertain held him fast. "Your master?" he asked. "What possible reason could you have for helping the Devoid?"

A cold sneer formed on Vertain's face. "I hate this world, Feywen Dery. Our lives mean nothing. We serve no purpose. My revulsion for this pitiful world brought the Devoid to me, and I, in turn, became its willful servant."

Vertain stood, pulling Feywen almost completely off the ground. Their gazes locked. The void of emotion in the Daraven's eyes revealed nothing except his intentions.

"My service to my master will continue," Vertain hissed. "That maugwrith explosion wiped out the rest of the Daravens. You are my last witness, traitor."

Vertain flung him away. Feywen landed hard but pushed himself up to his knees. If he didn't get help soon, Vertain would kill him. Worse, he'd go on sabotaging the Ictarians.

"I hope you cared nothing for that pitiful soldier helping you." Vertain's odd voice rang out from all around him. Feywen regained his feet. The Daraven's face, contorted with rage, materialized out of the dark. "I smashed the life completely out of him." Vertain's fist slammed Feywen back to the ground.

Feywen knelt, ignoring the pain. His eyesight cleared. A discarded spear lay a few feet from him. He reached out for it.

Vertain's boot landed on his hand, shattering the bones with a sickening crunch. Feywen rolled onto his back. Vertain's hideous figure stood over him. "After I've destroyed your fragile body, I'll send your Light to my master. The Devoid will consume your pitiful soul."

Vertain reached down, clenching Feywen's throat with his fist. His breath cut away completely. Vertain smiled, holding Feywen above his head. The grip on his throat tightened.

"You will beg me to end your life," Vertain said. His mouth formed a tight line. "You will beg the Devoid to swallow you whole."

Black haze closed Feywen's vision. He'd won the battle against Ictar's traitor, but he wouldn't win the night.

Shadows closed about Vertain's sneering face.

The iron grip released, and Feywen fell to the ground. White light exploded all around him, followed by screams of rage so foul they hurt his ears. His breath burned in his throat. His vision cleared enough to see Nidic Waq appear out of the darkness. Feywen laughed hoarsely.

Bathed in the red of the maugwrith flames, Nidic Waq held his fists before him, glowing like miniature suns.

"Leave him, Vertain," Nidic Waq commanded. "I know what you are. You will not leave this field. You have failed your master."

Vertain crouched on the grass in front of Feywen, his own fists knotted and beginning to glow brightly. "You are a fool, Prophet," he spat.

In a single fluid motion, Vertain rose and threw out a blinding white spear of fire before diving for the protective cover of a nearby boulder. Nidic Waq deflected Vertain's killing fire with his own. The prophet held his tall frame rigid against the night.

Feywen blinked. *Are Nidic Waq's eyes glowing green?*

The ground beneath Vertain suddenly erupted in a shower of soil and rock, flinging him into the air. His body hung limply for a brief second against the dark. Nidic Waq lashed out with both hands thrust before him, the white fire burning in a jagged line. The fire hammered into the Daraven, lifting him several feet into the air. With a terrible crack, the light enveloped Vertain and obliterated him.

An incredible weariness sunk into Feywen. Nidic Waq knelt down beside him, his face drawn. "Stay, Feywen," he said.

"Thank you," the Dwarf whispered. He smiled with contentment. His exhaustion took control. His eyelids, heavy, couldn't stay open. The pain wracking his body turned from a dull throbbing to emptiness.

Then blackness overtook Feywen Dery, and his thoughts scattered.

Interlude

All was quiet inside Exed's walls. The cloudy skies lightened faintly with the approach of sunrise. The din from the Ictarian soldiers, wild and celebratory, barely penetrated the solitude of this courtyard. With Vertain's death, there'd be a chance to rest and gather strength. When the Seekers came again, it would be an attack born of sheer desperation. For now, the Ictarian Army stood victorious over the ashes of a Seeker horde and bereft of Vertain's meddling.

Nidic Waq breathed deeply through his nose, letting a slow, even stream of air release through his lips.

The Currents reeked of the Devoid's disgust. The sheer strength of its hatred radiated from its prison. Darr Reintol's restoration of the Sephirs was having its intended effect, limiting the Devoid's reach into the physical world. Vertain's death limited it further. Balance returned slowly. With only the Sephir of Fire left to restore the Devoid's prison, it would do everything in its power to smash the Ictarian Army.

Nidic Waq still didn't know what shape that destruction would take. Even though balance returned to the Currents, confusion ran wild among the spirits. The Devoid, sensing the walls closing in around it, had done something lasting to the spirits. Their state of confusion should've lessened with all that'd happened over the last few days. Instead, it grew worse.

He glanced across the courtyard again, finding the dimly lit window where Feywen Dery slept. Nidic Waq laughed softly. Feywen showed such courage, or was it something else? The once-prince had set his eyes on the deadliest man on the battlefield last night. As a result, he'd saved the Ictarian Army.

Vertain. The name echoed like a curse in Nidic Waq's head. Jacova, Walvor Bridge, and Vanla had all been lost due to the Devoid and Vertain. They would've been lost eventually. Still, the deaths of thousands were on their hands. The Ictarians could've dragged out these battles for weeks, but Vertain had condensed them into a month of defeat after defeat. Even Exed wasn't safe. What other traps had Vertain set?

Nidic Waq lowered his head. As a Spirit Summoner, inexperienced and only barely aware of what he could do, made Vertain's motives impossible to detect. His hatred, a closely guarded secret, drew the Devoid to him, and through his hazy connection to the Currents, Vertain listened to the Devoid's seducing words, promising power and revenge for all his perceived wrongs.

Vertain's battle prowess made him more dangerous. He gave the Devoid the exact tools it needed to infiltrate and destroy the Ictarian Army. In exchange for his master's promises, Vertain surrendered himself. His body became a host, and the Devoid became a parasite that could control its host body. It was unfortunate to lose such a skilled warrior and leader, but Nidic Waq felt no pity for Vertain. He chose to accept the Devoid's call.

As for Feywen, the Elven healers expected him to make a full recovery, though he'd likely lose the ability to use his right hand. The bones, crushed by Vertain's boot, would never heal properly. Nidic Waq rubbed his chin. Feywen didn't seem the type to be limited by a battle wound.

A sudden tearing sensation ripped through the Currents. Somewhere, an unused door opened. Nidic Waq cringed physically. This was not a good sign.

He plunged into the spirit realm to investigate...

...The spirits buzzed madly around him, in uproar of what was taking place. Beyond them, the Lights of the living creatures of Ictar shone faintly, frozen in perceived time.

Nidic Waq rose above it, ignoring the mangled cries of the spirits. They couldn't help him in this state. He let his Light drift, focusing on the source of the irritation, searching for the break in the lines of power that bound the realm.

The presence of the spirits and the living creatures of the land disappeared, leaving him with the intertwining magic of the Sephirs. The colored streams of light--blue, red, yellow, and green--wove across the fabric of the Currents. The Sephirs' power, unbalanced still, but nothing indicated a break.

No. The breakage came from somewhere else. Somewhere darker.

The prophet sheathed his Light in iron emotion, in strength of purpose. Nothing would deter him. The Currents had many levels, many places only the spirits could go, places forbidden to souls still connected to the physical world.

Protected and focused, Nidic Waq plunged himself deeper into the Currents. The faint purple glow darkened into a steel gray. Farther down, the gray would turn to sheer blackness. He wouldn't delve that deep.

Even here, the magic of the Sephirs intertwined and bound the realm. The spirits, languid and sluggish, moved about unresponsive to his presence. It was from here that he'd felt the break, where the Currents bordered on the Devoid's prison. The crack was small, but a draft of venomous anger wafted through, coupled with sinister joy. Nidic Waq lingered, taking measure of what he needed before retreating to the familiar wisteria lights.

Safely away, he reached out to each of the Archons in turn, showing them the brief memory of his discovery. Their power must stretch further. The binding powers of the Sephirs must prevent the Devoid from reaching Ictar.

The Archons responded without hesitation, all but one. The Archon of Fire, its Light too weak to comply, faltered quickly. Nidic Waq reached out to it, pleading with it to find some reservoir of strength. The Archon remained silent, its Sephir unreachable. A terrible omen.

Caeranol would already know of the break. He might even find something to help. For now, Nidic Waq had done all that he could...

...When he returned to the physical world, something was amiss. Someone had cast a summoning. Its source came from deep within the Currents, from a place where a dark evil thrived and pressed against the boundaries of reality.

From the distant south, faint thunder rumbled through the skies.

Nidic Waq threw back his cowl and sprinted through the courtyard. The buildings disappeared behind him, and before him, the dark line of the city walls rose up. Nidic Waq ran hard, his breathing even and his heartbeat steady. His mind, for the moment, was free.

When he reached the city's inner wall, he climbed the stairs to its top. Soldiers standing on guard recognized him and let him pass without explanation. Nidic Waq rushed past them, already discovering Ariel Forn's presence.

At the top of the wall, he found the Cortazian King with his guard, Roelian, both facing the southern skies. Nidic Waq's breath caught in his throat, and his gaze froze, not in wonder, but in fear.

The skies rapidly brightened with the approach of dawn, but to the south, a great dark mass of storm clouds boiled and expanded across the horizon. Great flashes of lightning danced across the mass followed by horrendous bouts of thunder that shook his chest. The clouds had the look of a massive blanket, shaking itself before preparing to enfold something huge.

It headed straight for Exed.

"I'll forget for the moment that you lied about finding the traitor," Ariel said, his voice low and even. His eyes showed some relief. "Prophet, what is this?"

Nidic Waq pursed his lips, trying to mask the feeling of doom building within him. "It is a summoning."

"A summoning? By whom?" Ariel asked, leaning close.

Nidic Waq pointed past the walls to the fields below the Angleire. Soldiers milled around, but most looked southward at the approaching storm. They were completely missing what else approached.

From the eastern end of the Ladornaleah, a wall of Seeker mist moved sluggishly towards them, its breadth sweeping up the horizon. In a few days, it would sit before them if it didn't swallow them whole.

"What in Chaos is going on, Prophet?" Ariel hissed.

Nidic Waq tilted his head up, his jaw set. "This is the Devoid's final move. It intends to destroy us." He pointed to the coming storm. "That storm has been summoned to blot out the sun. It will give the Seekers the ability to fight during any hour of the day."

Ariel shook his head fiercely. "The Soul Seekers have never fought in daylight."

"They have not," Nidic Waq replied. "They will be weaker, and that storm will not last long, but the Devoid hopes to crush us with sheer numbers."

Ariel's eyes narrowed and his lips curled. "How do you know all this?"

Nidic Waq smiled sadly. "I'm sorry I lied to you, Lord Forn. I could think of no other way to draw out our traitor."

Ariel shook his head violently. "It doesn't matter. I trust you now. How do you know the Seekers are coming?"

Nidic Waq turned his gaze fiercely on Ariel. "Time is running short for the Devoid. Its eyes and ears on the field have been destroyed. The last of the Sephirs will soon be saved, and two of the Chosen of the Light remain to be found. The Devoid has been backed into a corner, and its teeth are bared. It has summoned all of its strength, all of its power, to do what it's about to do."

"And what is that?" Ariel asked warily.

Nidic Waq let the question hang in the air for a moment. He loathed answering it.

"The Devoid will smash Exed with every ounce of strength it has left, and when it does, it will free itself from its prison."

Darr's journey, the coming together of the Chosen, and the struggles of the Ictarian Army will come to a conclusion in Book Three of The Chosen of the Light: Devoid.

Author Bio

Over the last twenty years, Jon Carlin Shea has been putting his love for fantasy stories down on paper. With interests in writing, woodworking, parenting, comic books, movies, and RPG video games, he always has something new to inspire him.

We lives in Western Washington with his wife and son.

You can learn more about him at www.joncarlinshea.com.

www.ingramcontent.com/pod-product-compliance
Lightning Source LLC
Chambersburg PA
CBHW030014180626
46810CB00001B/39